Play the Monster Blind

Play the Monster blind

STORIES

Lynn Coady

Doubleday Canada

Doubleday Canada and colophon are trademarks.

Canadian Cataloguing in Publication Data

Coady, Lynn, 1970–
Play the monster blind

ISBN 0-385-25867-4

I. Title
PS8555.O23P52 2000   C813'.54   C99-932780-1
PR9199.3.C62P52 2000

Jacket photograph reprinted with permission from *The Globe and Mail*
Jacket design by Sputnik Art + Design Inc.
Text design by Susan Thomas/Digital Zone
Printed and bound in Canada

Published in Canada by
Doubleday Canada, a division of
Random House of Canada Limited
105 Bond Street
Toronto, Ontario
M5B 1Y3

The quotation on page vii is from "Rougeur des Matinaux, XXIV" by René Char, translated by John Thompson. Reprinted from *John Thompson: Collected Poems and Translations*, Peter Sanger (ed.), with the permission of Goose Lane Editions.

Material in this collection has been previously published as follows: "Play the Monster Blind," *Turn of the Story* (anthology), Anansi, 1999; "Ice-Cream Man," *This* magazine, 1998; "Batter My Heart," *Fiddlehead*, 1994 and *Fiddlehead Gold* (anthology), Goose Lane Editions, 1995; "A Great Man's Passing," *The Antigonish Review*, 1994

FRI   10   9   8   7   6   5   4   3   2   1

For Mom, Dad and the boys

"When the ship sinks, its sails survive, within us. They are hoisted on the mast of our blood. Their fresh impatience draws itself up for other obstinate voyages. It's you, isn't it, who is blind on the sea?"

— René Char

Contents

◆

Play the Monster Blind

◆

DRINKING

THE FATHER WAS DRINKING AGAIN, in celebration. John said it bothered him. He remembered being three, tooling around town in the green station wagon with fake wood on the sides, watching his father drink. He would drink and visit his friends, at their homes or at the boxing club. He would pull into the driveway, pause to smile at John, take a quick couple of swallows before reaching over to unbuckle the boy. And he would hoist his young son inside to show him off, both of them pink-cheeked. He showed her a picture of himself then, his little hands tied inside of a pair of enormous boxing gloves, his father perched behind him, holding them up to take aim at a smiling, sweaty man in trunks.

John was strapping then, and he was strapping now. One of the first things the father told her was that they used to have to pin John into three layers of diapers, he was such a big eater. It was obvious the old man and he were close. The second evening after she and John arrived, she stayed inside doing dishes with the mother, and saw the two of them sitting out in plastic chairs on the lawn, facing the shed with rums in hand. The mother said, "That should keep him happy for a while," and the plastic chairs sagged and quivered from the weight of men. The father was built all of hard, stubborn fat, but John was just big. They sat quietly torturing their lawn chairs together.

He told her he used to be fat. He was very sensitive about it. He told her he had never told that to anyone. In high school he stopped eating and started taking handfuls of vitamins, which made him thin and absentminded, but his mother stopped buying them and he had no choice but to go back to eating. In university he just gave in to everything and ate and drank until he ballooned. Now he was approximately in the middle, a big man with a thick beard. When he was fourteen, his father had him collecting UI for all the dishwashing he had done at the family restaurant, because the workers didn't know any better from the size of him. She had thought, when she met John, that he looked like a lumberjack. He wore plaid shirts and work boots whenever she saw him in class, not because it was fashionable, and not fashionably, but because it was what he wore. She learned where he was from and imagined they all must dress like that, that it must be a very welcoming place, rustic and simple and safe, like John himself.

When his sister showed up, pasty and in leather pants despite the August swelter, the first thing she said to him was, "Hey, you fat shit." Bethany knew that they had not seen each other in a couple of years. He reached over and grabbed one of the sister's wrists. Her knees buckled at once and effortlessly he turned her around, already sinking. Then he grabbed the other wrist and held them together in one large paw while guiding her face-first to the kitchen floor, using her wrists as a sort of steering apparatus. Then he sat on her.

"Pardon?" he kept saying.

"You fat bastard."

The father sat nearby, laughing. The mother saying, "Johnny, Johnny, Johnny," now, as she tried to move around them to the stove. Bethany and the sister were exactly the same age. She felt she should have something to say to her.

When the brother arrived, he at once began to beat and contort the sister in the same way, as if this were some sort of family ritual. She railed at him as he pulled her feet up behind her to meet her shoulders. Whereas John just used the sheer force of his bulk and his size, Hugh, smaller and wiry, was a dabbler in the martial arts. He said he used to box, like his father, but got bored with all the rules. Now he was interested in something called "shoot fighting," which scarcely had any rules at all. He knew all sorts of different holds and manoeuvres, some of which he demonstrated on the sister for them. When he was finished — Ann yanking herself away, red-faced and hair awry and staggering towards the kitchen for a beer — he darted at John, head down and fists up. John responded in the way she had seen him do at bars whenever drunken men, maddened by his size, ran at him. The strategy was to reach out his big hands and simply hold the opponents at bay until they got tired and embarrassed.

Bethany thought of herself as an easygoing person and tried not to be nervous, but she and John were going to get married, and she knew that the family was striving to be civil in a way they were not used to. John kept cuffing his sister in the head whenever she said "goddamn "or "cocksucker," and quietly stating, "Dad," when the father did the same. Bethany and the sister tried and tried to talk to each other, bringing up woman-things like belts and shampoo. She knew that the sister worked in theatre in Halifax and lived with a man who was thirty-five, and everyone was disappointed in her, but hoped she would soon turn her life around. It was touching the way the family spoke of Ann when she was out of the room. The father, overwhelming his armchair, ponderously clinking his ice cubes and turning to John.

"What do you think, me boy?"

"Well, who knows, boy."

"She's getting by," the mother would say.

"But for how long?"

"We'll talk to her at some point," John promised, this being what the father was waiting to hear. The father was always turning to John and waiting to hear the right thing, and John always seemed to know what it was.

The father didn't ask the other son to talk to the sister, and Hugh didn't seem interested in doing it anyway. Hugh and Ann presented themselves as allies, of sorts, against John's authority, even though they fought with one another more furiously than they did with him. They rolled around the living room, knocking over lamps and bothering the mother's nerves, as she complained from the kitchen, and John would come in and bark at them to smarten up. They would call him a big fat fruit and he would sit on them both, the sister on the very bottom of the pile. At one point she looked up at Bethany, blood vessels throbbing to burst in her face, and squeaked, "Can't you control him?" Which Bethany lightly laughed at.

When the parents went to bed, the four of them sat around the table drinking rum. She had never had so much rum in her life. She normally liked spritzers, which John said were for pussies. John tried to talk to his brother and sister seriously about the father. How the drinking bothered him.

"It keeps him in good cheer," said Ann.

"You two don't remember how he used to get. I remember how he used to get."

"Maybe he's too old to get that way now."

"It bothers Mum's nerves."

"I think he's been dandy," said Ann.

"Just because he's not yelling at you all the time doesn't necessarily make it fine and dandy."

"I disagree," said Ann.

Hugh said nothing, waiting for the conversation to turn to sports or parties. Bethany noticed how jolly Ann looked when she said she disagreed with John. She thought, once or twice, that John might grab his sister's head and slam it into the table a couple of times. Ann looked capable of disagreeing with John in her sleep.

Hugh never seemed to bother getting into a conversation with his brother. He merely lurked in corners, behind chairs, waiting for an opportunity to get him in a paralyser hold, but John would always shrug him off like a summer jacket. Hugh showed some of his holds to Ann, who in turn tried them out on her mother, but the mother complained loudly about her arthritis whenever this occurred.

"Hugh said they're not supposed to hurt — they just immobilize," the sister protested, chin digging into the mother's head.

"Well, they do. Get away before I clout you."

Ann released her mother with much reluctance, sorry to loose the fleeting power. The mother had just stood there politely the whole time. She probably could have broken out of it if she wanted to. Like everyone else in the family, the mother was bigger than Ann.

Ann wore combat boots with her sundress. The father made fun of them, and the mother wanted to know if her feet didn't get overheated. Bethany felt sorry for Ann, because when they all were sitting around the picnic table eating lobster, Ann couldn't open hers but she wouldn't ask any of them for help. Bethany finally passed her a cracking utensil under the table.

"I never used to eat lobster until last year," Ann explained. "It grossed me out. Then I decided I want to be the kind of person who'll eat anything she's given."

"She won't eat the pickled alewives," said the father through a mouthful of roe.

"Don't count as food," said Ann, sullen. Hugh was sneaking up behind her with a lobster that had not yet been boiled alive.

Boxing

THEY WOULD PICK UP THE UNCLE and the bunch of them, some in the father's car and some in John's, were going to tour around the trail, staying in cabins and eating in restaurants and swimming at beaches. This was the father's gift. John told her that doing it was important to him and she would have to have fun. She was surprised he would put it this way, because she was looking forward to seeing the island. She was worried about being in the car with the father, however. At the airport after they arrived, he made them stop at the duty-free liquor store and purchased an armload of tiny bottles of Crown Royal. Once they were in the car, he handed one to each of them and said, "Slug 'er back, you two. The vacation has officially begun." Bethany had never drunk straight whisky in her life and had no idea how to properly respond. She looked at John for help and he took it from her and dropped it into her purse.

"Can't be into this on the road, boy," he said, smiling and blinking ahead of him.

"Ach, I'd need fifty or so of these before anything good started happenin."

"Let me drive, boy."

"No, we can't have you drinkin and drivin."

"I don't need to drink."

After scant argument, the father declared, "Betty, it's just you and me!" turning around in his seat to beam at her. "My God," he added, "did you down yours already? Well, good boy, yourself."

So the father sat in the back seat with her the whole way, making jokes that John was their chauffeur and kicking his seat and telling him to step on it while Bethany watched the innumerable veins road-mapping his nose and cheeks begin to glow as if filling up with lava. She was terrified of everything. They were on a stretch of road where one sign after another read things like: JESUS IS COMING! PREPARE THYSELF! REPENT! SAITH THE LORD.

All the way to the house, he told her about boxing. He rhymed off one boxer after another, not famous boxers like Muhammad Ali but ones from, as he said, "nearby." Men with names like Sailor Dave and Fisher MacPhee and Ronnie the Dago. He said he had met more than a few of these fellows in the ring, and could tell her something about the style of each if she was interested. The Dago, for example, was a smart fighter, a thinking fighter. Always went in with some kind of strategy. Archie the Rigger, however, had nothing going for him but a hard head and had the record to prove it. Fisher was the prettiest of fighters, floated on air. Sailor Dave was like a goddamned bull, just an ox. The father went on and on in this vein. He handed one little bottle after another to her so that when they finally got out of the car her purse clinked and sloshed.

"Johnny," the old man pronounced, holding the kitchen door open for her, "this is a goddamned good girl right here." He went to bed almost at once, and so they sat up and had cornflakes with the mother.

◇

The sister very much admired Bethany's luggage as they loaded up the car. She marvelled at it, it was so nice, so much that Bethany was embarrassed. John intuited this and kept making jokes that some people had moved beyond Glad bags and cardboard.

"It would never even *occur* to me to have bags like that," the sister persisted, and finally John told her to shut the hell up and she told him to kiss her rosy red arse and he strode over to her and picked her up and placed her, barely able to squirm, in the trunk of the car and then held the hood down, not completely closed, until Bethany told him, for Pete's sake, to let her out of there, and Ann, who throughout the performance had not made a sound, flung one bare leg out and then the other and hopped away like a crow. Hugh stood by looking pensive, as if he wished he had thought of it first.

Hugh himself was a strange one, because, although he had gone to university, he spoke with an insanely nuanced accent that was nothing like the rest of the family's, and every second thing he said had something or another to do with his hole, and he wore an Expos cap just perched on the top of his head, but when she asked him what he did for a living, he replied that when he was not "partying his hole out," he worked with computers. Bethany asked John about it later on and he said, "Oh, yah. He's the brain. Straight A's. Could have done anything he wanted." What he chose to do was teach courses at the vocational school and help people around town with their systems. He didn't go anywhere after university because, he said, all his friends were here. "Friends're pack a retards," John once remarked. And after a few days Bethany began to realize that Hugh didn't own any shirts except T-shirts with sayings on them. He sat around in T-shirts that said things like: I'D RATHER PUSH A FORD THAN DRIVE A CHEVY and IT'S NOT HOW DEEP YOU FISH, IT'S HOW YOU WIGGLE YOUR WORM!

After the mother, the uncle was the one she felt most comfortable with. They picked him up at a group home where he stayed in Port Hastings the night before the trip. Bethany knew in advance that he was Mentally Handicapped, and having this foreknowledge made her calm about meeting him, far less nervous than she had been about the rest. It was good to have a label, something her mind could scrutinize. It was good to have an idea what to expect.

Lachie was his name, and she found him delightful. He reached out one hand and wished her Merry Christmas as she shook it, and then he extended the other to wish her Happy Easter. He puttered away, then, announcing, "There now! He knows Betty!" to all present. For the rest of the evening he sat in a chair in the corner of the living room and raised his eyes every once in a while to ask if it was time for cornflakes. Bethany felt at home in the chair beside him. Now and again he would show her the fingers of his right hand to let her know that he'd been nibbling at the nails. Apparently this was a great pastime of his, much frowned upon by the rest of the family, and he seemed to enjoy the disapproval it provoked.

"Breaks his nails," he remarked more than once.

"Tch. Isn't that terrible," Bethany answered.

Lachie would smile back and reach over quickly to poke her in the cheek with a ragged fingertip before reclining again.

"You kick his arse if you catch him at that!" the sister yelled from across the room, the uncle plunging both hands into the tucks of his armchair and closing his eyes.

The uncle was the fattest. John said that his grandmother had spoiled him from birth, heaping his plate and feeding him entire pies, and Lachie had never done anything but follow a few cows around on the farm for exercise. Now he had arthritis in his knees, and he could hardly walk around any more. The fat hung off Lachie in an unpleasant sort of way, like it wasn't quite a part of him, something that had to be strapped on in the morning. John said that was how *he* would be if he let himself go, how would she like that? He said it was in the genes. He constantly had to be working against it.

"Your sister's a bone rack," Bethany pointed out, "and she looks more like your uncle than you do."

"She had the anorexia all through high school," John explained, dismissive and also somewhat grudging. "Sees the nutritionist once a week."

"All she talks about is eating," Bethany said.

"I know."

"What about Hugh?"

"Works out every day," John said with a bit of contempt, because anyone could see this with one look at the chest beneath the T-shirt slogans.

◇

At the dinner table the father congratulated Bethany for her fine appetite, unaware that she was only eating so much because he kept insisting more be offered to her and she was afraid of offending him.

"Get Betty some more potatoes, Annie. Jesus Christ, she's wasting before our eyes."

"Do you want more potatoes, Betsy?"

"Ummm ... sure."

"She doesn't want any more, Dad."

"She just said she did, for the love of God!"

"Quit forcing food down the woman's throat."

10

"Well, Jesus Christ, I'll get her the potatoes if you're not up to the challenge," said the father, practically spreading himself across the table.

"No, no, no! I can get them for myself!" Bethany exclaimed, horror-struck.

"There now," the father said, emptying a greyish, steaming mound out of a Corningware dish and onto her plate. "Some of us know how to be civil to a guest."

"You're making her sick," said Ann.

Bethany was a big eater most of the time, however, and only went to bed in slight discomfort, having eschewed the evening's cornflake ritual. She asked John if he thought she needed to lose weight and he said who gave a shit one way or another. He would not have asked her to marry him if he thought she was a tub of lard. It was being around Ann and the mother that made her feel that way. The mother said having her "nerves on the go" all the time was what kept her skinny, and Ann, meal-obsessed, hopped about the kitchen a pale crow, swallowing the occasional fastidiously selected morsel. John had said that he and Hugh had teased her about being fat all throughout their childhood but had to stop once she decided to forgo eating altogether, and felt guilty for the rest of their lives. Now John would wrap a hand around one of her thighs whenever she passed by and squeeze, feeling for meat. "Get in the kitchen and eat a tub of ice cream or something, ya stick," he'd say, thinking he was being kind. And the sister Ann would smile at her brother as if she were thinking it too.

Swimming

LACHIE COULDN'T GET HIS CLOTHES OFF fast enough. Scarcely had she put the picnic cooler down than his shirt was in a heap on the sand and rolls of white flesh sprouting the coarsest of black hairs gave salute to the sun and the ocean. The effect of the sight of so much exposed skin caused her to reach instinctively for a bottle of sunscreen. She tried to hand it to him, but the uncle was busy unbuckling his pants and muttered, "No, you put it on me. He can't get his pants, can't get them." She waited a moment to see if any of the family would come down the path before finally squirting a little onto her fingertips and trying to apply some to

Uncle Lachie's shoulders, but he had the pants around his ankles and staggered out of her reach a second later. Then he regained himself, muttering about the ocean, and, in his haste, yanked off his swimming trunks on top of everything else. Bethany was not so embarrassed as to be unable to imagine her embarrassment if someone other than John came down the path at that moment, so she said calmly to the uncle, "Put on your trunks, Uncle Lachie. You need to put your trunks back on."

Lachie was irritated at anything keeping him from the sea at that point and protested vigorously for a good minute or so as Bethany stood there beside him, trying to come up with a persuasive argument. She thought it strange that he would argue so much and yet not actually defy her outright, trundling away, a white blur against the blue sky like a walking snowman. Finally she just said, "You can't go *swimming* without your *swim* trunks, Uncle Lachie," like it was the most logical thing in the world, and he gazed meditatively down at the shorts for a bit before hauling them back up about his hips and plunging towards the Atlantic. Bethany thought this a profound triumph and almost wished there had been someone around to witness the crisis, and her unexpected competence. At that moment, Ann appeared. Struggling with a cooler and in a polka-dot bathing suit with moulded bra-cups that must have belonged to the mother in 1968. She lingered beside Bethany for the briefest of moments before taking in the sight of Lachie. White like a plump cloud had fallen directly out of the sky and now bobbing free and independent with the waves.

"Lord lifting Antichrist, he'll fry like a pork rind!" she hollered, seizing the sunscreen out of Bethany's hand and giving chase. Bethany could see that he was seated up to his belly now, and seemed to be looking down at the point where the water divided him up.

Eating

THE FATHER DRANK TOO MUCH at dinner and made the waitress cry. She wouldn't come back to the table and John had to get up and walk across the restaurant and talk to her and talk to the manager. She watched him standing there with them, grinning under his beard, gesturing in an open and accepting sort of way with his enormous hands. The girl was being charmed by him and the manager was being charmed by him in a different manner. She knew how he was charming the waitress, because she had been charmed like that too. How a big man like that could grin so open-handed and vulnerable. He could take your head between those two hands and pop it like a zit, but he was decent enough not to do that, not to even remind you that he could. He smiled, instead, and cajoled. He had no interest in bullying you — the easiest thing in the world for him to do. Everything about his demeanour said: *I am just a great big guy with a drunk dad and a new fiancée and nobody wants to feel like this, so let's not.* It was brave of him. It was exactly what made him so good.

Pretty soon the girl was laughing with tears still in her eyes and John was laughing and picking her up from the ground with a bear hug which made her shriek and laugh even harder. She could not have been more than seventeen, and was in love now. He sauntered back to the table, his mouth pursed in a comical sort of way.

"A little thing out there called PR," he said to his pink, smirking father.

"A little fucking thing called incompetence in the work force," the dad shot back. "If one of my girls had ever pulled any of that kind of shit back when I was running the Bluenoser ..."

"Boy, boy," said John. "Jeez, eh?" He went on making inarticulate noises of comfort and reprimand. The father made noises of declining outrage and increasing shame, as his awareness of the situation grew. But she could see that he wasn't going to acknowledge it, blustering about incompetence all throughout dessert and, while waiting for the bill, about teenager girls with earrings in their noses instead of their ears where God intended them. Blustering all the while but now drinking out of his water glass instead of the other one that was poised beside the wreckage of his meal. Bethany could tell he hoped to bluster until he was blustering on a different topic, one that made everyone more comfortable and jovial. Blustering wittily and cheerfully, no longer blustering at all — a benevolent father regaling the family with priceless and innumerable anecdotes from a rich and varied life.

❖

The sister puked for what seemed like hours. Bethany in an agony because she thought she should go and see if she was sick, but on the other hand, John had said she used to be anorexic, and she knew that this was what anorexics sometimes did after big meals. It was an impossible situation. It was almost dawn, and she and John and the sister had made a deal — that Bethany would sleep with John for a little before slipping through the bathroom that joined their rooms and crawling into Ann's bed. This being the arrangement the parents would be expecting when they arrived from the other cabin to make breakfast. But now it was getting light and Ann was still in there, puking away, and Bethany was in an impossible situation. John snored.

Lying there angry, it took her a couple of seconds to realize that the retching echoes from the bathroom had ceased. The bedroom was now almost fully illuminated, and she flung the blankets away, fully awake, deciding she didn't care if Ann knew she had heard her puking or not. When Bethany didn't get a good night's sleep, it did terrible things to her body. It gave her indigestion, made her cranky and intolerant, red-eyed and snippy. She had to catch a good couple of hours in Ann's bed before the parents stormed in wanting to take pictures and see them splashing around in canoes.

"Ugh," said Ann as Bethany crawled in beside her.

"Are you okay?"

"The *dreams* I was having!"

Bethany licked her lips. She wasn't going to pretend she was stupid. "But you were throwing up, Ann."

"Before I was throwing up," she said. "Sick dreams. It has to have been the scallops. Sometimes my stomach doesn't welcome the shellfish."

"Hm," said Bethany, in a way she hoped sounded as if the explanation had been accepted and the incident forgotten about in almost the same moment.

"Ohg," moaned Ann some moments later. "Did you ever dream that you were *where you were?*"

"I don't know what you mean," Bethany said around a yawn.

"You're not supposed to dream about being where you are. It's not natural. I'm not supposed to be dreaming about being in this cabin with all of you. In my grandmother's house. Or in school, or in Halifax or something, or somewhere I've never even been. Nobody dreams literally, for Christ's sake."

"What were we doing?"

"Oh God, it was horrible. We were just doing all the things we've been doing all along."

She was snoring not five seconds later.

DRIVING

THEY DROVE ANOTHER FEW MILES, on their way to still more rented cottages. The father made a point of repeating all through breakfast he hoped these would be more amenable than the ones they had spent the previous night in.

"No TV, no radio," he kept saying. "Nothing but four walls and a goddamn bed. I can haul a cot into the closet at home, if that's what I want. Charge people fifty bucks a night to use it."

"It's a *cabin,* boy," John said. "You're supposed to sit on the porch and watch the sunset. What do you need a TV for?"

"It's the principle of the thing. What if it rains? What if there's a ball game? Beds not fit to piss on — I can see plain as day that poor Betty didn't get a moment's sleep. I should have complained. I should have complained at that goddamn restaurant, and I should've complained the moment we showed up here. Reservations two jeezly months in advance and this is the best they can give us."

"You *did* complain at the restaurant," Ann reminded him, looking around to confirm that no one else was going to do it. "Don't you remember?"

"To the manager, not to that young one. Poor girl didn't know what I was talking about."

"You might have thought about that before you called her a useless twat."

"Well, goddamnit, I was mad!"

"Leave it now, Ann," said John. Bethany was beginning to see that this was the way they commenced most mornings. John saw her understanding this.

"All I wanted," rumbled the father, "was a good dry chip. That's all I wanted. What do they bring me? *Potato wedges!* What the Jesus? Greasy old potato wedges with some kind of crap sprinkled all over them. That's not chips. I asked for chips. I just wanted a *good dry chip!* Not that gourmet crap swimming in Christ knows what."

15

"Well, it's done with now."

"Well, I'm not letting them get away with that shit."

"Good, then, boy."

"You have to let them know, Johnny. You can't just let them keep on with that kind of shoddy service."

"All right."

"You have to remind them — I'm the customer. I'm payin' your salary. You need me. I don't need you." The father seemed to whisper to himself for an instant as if imagining some outlandish response, and then turned to Bethany and smiled suddenly. "You just ignore me, Betty," he said. "John here's the family dip-lo-mat. We'd get kicked outta where-all we went if the dip-lo-mat wasn't around."

"I guess to God," said John.

"I'm just an old boxer," said the father, manoeuvring his bulk from the confines of their picnic table. "I hit people. Don't take mucha the dip-lo-mat for that," he chuckled, moving off to examine the workmanship of the cabin's front step. Intermittently they heard quiet exclamations of disgust from his direction as they cleared away the breakfast things.

He wanted John and Bethany to ride with him to Dingwall because he felt as if he wasn't spending enough time with them. He told the mother to take the car with the other two. The mother announced that she would have to drive, then, because Hugh was a maniac and Ann had always been too stubborn to learn, and they couldn't expect her to go for very long because her nerves were bad. The three of them chewed at each other for a bit, but Bethany got the feeling that they were pleased to have been thrown together — a day off from the father's gruff bullying and the more genuine authority of John. Lachie was content to ride with herself and John and the father, however, because he didn't care either way. They were taking John's Escort, and that was the one he had climbed into immediately after breakfast, and so that was the car he was going in.

"Come on, come on, come on," he kept saying, watching them load the baggage. "Ding-Dong. Going Ding-Dong now."

They stopped at a lookout point, and Bethany climbed out of the car before the rest. In every direction she turned, she could see nothing but dark, fuzzy mountains. The ever-present ocean was nowhere in sight, and it disoriented her. She didn't know if this was beautiful or not. The green mounds sloped upward uninsistantly, and then came together in dark, obscene valleys that reminded her of the creases in a woman's flesh — her own. Reminded her of sitting naked and looking down at the spot where her stomach protruded slightly over her thighs. She didn't like how these low mountains were everywhere, their dark rolling motion completely uninterrupted by a view of water, or patches of field. John suddenly moved past her and jumped up onto the wooden railing, framing himself against them.

"Get down. John, get down. Get down now," she said.

"What? Take my picture!"

"Get down," she hissed, queasy at the sight of him poised there, ready to disappear into one of the dark creases. Meanwhile, Lachie refused to get out of the car to look. She could hear the father's persistent cursing as he tried to yank him by the hand, then coming around to the other side of the car and trying to shove him out the opposite door. Lachie remained where he was, however, unmoved and only a little irritated with the father's proddings. All he wanted to do was go, to drive in the car. "Come on, come on, come on," he said, and, "No, no, no." With their arms around each other, Bethany and John watched him easily resist the father. Bethany was thinking that John could probably go over there and lift him out, but she hoped that he wouldn't. By this time the father was laughing with frustration. He said that they were going to stay there and see the view and Lachie could drive the friggin' car to Ding-Dong all by himself, if he wanted to go so badly.

The rest of the trip, the father told her the story of Archie "Fisher" Dale, a fine boxer he knew out of the Miramichi, "who some people called Tiny because he was such a little fella, in fact his manager had wanted to bill him as Tiny Dale, but Archie would have none of it. In actual fact, he wasn't all that small — five-six — but smaller than what you'd usually see hanging out at the boxing clubs and whathaveyou. Well this one — you wouldn't find yourself taking him too-too seriously to look at him, I mean, some of the fellas you'd see at those places were like Johnny here, great big bastards, and a lot of them figured they could fight simply by virtue of the fact that they were bigger than anybody else. But that's not always the case, you know, and there's nothing more pathetic than seeing some big lumbering bastard getting all tangled up in his own legs trying to keep up with some little lightning rod like Fisher himself who lands you a good right cross before you even see him in front of you."

Because, besides height and mass, this little fella had it all. John's father had never seen a fighter so well equipped for greatness. He fought single-mindedly. He often appeared vicious, but he never actually got angry — to get angry at your opponent was just foolishness, the quickest way to spot an amateur. He was fast, he was graceful, he had arms like steel cords lashed together, but for all that grace he was *tough*. You could just *hit* him. He didn't care. John's father and Fisher Dale would go drinking down-town in Halifax, and after downing a few, the little prick would just grin at him with his gap-filled mouth and say, "Hit me, John Neil. Hit me a good one, now." Well, John's father was never one to oblige in this respect, but there would always be one or two fellas nearby just chompin' at the bit to take a poke at Fisher Dale. You couldn't drop him. You just could not drop him. He'd weave and teeter, blood pouring out of his mouth, and, by Jesus, that grin would never leave his face. "Hit me again, why don'tcha?" was all he'd say.

"What would he do that for?" Bethany asked, genuinely mystified.

"Because," John's father told her with very precise enunciation to give the statement weight, "Fisher was crazy as mine and your arse put together. Everywhere except the ring. He was Albert Jesus Jesus Einstein in the ring. The drinking, you know. What it does to some people. Archie Dale was such a one."

"This is the saddest story I know," the father reflected, after having paused for some time. "Now that I think of it. What that boy couldn't have done. And he was one of the hardest working in them days too. The stamina. Fight in Halifax one night, under one name, hop on the train right after for one in Yarmouth or somewhere, callin' himself Wildman Dale or some such thing. You could only fight a certain number of matches in them days if you wanted to keep your licence, but the more ambitious and greedy of the bunch — Dale was both — would just hop from town to town, fighting under different names. Sometimes he'd go ten, fifteen fights a week. Outlandish, if you knew anything about the circuit. I could never go more than five.

"You know, the only time he had the boozin' under control was when he was fighting that way — hopping from town to town, sometimes going two a night. Kept him busy, kept him focused. See, he wasn't the type a fella could just fight a couple times a week, and then head down to the tavern for a couple of beers with his buddies, waiting for his manager to call about the next one. It was all or nothing with Dale. That was his problem right there. If he stopped fighting, he started drinking, it had to be one or the other. Manager shoulda just kept putting him up against one guy after another till he dropped dead of a brain clot — least he wouldn't've ended up a drunken failure."

"What happened?"

"What happened was that he got caught, they found out he was fighting illegally like that, and he got his licence suspended. And howls just went up all across the country, you know, with the gamblers and everything, because the boy was on a streak — he was winning every match he fought. He'd pounded me long ago, I don't mind telling you, not to mention pretty near every other fella on the circuit, and his manager was talking about taking him over to the States. "But that was that — suspension for a month."

"That's not so bad."

"Ach, no. Most boys'd take their winnings and go off on a tear. Well, that's what he meant to do at first, but, like I said, with Dale it was all or nothing. I went downtown with him the one night, we drank ourselves stupid, and the last I seen of him" — John's father began to heave and shake at this memory — "he was chasin' a cop down Gottingen Street at four in the morning. He was chasing the cop! Somehow he got his nightstick away from him, and he was chasing him down the street, waving it around his head like a lasso! Cop hollerin to beat hell."

"So what happened to him?"

" *That* happened to him. Like I said, it was the last of him I seen. Never fought again, I can guarantee you that much. Disappeared into the night."

"You saw him again, Dad," John's voice came from the driver's seat. It was as if he were repeating something by rote.

"Oh, yes, wait now, I did see him again. Eight or so years later, in Inverness, of all places, walking home from a square dance. This little frigger in a trench coat shuffling towards me with great deliberation, you know. I didn't know who it was, some queer or something, I was getting ready to pop him. Well, isn't it Fisher Dale. 'John Neil!' he shouts. 'Whad'llya have?' Then he yanks something from the pocket of his trench-coat" — the father began to act out the role of Fisher Dale, now. "'A little *puck* a whisky? Or — reaching into his other pocket with the opposite hand — "'a little *puck* a rum?'" The father shook and heaved and gasped. He repeated the gesture a couple of times for effect, the yanking of one bottle out of the right-hand pocket upon the word "puck," and then another from out of the left. It was like Lachie wishing her Merry Christmas and Happy Easter in succession.

"This is all he has to tell me after eight years," John's father finished, jovial and refreshed from the story's telling. "Ah — Jesus, though. Lord save us if it wasn't a shameful waste of a beautiful fighter. Just a beautiful little fighter."

John told her later that he told that story to everyone. It was his favourite story. She would hear it a hundred more times in the upcoming years, he said. In the meantime, the road rose and sunk like a sea serpent's tail. Every so often they would come around a craggy bend, after miles of nothing but the low, fuzzy mountains, and all of a sudden it would seem as if the whole of the Atlantic Ocean was glittering before them, so big it eclipsed even the sky. And then the road would sink lower and lower imperceptibly, until they were trundling through some infinitesimal community and she'd see grey, half-demolished barns with black letters spelling CLAMS painted across the roofs and little stores with Pepsi-Cola signs from the early seventies in the windows, the red in the logo faded to pink and the blue now a sick green. She went into one of them to get lemonade and ice-cream bars for every-body, and the woman behind the counter was not nearly as friendly as Bethany had been expecting. The woman had a little girl sitting with her back there, and every time the little girl did something other than just sit there the woman would bark, "Whad I tell ya? Whad I tell ya?" at her — oblivious to Bethany's presence — so the little girl would place her hands at her sides and arrange her legs and sit chewing on her lips until the fact of being a child got the better of her and she would once again reach for some-thing with absent-minded curiosity. Then the woman would bark again.

"You've got a lovely place here," said Bethany, and the woman regarded her with terror. She thought Bethany was talking about the store, and not the island, and therefore must be insane. She added, "This is my first visit," to make it more clear. The woman looked down at the little girl, as if hoping to find her trespassing again so that she could yell at her and ignore Bethany. But the girl was being good, so the woman ignored Bethany anyway, a confused and queasy look taking over her ruddy, mean face. "Six sevenny-five, wha?" she said. Bethany gave her a five and a two, hoping she had understood correctly. She gathered up her ice-cream bars without asking for a bag and staggered out the door and into the sunshine, cowbells clunking rude music behind her.

FIGHTING

SHE ATE BARBECUED BOLOGNA for the first time in her life. John was trying to convince her it was a delicacy of the area as he slathered Kraft sauce onto it, splattering the coals. She kept telling him in a low voice not to lie to her, to quit lying to her. She made her voice low because if he was telling the truth, she didn't want the rest of the family to know she hadn't believed it.

"Listen here," he kept saying. "You haven't *lived* until you've scarfed a good feed of barbecued bologna."

"Shut up," she said, giggling and looking around. "Liar." She saw that Ann was nearby, sprawled in a sun-chair and drinking a beer. She had probably heard everything, and so Bethany took a chance and looked seriously at her for confirmation. Ann smiled and raised her eyes to heaven. She turned back to John.

"I knew you were lying!"

"What?"

"Ann says you're lying."

"Ann's not gonna get her share of barbecued bologna."

"Quit teasing the woman," said Ann. "You're always teasing her. How long do you think she'll put up with it before she kicks your arse?"

Bethany smiled at Ann. They were getting somewhere. Most of the time the sister had seemed too high-strung to even talk to, but Ann had started taking long, slow draughts of beer early in the afternoon, and now her movements were easy and fluid — nothing of the crow remained. She had been in the sun-chair most of the afternoon, letting the sun burn it out of her, while the rest of them played badminton and lawn darts. Her smiles became slow and amused instead of fleeting and anguished. Bethany sat on the grass beside her every once in a while to drink a beer of her own and together they would holler insults at John about whatever he happened to be doing at that moment. Hugh came over and capsized the chair at one point, but Ann simply rolled away from it and fell asleep a few feet away in the grass.

They must have eaten the red, charred flesh of every beast imaginable that evening, and the lot of them sat exhausted in chairs they had each pulled up around Ann's chair as if she had become some sort of axis during the afternoon. The father's face was the same colour as the meat they'd consumed, and bloated, and he blinked constantly as if a breeze was blowing directly into his eyes. While Ann had relaxed herself with long, slow, sunny draughts of beer, the father had done the exact opposite — disappearing without a word at steady intervals throughout the day in order to shoot rum in the kitchenette, the imperative of it seeming to make him more and more anxious. She knew he was doing that, because she had stupidly kept asking, "Where's your father gotten to? Isn't it your father's turn? Where's your father?" until John finally had to tell her. He said this was the only way the father had ever learned to drink — like a teenager sneaking swigs at a dance. He'd never sipped a cocktail in his life, much less enjoyed a beer during a fishing trip or something. John said that his father had never understood the purpose of beer. He didn't see the *point* of an alcoholic beverage with so little alcohol in it. Why something should take so long to do what it was intended to do.

"He's an alcoholic," said Bethany, epiphanic. They were walking along the beach when he told her this.

"Oh Christ," John said, then, letting go of her hand. "You don't know much." It hurt her feelings but she didn't tell him.

On the path back to the cabin, they saw the father coming towards them. The sun had set moments before and their eyes were used to the dark, but the father's weren't. They saw him first, walking with great clomps, his arms stretched out in front of him like Boris Karloff in

Frankenstein. Bethany remembered hearing that, in *Frankenstein*, Boris Karloff had stretched out his arms before him like that because the film-maker had at first wanted to have the monster be blind. They never followed up that aspect of the story, but they kept the footage of Lugosi playing the monster blind anyway, and that was why the enduring image of Frankenstein ended up being this clomping creature with his arms stuck out in front of him. The problem was that this was what John's father looked like, coming towards them — a frightened, blind monstrosity. John made a sound beside her, before speaking to him in a loud, fatherly voice. She almost thought she'd imagined that sound. It could have been mistaken for a brief intake of air which would have been necessary before speaking so loud to the father. But it hadn't been that.

"Jesus, Jesus, Jesus, boy!" was what John said. "You stumbling around looking for some place to take a piss or wha?" Bethany jumped at the "wha." High-strung like the lady at the store.

The father tittered, focused in on their dark outlines, and came forward, blustering jokes about getting lost in the raspberry bushes and their having to send in a search party for him in the morning. He had just wanted to walk with them on the beach, he said. Was he too late? Were they on their way back?

"We'll have another walk," said John.

"No, no. Betty's tired. Are you tired, Betty?"

"No, no." So they headed back to the beach.

She couldn't remember what he said. All she could think about was Boris Karloff, clomping around confused and horrified, chucking a little girl into a pond. She pretended to be enthralled with the moon on the water. The truth was, the old man was incoherent. She could hear John mm-hmming in response to him. It seemed as if he had something very important to say, a zillion different things, none of which he could keep straight. He said that they were blessed. He said that they were lucky. He said that he would help them. He said that family was the only important thing. He kept saying that he was old, and that life could be difficult. He said wouldn't it be nice if people sometimes understood each other. Nobody had ever come close to understanding him in his godforsaken life. But at some point he'd decided that being understood wasn't as important as being good. So just because nobody gave a shit about him and had no respect for him and thought him a foolish old bastard — he'd decided that wasn't what was important.

"Boy, boy," John kept saying. "You need to get to bed."

At the cabin they shared with the brother and sister, they found the same two locked in violent combat, the worst Bethany had seen so far. The two of them laughed hysterically throughout, Hugh with a giddy and unrelenting "Huhn! Huhn! Huhn!" and Ann with an ongoing, high-pitched shriek. John was not in the mood for it. There was a broken glass on the floor and a lamp on its side. Hugh was trying to manoeuvre Ann into one of his paralyser holds, but Ann was resisting heroically. Bethany had never seen her quite so nimble — just as he managed to position his arm about her throat, or somewhere equally critical, she would slither away as though greased. "I've uncovered the secret!" she kept shrieking when she could speak. "I've uncovered the secret!" And Hugh would gasp, "Shut up! No you haven't! Shut up! No you haven't!" — so that for an instant Bethany thought there must be some hideous secret about Hugh that Ann was threatening to reveal. But Hugh was laughing too hard for it to be that. He seemed to be hysterical with disbelief that Ann was suddenly able to wrench herself out of his every grip.

"Settle the fuck down!" John was shouting.

"You just move ..." Ann sputtered, near to the point of being too winded to speak, "where *he* moves...." She dove around her brother and jabbed a fist into his solar plexus, Hugh howling pain and laughter. "You just move" — she threw her hands into the air and brought them down onto his ears — "*with* the hold! You move *with* the hold!"

"Shut up!" Hugh roared, holding his ears as if he couldn't stand to hear it. Giggling and panting, she scrambled for a phone book to defend herself from his next onslaught. John stepped forward and wrenched it out of her hands and hit his stampeding brother with it himself, which stopped both his laughter and his forward momentum at exactly the same time. Ann flew across the room, but might have caught her balance if not for staggering against an end table, which propelled her, arms like windmills, into Bethany, who caught an elbow in the mouth.

All night she lay wriggling the tooth with her tongue, tasting for blood. Everyone was deeply upset with Ann, but Bethany didn't care. She could hear them in the next room yelling at each other. She could hear Ann crying like one betrayed and broken-hearted. Tomorrow, Bethany thought, she would have to go up to her and assure her that she was all right, that it wasn't her fault and all that. But she didn't feel like doing it at the moment. Hugh had given her a 222 that he had been carrying around from the time he sprained his wrist, and now the pain had transformed itself into torpor. But she didn't feel as if she could sleep. She wanted to just lie, in the dark, away from the bunch of them.

Ann kept whining that it wasn't fair, Bethany could hear her. Whining and sobbing. "Just because you guys can beat up on anybody you want without actually hurting them!" she was saying. Then John crawled into bed and issued almost a formal apology.

"Everybody's fuckin' drunk," he sighed afterwards.

"I know."

"Well, again, I'm sorry."

"Again, it's all right."

She could feel him picking up a handful of her hair and pressing it into the centre of his face.

"I'm lucky to have you," he said. "I don't tell you that enough — I know it."

Bethany wriggled her tooth and felt pleasure at the sudden bit of power. She smiled involuntarily, separating her split bottom lip and receiving a thread of pain. Perhaps she would be mad. Refuse to say another word. Keep him up all night with worry, her very need for him in question.

◈

Ice-Cream
Man

◈

YOU THINK YOU MUST NOT LOOK the way you feel. People the same height as you are still sometimes place their hands on their knees and lean their faces into yours and ask: "And how old are *you?*" You must somehow still look like you're small, a child. To be a child is not necessarily good, because it means getting more attention than someone more grown and established. Children are the only people that other people just stare at without worrying about it. Children aren't supposed to notice, or care.

But you always cared, remember, because you never liked being the centre of attention, you were just like him that way. People used to come into the shop and compliment him on what a fine job he had done on their shoes, and he would just say, "No, no, it's not true," confusing them because it was obvious that he had. But pretty soon they realized that was just what he said if you were nice to him. Great heels you put on these, Danny — No, no they're not. That's a nice coat you're wearing — No, no it isn't. It was like: Please, please, don't remark upon me. People learn not to. When they like someone, someone quiet who does a good job at things, they put up with what's strange about them. You notice that. It was the opposite with her, when she was alive. Nobody liked her, she didn't do anything, any kind of work, so they wouldn't put up with what was strange.

Locking you out of the bathroom for hours in her big tub full of suds and oils. Thick perfume smells wafting through the keyhole. Let me in, Mother. Pee, pee, pee.

Go to the other bathroom. There is no other bathroom! She knows. You've all lived here for years. She pretends.

Tooralooraloora she sings. You peek at her through the keyhole. She fills up that whole damn tub.

That's why no one cared for her. Let herself go. Wearing the bright clothes to the Co-op when she was supposed to be hiding herself. You used to hear ladies in the store. You knew they were talking about her, because they always called her "Herself."

Oh, look, if it isn't Herself.

What's Herself into today?

Lord bless us and save us if she isn't into the make-up!

Oh my dear God!

It was funny, because she was so enormous. To them it was like washing down a banana split with a diet cola.

But the good thing was that nobody ever noticed you with her around. You were like him, hidden away in the shop, hunched over soles. Everyone likes him, hidden down there. Now that you're tall and she's dead and people see you, they don't mind you too much either.

◇

It is probably important to keep it that way. You never used to have to worry about all this. When you were a child, you could be as weird and stupid as you wanted, but you never actually wanted to. You were practising to be like him, for when you got tall. Because you could see who they put up with and who they didn't. You can see it now, too.

You used to play with Paula Morin all the time because she lived next door and your mother called up and asked her to because you were "too stubborn" to go find anyone yourself. So she'd come over in the winter and ignore you and play with all your toys. It seemed perfectly natural, because she was three years older than you and didn't have any really good toys of her own. So the two of you would just sit on different sides of the living room, you building stuff with Lego and her in the middle of a circle of all these toys you'd forgotten about long ago that she pulled out of the cubbyhole. You'd sit like that in silence for hours. You thought she was great. You begged to have her come over after a while. When the weather got warmer you'd go outside and she'd involve you in all her imaginary games. You would be her baby, or her dog, or an evil arch rival who was not quite as powerful as she was.

She moved to the trailer park on the other side of the town to live with her dad. When she was next door to you, she was with her grandmother. Her mother was, for some reason, in Sydney. It didn't make much sense at the time. So she was one of those people you just forget about for a long time and then in junior high you see them again and you look at each other and say hi and just know somehow that it's as if you have been reincarnated as different people, and it would be in bad taste to act as if you've known each other in the past.

She had these boobs and a perm and wore tops that showed her stomach. The only difference with you was that you were tall. She hung out with the guys that stuck out their feet to trip you if you were passing them outside or in the hall. They were the worst kind of guys, because it didn't matter if you were someone like your mother or someone like you or someone like anyone, they'd trip you and laugh their holes out no matter who you were. One of the guys was Bernie Heany. You used to play skipping with him when you were around eight. He was the only boy who ever played skipping. He used to love it.

The point is that now Paula Morin can't leave her house, because she gang-banged and everybody knows. They used to call her "Paula More 'n' More" and sometimes "Ball-a," and laugh about her all the time, but she still was able to linger in the halls and the smoking area with Bernie and everybody, sticking out her foot right along with them and having a great time, but now she can't leave her house. She used to go to school but she can't even go to school any more. People were saying they were going to kill her. They left stuff in her locker and in her desk. One day when she was still in school, everybody knew about the plan to kill her. People were passing notes all over the place, because they wanted everyone to be in on it. Some girls were going to trick her into going outside behind the rink and then the guys were going to get her. You sat there reading the notes thinking: Why doesn't she call the police? It's against the law to threaten to kill someone. It's written all over her books and her locker. She's got proof. I would just call the police. All she has to do is call the police.

But nothing ever happened. A lot of people went to the rink, but there was nothing going on, the girls couldn't find her. She just stopped coming to school after that.

◇

He feeds you soup every night for dinner and doesn't worry too much about anything. You have to keep reminding him he said he would drive you to the hockey game after you eat. He says he'll do things and then forgets. Oh my, I can't wait to sit and watch the news right after this. You said you'd drive me to the hockey game. Oh yes.... Well, now, I think I'll take another shot at fixing that zipper on Mary MacEachern's bag after dinner. You said you'd drive me to the hockey game. Oh yes.

It's because he never had to do it. She would always do it, if she wasn't in the tub. She loved doing it. Sometimes when you had nowhere to go she would invent stuff for you. She signed you up for step dancing because the lessons were in Antigonish and she enjoyed the drive. She'd get to fart around in the mall while you were dancing. You could never get the hang of it. You hated it. Toe-heel, toe-heel. People said you looked as if you were killing snakes. But she didn't mind one bit.

She'd drive you to the games and you'd sit with Peggy Landry and Gus MacPhail and she'd be standing around talking to the Mountie who took tickets or to Rory McKay who drove the zamboni, not even caring that they were trying to see who had the puck. You used to wish she would go so that you could concentrate and not see which people were looking at her, or what kind of face the Mountie had on him while she was talking. But it was better that she would drive you there and wait and drive you home again than having him taking off his shoes and picking up the newspaper when you're standing there with your coat on.

She'd anticipate the next bath in the car, shivering. Mmmm ... my warm bath calls, she'd growl. Mmmm, the pleasure of a hot bath after having to stand in that cold rink for hours. (You didn't have to stay.) Oh, but the longer I stay, the better it is. Mmmm, I can't wait. The simple pleasures. Pleasure is the absence of pain, Socrates says. All the little things you can indulge in to decrease the pains of living. Oohhhhh yes yes yes, my dear, if that isn't what it's all about, I don't know what is.

And the whole hallway saturated with the smell of lavender and honey and Jim Beam, still hanging in the air when you're getting up for school. Cookie crumbs under your feet as you stand brushing your teeth at the sink.

✧

Gus MacPhail doesn't sit with you any more. Now he's on the ice. But he probably wouldn't anyway. It's just like it was with Ball-a More 'n' More. You used to go over to his house and listen to Bay City Rollers albums on his brother's turntable and he had posters of the Bay City Rollers all over his bedroom. Then you lost track of him and saw him again when you started junior high and the only thing you could think to say was, So, ya still like the Bay City Rollers? And Gus had said, The Gay City Blowers? And that had been the end of that. Now he's a goalie.

You still sit with Peggy, but there's all these other girls there who want to sit with Peggy too. You and Peggy glance at each other sorrowfully every once in a while, because you have less and less to talk about these days. You used to spend days on end together, completely content to be in one another's company. You used to be like the same person. Now the games are pretty much the only thing you have in common and both of you know it.

One of the girls is talking about Paula, that she saw her or something at MacIssac's Variety buying an ice-cream bar and Mr. MacIsaac shot a porno mag down on the counter in front of her and asked if she'd like that too. All the girls go, Oh my God, oh my God for a while, and then talk of other things. When you think about people gossiping, you think of them sitting around talking and talking about people until it makes everyone sick, but that's not really how it works at all. All it takes is one sentence every couple of days, a passing remark or joke. And then that person and all that is wrong with them is riveted inside your skull and if anyone ever says their name around you, it triggers all the remarks and the jokes in a flood — that's what you think of when you think of them. That's how it works.

It's getting hard for the girls to talk, because the game is getting exciting and the men all around you roar. Alan Petrie gets sent into the penalty box, and everyone wants to kill the referee. He's the most judicious and fair referee there's ever been, and most of the time they go around singing his praises, but when he calls against the team they all want to kill him anyway. He is the elementary school math teacher, and the only black man in town. You really hear about it with this sort of thing. Gus MacPhail's mother is hollering that they're going to melt him down and make hockey pucks out of him.

And it's one–nothing for them and the guys try and try to get a goal before the end of the first period, but they can't do it without Alan. When the buzzer goes off, everyone howls with rage and frustration, and then there's a crush to get at the canteen for the pop and chips.

◇

For as long as you've been coming to the rink, the guy at the canteen has always thought it was funny to pretend to refuse to give you whatever it is you come asking for. He never cares how many people are waiting in line behind you, he has to get his joke in. He stands there smoking and grinning, the cigarette bobbing up and down as he talks.

"Chips."

"Chips? Nah, you don't want chips."

"Hot chocolate."

"Oh, no, I don't think so."

"Chips and hot chocolate!"

"I've never heard a more disgustin' combination."

"Just give her her goddamn chips and hot chocolate, Hughie, and stop flirting with the young girls!" some old guy hollers from the throng behind you. All the old drunks retching laughter.

"Wouldn't you rather have a nice ... cold ... ice-cream sandwich?" This same joke since you were seven years old.

"It's too cold!"

"What are you talking about, it's a sauna in here!"

"Give her the Jesus chips, ya pervert! Haw haw haw."

He winks and hands them over. You have to smile at this guy because it's nice to talk to someone who says and does exactly the same thing he's been doing and saying ever since you've known him, without exception. The canteen guy is the only person you know like that. This is a revelation. You'd like to crawl back there behind the counter with him and to hell with the rest of the game.

34

The nice feeling stays with you for the next two periods. Alan Petrie's back in the game. They score, one, two, three goals, and the other team can't score any. The final buzzer goes off and the surrounding crowd writhes and roars in ecstasy, filling up your ears and brain with nothing but them. You're in such a good mood you wave to the canteen guy from the middle of the stampede to get outside. He's lingering in the kitchen door with a smoke behind his ear and one in his mouth. He tells you come here with his finger and there's a look on his face like he's finally going to give you the ice-cream sandwich he's been talking about all these years.

◇

He's not there. The throngs have long since broken up into their cars and gone to their separate homes, the parking lot's empty, he's not waiting. He's at home examining the holes in his slippers. Baffled, probably. What on earth does one do when there's holes in one's slippers? Completely engrossed with the problem.

You're still standing there, too angry to walk when he comes up behind you. You're not surprised, because you listened to him slam and lock the arena doors, and you can smell his duMaurier.

"Still here?"

"He didn't come."

"Boyfriend?"

You actually giggle at this and instantly feel stupid. "No, no. Him, him — my father."

"Just left you here to freeze!"

"Yes."

"Well that's a frigger right there, now."

"I know," you say, feeling grateful.

"I can take you home," he says.

"Oh, good."

"Least I can do, isn't it?" You don't know what he means by that. "Have to be there right away?"

You picture him in the recliner with his slippers in his hands. Open mouth.

"Nope." And off you go.

At ten to twelve, he's asleep in front of the late news, Mrs. MacEachern's bag on his lap. You're lucky he didn't lock the house and go to bed. After a couple of seconds of standing in the hallway regarding him, you walk back to the door, open it, and slam it harder and louder than when you first came in. When you get back to the hall, the bag is on the floor and his eyes are open and he looks about six years old.

"Frigger," you say.

"Now, now...." He picks up the bag and automatically starts experimenting with the zipper again.

"Left me up there to freeze."

"I thought you'd get a ride," he says, furiously yanking the zipper back and forth.

"You didn't think that at all, that or anything."

He stops yanking on the zipper and looks around, still fingering the bag's soft leather. "You have to understand. It never used to be my job."

"It's just common friggin' courtesy. Can't you think of it as just common friggin' courtesy?"

"I've never *had* to think of it."

You decide to go to bed now.

It occurs to him to call, "How did you get home?" when you're at the top of the stairs.

"Got a ride," you call back. "I'll get a ride all the time from now on."

You can hear him making pleased noises to himself down there.

❖

You sit on the toilet across from the enormous claw-foot bathtub Herself had installed before you were born. It would be nice to dump a ton of smelly crap in there and sit in the steaming water, your bones are cold from sitting in his truck, your muscles stiff — but you want too much to go to sleep. It's dangerous to fall asleep in the tub, somebody told you that when you were six and you thought instantly of Herself and never forgot it. You crouched outside the locked door night after night, peeking in the keyhole occasionally to check on her.

"You better not fall asleep in there!" you'd holler, if she appeared ready to nod off. Water would splash everywhere as she jerked up.

"Jesus Murphy! Go play with something and give me some peace."

"Well, you looked as if you were going to sleep."

"Git! Go with you!" You'd watch her sink back down beneath the froth.

You haven't sat in that tub since you were so little you had to be bathed. You always take showers downstairs, quick, without even giving the process a second thought. Him too, every evening after coming up from the shop smelling like dye and leather and polish and glue. It would no more occur to the two of you to sit in Herself's tub than it would to put on her clothes and walk around in them. Why was that?

❖

The first thing to change is the hockey games. You feel foolish just going up and getting your chips and hot chocolate now, and you were afraid, because you didn't know if he might say something new, something that he had never said before, in front of the bundled, hockey-maddened throngs. So for the first little while you had other people get things for you if they were going, and then you'd go and see him afterwards, while everyone else was watching the ice.

"Where were you? I had your chips waitin' right here."

"I don't know."

"Well, here, have them now, eat them with me."

"Good, then."

You rip open the bag and the two of you pass it back and forth. He doesn't even care about the game. He is the only such person in the world. He gives you a hot chocolate and gives himself a coffee and he pours a bit of rum into both. Which tastes awfully good. You try his and you try yours, and yours is better. You're looking at his teeth. They're very long, and each of them is clearly outlined, almost framed by the brown nicotine stains between every one. Cigarettes seem to have given him all the character that is in his face. It's a yellowish colour and the most prominent wrinkles he has are the ones that show up around his mouth when he takes a long drag.

"How long have you been smoking?"

"Since I was ten."

37

"How old are you now?"

"Thirty ... two."

"Pretty old."

"Ya got that right. How 'bout yerself? Just kiddin'."

So this is what you look forward to more than the games themselves. You never would have imagined such a thing. Sitting in back of the canteen with the sound of coffee dripping into the pot louder than the wails and moans of the entire town every time a goal is scored or missed.

One dinnertime at the house in the middle of the soup, he suddenly looks up. "What about your chips?"

"Wha?"

"What about your chips? Don't you still get your treats up at the game?"

"Yah, I get em." You take a half-package of crackers and, holding them above your soup, demolish them into dust and salty fragments.

"Don't you need any money?" he asks.

"Where'd this come from all of a sudden?" you say, because it's been two months since you had to pay for your chips and hot chocolate. "You should be happy."

"It's a boyfriend or something," he says to himself. "Giving you the drives home as well, I suppose."

Two whole months, you think.

"Isn't that nice," he says after a little while. "That'd be your first, if I'm not mistaken." He looks directly at you and bobs his eyebrows. He's impressed with himself for possessing such intimate knowledge of your comings and goings.

◇

It's different at school as well. Since you scarcely see Peggy at the games any more, there are almost no ties left between you at all. It used to bother you, but it now doesn't so much. Sometimes she looks like her feelings are hurt when you don't bother going up to her after French, and all the oh-my-God girls who try so hard to be with her as often as possible must think you're crazy.

Bernie Heany sticks out his foot and you leap over it like a ballerina. They laugh at you, but they laugh at you no matter what, and it's better than falling on your face.

It just seems natural when it's spring and the hockey's all over for the season to traipse past the Kentucky Fried Chicken after school and visit him at the apartment. You have nowhere else to go in particular. Sometimes you just shove the beer boxes and dishes aside and sit at his kitchen table with a cup of tea and do homework and wait for him to wake up.

He says, "Why don't you ever bring me some chicken, you go right past."

"I didn't think of it," you say.

"Don't you think it would be a nice gesture?"

"I suppose."

He's smoking on the couch, watching TV, wearing a sweater, but no pants. "Every woman I've known," he says, "has always tried to do nice things for me."

You put your pencil down and sit there for a second.

"It's not like that with me," you say after a while.

"Well, obviously, eh?"

"It's bad?"

"No, it's not bad. I just think it's interesting, that's all."

A fat boy at school has been sticking notes in your locker. *I like you you are very prety.* That's the sort of thing he means. All that sort of foolishness.

❖

The grandmother used to come over and watch her swirling around the kitchen, her hair coming and going like a black tide. My Jesus, won't you cut that hair, she'd say. Letting it get all over the kitchen. Into the girl's food.

It was true. Every mealtime of your life spent pulling two-foot hairs from the plate.

"I just have to check the bird, and then I'll pin it back," she'd say.

It's hanging into the pot!

Grandmother would gag. Herself used to say that the grandmother spent her whole life making herself sick worrying about germs that would make her sick. When you were a baby, the grandmother would come to visit, and Herself would have spent a week preparing it, filling bucket after bucket with hot water and bleach, sanitizing the whole house. And then the grandmother would arrive and some sort of radar would kick in and she would head straight for underneath the sink and pull out the rag that had been used for cleaning. My good Lord, dear, what's this doing just sitting here? Throw it in the wash! Do you know how many germs could live in here?

It's full of bleach. There's no germs.

Well, it's filthy. The girl would have that in her mouth in no time.

Then, for no reason in particular, the grandmother would raise her head and peer at the light fixture. Herself would follow her mother's gaze, and the two of them would stand regarding the bodies of dead flies all around the bulb. Like they'd been laid there as sacrifices.

Dear, dear, dear, the grandmother would say. *Tch.* She'd wander off to find a bucket and rubber gloves.

But the worst thing, the dirtiest thing for the grandmother was always hair, and the house was always full of it. The kitchen, the bathtub, the laundry. The food. There is still quite a bit of it around. You had to untangle one from the button of your sweater just the other day. You still use one of her brushes, and there's no getting all of it out. You could hypnotize yourself if you think too long about the drain of the bathtub, of how much of Herself remains clogged down there.

Then later the old woman would say, Aren't you a little old for that sort of hair, dear? Couldn't you do something a bit more conservative with it? She was always saying a little, a bit: Oh, just a little wee drop, if you don't mind. I think I'll take a little nap. I think I've got a bit of a cold. Couldn't you stand to lose a bit of weight?

For the first few months after the funeral, she used to come over to the house all the time, thinking that you and he would have it in a shambles, unable to care for yourselves. But much to her surprise, it was in very good order. It remained so. It was like you didn't even live there at all. The grandmother was so impressed that she decided she was no longer needed and went away to live in British Columbia.

◇

It's late when you leave his apartment, hands greasy with chicken, and see Ball-a More 'n' More standing there in the hall. All around her is the smell of cigarette smoke and cheap clothes detergent, which wafts up from the laundry room downstairs. You don't know what to say to her so you just keep heading towards the stairwell, zipping up your coat. She calls, "Hello, hello," sarcastically at you, and you turn around and say that you didn't even recognize her. It is a reasonable thing to say, you think. The last time the two of you had a conversation, you were seven years old and she was making you scamper around on your hands and knees fetching sticks and rocks in your mouth.

She says, "I live just across the hall," but she is in her boots and jacket, and following you down the stairs.

"I didn't know that. Where are you off to now?"

"Out to get smokes. Wanna come for the walk?"

"I've got to get home."

"Fine, then." She's insulted, oddly. "Actually, I saw you coming in a couple of hours ago. I was walkin' right behind you."

"Oh yah," You don't say: *I thought you couldn't go outside any more.* But maybe people are finally starting to forget about Ball-a and how much they want to kill her.

"I know the guy that lives in there," she says.

"Yah, me too. He's nice."

"How do you know him?"

"Oh, I know him from the rink. I just brought him some chicken." Ball-a snorts, but it's not as if you're lying.

"Aren't you good," she says.

"Aren't I though."

"That's what the good people do, I suppose," she says. "The good people bring each other *chicken.*" There's so much hate in her voice that your instinct is to run. But abruptly she laughs and dashes across the field to the variety store, her boots crunching holes through the crust of the snow. You can hear her tossing words over her shoulder, and at first it just seems like an echo — *Chicken! Chicken!* — but then you realize she's calling you names. Just like when you both were little, and you wouldn't touch a cat that had been laying split open on the street.

Now all of a sudden he decides he wants you to go back to religion classes. You haven't gone since Herself stopped being around to take you. You give him a look as if he's crazy and stupid. You've just walked in the door and he's standing there at the table in front of two bowls of soup, one empty, one full.

"Look," he goes, "I remembered."

"Isn't that dandy."

"But you didn't."

"I didn't remember the *soup?* Is that what you're on about?"

"Well, where were you?"

"Eating chicken."

"With himself, I suppose." That's what he has dubbed the new "boyfriend." He has built up a whole mythology surrounding this person and you have at no time spoken one word about it to him. He turns around suddenly. You watch him execute one full circle around the kitchen.

"What in God's name are you doing?"

"You're getting a mouth," he says, squeezing his hands together. "You're eating chicken. You have to go back to religion."

So that's what you do. You don't like seeing him walking in circles, looking this way and that, so you just go. They hold it on Wednesday nights, and that's what it is now.

You come in late, and all the worst kids are there. The kids whose parents are the most strict about prayer and chastity — they automatically become the ones who smoke and drink and curse. You'd think people would see this connection. Bernie Heany is seated behind you with his feet on the back of your chair.

The nun is going on about Abraham and Isaac. God told Abraham to take his son up to the pyre and sacrifice him like a goat, just to see what Abraham would do. Abraham said, Anything you say, God, and hauled him on up there. Then God sent an angel to say, For Pete's sake, Abraham, we didn't really mean for you to do it. But Abraham's all set to go and the angel has to hold him back. Praise be, says the nun, and shows us a picture of a famous painting. There's Abraham with his knife in the air, all set to tear in, the angel trying to wrestle him away. Bernie Heany is snickering because Isaac isn't wearing any clothes and he looks like a girl, all tied up there.

❖

You tell him you're not going back to religion, and you're not coming home for the soup, all the time, either.

"But I got it ready," he keeps saying. "You weren't even here, and I got it ready. I got the bowls down and I heated it up. I was thinking about you."

"I don't want to have soup every friggin' night."

He has to think about that for a moment.

"We can have something else!" It dawns on him: "We can order pizza." You're already stomping up the stairs, pulling off your sweater.

"I can get that when I'm out."

"But you should really have it with me," he says. You can tell by the way he says it that he doesn't even quite know why that is. He just knows that you should.

After a moment or so in front of the bathroom mirror, you holler, "Taking a bath now!" And he lets a couple of moments go by as well.

"What?"

"I'm going to have a bath."

"I wish you wouldn't," he calls immediately. So you turn on both taps at once and water thunders through the empty pipes, causing the entire house to shudder.

And for God's sake, it's great, once you get in there.

◆

Batter
My Heart

◆

YOU SEE IT THERE, every time on the way back to the old man's. Put up by Baptists or the like, about twenty miles or so from the tollbooths. What always happens is that you go away and you forget that it's there until the next time. Just when the fog and eternal drizzle have seeped deep enough inside your head and sufficiently dampened your thinking, it leaps out from the grey and yellow landscape — the same landscape that has been unravelling in front of your eyes for the last three hours. Lurid, over-sized letters painted with green and red and black:

> PREPARE
> TO MEET
> THY GOD

Then the bus zips past almost before you can be startled. And it makes you smile for a moment, just like it always has, and then you forget about it, until, presumably, the next time you've gone away and then come back again.

By the time it gets dark, you are driving through Monastery, so called because there is a monastery. You know when you're passing it because there is a large cross lit up by spotlights positioned on either side of the turn-off. Earlier in the day, the driver slowed down and the people oohed and pointed because a small (it looked small, in the distance) brown bear was scampering towards the woods. Just before disappearing, it turned around to glare. These are all the signs.

The monastery you remember from twice in your life. Once, a pious little kid with your family. You saw the crosses marking the graves of dead monks, you saw the building but didn't go inside that day. It hadn't looked like a monastery. Industrial, like a hospital or a prison. It had been built some time in the fifties. You drank water from a blessed stream.

Now they run some kind of detox program there, the drunks living with the monks. The second time, you were a less-than-pious teenager there to visit both your boyfriend and your history teacher. The two of them were actually related somehow — same last name. He had told you it was a disease that runs in his family. The history teacher, far worse than him, older, having had more time to perfect his craft. The monastery like a second home. Word was, this time it was because he had showed up at an end-of-the-year staff party at the principal's house and walked directly through a sliding-glass door. He had a Ph.D. and spoke fluent Russian. You walked into the common room with your boyfriend and the history teacher was sitting at a table playing gin rummy (ha, ha, ha,) with the other drunks. You and he chatted a moment, he condescending, as usual. But not nearly so much as when he was drunk. You can't remember why, but the last thing he said was that you would never make it in the big world. You could only agree, pliant. You still agree. What did that mean, though, *make it?* Did he think you would shrivel up like an unwatered plant? But at the time, you didn't care, you didn't care to defend yourself, you didn't care about any of it. It was liberating, that. It was almost fun. All of a sudden you didn't have to be nice to the boyfriend who used to seem so sad and fragile, who used to get drunk and then go and take a dirty steak knife from out of the dishpan and look at it.

◇

Now about Daddy, different people have said different things. He is the kindest man you could ever know. Well — he's got his own way. He's got his own opinions and, goddamnit, he's not afraid to express them. With his fists if it comes down to that. Quite the temper. Quite the mouth, if you get him going. A good man. The only honest man in town. A visionary. A saint. Would do anything for you, but if you disappoint him, I guess he'll let you know it. Stark raving mad. One mean son of a bitch.

You get home, and Daddy's throwing a man off the step.

"Mr. Leary, I implore you." The man is filthy, flabby, pale.

"Get offa my step, you goddamn drunk."

"Mr. Leary, I've changed. I've turned over a new Jesus leaf."

"And what d'ya know, there's a bottle of Hermit underneath it!" (a sometime wit, Dad.) "You're more full of shit than my own arse. I'm through wasting time with you, Martin. Offa my step."

"Another chance, Mr. Leary, that's all I ask." The bum straightens himself with boozy dignity.

The old fella has caught sight of you. "Hello, Katey! Martin, I'm telling you for the last time to fuck off. I won't have my little girl gazing on the likes of you."

Martin turns, he seems to bow, but may have just lost his balance. "Hello, dear. I'm sorry not to have a hat to tip at you."

Daddy steps forward with a no-nonsense air. His fists are clenched, his jaw is clenched. It should be laughable in a man this side of sixty, but here is the truth: he is terrifying.

"I'm not gonna tell you again," his voice breaks a little, as though any minute he's going to lose control. Again, it seems so put on that it should be ridiculous. You would think that, anyway. Martin is no fool. He retreats into the driveway.

"Mr. Leary," the bum says, actually resting his hand on his heart. "You were my last hope. I went around tellin' everybody who would listen, Jane at the hospital and them, I ain't worried, no matter how down I get, I know I can count on Mr. Leary to come through for me."

"Don't you try to make me feel guilty, you sick bastard!" Daddy shouts. "I broke my ass for you, Martin, I put my ass on the line!" But Martin is stumbling down the driveway. He has his pride.

"Jesus bum." Dad looks like he wants to hit something. He always looks like that. "Come in and have a bite of tea, now, Katherine."

Daddy had done all he could for Martin. This is what you hear over tea and bannock and Cheddar. Put his ass on the line. Tried to get him straightened up. On his Jesus feet again. Martin lived in an old pulp-cutter's shack out in the woods with no water or electricity. His wife dead of a ruined liver. Both boys in jail for the drunk driving. His girl off living with someone. Dad spits, sickened.

Dad normally wouldn't have done a blessed thing for the drunken idiot, but there had been something rather enchanting about him when they had met over the summer. "Lyrical," Daddy says around a mouthful of bannock, surprising you with the word. Daddy had been on the river helping out a friend with his gaspreaux catch. This was etiquette — everyone who had a fish trap helped everyone else load their vats. Daddy didn't begrudge his friend this, particularly because his own catch, brought in last week, had been larger.

Dad had been sitting on the edge of the trap once the last vat was filled, wiping sweat from his pink, hairless forehead, when Martin Carlyle appeared from out of nowhere and greeted him. The two men had never actually come face to face before, but, as both had attained a kind of notoriety within the community, they recognized one another, and each knew the other's name. Now Daddy puts on a show, acting out the two parts:

"Good day, Mr. Leary, sir!"

"Hullo, Martin."

"By the Lord Jesus, it's a beautiful day!"

"Yes."

"Did you catch a lot of fish today?"

"One or two, Martin, one or two," Dad says, squinting up at the man, who had a terrible matted beard and pee stains on the front of his pants.

Now Martin stands in silence, weaving just a little bit, and appears to be thinking very deeply about something.

"Mr. Leary," he says at last, "I put it to you. Would this not be the perfect day to be bobbing along down the river in one of those vats with a big blonde in one hand and a bottle of Captain Morgan in the other and a pink ribbon tied around your pinocchio?"

Daddy concludes the performance, sputtering bannock crumbs from his laughter. "Lyrical," he says. "That's what you would call lyrical, isn't it, Katey?"

◇

There you were in the monastery, once upon a time, a walking sin.

Defiling the floor tile upon which you tread. A sin taking life in your gut. No one can see it, which is good. Being a girl is bad enough, in a monastery. The drunks turn and stare.

Martin Carlyle among them at the time. A pink ribbon tied around his pinocchio. Sitting on the bridge that crosses the blessed stream as you and the boyfriend traipse by along the muddy path. Spring. Grimy, miserable season. You irreverently spit your gum out into an oncoming mud puddle, and he shoots you a dirty look. Impiety. He's religious now, after two weeks among them. Martin is on the bridge with a fishing pole between his legs. He calls:

"Hey-ho, Stephen, boy!"

"Martin!" Raises his hand.

"Whee-hoo! You got a little friend!"

"How are you, Martin?"

"Ready to break into the vestry, that's how. Get meself a little taste of wine!"

"Don't do that, Martin, don't do that now."

"No —"

Together, you walk up the hill to look at the stations of the cross. He is insistent that you pause at every station. The women clamour at the feet of the suffering Christ. He keeps telling you about how different he is. He keeps saying things like: "I pray now. I honestly pray," and, "Everything seems right. Like all my problems were meaningless."

And you say, "Of course it does," and he says, "What?" and you say, "You get to be in a monastery."

He tells you, "The monastery doesn't have anything to do with it. You just have to learn to pray. I mean really pray. What that means is accepting God."

Well, you are certainly too much of a hardened and worldly wise seventeen-year-old to go for that. "No way," you say.

"Why?" He gives you a gentle look, and you see that he thinks he is a monk. Wise, wizened. Sleeping in a narrow bed, in a little cell, humble. But when you spit your gum out onto the path, and were impolite to Brother Mike, he wanted to hit you. You could see that. Any fool could see that.

"Nothing to accept," you say.

"You can't believe that," Misguided woman. Is there no one left to condemn you? No one, Lord. Then I will condemn you.

"Belief," you say, "doesn't come into it."

He attempts to look at peace with himself yet disappointed with you all at once. Then: "Do you want to go see the shrine to the Virgin?"

Why not? Very nice, very pretty. Easily the prettiest thing here in manland, white stones and plastic flowers all about. He tries to hold your hand, to create some kind of moment, sinner and saviour. He looks over: "Do you want to kneel?"

"No, I don't want to kneel!"

◇

He smiles when you leave, all benevolence, alongside of his favourite monk, Brother Mike. He had wanted you to talk to Brother Mike for some reason, but you said no. He was disappointed, but he said he understood. He thinks that you're making the wrong decision, going away, but he understands that too. He understands everything. He and the monk stand side by side waving goodbye.

When you first arrived, it was Brother Mike who intercepted you. You had gone into the chapel instead of the main entrance, and stood overwhelmed by the height of the ceiling, the lit candles, the looming statues of saints looking down from every corner, the darkness. For want of something to do while you waited for someone to come and find you, you went over and lit a candle for your dead Gramma.

Brother Mike had been kneeling up front, but you didn't even see him, it was so dark. He was standing right beside you before you noticed him. He spoke in a natural speaking voice, not a whisper, which in a church seemed abnormal. "Are you Katherine?"

He led you to the common room, and that was when, watching your feet hit the grey industrial floor tile, it occurred to you what a desecration your presence constituted. Every heartbeat, every snoutful of sanctified oxygen you took went blasphemously down into your bellyful of sin to give it strength. Brother Mike looks around to see if you are still following and gives you a kindly smile.

"Well, the boy had a lot of anger when he came here. A good deal of anger with himself and the world. I think you'll see a big difference."

Now, a few years gone by, the phone will ring late at night. Not often, but every now and again. Bitch. Heartless, stupid .... Just like old times!

The day after you arrive is Sunday, and it is clear that he expects you to accompany your mother to church. No argument. *My, hasn't Katey changed.* Because then it used to seem like there was some kind of moral imperative to jump up and down on the backs of their sacred cows. Isn't it, you used to argue into Daddy's pulsating face, more of a sin to be sitting there thinking the whole proceeding is a pile of shit than to just stay at home? And now you don't care if it is or not, sins and moral imperatives alike being figments of the past.

But when the choir isn't present, ruining the peace, church can be nice, the sun coming in through the fragmented window. You can sit alone among everybody, enjoying your mild hangover. Everybody murmuring responses to the priest in unison. You do it too and are not even aware. That's nice. The powdery smell of clean old men and old ladies all around. The feel of their dry hands when it comes time to extend the blessing to one another. You love the sight of old men in glasses, kneeling, fingering their beads.

But one of the last times you were to mass, also sixteen, Mommy insisted for some reason on going to the early one and there you are with the worst hangover in the world. Ever, in the world. Mother, God love her, with no idea. You say in the car: Hm, Mom, I'm not feeling so good this morning. She says, Yes, Margaret-Ann's kids are all coming down with the flu.

Inside, everything makes you nauseous. You remember that your Gramma had this bottle of perfume that she only wore on Sundays, for mass. She said that she had been using the same bottle for thirty years, and only on Sundays and for weddings and for funerals. You remember that because it smells like the old women sitting on all sides of you must do that too — don thirty-year-old scent for mass. Everything smells putrid. You think that the old man in the pew ahead must have pissed himself a little, as old men will. The priest waves around incense. You stand up, you sit down, you stand up, you sit down, you mutter the response to the priest.

You turn to tell your mother that you need to go outside for air — dang flu bug. Halfway down the aisle, bile fills your cheeks.

Outside, you run around to the back of the church where no one will see you because it faces the water. It's February, the puddle steams. Your breath steams. You eat some snow and gaze out at the frozen strait, mist hanging above it. Hm, you think.

Today, it's not like that. You feel pleasant, dozy, as soon as you take a seat beside your mother in the pew. You pick up the Catholic Book of Worship and read the words to the songs. You've always done that, every since you were small.

Sadly, the choir will be singing today. The well-to-do matrons with sprayed, silver hair and chunky gold jewellery. Most of them are members of the Ladies Auxiliary. You don't know what that is. Mrs. Tamara Cameron approaches the microphone and tells everybody that the opening hymn will be "Seek Ye First." This is the one where they all try to harmonize one long, high-pitched "ALLLLL-LEEEEE-LOOOOO-YAAAAA" with a whole verse. They think it sounds ethereal. The organist is a stiff, skinny fifteen-year-old outcast who appears to be scared out of her mind. You lean over to ask Mommy where the real organist is, Mrs. Fougere, who has been there for as long as you can remember, and your mother whispers that she is dead, as of only two weeks ago.

The first chord that the fifteen-year-old hits is off-key, causing Mrs. Cameron to glower. The girl is going to cry, maybe. No — the song begins.

The congregation has always liked the choir because it means they don't have to sing. They are content to stand there, holding their books open in front of them. But Mommy always sings, choir or no, and she holds her book at an angle so that you can see the words and sing too.

A wonderful thing happens now. You notice Martin Carlyle, shuffling unobtrusively into the back row of the choir box. He is wearing the same clothes as you saw him in yesterday. He blows his nose quietly, with deference, into a repulsive piece of cloth and then tucks it back into his sleeve, where he got it. He picks up a hymn-book, flips it open to the correct page after peeking at someone else's, and decides to join in on the high-pitched "Alleluia" rather than the regular verse. Except that his voice isn't high-pitched, like the ladies'.

54

Seek ye first the Kingdom of God
And his righteousness
And all these things will be offered unto you
Allelu, alleluia.

Mommy says into your ear, "There's Martin," unsurprised, which must mean he shows up for this every Sunday. That is why Mrs. Cameron has failed to glower, and only looks a little put out. What can she say? They are all God's children.

❖

After you've been around for a while, Martin seems to turn up everywhere. He's the town drunk, is why, and the town is small. Every Sunday, you see him at church, singing in the choir, his voice even more off-note than the ladies'. Half the time he doesn't even know the words and sort of yah-yahs his way through. One day you do an experiment and go to the nine o'clock mass instead of the later one. There Martin is, singing away.

He never recognizes you, even after the time on the step. One time you see him at the bar bumming for drinks and you are so pissed that you say to the assholes you are with: "Look! It's my soulmate," and you go over and fling your arm around him and call for two scotches and sodas. You remember him blinking at you with reservation and saying, "Thank you, dear. Thank you, Miss."

Another day you go to the bar — even though you have been saying to yourself all along: I probably shouldn't go to the bar — and of course on that day you see him there and he comes and sits down at the table you're at. So then you go and sit down at a different one but then he comes and sits down there too. All he does is look at you and smoke. It is the first time you've been face to face in two years. At a third table, he sits down right beside you and tells you, in a number of ways, that you are a terrible person and why. The assholes you are with examine their drinks. If one of them would at least move, you could get up from the table.

⬦

For a long time, nothing much happens.

Then, word comes around that Martin has shot himself in the head.
Doctor Bernie, a second cousin, calls from the hospital and informs Daddy
that the patient has been asking for him.

"Holy shit!" says Dad.

"Yes,"the doctor replies. He has an implacable, sing-song voice which
has always annoyed you and your father equally.

"He's been asking for you ever since they brought him in here, Alec."

"Well, holy shit, Bernie, is he going to live or what?"

"Oh yes, he's sitting up having a cup of tea."

Dad has to get you to drive him to the hospital because he is "so Jesus
pissed off I can't see straight."

"Holy shit," he keeps muttering, and, "Stupid bugger."

In the hospital, you hang around the reception desk listening to his
voice resound in the corridor. It is a small hospital. Nurses rush past to
silence him, not understanding that their pasty, wrinkled faces and harsh,
hushed voices and fingers pressed against their lipless mouths are just going
to make him angrier. You remember this from all your life. Shrinking down
in the front seat of the car while Daddy yells at a careless driver. Shrinking
down in the wooden desk while Daddy yells at your math teacher.
Shrinking down into the chesterfield while Daddy yells at the television.
Everything making him angrier and angrier and nobody getting it right.

But when Daddy emerges, trailing flustered and ignored nurses, he is
laughing.

"Leave it to Martin," he says. "Shoots himself through the head and
even that doesn't do him a bit of good."

"So are you going to help him again, Daddy?"

"Well, Jesus Christ, Katey, what are you gonna do, you know?"

⬦

He doesn't really know what to do any more, he's done so much already.
He used to drive Martin to AA meetings (much as he had hated them

himself in the old days) but was soon informed by such-and-such that Martin took advantage of the trips into town to visit the liquor store and drop in at Buddy's Tavern. And everything ended up like that. Daddy had badgered social services into boosting Martin's allowance so that he could buy some soap and deodorant and Aqua Velva and clothes to get himself cleaned up for the job Dad had managed to get him sweeping up at the mill. Then, when Dad heard about the new public housing units that were going up, social services found themselves duly annoyed into putting one aside for Martin, even though they were being clamoured for by single mothers and the like.

So Daddy drove out to Martin's shack in the woods, which had no water or electricity, and laid all of this at his feet.

"By God, Martin," he said, "you'll get the new place all snugged up nice and pretty soon you'll be having your daughter over for Sunday dinner."

"No, Mr. Leary, my daughter wouldn't come over so she could spit on me."

"Well, goddamnit, you can have me over to dinner!"

"Proud to, Mr. Leary."

Daddy handed him the keys and, looking around at the differing piles of junk that served as Martin's furniture, told him to just give social services a call once he got everything packed away and ready to go. They'd come and get him moved in. "By the Jesus, I'll come and help too," he added.

"God bless you, Mr. Leary,"

"Aw, well, what the fuck."

Dad left, feeling good, stepping over Martin's sick, emaciated dog, King.

But months went by and social services called up: "Mr. Leary, there is a list of people as long as my arm who are waiting to get into that unit, and it just sitting there...." Dad barks something that shuts the sarcastic little bastard right up, and then hangs up so he can phone his buddy at the mill. How has Martin been getting along? Martin Carlyle? He didn't show up, Alec, and I wasn't expecting him to.

Outside the shack with no water or electricity, Daddy found Martin asleep on the ground while King sniffed daintily at the surrounding vomit. Martin's drinking friend, Alistair, was leaning against the side of the house, taking in the sunshine. A beautiful spring day. He was not passed out, but cradled a near-empty bottle of White Shark against his crotch, serene and Buddha-like.

He squinted up at Daddy and said that himself and Martin had been having "a regular ceilidh" all month long with the extra welfare that Martin was now getting. Daddy kicked the dog into the woods and threw the bottle of White Shark in after it. This having been the incident that preceded the throwing of Martin Carlyle from Alec Leary's step, where you came in.

◇

Daddy has a sore knee. It makes him hobble when he walks, and it makes him angry. You have to go out and help him bring the wood in because none of your brothers are about. If you were one of them, it would be a bonding moment between you and he. It might be anyway. He likes you when you work. Here is one thing you know: Men love work. You might not know anything about what women love, but men love work.

You can always tell when it's Martin phoning, because Daddy's tone will become reserved. You hear him say things like: Well, I'll do what I can, Martin, but I'm not making any promises, you hear me? I can't just give give give. Then Dad will hang up and turn to you.

"If that Martin Carlyle ever comes around when I'm not here, don't you let him in."

"No."

"Do you know what he looks like?"

"Yes, I've seen him a million —"

"A big fat hairy ugly bastard and he's got a hole in his head" — Daddy points to a spot above one of his eyebrows — "where the bullet went in."

Daddy is busy these days with Little League. The head of the recreation department called him up and asked him to coach. "Nobody else wanted to do it, I suppose," he grunted into the phone. "Selfish whores."

And your mother, observing that you never seem to go out any more and have absolutely nothing to occupy your time, ever so delicately suggests that it would be nice and he would like it if you attended the games. So you do, even though you have no understanding of baseball and don't know when to cheer or when to boo and are the only woman there who isn't somebody's mother and almost get hit on the head with a foul ball twice. You watch him hobbling back and forth in front of the dugout, hollering at both teams and causing the little guy at bat's knees to knock together. At the end of every game, win or lose, he takes them to the Dairy Queen and buys them all sundaes. You get to come along too. You have coffee. The little boys look at you and ask you questions about yourself. Are you married? What grade are you in? They can't quite figure out where you fit. You answer every question as honestly as you can, but it doesn't help them any.

Soon, you're attending the practices. Maybe you are the unofficial mascot. Dad gets frustrated with them one day and steps up to the plate to show them how it's done. He can't throw any more because his arm cramps up when he raises it above his shoulder, and he can't run because of his knee, but he gets the best pitcher on the team to throw him one so they can see how to hit. The clenched fists and clenched jaw all over again — overweight, balding man clutching a child's tool in his large, pink hands. When he swings the bat, it makes a sound that frightens you and you look up from picking at your nails and see that all the little round faces are turned upward in awe.

❖

Jesus Christ,
Murdeena

❖

HER MOTHER WOULD TELL YOU it started with the walks. Just out of the blue, not too long after she got fired from the Busy Burger and had been kicking around the house for a few days. Out comes Murdeena with, "I think I'll go out for a little walk." Margaret-Ann was just finishing up the dishes and hurried to dry off her hands when she heard it, thinking Murdeena was being sly about asking for a drive somewhere.

"Where do you want to go?" asks Margaret-Ann.

"I don't know, I'm just going to walk around."

"Where are you going to walk around?"

"I'll just go down by the water or somewhere."

"Here, I'll take you down," she says, reaching for the keys.

"Pick me up a Scratch and Win!" Mr. Morrisson calls from the couch, hearing them jingle.

"No, no, no," goes Murdeena. "I'm just going for a walk, to look at the water."

"I'll drive you down, we can sit in the car and look at it," says Margaret-Ann. She doesn't know what her daughter is on about.

"I want to go for a *walk,*" says Murdeena.

"Who goes for *walks?*" points out Margaret-Ann. She's right, too. Nobody goes for walks. The only people who go for walks are old women and men who have been told by their doctors that they have to get more exercise. You can see them, taking their turns around the block every night after supper, looking none too pleased.

"What's the matter with you?" asks Margaret-Ann. She's thinking Murdeena is feeling bad about getting fired and wants to go mope.

"Nothing, Mumma. It's a nice night."

"Go sit on the porch, you don't have to go traipsing about."

"I *want* to."

"Go on, I'll bring you a cup of tea."

"I don't want to drink any more tea. I want to walk."

Thinking of the seniors, it occurs to Margaret-Ann that walking is a healthy pastime, and maybe she should encourage it.

"You're on some kind of new health kick, now, are you?"

"No."

"Well, if that's what you want to do," she says, doubtful. "Are you going to be all right?"

"Yes." Meanwhile Murdeena's digging around in the porch, trying to find something to put on her feet.

"Do you need a jacket?"

"Yeah, I'll put on my windbreaker."

"Maybe you should wear mine," says Margaret-Ann, fidgety about the whole performance.

"No, I'll be all right."

"What do you got on your feet?"

That's a bit of a problem. Nobody walks, so nobody has any walking shoes. Murdeena settles for a pair of cowboy boots she bought in Sydney back when they were in style.

"You can't walk in those."

"They're *made* for people to walk in. Cowboys. They walk all around the range."

"They ride around on their horses," protests Margaret-Ann.

"Well, they'll do for now." Murdeena puts on her windbreaker.

Then Ronald pipes up again. "She's not going out by herself, is she?" he calls from the couch.

"Yes. She wants to go for a *walk*."

"Where's she going to walk to?"

"Jesus Murphy, I'll bring you back a Lotto!" Murdeena hollers before the whole rigmarole can get under way again, and she clomps out the door in her boots. So there's Margaret-Ann left to do all the explaining.

Margaret-Ann will tell you that is where it all started, although it didn't seem like much of anything at first. Murdeena walking. By herself, in the evening. Perhaps it was getting fired, that's what Margaret-Ann thought. Murdeena had never been fired before, although the Busy Burger was only her second job — before that she was a cashier at Sobey's, for four years, right up until it closed down. She was great at it, and everybody liked her. She liked it too because she got to visit with everyone in town and catch up on their news. The Busy Burger wasn't so much her style because most of the people who came in were high school kids and Carl Ferguson who ran the place was a big fat shit. She used to get along so well with her manager at Sobey's, because they'd gone to school together, but Carl Ferguson was just this mean old bastard she couldn't relate to who didn't like girls and treated them all like idiots. He picked on Murdeena especially because she couldn't count. Even with the cash register there giving a read-out, she never gave anyone the right change. Murdeena could never do math, none of the teachers at school could figure her out because the math teacher assumed she was borderline retarded while the rest of them were giving her A's and B's. There must be some kind of condition where you can't do math, just like the one where you can't spell, and that's what Murdeena had. If you asked her anything having to do with numbers, she'd change the subject. If you asked her how many people lived in her town, she'd say, "Oh, quite a few," or else, "Oh, it's about the size of Amherst, I'd guess. Maybe more." If you'd try to pin her down on a figure, she might say something like, "Oh … maybe … a … couple of hundred." It was a good way to get her back in high school. We'd all laugh.

But her mind just didn't work that way, some people's minds don't. It didn't make her a moron, but Carl Ferguson treated her like one anyway. She was always careful to check the register and count out the change meticulously, but sometimes the bastard would stand there watching her making slow calculations as she moved the change from the register to her palm and he'd wear this disgusted smirk and make her all nervous. So one day, right in front of him, she handed Neil MacLean a twenty instead of a five. Neil said he could see her hand shaking as she did it, and he tried to nod to her or something, let her know in some way that the change was wrong. Before he could do a blessed thing, though, Carl Ferguson tears the twenty out of her hand. "For Christ's sake, woman," he goes. "You trying to make me go broke?" And Murdeena cried and Neil, probably trying to help out, told Carl he was an arsehole, but that's when Carl told her she was fired — probably just to shut Neil up and prove that he could do or say whatever he damn well pleased in his own establishment.

Everyone hated Carl after that because everyone liked Murdeena. Whenever she gave people back the wrong change at Sobey's, they'd just say, "Oops, dear, I need a bit more than that," or a bit less, or whatever, and then they'd help her to count out the right amount, and then everyone would have a big laugh together.

So then she was on UI again and there was talk in town about a big bulk-food store opening up, and Margaret-Ann kept telling her there was no need to worry.

"I'm not worried anyways," says Murdeena.

"Then why all the walks?" This was after the fourth walk of the week. Murdeena was going through all the shoes in the closet, trying to find the best pair for walking. Tonight she had auditioned a pair of her brother Martin's old basketball sneakers from eight years ago.

"I'm not walking because I'm worried about anything!" says Murdeena, surprised. And the way she says it is so clean and forthright that Margaret-Ann knows she's not lying. This makes Margaret-Ann more nervous than before.

"Well for the love of God, Murdeena, what are you doing stomping around out there all by yourself?"

"It's nice out there."

"It's nice, is it."

"Yes."

"Well, it seems like an awful waste of time, when I could be driving you anywhere you wanted to go."

Murdeena has never gotten her driver's licence. This is something else about her that's kind of peculiar. She says there isn't any point because she never goes anywhere. Margaret-Ann and Ronald like it because it means that she still needs them to do things for her from time to time.

"If I wanted to go for a drive," says Murdeena, "I'd go for a drive."

"It just seems so Jesus *pointless!*" bursts out Margaret-Ann, wishing Murdeena would quit fooling with her, pretending everything was normal. People around town were starting to make remarks. Cullen Petrie at the post office:

"Oh, I see your girl out going for the walks these days."

"Yes, it's her new thing, now."

"Well, good for her! I should be getting out more myself."

"Yes, shouldn't we all," says Margaret-Ann, officiously licking her stamps.

"Isn't she tough!"

"Yes, she is."

"Every night I see her out there," marvels Cullen Petrie. "Every night!"

"Yes." Margaret-Ann gathers up her mail in a pointed sort of fashion, so as to put Cullen in his place. "Yes, she's tough, all right."

Cullen calls after her to have Murdeena put in an application at the post office — he'd be happy to see what he could do for her. Margaret-Ann would like to kick him.

"You don't *need* a job right now, in any event," Margaret-Ann keeps telling her over and over again. "Your UI won't run out for a year, and you've got enough to keep you busy these days."

"That's right," agrees Murdeena, clomping around in an old pair of work boots to see how they fit, and not really paying much attention. "I've got lots to keep me busy."

Murdeena is always on the go, everyone says so. She plays piano for the seniors every weekend and always helps out at the church teas and bake sales. She'll do the readings in church sometimes, and plays on her softball team. It used to be the Sobey's softball team before it closed down, but they all enjoyed the games so much that the employees didn't want to disband. They ripped the cheap SOBEY'S logos off their uniforms and kept playing the other businesses in town anyway. Nobody minded. For a joke, they changed their name to the S.O.B.'s.

Some people are concerned that she doesn't have a boyfriend, but Margaret-Ann and Ronald are relieved, they like her where she is. She went out with a fellow in high school for three years, and it looked as if things were pretty much all sewn up for after graduation, but didn't he go off to university — promising they'd talk about the wedding when he came home for the summer. Well, you don't have to be a psychic, now, do you?

So Murdeena hasn't been seeing anyone since then — almost five years now. She has her own small group of friends, the same ones she had in school, and they all go out to the tavern together, or sometimes will take a trip over to the island or into Halifax. There are a couple of young fellows that she spends time with, but they're all part of the group, one with a girl-friend and one married.

So no one can think of anyone Murdeena might end up with. Murdeena knows everyone in town and everyone knows her. Everyone has their place and plays their part. So it's hard to think of changing things around in any sort of fundamental way. Like starting something up with someone you've known since you were two. It doesn't feel right, somehow.

◇

"To hell with it," she announces one evening after supper. She's got every pair of shoes in the house lined up across the kitchen floor.

"What is it now?" gripes Margaret-Ann, even though Murdeena hasn't said a word up until now. Margaret-Ann always feels a little edgy after suppertime, now, knowing Murdeena will be leaving the house to go God knows where. "What's the matter with you?"

"None of these are any good." She kicks at the shoes.

"What do you mean? Wear your nice deck shoes."

"No."

"Wear your desert boots."

"They're all worn out. I've worn them all. None of them feel right."

"Do they hurt your feet? Maybe you need to see a doctor."

"They don't hurt, Mumma, they just don't feel *right*."

"Well, for Christ's sake, Murdeena, we'll go out and get you a pair of them hundred-dollar Nike bastards, if that'll keep you quiet."

"I'm going to try something else," says Murdeena, sitting down in one of the kitchen chairs. *Thank God!* thinks Margaret-Ann. *She's going to stay in and drink her tea like a normal person.*

But Murdeena doesn't reach for the teapot at all. What she does is take off her socks. Margaret-Ann just watches her, not really registering anything. Then Murdeena gets up and goes to the closet. She takes out her windbreaker. She puts it on. Margaret-Ann blinks her eyes rapidly, like a switch has been thrown.

"What in the name of God are you doing now?"

"I'm going for my walk."

Margaret-Ann collapses into the same chair Murdeena had been sitting in, one hand covering her mouth.

"You've got no *shoes!*" she whispers.

"I'm going to give it a try," says Murdeena, hesitating in the doorway. "I think it'll feel better."

"For the love of Jesus, Murdeena, you can't go walking around with no shoes!" her mother wails.

Murdeena makes her lips go thin and doesn't ask her mother why, because she knows why just as well as Margaret-Ann does. But she's stubborn.

"It'll be all right. It's not cold."

"There's broken glass all over the street!"

"Oh, Mother, there is not."

"At least put on a pair of sandals," Margaret-Ann calls, hoping for a compromise. She follows Murdeena to the door, because she's leaving, she's going out the door, she's doing it. And she's hurrying, too, because she knows if her mother gets hold of that windbreaker, she'll yank her back inside.

"I won't be long," Murdeena calls, rushing down the porch steps.

Margaret-Ann stands on the porch, blinking some more. She thinks of Cullen Petrie sitting on his own front porch across the street, taking in the evening breeze.

◇

Murdeena Morrisson has been parading all over town with no shoes on her feet, everyone says to everyone else. They marvel and chuckle together. They don't know what she's trying to prove, but it's kind of cute. People will honk their horns at her as they go by and she'll grin and wave, understanding. "You're going to catch cold!" most of them yell, even though it's the middle of summer. The only people who are kind of snotty about it are the teenagers, who are snotty to everyone anyway. They yell "hippie!" at her from their bikes, because they don't know what else to yell at a person without shoes. Sometimes they'll yell, "Didn't you forget something at home?"

Murdeena hollers back: "Nope! Thanks for your concern!" She's awfully good-natured, so nobody makes a fuss over it, to her face anyway. If that's what she wants to do, that's what she wants to do, they say, shaking their heads.

Margaret-Ann does her shopping with a scowl and nobody dares mention it to her. Murdeena won't wear shoes at all any more. She'll go flopping into the pharmacy or the seniors home or anywhere at all with her big, dirty feet. The Ladies Auxiliary held a lobster dinner the other night, and there Murdeena was as usual, bringing plates and cups of tea to the old ladies, and how anyone kept their appetites Margaret-Ann could not fathom. Murdeena stumbled with a teacup: "Don't burn your tootsies, now, dear!" Laughter like gulls.

◈

"I don't want to hear another word about it!" Margaret-Ann announces one evening at the supper table. Murdeena looks up from her potatoes. She hasn't said a thing.

It is obviously a signal to Ronald. He puts down his fork and sighs and dabs his lips with a paper napkin. "Well," he says, searching for the right words. "What will you do in the winter? They're'll be snow on the ground."

Margaret-Ann nods rapidly. Good sound logic.

Murdeena, still hunched over her plate — she's been eating like a football player these days, but not putting on weight, as she tends to — suddenly grins at the two of them with startling love.

"I'll put on *boots* when it's wintertime!" she exclaims. "I haven't gone crazy!" She goes to shovel in some potatoes but starts to laugh suddenly and they get sprayed across the table.

"Oh, for Christ's sake, Murdeena!" complains her mother, getting up. "You'd think you were raised by savages."

"That's politically incorrect," Ronald articulates carefully, having done nothing but watch television since his retirement.

"My arse," Margaret-Ann articulates even more carefully. Murdeena continues to titter over her plate. This quiet glee coming off her lately is starting to wear on Margaret-Ann. Like she's got some big secret tucked

70

away that she's going to spring on them at any moment, giving them instant triple heart attacks. "And what's so Jesus funny inside that head of yours, anyway?" she stabs at Murdeena suddenly. "Walking around grinning like a monkey, like you're playing some big trick on everybody, showing off those big ugly feet of yours."

Offended, Murdeena peers beneath the table at them. "They're not ugly."

"They're ugly as sin!"

"Since when?"

"Since you decided you wanted to start showing them off to the world!"

"Why should anybody care about seeing my *feet?*" queries Murdeena, purely bewildered.

"Exactly!" shoots back her mother. "Why should anyone care about seeing your feet!"

It ends there for a while.

❖

She had always been the sweetest, most uncontentious little girl. Even as a baby, she never cried. As a child, never talked back. As a teenager, never sullen. She was their youngest and their best. Martin had driven drunk and had to go to AA or face jail, and Cora had gotten pregnant and then married and then divorced, and Alistair had failed grade nine. And all of them moved far away from home. But Murdeena never gave them any trouble at all. *Agreeable* was the word that best described Murdeena. She was always the most agreeable of children. Everybody thought so.

Gradually, however, she takes to speaking to Margaret-Ann like she believes her to be an idiot.

"Mother," she says, slow and patient, "there's things you don't understand right now."

"Mother," she murmurs, smiling indulgently, "all will be explained."

Margaret-Ann rams a taunt, red fist into a swollen mound of bread dough. "Will you take your 'mothers' and stuff them up your hole, please, dear?"

"Ah, Mumma," Murdeena shakes her head and wanders away smiling, her bare feet sticking to the kitchen linoleum. Margaret-Ann fires an oven mitt at her daughter's backside, and feels around the counter for something more solid to follow it up with. She can't stand to be condescended to by Murdeena.

The world seems on its head. She can hear her in the living room with Ronald, solemnly advising him to turn off the TV and listen to her tell him something, and Ronald is trying to joke with her, and play round-and-round-the-garden-like-a-teddy-bear on her hand to make her laugh. She won't give him her hand. Margaret-Ann can hear her daughter speaking quietly to her husband while he laughs and sings songs. Margaret-Ann feels dread. She goes to bed without asking Ronald what Murdeena had tried to say.

It is reported to Margaret-Ann later in the week. The folks at the seniors home were enjoying a slow and lovely traditional reel when the entertainer abruptly yanked her hands from the keys and slammed the piano shut. The loud wooden *thunk* echoed throughout the common room and the piano wires hummed suddenly in nervous unison. A couple of old folks yelped in surprise, and one who had been sleeping would have lurched forward out of his wheelchair if he hadn't been strapped in.

"Murdeena, dear, are you trying to scare the poor old souls out of their skins?" gasped Sister Tina, the events organizer, and Margaret-Ann's informant.

"There's just so much to tell you all," Murdeena reportedly answered, staring down at the shut piano, which looked like a mouth closed over its teeth. "And here I am playing reels!" She laughed to herself.

"Are you tired, dear?" Sister Tina asked in her little-girl's voice, always calculated to be soothing and inoffensive to those around her. She moved carefully forward, using the same non-threatening gestures she approached the seniors with.

With unnerving spontaneity, Murdeena suddenly cried, "There's so much news!"

"What's wrong with her?" barked Eleanor Sullivan, who loved a good piano tune. "Get her a drink of rum!"

"Give her some slippers, her feet are cold," slurred Angus Chisholm, groggy from being jolted out of his snooze.

"I have some good wool socks she can put on," Mrs. Sullivan, the most alert and officious of the bunch of them, offered. "Run and get them for her, Sister, dear." All of a sudden, all the seniors were offering to give Murdeena socks. A couple of them were beckoning for Sister Tina to come and help them off with their slippers — Murdeena obviously had more need of them than they did.

"I haven't been able to feel my *own* goddamned feet in years," Annie Chaisson was reasoning, struggling to kick off her pom-pommed knits.

"For the love of God, everyone keep your shoes on," commanded Sister Tina. "You'll all get the cold and there won't be enough people to look after you!"

"I don't need your footwear!" hollered Murdeena. "I need to be heard! I need to be believed and trusted and heard!"

It was an outlandishly earnest thing to say, and the old people looked everywhere but at the piano. Murdeena had swung around on the stool and was beaming at them. What came next was worse.

❖

"I take it you've heard," says Murdeena to her mother. She'd gone for a walk after her time with the seniors and stayed out for two and a half hours. Margaret-Ann stands in the middle of the kitchen, practically tapping her foot like a caricature of an angry, waiting mother. You would think Murdeena was a teenager who had been out carousing all night. Ronald is sitting at the kitchen table looking apprehensive because Margaret-Ann told him to and because he is.

"I take it you have something you'd like to say," Margaret-Ann shoots back. "You're father tells me you've already said it to him. And now that you've said it to a bunch of senile incontinent old friggers, perhaps you can say it to your own mother."

"All right," says Murdeena, taking a breath. "Here she goes."

"Let's hear it, then," says Margaret-Ann.

"I am the Way and the Light," says Murdeena.

"What's that now?"

"I am the Way and the Light," says Murdeena.

"*You* are," says Margaret-Ann.

"I am."

"I see."

Ronald covers the lower part of his face with his hands and looks from one woman to the other.

"Now what way and what light is that?" asks Margaret-Ann with her hands on her hips.

"What — ?"

"What way and what light is it we're talking about?"

Murdeena swallows and presses her lips together in that stubborn but uncertain way she has. "The way," she says, "to heaven."

Margaret-Ann looks to her husband, who shrugs.

"And the light," continues Murdeena, "of — well, you know all this, Mother. I shouldn't have to explain it."

"Of?"

"Of salvation."

Murdeena clears her throat to fill up the silence.

They are up all night arguing about it.

◇

First of all, the arrogance. It is just plain arrogant to walk around thinking you are "the end-all and be-all," as Margaret-Ann insisted on putting it. She would acknowledge it in no other terms.

"What you're saying is you're better than the rest of us," was Margaret-Ann's argument.

"No, no!"

"You're walking around talking like you know everything. No one's going to stand for it."

"Not *everything*," said Murdeena. But she was smiling a little, you could tell she thought she was being modest.

"People aren't going to stand for it," Margaret-Ann repeated. "They're going to say: 'Murdeena Morrisson, who does she think she is?'"

"Oh, for Pete's sake, Mumma!" burst Murdeena with uncharacteristic impatience. "Don't you think back in Nazareth when Jes — I mean me, when I was telling everyone in Nazareth ..."

Margaret-Ann covered her ears.

"... about how I was the Way and the Light back then, don't you think everyone was going around saying: 'Humph! Jesus Christ! He must think he's some good! Walking around, preaching at people.'"

"This is blasphemy," hollered Margaret-Ann over the sound of blood pumping through her head. She was pressing against her ears too tightly.

"That's what they said back then, too."

Margaret-Ann was right and Murdeena was wrong. Nobody wanted to

74

hear it. Everyone liked Murdeena, but she was taking her dirty bare feet and tromping all over their sacred ground. Word spread fast.

❖

Pouring tea for Mrs. Foguere in the church basement, she leans over to speak.

"Once upon a time, there was a little town on the water...." she begins.

"Oh, please, dear, not now," Mrs. Fouguere interrupts, knowing by now what's coming and everybody looking at her with pity.

"No, it's okay," says Murdeena, "I'm telling you a story."

"I just want to drink my tea, Murdeena, love,"

"There was this whole town of people, you see ... and they were all asleep! The whole town!"

"I don't believe I care for this story, dear," says Mrs. Fouguere.

"No, no, it's a parable! Just wait," Murdeena persists. "This whole town, they were all asleep, but the thing is ... they were sleepwalking and going about their business just as if they were awake."

"I don't care to hear it, Murdeena."

"Yes, for God's sake, dear, go and have a little talk with the Father, if you want to talk," Mrs. MacLaughlin, seated at the next table and known for her straightforward manner, speaks up.

"But it's a parable!" explains Murdeena.

"It doesn't sound like much of a friggin' parable to me!" Mrs. MacLaughlin complains. The women nearby all grumble in agreement.

Murdeena straightens up and looks around at the room: "Well, I'm only starting to get the hang of it!"

The ladies look away from her. They take comfort, instead, in looking at each other — in their dresses and nylons and aggressive, desperate cosmetics. Someone snickers finally that it was certainly a long way from the Sermon on the Mount, and a demure wave of giggles ripples across the room. Murdeena puts her hands on her hips. Several of the ladies later remark on how like Margaret-Ann she appeared at that moment.

"To hell with you, then," she declares, and flops from the room, bare feet glaring.

Murdeena has never been known to say anything like this to anyone before, certainly no one on the Ladies Auxiliary.

Sister Tina comes to the house for a visit.

"Seeing as I'm the Way and the Light," Murdeena explains, "it would be wrong for me not to talk about it as often as possible."

"Yes, but, dear, it wasn't a very subtle story, was it? No one likes to hear that sort of thing about themselves."

"The point isn't for them to *like* it," spits Murdeena. "They should just be quiet and listen to me."

At this, Margaret-Ann leans back in her chair and caws. Sister Tina smiles a little, playing with the doily the teapot has been placed upon.

"They *should*," the girl insists.

"They don't agree with you, dear."

"Then they can go to hell, like I said."

"Wash your mouth out!" gasps her mother, furious but still half-laughing.

Sister Tina holds up her tiny hand with all the minute authority she possesses. "Now, that's not a very Christian sentiment, is it Murdeena?"

"It's as Christian as you can get," Murdeena counters. Scandalously sure of herself.

The next day, the Sister brings the Father.

"I hate the way she *talks* to everyone now," Margaret-Ann confides to him in the doorway. "She's such a big know-it-all." The Father nods knowingly and scratches his belly. The two of them, he and Murdeena, are left alone in the dining room so they can talk freely.

Crouched outside the door, Margaret-Ann hears Murdeena complain: "What are dining rooms for, anyway? We never even use this room. Everything's covered in dust."

"It's for *good!*" Margaret-Ann hollers in exasperation. Sister Tina gently guides her back into the kitchen.

The Father's visit is basically useless. Afterwards he keeps remarking on how argumentative little Murdeena has become. She would not be told. *She simply will not be told,* he keeps repeating. The Father has little idea how to deal with someone who will not be told. He makes it clear that his uselessness was therefore Murdeena's own fault, and goes off to give Communion to the next-door neighbour, Allan Beaton, a shut-in.

"Everyone's too old around here," Murdeena mutters once the priest is gone. She's watching him out the window as Allan Beaton's nurse holds the door open to let him in. The nurse is no spring chicken herself. The father is mostly bald with sparse, cotton-ball hair and a face like a crushed paper bag.

"You're just full of complaints, these days," her mother fumes, hauling a dust rag into the dining room.

❖

So now Murdeena is going around thinking she can heal the sick. She figures that will shut them up. In the parking lot at the mall, Leanne Cameron accidentally slams her seven-year-old boy's finger in the car door and Murdeena leaps from her mother's Chevette and comes running up, bare feet burning against the asphalt, a big expectant grin splitting her face. This scaring the piss out of the little boy, who starts to scream at the sight of her, twice as loud as before. Murdeena tries and tries to grab the hand, but Leanne won't let her anywhere near him. It is a scene that is witnessed and talked about. Margaret-Ann vows never to take Murdeena shopping with her again, or anywhere else, for that matter.

Margaret-Ann declares that she has officially "had it." She experiments with giving Murdeena the silent treatment, but Murdeena is too preoccupied to notice. This hurts Margaret-Ann's feelings, and so she stops experimenting and quits talking to her daughter altogether. Her days get angrier and quieter, as she waits for Murdeena to take notice of her mother and do the right thing. See to her.

"See to your mother," Ronald pleads with her at night, lowering his voice so that the television will keep it from carrying into the kitchen. "Please go in and see to her."

Murdeena's head snaps up as if she had been asleep and someone had clapped their hands by her ear. "Did she hurt herself? Is she bleeding?" She wiggles her fingers eagerly, limbering up.

She starts lurking around the children's softball games, hoping someone will get a ball in the face or sprain their wrist sliding into home. She hovers like a ghoul and the children play extra carefully all summer long as a result. Murdeena watches toddlers waddling away from their parents, toward broken bottles and the like, with her fingers crossed.

By now, though, people know to keep their kids away from Murdeena Morrisson. In the space of a couple of months it has become the community instinct. She stalks the adult softball games too, even though she has long since stopped playing for the S.O.B.'s.

❖

No one can very well tell Murdeena to stop coming to play piano, since she has been doing it since she was thirteen and on a volunteer basis — Margaret-Ann thought it would be a good way for her to get some practice and do something nice for the senile incontinent old friggers at the same time. So Murdeena headed over every Sunday after supper, and for the next ten years there never arose any reason for her to stop. It was a perfectly satisfactory relationship, if somewhat stagnant. The seniors asked for, and Murdeena played impeccably, the same songs, Sunday night after Sunday night. "Mairi's Wedding" and "Kelligrew's Soiree" and such. Some of the seniors who were there when she first started playing had died, but most of them were still around — living out the final years of their lives while Murdeena was experiencing practically the whole of her own, a bland and inoffensive local girl for them to tease about clothes and boyfriends, sucking up her youth.

But Murdeena will no longer be teased. Her friends have abandoned her in response to the "high and mighty" tone she's adopted with them, her mother is angry, and her father has never spoken to her much in the first place. The seniors are the only captive audience she has. For the first little while after the night she slammed the piano shut, she'd make a slight pretence of being there to play for them, but the tunes would usually trickle off after a few minutes. She'd stealthily start making inquiries about Angus Chisholm's knee, Annie Chaisson's hip, Eleanor Sullivan's arthritis.

"If you'd just let me hold your hands for a couple seconds, Mrs. Sullivan," she'd plead.

"My dear, I'd love for you to hold my hands, but not in the spirit of blasphemy."

They listened, though. The seniors are the most tolerant of the town, for some reason neither threatened nor scandalized by what Murdeena has to say. They don't tease her about the way she looks either — they don't mention her feet. Murdeena's lips are now always thin, and so is her body — she has finally lost all her baby fat from walking the streets for hours into the night and sometimes forgetting to eat supper. It's October, and there's no sign of shoes as yet. The seniors decide it's her own business and they don't say a word.

And so, stymied by the town, she gradually turns all her attention and efforts to the attentive oldies, stuck in their chairs every Sunday night until the nurses come along to help them to bed, waiting to hear Murdeena. Sister Tina — who writhes and jumps like she's being jabbed with hot pokers at every word out of Murdeena's mouth — soon realizes that she needn't be worried about the girl giving them offence. The seniors greet the blasphemy with more good humour than anyone else in town. Born in farmhouses, raised up on hills or in remote valleys, where to come across another human being, no matter who they were or what they had to say, was a deep and unexpected pleasure — therefore humble, charitable, and polite — the old folks listen, lined up side by side in front of the piano.

It's like Murdeena figures that the seniors represent the front lines — that if she can just plough her way through them, everything else might fall into place. The world will become reasonable again. So Sunday after Sunday, she abandons the music in order to plead. Sunday after Sunday, now, she pleads with them until dark.

And they're good about it. They let her talk and hold out her hands to them. They don't complain or interrupt. They smile with their kind and patient old faces and refuse to let themselves be touched.

◇

Look,
and Pass On

◇

Inferno, CANTO 3, 1.51

THE THING WAS EIGHTEEN and she wore her dead grandmother's underpants.

"I like them," she enunciated to him over and over, because he would not let up about it. "They are comfortable."

They didn't bunch?

"Bunch where?"

Up her ass?

"I don't notice."

He was always leaning back and looking at the sky in a theatrical prayer for her. He drove a car with a window for a roof, could see the clouds fly past, if there had been any clouds. He said he was going to buy her some different ones.

"I don't need any."

But he would like to buy her some different ones. Her bare feet were up on the dashboard of his mother's car, dirty. She squinted, thinking about discomfort.

"Not those ones ... not the ones with no arse ... with the little bit of material that goes up your arse...."

Thongs, Thing. Lots of women wear them.

"I don't like them."

She would like them.

"No, no. I don't think I would."

He saw her underwear at night in the hotel. He hooted and yanked at them, like diapers. The elastic waistband came up almost underneath her breasts, her whole lower torso obscured by white cotton. One time when she turned to go to the bathroom, he grabbed a cushion from the chair and shoved it in there, and there was plenty of room left. She had reached behind herself and removed it and put it back down on the chair. Fifty other women would have thrown it at him. She was eighteen, however, and she did not have a playful bone in her body.

But he wanted to buy her some. He had all sorts of money. It was no problem. He could buy her all sorts of things. Whenever they pulled into an Irving for gas, she would wordlessly try to hand him twenty dollars like her father had told her to do, and he would say, in the phlegmy Cape Breton accent he used to mock her with, to take that thing and shove it up her hole. At this she would laugh. Hole-humour was big where she was from. She did not insist about the money because, he was aware, she was too young to know that she should insist.

It was late August and stifling in New Brunswick. They drove past the long Saint John River with boats on it and she said that the sight of water made her sad, because she always wanted to be in it. He said they could stop somewhere and swim but they shouldn't make a habit of it, if they wanted to make it to Guelph in good time. Anyway, they would go for good swims in the Georgian Bay once they arrived. He would have a long weekend to show her the sights before she had to be at the university, to start her first year of school. Alan was excited about this. He would take her to his parents' cottage on the bay, show her the beauty. He would take her to bars where his best friend Trent's band was playing for the Labour Day celebrations. His friends would see her and she would see them.

She wanted to stop at everything that was big. They had to stop at the big blueberry and the big potato. She insisted. The blueberry was friendly, but the potato was an evil-looking thing. She took a picture of him cringing before it. This was the kind of thing she enjoyed.

She enjoyed the hotel rooms for different reasons than him. The father had not agreed with the hotel rooms, with her blithely factoring them into the travel itinerary. The father had looked Alan in the eye and made it clear that he did not see any reason for hotel rooms. They could make it straight through without stopping if they got an early start, didn't take too many breaks. Alan was agreeing with him, but she vetoed them both without looking up from the map, spread out across her family's kitchen table with the innocent bechickened tablecloth. "I *want* to stay in a couple of hotels," she had said. Her father silenced by her lack of shame, hands placed palms-down atop the chickens, as if to keep him from falling into them. It was clear she scarcely noticed him any more. In all likelihood he hadn't agreed with any of her travel plans to begin with. To get this *friend*, six years her senior, to drive her out to school.

What had he said when she told him this? Alan wanted to know.

"What could he say?"

What had *she* said?

"I said I'm eighteen." Smiling at her dirty feet. Not really smiling at all. "He can't say too much these days. Right numb."

She insisted on the hotels the way she insisted on her grandmother's underwear. It was what she liked. It turned out that it was actually the old man's own fault, this particular penchant in the thing. He used to take them on vacations all the time. It reminded her of being on vacations with her family, she said. Mother, father, sister, brother. At their first motor inn, she had shocked him by making a beeline to the bed and jumping furiously up and down on it. "This is how we always used to christen the room." she said, voice hiccuping from the bounces. She didn't really smile or look as if she were enjoying herself. But she did it every time, no matter what, he would come to know, bouncing, looking straight ahead.

They'd spent time together before, but not time like this. Car time. He could talk to her about whatever came to mind. Books he'd read. Music she should listen to. Interesting ideas he sometimes had about things — what he liked to call his "little philosophies." She enjoyed listening. They stopped at a beach and he got to see her in a shiny pink bathing suit. It was a one-piece, but he could see the unstable protrusion of her little stomach, from a year ago. And there were still stretch marks on the backs of her thighs, making them strangely dimpled. There was a pleasant layer of fat — although diminishing — all over her and he thought to himself, *like baby*

fat, and then he tittered when he realized it literally was. He read somewhere, later, that stretch marks never went away. The stomach reminded
him of pictures and statues of the Catholic Madonna, her abdomen always
prominent, the flowing robes moulded around it, emphasizing. He saw why
they made them like that now — the pictures, the statues. He told her at
one point that he thought a prominent abdomen was sexy.

"Oh, good." she said, serious. "How about stretch marks?"

They sped on through the haze. It was his mother's Lexus. She gave it
to him for the summer, for his great trek through Maritime Canada. He
had not planned on going back to Bridget's town, where he worked for not
quite a year before having to flee the sulphurous egg smell of the pulp mill
and his sodden-eyed, violent co-workers, coming to work hungover and
beaten every Monday, always asking why he never went "out on the town"
with them on the weekends, did he think he was too good? But in the end
he placed a call from Smooth Herman's in Sydney after three pints and said
perhaps he could drop in on his way back to the causeway. And she'd said
without any ado, why didn't he take her with him. She had a train ticket
but it wasn't too late to cancel.

So she was leaving? he'd kept repeating. She was finally leaving?

"'Bout time, wha'?" she said.

He agreed that it was. It sounded as if she were becoming more illiter-
ate by the second. She replied something about her hole, to kiss it or play
it like a fife or something. He hung up the phone, surprised to be euphoric.

He remembered her then. Tar-eyed thing in a Woolco dress, sitting at
a chair and table set up outside the high school auditorium, vacantly
accepting his admission to see the Swedish fiddlers. He had said, "I can't
believe I am paying money to see Swedish fiddlers. I wonder what is
happening to me," and she'd looked up as if he had introduced himself as
an angel of the Lord. Later she came up to him to say that she had learned
the Swedish word for cheese and it was *oosht*.

Pregnant then but nobody knew it. All he had thought was *what a body
for a kid*. It turned out those changes had occurred only a couple of months
before and she was exasperated with them. He was the first person she told
about it. He had been flattered, but not really surprised. The people in the
town were like hornets in the hottest part of the summer, flying drunk,

bashing their prickly bodies into one another, buzzing enraged. He'd asked her about *programs, supports,* and she'd said, Programs? Supports? He had wanted, in a fanciful part of his mind, to take her away, but nothing about the situation allowed for it. She was seventeen then. He had someone who had been his girlfriend for three years, finishing up her BA in film in Toronto. Before all of that, however, he knew he needed more than air to get away from the sulphurous hornets' nest where she'd spent her whole life. So she went to Halifax alone in her sixth or seventh month, and, apparently, came back alone, too, but by that time he had gone.

❖

They hit a strawberry just before the Quebec border, at George's Famous Fruits. He rolled his eyes and pulled over without a word. Stepping out of the air-conditioned car, the heat threw itself over him like a quilt. She said, "Foo," and pushed her hair back. He could see on either side of her hairline that a good quantity of it had fallen out and was only now returning, tentatively. You didn't notice that when it hung down on either side of her face. He wanted to say, *My Christ, how many other things does it do to you?* but he didn't. She strode up to the strawberry, uncharacteristically purposeful. When she got there she did nothing but loiter in its presence, peering upwards, getting sun in her eyes. After a couple of minutes she said they could go.

There was nowhere to buy a thong in Quebec, not along these endless rural roads. They would have to go through Montreal, and they could stop there, but it could take forever, once they got in, to get back out again. He did not know the city well. But he was interested in the idea of a thong, in Montreal.

There is no reason to buy a thong, she had said in the hotel. I can just pull me underwear up to me chin and it'll go straight up me arse like so. She demonstrated. She was doing the big hick-voice now because she did it whenever they discussed her body.

❖

Ach, she said at him. He was telling her that he would be worried about her, up in University all by herself — driving after the first hotel, when the underwear had made its appearance and he'd almost died — and all she said in reply was "Ach."

87

Something else she must've gotten from her grandmother. He didn't remember hearing it last year, except for when Bridget imitated her, but now she used it all the time, now that the old woman was dead. Bridget used to come to his apartment and lie on his floor last year, clutching a glass of wine, and she would tell him all about cleaning up her grandmother's defecate.

He thought it a wonderful word. The retch of it embodying pure disdain. Complete dismissal.

"Acccchhhhh," he repeated, relishing the cat-hiss feel in the back of his throat. "What do you mean, "'ach'?"

"It's just school. And you'll be close by."

"I can come see you on the weekends."

"Sure."

"Make sure those university boys don't step out of line."

"Ach," she said, smiling.

They drove in silence for a couple of minutes, during which time Alan was thinking, What am I talking about?

"We're friends," she said. "We've always been friends." She said that about a half-hour of Trans-Canada later.

"Oh, yes," he said, trying a bit to sound ironic. *But I have been acquainted with your underwear and what about that?*

A while later he proposed they get a room in Montreal. It was completely gratuitous. They could be in Guelph at a reasonable hour if they kept on at a steady click. The little thing opened her mouth at the prospect of a just-for-the-hell-of-it hotel room.

So he talked the rest of the way, in good spirits. The first hotel hadn't been perfect — they had both drunk too much beer and were road-tired, but Montreal would be better. It would be Montreal. He talked about CBC Radio and what his favourite programs were, which was what he always did when he was in a good mood. They listened to some of them, Alan greeting every announcer by name. She was reading a book that her English teacher had loaned her but she never gave back, and he had read it before, so he told her what he thought about it. It occurred to him that she might like to know about some other books he liked and it flattered him when she dug a pen out of the glove compartment and began compiling a list on the back page of the English teacher's book. She was going to take general arts for her first year, of course. He told her the key to university was to just read all the books and go to all the classes. There was no way you could fail. She laughed, but he said it wasn't as easy as it sounded: Listen to me, I know what I'm talking about. He told her that she would be kicking herself in a few years if she spent all that money only to have it come to naught.

"Ach," she said. "Government's money anyways."

"You're going to have to pay it all back, Bridget."

He could tell she didn't believe it.

He didn't know what world she lived in. Sometimes the words out of her mouth could be diamonds of the purest common sense. But most of the time she gazed around herself, never meeting anyone's eye and retreating into her accent and monosyllables. The casual observer might dismiss her as retarded — exasperatingly quiet and unfathomably stubborn. She was the only girl he knew who didn't insist people think she was smart.

"I never worry about going to hell," said Alan at some point. He had been talking books at her for the last half-hour. "Ever since reading *Inferno.*"

"Uh? Why? It doesn't sound so bad?" Like she'd been shaken out of sleep.

"No, it's bad. But it tells you how to get out."

"It tells you how to get out?"

"Oh yeah, it's a fucking road map."

"That doesn't sound right," she said. "I wouldn't think they'd just let you walk out."

He said nothing for the next ten minutes because she was right. Alan thought about the winged demons poking the souls back beneath bubbling pitch; and liars sunken up to their mouths in shit, and she was right. Dante had only been visiting. They were compelled by You-Know-Who to let him pass. The remark about not being afraid to go to hell was one he had often made in the company of well-read friends. Now he knew he couldn't make it any more, and was embarrassed at having said it so many times already. Because of her and her common-sense Catholicism. He pictured her mind at work, trying to reconcile the image of Alan taking a leisurely stroll through the pit — Dante under his arm to be consulted every now and again for directions — with what had been seared into her brain since childhood. That hell is not for tourists.

◇

On the bypass they sat watching heat rise from the pavement, from the hoods of cars. He was telling her they weren't going to be staying anywhere fancy. It wasn't going to be the Ritz, or anything. She didn't care. He had sunglasses on, but she didn't and the glare made her blind. She talked to him from behind her fingers.

Traffic crawled, and he saw other drivers panting out their windows, end-of-the-summer arms like cured sausages. Cursing and practically weeping at their lot. Alan kept the windows shut tight, air-conditioning at full blast. "It won't be fancy," he repeated to himself, out loud. "But there will have to be air-conditioning. I will spring for an air-conditioner," he said.

"And beer," her voice came faint from behind the fingers. He thought she had fallen asleep.

"And thongs!" He tried to shout this, lustily, but something about the permeating swelter would not allow it. "Mountains of thongs," he croaked. Her sleepy titters muffled by the fingers. He was thinking about the last hotel and how he could make this one better. Maybe not so much beer — if he let her have her way, she would drink the world. And the air-conditioning at full blast this time. He had turned the air-conditioning off at the last one, because it was one of those air-conditioners where the sound drowned out everything else. But now he knew it would be just as well to have it on, so heat would be no excuse and he couldn't hear the noises she never made anyway. Alan was a planner. He had always been a planner. By the time they escaped the bypass heat prison it was dusk, the city was cooling, and he knew exactly how their evening was going to go.

They would go to the Peel Pub because it was the one bar he went to the last time he was here, her age, with the Varsity rugby team. He and the rest of them had done shooters, thrown up and lit farts on the street. He kept in touch with none of them now, but remembered them fondly. Alan knew he was a rarity because he had always enjoyed this kind of idiocy with men, but never understood the alternating fear and indifference towards women

90

of some of them. Alan grew up running to the drugstore to buy tampons for his many sisters, picking up another's birth control while he was there. Certain male acquaintances were horrified at the fact that Alan had also lit farts with more than one girlfriend. Nothing was a mystery to him.

They found a Quality Inn, showered, and went out. There were prostitutes and pornography all over the street, which Alan didn't even remember from last time. He put his arm around her as they walked. They found the place, ordered chicken wings and Caesar salads and a pitcher. Alan told her they would have to go back to the room if they were really going to drink, because he probably should start being a little more careful with his money.

"Save it for the thongs," she said.

"Goddamnit, I forgot to ask someone where the thong warehouse is!"

"Are you really going to get one?"

He looked around him, thinking of the sex shops all up and down the street. "I could pop out and get one right now. It wouldn't necessarily be Victoria's Secret. I could get a few other things, while I'm at it."

"Like what?"

"Dog collars. Nipple-clamps. Two-foot pronged dildos!"

"People don't have those."

"They do, Bridget." He delighted in contradicting her about this sort of thing.

"No."

"Remember that girl I told you I went out with?"

"Yeah, but, just her."

"You are aware that you're not the most worldly person out there?"

"I don't care."

"I could show you."

"No."

"We can go outside and I can show you right now."

"Don't."

"If you don't know what's out there, you'll never know what you like."

"I don't want to like anything," she said.

The next day on the road was hotter. At 7:00 A.M. they sat at a picnic table outside of a Shell station (Irving Bigstops left behind with all the oversized produce) and struggled to get their coffees down before the heat made it unthinkable. Bridget could scarcely open her eyes, but he had maliciously insisted they get an early start. All of a sudden something fast and loud buzzed near their heads and Bridget leapt away from it, splashing coffee everywhere.

"Jesus Christ, Bridget!"

"What was it?" She looked around her in horror. If it was a bug, then it was a bug approximately the size of a golf ball. A black, clicking, whirring golf ball blur. She assumed a stance of readiness, waiting for it to come back. It did, and stopped directly in front of them, whirring and blurry. Alan realized that it had come up alongside some sort of water container, hanging from the roof of the garage.

"It's a hummingbird," he said.

"What? What?"

"It's a hummingbird. See?"

They watched it for a while as if a tiny whirring deity had appeared. The cautious, hovering motions as it jerked away made it seem as if it were watching them also, monitoring them for movement.

"Jesus H. Christ, I guess I'm awake now," she said, heading back to the car.

The morning was silence but for CBC Radio. He was thinking of the different things he could say to her. He felt like his fourth grade math teacher must've felt, drilling the simple concept of fractions into his brain, over and over again, Alan staring with complete incomprehension. He had eventually mastered math, but he would never forget the slow forward rolls his stomach had begun to perform once the world started breaking the numbers up and putting them on top of each other. This had seemed like sheer perversity to Alan. It was funny, he thought, how things like that affect you when you're small. His doctor and mother feared ulcers. The inside of his little boy's stomach all raw.

He began by asking her slow, gentle questions about what she thought, and about himself. Tender, like how the patient math teacher used to explain things. Like Alan back then, something within the thing wasn't willing to cooperate. She was irritated by the necessity to answer. She pushed her feet into the dashboard, wanting more room as the questions became more insistent. He had decided somewhere along the way that he wasn't going to let up, he wasn't going to let her drift away like she always did. The night had been a farce, him hovering above, not knowing what to do, what was good and what was bad, Bridget offering nothing. He didn't think it was fair. There was no way he could let himself continue like this, hovering, in doubt. But instead of drifting away, she shut down. Her answers became as meaningless as she could possibly make them, and he felt himself getting angry. Deliberately. She was like this on purpose. It was not emotional laziness, as he had once supposed. Her mind was constantly in action, behind the heavy eyelids, forming strategies of avoidance. It was like trying to grab hold of a goldfish. Finally he said, "Your feet are fucking filthy," and she put them down.

"I didn't mean you had to put them down."

"That's okay."

"All I want to know is" — he wanted to kill her for just putting them down like that — "I mean, I always try to help...."

"But you don't have to."

God. God. God. "Well, I thought we were friends."

"Well, we are."

"Well, it seems like I'm the one who's doing all the giving here. Don't get me wrong, I'm not saying I'm in love with you, but it just seems like —"

"I'm eighteen," she said abruptly. His entire train of thought halted at once.

"Right," he said, listening. He meditated on the road.

"I just wanna get to school," she said.

❖

She did not fit in with anybody at the bar, but they loved her anyway because they were accepting, friendly people like himself, and because of her youth and supposed shyness. Alan's friend Trent tenderly brought her a Chocolate Monkey like a nurse bringing a patient a wee cupful of pills. It was a Polynesian bar, the kind of campy place a band like Trent's was

93

perfectly at home in, stuffed full of youngish Labour Day partiers. There she sat, never having drank anywhere that wasn't called a tavern, looking around at the umbrellas and plastic hula dancers. He knew that she thought it was a bunch of foolishness, if she was thinking anything at all. That was something he would not have known about her a week ago. She sat alongside of Trent's delicately tattooed girlfriend wearing a Jack Daniel's T-shirt, once the property of the shit-kicker who had impregnated her, he imagined.

Everyone paid him compliments on Bridget whenever they caught him alone, because she was so adorable. No one knowing about the nastiness of the thing, or suspecting what the previous eight hours might have done to him.

"Sexy in that wholesome kind of way," said Trent's green-eyed girlfriend Quentin, who took art photos and wrote haiku and had been known to like girls sometimes, according to Trent anyway. Alan understood entirely why she said that and wanted to tell her that it wasn't true, that she wasn't wholesome at all. He was feeling cynical, as though in the last few days he had learned enough about the world to make him not want to know any more. He had used to feel impervious with knowledge, "existentially at ease," he used to tell his friends — when he wasn't being pretentious about Dante and espousing his indifference towards hell. He knew they envied him, using their fabricated traumas to add substance to their lives, turning to him for the advice of someone capable of accepting the world for what it was. Now he felt like a fraud. But he did not feel like a fraud. He felt like a dupe. He felt a way he had not felt since being introduced to fractions.

He saw her watching the band and thought that all she ever did was wait for everything to be over. It was grotesque. It was grotesque to think about the car and doing things with people who didn't care if you did them or not. They who practically said Ach when you asked your gentle well-thought-out and carefully worded questions. Like, *What do you need from me? What do you need me to do?* The *ach* palatable in the air, all over them like sweat. Impervious. Contagious. Dangerous to have this kind of realization on a highway in the middle of Canada. He had wanted to drive into an oncoming truck, and the thing, he knew, would not have spoken as he did.

◆

A Great Man's Passing

◆

PEOPLE WHO DIDN'T KNOW, and that was mostly tourists, thought that the Sloane house, about a hundred feet backed up from the main road, had to be deserted. They didn't even think this in a conscious way. They processed it the way drivers process the things they see on a long, empty country road. House. Cow. Mailbox. Deserted house. It never occurred to anyone that such a place could be inhabited.

But it was, and the truth is, it had become so decrepit precisely because of how inhabited it was. This never occurred to anyone either. No one thought that a house could gradually be destroyed by how lived-in it was. People passed the Sloane house and thought: deserted. That house has no one looking after it. The people who drove by the Sloane house and thought that were the kind of people who assumed that if there was somebody living in a home, it was automatically being looked after.

But it wasn't, because the overriding concern of the Sloane family was looking after itself. And if the passing tourists had been aware of the size of the Sloane family, they would understand why there was no time for looking after anything else.

Bess never thought that the Sloane house was deserted because she had always known better. In the summers, when she and her parents would drive by on the way to Gramma and Grampa's, Bess would shout, There's the Sloane house, because it was a landmark that told her they were almost to the farm, and also because she had been in it before, and, in her little-girl consciousness, this fact made the house hers.

She knew the Sloanes, too, she knew the name of every single child living in that house. So they were hers, too. The youngest was Terry, then Margaret, then Mary Catherine. Then came some boys, Robert and Angus and Roland, who was Bess's age. Then they started getting older than her. Dougal and Jn'-Pat. Ann Rose. At that point they reached an age where the names came easier than the faces. Elizabeth. David. Ian. Joseph. Carrie and Stephen. That was it. Bess bragged to her friends about knowing so big a family.

We go down there every month, almost, she would say. We bring them our old clothes and other stuff. Mary Catherine always gets my old clothes and whatever toys I'm sick of. There's babies and clothes everywhere, in every room. And one of those boys has a weird eye. It doesn't go right. He wears glasses a hundred feet thick. His name is Angus but they call him Cookie 'cause his eyes make him look like the Cookie Monster.

At that point, Maureen MacEachern would always try to steal away a little bit of Bess's spotlight. I know! she'd say. 'Cause my mom is always filling up garbage bags with all of our old stuff and giving them to your mom to give to them.

Yeah, but you've never been there. I've been in the house and I know them. Dad says they're my third cousins. So I've got fifteen third cousins.

It made Bess mad because Maureen had so much to brag about already, why did she have to take what Bess had. She had lived in the nicest house in town and her dad was deputy mayor. Bess's dad was on the town council. Their families went on vacations and camping trips together. Plus, Maureen had five brothers and two sisters. That was a pretty big family, too, but it wasn't the same.

Bess had never known what Mr. Sloane did, and she hardly even knew what he looked like. He was never there when they came in to drop off their garbage bags, or maybe he was, but had just been obscured by children. Mrs. Sloane was always there, her stomach perpetually large because it never had a chance to get small again. She and Mom would talk. She would say, Thank you so much, Ellen, you are always thinking of us, to Mommy. The little girls would follow Bess around and ask her questions and try to show her things while the boys would yell at her and make fun of her and try to get her to chase them. Sometimes she would and sometimes she wouldn't. One time she was chasing Cookie, and he scrambled up onto the trunk of one of the rusted old automobiles that were sprawled alongside of the house. So Bess had reached out and grabbed Cookie by the belt of his pants, and down the pants came, and Cookie's underwear had the silliest patterns and most lurid colours on them that Bess ever could have imagined. Embarrassed more by the shorts than by the fact that she had pulled a boy's pants right off him, she turned away and pretended to be interested in what the little girls had been trying to tell her ever since she'd arrived. When she looked back, Cookie was returning, hoisting up his pants with a little smile. He didn't care. He wanted her to chase him some more.

◈

When Bess got older, and it began to seem like less of a treat to go see Gramma and Grampa on the weekends, it also became less of an adventure to drop bags off at the Sloanes', which had been par for the course during such visits, just as it had been par for the course to do things like swinging on the thick rope with the hook on the end of it in the barn, which Grampa said never to do and Dad always said, Oh, go ahead and do it anyway. Like attending mass on Sundays at the small Catholic church down the road where you would always see Mrs. Sloane with what Daddy called "her litter" and Mom would say in the awed, quiet voice that she used when saying prayers with Bess, That woman makes it to church every Sunday. All this was part of the adventure. But when Bess got older it became part of the routine. That's the problem with getting older, Bess thought.

And now, living here in her childhood vacationland, everything was different altogether, and it was strange that she had seen more of the Sloanes when she was a child and living in town than she did now that she was an adult and living only a few miles down the road. Every once in a while Mommy would say to her something like, "Jn'-Pat Sloane's supposed to be getting married. A little girl from the Forks, Cameron, I believe."

And Bess would have to think for a minute before honing in on his identity. "He's the dark one?"

"They're all dark, Bessie. Except for Angus and Ann Rose."

"No, I know which one you mean. Which Cameron girl?"

Dad would say, "Pregnant, I suppose."

"Oh, let's not be cynical," Bess would reply.

And every time Mommy would share some Sloane tidbit of news with Bess, she would always bring the topic to a close with the words "Poor Mary Kate." Which was Mrs. Sloane's first name. Every time something happened to one of the Sloane children, Mommy always spoke as if it had in some deeper, more significant way, to Mrs. Sloane. But as far as Bess knew, Mommy hardly ever saw Mrs. Sloane any more. And there they were, just a few miles down the road.

⬥

Mid-fall, Bess had a job. There had been no getting around it. It had fallen into her lap, such a rare thing that to refuse would have been like showing your middle finger to God just when he was in a good mood. The man who owned the Bonnie Prince Inn was an American named Rufus Bank, who asked that you call him Ruf. He had come to Daddy in the summer wanting to know where he could catch trout, and so Dad asked the man over for dinner and took him behind the house and down the side of the hill and they fished about a mile upriver from where Dad's gaspreaux trap was set up. Everyone but the American knew there wouldn't be any trout, but they also knew that he would be just as satisfied if he caught even one bony gaspreaux, which he did, and he was. They came back up to the house and fried the fish up for Mr. Bank's dinner. With it, he drank one of Bess's beer.

"You people have a paradise here, do you know that?" said Ruf, looking around at them all with good-hearted reproach, as though perhaps they were guilty of not knowing it. "I've wanted to live here all my life. When the Bonnie Prince came up for sale, I said to myself, there's my retirement. Right there. Couldn't believe my luck." He looked at Bess and told her that she couldn't have picked a better spot to raise her little boy. Then he looked at Dylan, chomping on a pork-chop bone in his high chair. Bess looked at him too.

In the winters, Ruf had to close the Bonnie Prince, but he left the lounge open for the locals. The previous owner hadn't done that, and if you wanted to get drunk, you either had to drive to Inverness, or go to one of the dances in the South-west Hall, or stay home. Bess had gone to one of the dances, once, in the early summer, with her second cousin, Meg, who was trying to help her to feel welcome. When they arrived outside the Hall, Bess said to Meg, "Is it an outdoor dance in this weather?" Because it looked as though everyone had gathered out in front instead of inside. Then Bess saw that the crowd was standing in a circle and in the middle one young man was jumping up and down on another man's head. Meg parked the car close by and the two of them sat in it, passing a bottle of rum back and forth until the fight was over.

"That was Dougal Sloane," Meg commented, capping the rum and dropping it back into her purse.

"Who?"

"The guy who won."

"He's gotten big," Bess said after a moment.

◇

But now there was Ruf's lounge to go to, and he had painted it, and installed a full-time DJ and every other week a band from Blue Mills called Ryder would play there. Also, Ruf had changed the name from the uncomplicated "Bonnie Prince Inn Lounge" to "Red Ruf's" because, he said, he used to have red hair and he noticed that everyone "around here" had nicknames and that was one of the things he loved about the place. Bess was to learn that the best way to endear yourself to the American was to refer to him affectionately as Red Ruf, as often as you could get away with.

Red Ruf had offered Bess a job because Daddy had asked him to during one of their fishing trips. Daddy wanted Bess to be clear about that.

"There we were in our hip-waders and Ruf's going on about the lounge and how there'll be people coming in from as far away as Whycocomah once he gets his whaddayacallit sound system installed and he's pretty damn sure he's going to be needing some extra staff to help serve the liquor up, and I say, 'Well, goddamnit Ruf, our Bessie's been looking for a job ever since she landed here and the little fella started getting more independent. I know she'd appreciate getting off the welfare. It's been hard on her, you know, what with the little guy....'"

101

Lies. Bess hadn't minded the welfare so much at all. It had kept Dylan clothed and fed all summer long, and she earned her own keep by working at home and helping with Gramma and Grampa. Best of all, it allowed for her to be with him every moment, and so Bess, although she heard things on the radio about Welfare Queens, and talk that the government would no longer tolerate her kind of inertia, could not feel guilty about her own reluctance to enter the work force. She knew this was a great sin in her society, but didn't quite understand why. She saw men on television who said that all they wanted to do was work. They would do anything, clean out toilets, mop floors, but they could not stand the ignominy of welfare. They said they felt degraded.

All Bess knew was that Dylan was being fed and that she was able to spend as much time with him as she needed, which was all the time. It seemed to her that if there had to be a government, this was the kind of thing it was supposed to be doing for people. Daddy said that this was naive.

"You have to participate. You can't just live off the sweat of honest, working people."

"I'm an honest working person, too."

"You're a hippie that thinks the world owes you something...." She saw him stop himself, and filled in the rest. Going around having babies, thinking the government's gonna look after them. Free love and all that. He's talking about himself, him and me, Bess thought, smouldering as she always did when she thought about the two of them, playing tug-of-war, and if one person lets go of the taunt rope, the other will suddenly go flying. As if I'm not cleaning up your mother's pasty yellow poo every night, spoon-feeding her curds and potatoes. As if I have not conceded to raise my boy in a funeral home, with the two corpses propped up in front of the TV set, one saying a rosary, the other smoking a cigarette. As if I couldn't have stayed away if I wanted to. As if I still couldn't go.

Ruf didn't know about any of this. All Ruf knew was that he was giving a job to someone who needed it.

"That's very nice of you, Mr. Bank," stunned Bess had said into the phone when he called up with his offer.

"Oh, well," said Ruf. "It's nice to know that I can do some good around here, what with the unemployment situation and everything. It's nice to know that I'm not just here for myself, that I can make a little bit of a difference to some of the people — if you know what I mean. You know — you people are my neighbours now, and I want to help you in any way I can."

"That's very nice of you," Bess said again, beginning to panic, looking down at Dylan who was on the floor in front of her playing with her shoe. How long will he want me to work, she wondered. How many hours out of the day? Then there was the fact that she had always thought that the last job she would ever choose for herself would be that of a bartender.

But there was no saying no, there simply wasn't, and she didn't. While she had been talking on the phone to Ruf, the members of her family had all quietly materialized, and when she looked up they were standing there with smiles, as if she had just opened a gift from the three of them.

"Who was that, now?" asked Daddy, smiling most of all.

So now Bess had a job, and even though that was more than could be said for the rest of the family, they still seemed to possess a sort of moral high ground that she would never be able to attain. She thought that it was probably because they were old, and had all worked in the past. A million years ago Aunt Marg was a nurse and Dad had done a lot of different things before having enough money to buy a hotel/restaurant, and becoming the kind of upstanding citizen who sits on town councils, and then losing the hotel/restaurant a few years later and not being that kind of citizen any more. Then Daddy became disillusioned and didn't do much and said that if he couldn't do things his way, he wouldn't do anything at all. And then he lost the house and he said that it was just as well because Mumma and The Boss were getting on and needing someone to take care of themselves and the farm full-time anyway. Plus, moving to the farm meant no mortgage, no rent. "Now I do what I goddamn well please," Bess had heard him say to Red Ruf Bank.

But Bess was young and had to work. It was, Dad said, "a shame" for her not to work, and worse for her not to want to. After Red Ruf's phone call, Bess had been cranky all day and drank all the beer that was in the fridge. She looked outside at the dead, empty field which no snow had the decency to come and bury yet. In a way, the job had come at a good time, she supposed, with winter on the way and the snow piled up at the doors and windows and no way for her and Dylan to escape down to the river for a swim or even out to the field because Bess hated snow and the idea of plodding along in the wet cold stuff just for the hell of it made no sense to her. So that meant more time spent indoors, but more time spent indoors meant more time in the funeral home, so maybe it would be a good thing to have somewhere to go. Mommy had said, "It will be good for you to get out."

What irked her, though, was the momentousness of it all. Mommy making a special Bess-got-a-job dinner that night, and Daddy telling the stories of how he had wrangled the offer out of Red Ruf, reeling him in as they stood in the middle of the river with the pathos of Bess's "situation." Bess having to think about what she was going to wear for the first time in months, and everybody happy for her, happy that she was going to be serving up Moosehead to head-stomping pulp-cutters and cod-jiggers. And it wasn't even that. Just happy that she was going to be doing something. Not understanding that time is going to go by and that days are going to pass whether you are doing something or doing nothing. And when you are doing nothing, they go by just as quick, if not quicker — a fact that people who are always doing something will not believe if you tell it to them.

◇

The first two shifts she did for Red Ruf, she had to go to and sit in the employees' bathroom and cry because she was wondering what Dylan was doing. She imagined Mommy and Aunt Marg gleefully following him around with aprons full of cookies to be offered in case he fell down and hurt himself or threw some kind of tantrum. It's like being in love, she thought to herself, rubbing her eyes unrestrainedly because she was unused to wearing make-up and forgot that she would be smudging black mascara and blue powder all over her stupid face. Washing she thought. It is, but it isn't.

The next couple of shifts she did were on the weekend, and Bess got her first taste of culture shock, the shock of someone who has been in hiding for over a year and suddenly finds herself at the centre of a large, oddly unsociable party where people seemed to expect more from her than drinks. They wanted to banter, they wanted her to smile and chat and learn their first names and tell them where she was from and who her father was. It seemed most of them would rather talk to her than the people they were there with.

Sometimes, Red Ruf would show up with the intention of helping her at the bar, but most of the time he forgot about that and ended up perching on one of the stools and holding a sort of court among the locals. Most of the locals loved him. He was afforded the status of "a character" because he was rich and American. This was something you could tell Red Ruf had always longed for but had never been able to attain when he had lived among other rich Americans.

There were awkward moments, like when she noticed her second cousin Meg there with all of her brothers and didn't know if she should speak to the brothers, who were virtually strangers in the way people are expected to speak to relatives that they haven't spoken to for ages, or, if she should just behave towards them the same way as she did to everyone else in the bar. She prayed that Meg would come up to the bar with the brothers in tow and initiate some kind of dialogue that would take the onus of Bess, but things never happen that way. The first time Bess noticed that her cousins were in the lounge, Meg hadn't even seen Bess working the bar and they went right past her, to a table. Then, a little later, one of the older brothers who, Bess was pretty sure was called Findlay, came up to get beers for everybody and looked right thought her. Bess took his order, began setting the beer down in front of him, and, watching the beer bottles very closely, said, "Do you remember me, Findlay?"

When she looked up, she saw that his gaze had focused in on her a little, even though his face hadn't changed.

"Of course I do, Bess," he said, and then he took his beer and returned to his table. Bess thought about it for a while before coming to the realization that she had forgotten all about the completely familiarizing power of gossip. Findlay had probably been hearing so much about Bess all throughout the summer from his sister Meg and father Alistair — who liked to talk about anything as often as possible — that it was impossible for him to have lost track of her existence in the way that she had of his, and of so many other people that her parents insisted she knew, and remembered fondly.

When the Sloanes began popping up, Bess had been expecting pretty much the same treatment she'd received from Meg's brothers, who, she could tell right away, had listened intently to every opinion their father Alistair had espoused regarding Bess. She had a pretty good idea as to what these opinions were, because he had also espoused them to Bess numerous times over the summer when he would be sitting across from her at the dinner table tossing back some of Aunt Marg's whisky after he and Daddy had come up from the trap. In any case, Bess was not bothered with what Alistair's sons thought, she was only relieved to know that she wasn't going to have to be friendly towards them as she had at first feared. As the week-end shifts went by, she came to see from their constant sponging of drinks and groping of randomly passing arses that they were only slimmed-down, less shambling versions of Alistair, and this made it easy to be unconcerned by them.

But late into one evening, Findlay came weaving up to the bar to have a rare word with her. "How's she going?" he initiated.

"Good, Findlay. How're you?"

"Well, well, well. She's talking to me."

"And you're talking to me."

"I never thought you'd lower yourself."

"Say hi to Alistair next time you see him."

"Don't you say nothin about Daddy."

"Okay."

"Okay. Some good, you."

"What — Findlay — what's the problem?"

But Findlay gave her a look as though to say that it was hopeless trying to talk to her, she was too low, or too high, or something ignoble like that, and he shambled away. Whoo, big confrontation, Bess thought, mopping beer up off the counter. But she was grimacing because it hadn't been good. You people are my neighbours now.

The first night she noticed the Sloanes had begun to frequent Red Ruf's was one time when somebody hollered, "Foit!" and everybody in the lounge bolted for the door.

"Oh my gosh," said Red Ruf, gazing out one of the windows. "Maybe you'd better call the police, Bessie. I don't think I want this kind of thing going on."

"What's happening?" said Bess, having to stay behind the bar.

"Some young lad's kicking a man's head in out there."

At that moment Cookie Sloane hurried in from outside. Bess thought that he had only grown about a foot since the time she had pulled down his pants. Otherwise he looked completely the same, peering though his thick glasses like they were fog.

"Don't call the Mounties," he said, rushing over to the bar. "Okay, Bessie? Please? The guy was a fucking arsehole. Dougal will finish up in just a bit. Okay?"

"Okay," said Bess, forgetting to consult with Ruf.

Cookie smiled, all dirty teeth — "God love ya, dear!" — and ran back outside.

✧

Dougal and Cookie sat on bar stools beside one another, Dougal with his head down, looking at his beer, smiling very happily at all the things Cookie was saying to Bess about him.

"He's just a big idiot," Cookie was saying. "Stupid as mine and your arses put together. That's what he is. Doesn't know how to do anything except pummel the shit out of some poor bastard who doesn't know how to keep his tongue in his head. Isn't that right, you hopeless fucking dummy?"

"Yes," said Dougal, smiling.

"How you been, Bessie?" Cookie went on without blinking. When you looked into his freaky eyes through the thickness of those glasses, you expected his voice to sound like it was coming from a mile away. "Are you good? Mummy told me you was living down here now, up at Iain and Lizzie's place. Said you got knocked up and have a little boy now. That can be tough, eh? Same thing happened to Ann Rose and Elizabeth, but they're living together in town and doing okay. Sort of a joint effort. Still, it gets me cross. I'm saying to Mary Catherine all the time, 'Now don't you fuck! I don't care how bored you get, don't do it.' It's not all that much fun anyhow and it gives a lot of stupid bastards something to talk about and a person to feel superior to. But I suppose the girls've gotta get their rocks off somehow, too, that's only fair. Somebody told me that girls don't like it, and I used to think that was true but then I had a girlfriend and — Jesus, Mary, and Joseph — how we used to go at it. It was always her wanting to. She's gone now, though, up to Halifax to study the nursing. She wanted me to write letters but I'm no damn good at it. How's your Grammie and Grampie, Bess? Christ Almighty, they must be getting up there, eh? Your mum's helping to take care of them, my mum was saying. My mum says your mum's a saint, did you know that? She's always saying what a saint your mum is, and how you guys always used to help us out. I always remember, we'd see you and your mother driving up in the station wagon and it was just like fucking Christmas. The girls would go into hysterics and Mary Catherine would always have to have a lay-down after you left. Anyways, I know I talk too much, but someone's gotta make up for the wordless idiotic wonder over here. I'll have another beer, Bessie, me mouth is pretty dry. That was a good fight, though, you have to admit. The guy didn't look too bad. Listen, Bessie, how are you, though, dear, how are you really?"

With Cookie — and it hadn't been like this with anyone else since she had arrived in the late spring — it was just like picking up where they had left off. Like any second he would jump up and pull her hair and say, blah-blah, dumb old ugly old stupid old Bess, there she is, and she, delighted, would jump up too and chase him all over the yard until they got so tired that one of them would gasp, "Times," and then, after they had rested, Bess would abruptly scream, "Off times!" and pounce on him. She had not felt as if she could feel like that again in a very long time.

✧

Bess saw Cookie at Red Ruf's almost every weekend, usually with Dougal in tow. Although they caused no more fights, Red Ruf sometimes frowned in a worried, slightly disappointed way when he came in to hold court and spotted Bess haunched over the bar, straining to hear one of Cookie's observations, blatantly ignoring an older patron down on the far end, one of Ruf's own courtiers.

"You know those boys?" he wondered to her one day, in an almost laughingly casual tone. Bess had been watching Cookie with glee, out on the dance floor with one of the local girls. Cookie was, by his own admission, "a dancing fucking fool," and whenever he wasn't huddled on a bar stool beside Dougal, he would sweep into the crowd and descend upon any one of the girls, every one of whom loved him, and lead them, shaking their hips and clapping their hands, out onto the floor where Cookie would commence to stomp up and down in his work boots, shaking his frail blond head in ecstasy and pausing every now and again to adjust his glasses.

"Which boys?"

"The boys who started that fight," Ruf said pointedly. He referred to it as "that fight" because it was the first one ever to occur at Red Ruf's and there was no doubt in his mind that if it hadn't been for that first fight, none of the other ones that broke out regularly each weekend would ever have come about.

"Cookie and Dougal. They're great guys, Red Ruf. Look at Cookie out there. I don't think you'd get any women in here if it wasn't for him."

Ruf squinted out at the dance floor with all the ill-concealed befuddlement that all big men demonstrate when they see women obviously enjoying themselves with the kind of man that Cookie was. It made Bess laugh out loud, which made Ruf jump and stare at her. As if Cookie was a man at all and not a sexless little sprite who made you feel as if he valued your company over everyone else's and told you everything as though it were the greatest of secrets and talked dirtier than anyone you've ever met, yet with an absolute innocence.

"You like that little fella, Bessie?" Ruf asked, turning his squint her way.

"He's adorable."

"I don't know," said Ruf, his big white head swivelling back towards the dance floor. "The first time I saw him and his lunkhead brother in here I kinda figured he was what your dad would call a shit-disturber."

Bess folded her arms coolly and gazed off in the same direction as Ruf. "They're my cousins," she said.

"Oh, Bessie, dear," he said, jumping again. "Why don't you set yourself up with a beer, dear."

Bess smiled, setting herself up with a beer. Ruf had yet to understand that everybody was cousins.

❖

One night Bess arrived from work to find the funeral home minus one ghoul. Gramma sat on her side of the room, rocking in time with her prayers to the Virgin, and Mommy sat close beside her on a chair she had brought out from the kitchen, nodding at the garbled prayers and watching Dylan play with trucks. The television was on, babbling news. Bess came in and leaned against Grampa's empty chair, the stink of ancient smoke and piss emanating from its fibres. On the floor beside it sat the emptied stewed tomato can which he used to hork his old-man's juice into. Beside that was a pack of matches. Dylan came up and wrapped his body around Bess's leg.

"They took him to the hospital, did they?"

"Yes, God love the poor soul."

"When was this?"

"Around suppertime."

"Poor Iain," said Gramma to nobody. "*Croc a nian, scat a nean*" — which was a song about salt cod that she recently had been mistaking for the Our Father.

◇

Saturday night she made a mistake that fated Sunday morning into being a bad one. She had been setting herself up with beers during most of her shift, as Red Ruf often invited her to do so, and when the time came to take off her apron and accept a lift home from him, Cookie, instead, instructed her to sit at a table with himself and Dougal, down a few, and they would take her home in a bit. Loving Cookie and Dougal as she did, this seemed at first a reasonable idea, but once she got out from behind the bar and into the centre of the crowd, the culture shock resurfaced and everything was terrible again. All of Cookie's many friends approached the table to talk to him, and when they saw Bess there, they tried to talk to her too. Sometimes Cookie went off to dance, but the friends stayed, talking to Bess and asking her questions. She knew them all remotely from working the bar, but now felt that this pleasant remoteness had been ruined. There would be no more of these people coming up, smiling at her, asking for a beer and saying please, and no more of Bess obliging them with another smile and their going away.

Cookie, indicating the dance floor, said to her at one point, "Let's get on out there for Jesus' sake," and she thought that she might as well, but once Bess found herself standing there across from Cookie doing his sweaty work-boot stomp, she felt very large and vivid with the lights flashing on her and the music all around, and so she reached over to pull on Cookie's sleeve and tell him that she was going to sit back down again. He nodded and bounded off towards the tables to get someone else.

And it was terrible because she had no way home except for Cookie and Dougal's father's fish truck parked outside. When she had told Ruf, no thanks, she'd be staying, he blinked at her in a kind of lost way and then said, All right, pulling on his jacket. She saw now that she should've gone home when Ruf offered his customary lift, like she always did — that would've been the right thing to do because now she was trapped with all these people and the road home was three miles long, unlit and lined on either side with woods. And, this was what always happened, the more nervous she got, the faster she finished her beer. Dougal, who sat always at the table, smiling, never getting up to dance or do anything except go to the men's room, looked over at her accumulation of empties and commented that she was "quite the Jesus partier."

Cookie bounded over, sweaty, and sat down. He leaned over and punched Bess on the shoulder: "Wouldn't even gimme a dance!" He laughed like it was a joke, which was a trick of his Bess had come to know. He used it when he sensed someone was uncomfortable. Just saying things and laughing at them, but making you feel as if you were actually the funny one, the clever wit. She smiled and shrugged and told him she was sorry as though what she had done was natural and excusable. They all pretended this. On the other side of her, her second cousin Findlay thumped into a chair.

"Findlay, ya crazy cocksucker," Cookie yelled above the music.

"Meg's wonderin' how you're doin'," he said, leaning towards Bess.

"Oh, is Meg here?" Bess stretched her neck and peered into the crowd.

"Oh, is Meg here?" Findlay repeated, pretending to look desperately around.

"Oh, for Christ's sake," Bess, who was now drunk, said.

"Now what's that supposed to mean, eh? We been here all night, looking y' right in the eye. I wonder what yer dad would say, hearing you turnin' up yer nose at Alistair's kids."

"Here's a beer for ya, Findlay," said Cookie.

"I don't suppose you'd lower yourself to dance."

"No thanks," Bess answered helplessly.

"Turned me down too, jeezless teaser!" shouted Cookie, still holding out Findlay's beer. "Walked right off the dance floor, me standing there with my dick in my hand! Trying to make me look silly or something is my guess."

"That's about what I figured." Findlay attempted to stand up, and, after a few minutes, succeeded at it, finally accepting the extended bottle. "Cookie," he said, pointing with it, "you don't talk to me, you little fairy bastard."

Dougal stood up, still smiling.

"Oh, no, no, no," Bess shouted, shaking her head extravagantly.

But Findlay had already lumbered hastily off towards his table, wherever that was. And Bess got up and went behind the bar to use the phone. She called her father who said that they hadn't even known where she was and here's the poor little fella squalling for his mother and nobody knowing what the Jesus to tell him, had to let him cry himself to sleep and Mommy pacing the floor half in tears and everybody worried sick to death about The Boss until finally he decided to give Ruf a call: "Oh my! She's out drinking with the Sloanes, Alec, didn't you know? Didn't she even call?"

"Daddy, won't you come get me, please?"

So Sunday morning was fated to be a bad one. Bess woke at around six in the morning, the sun still pale, and stayed awake even though she had several semi-dreams which were about ridiculous things like walking across the yard with the dumb chickens that her grandparents used to keep, scurrying behind her thinking she would feed them and then turning abruptly around and running at them, causing them all to cluck and scatter hysterically. On the other side of the room, the little boy breathed with comfortable steadiness. Bess tried to convince herself that, because of the dreams, she was really asleep, unaware of any headache.

At around eight o'clock, the house came awake, the first stirrings taking place in the bathroom down the hall and then extending into the kitchen downstairs. Bess had a brief dream about their dead black steer, Uncle Remus, who tried to kill her in the summer Daddy and Alistair had to shoot it. In the dream she got Uncle Remus mixed up with Candy, their pony, and she was standing alongside of Uncle Remus out in the middle of the field, stroking his nose and feeding him a carrot. Uncle Remus chewed on the carrot thoughtfully before looking up at Bess and saying, Well, of course you must understand why. And Bess was embarrassed for him and stroked his nose furiously. Of course, of course, don't give it another thought.

Downstairs, the phone rang. It was their line, one long and two short, and she heard Marg scurry to answer it. Dylan turned over, sighing, would be awake soon wanting Bess to play and watch the sparse Sunday morning cartoons. Things were quiet downstairs for a little while, maybe a half an hour, and then Bess could hear Mommy clear her throat, get up from the chair, and cross the floor. Then Bess heard her feet on the staircase, *creak, creak*, and she cleared her throat again. She was coming very deliberately, to wake up Bess. Bess heard her coming down the hall, pushing aside the already half-open door. Dylan turning over again and probably opening his eyes and looking at her as she sat down on the edge of Bess's bed. Mommy touching her shoulder and clearing her throat a third time and then leaning over to kiss Bess soft on the cheek, which was the way she had woken up Bess since the beginning of everything.

"I have some bad news."

"Grampa's dead."

"An hour ago. Daddy says we're going to wake him here."

Bess sat up. "Jesus Christ." Dylan was awake and smiling at her.

Mommy ran her thin hands through her short hair. "I know," she said. "We're going to have to start the cleaning today, as soon as you're dressed."

Mary Kate Sloane brought six plates of sandwiches and two large bowls of potato salad. She also brought a banana bread and a cinnamon loaf and two tins full of biscuits. She also brought a bottle of rye and a bottle of scotch, which she presented to Aunt Marg.

"I couldn't remember, Margaret, was it the Jack Daniel's you liked? Or the Johnnie Walker?"

"It's the Johnnie Walker, dear, God love you. It all goes down the same hole, in any case."

She had pulled up wedged between Cookie and Dougal in her husband's fish truck. When they got out, Bess saw that the back was full of boxes with food in them, and her daughter, Mary Katherine, had ridden back there too, partly to hold the boxes in place but mostly because there was no room in the front. She sat primly on top of a box, wearing a jacket that certainly couldn't have kept her warm enough during the ride, and high heels, and smoothing down a black skirt. Bess was very pleased to see her, for some reason, and wanted to stay close to her the whole time she was there and ask her questions about how she was doing in school and whatever else she was up to these days.

"We're here to help, not as guests," Mrs. Sloane said. "Not that we don't want to pay our respects to Iain, God love his soul, but anything you need done, you tell me or one of the boys or Mary and we'll see to it. Now you get back to your guests and we'll serve this here food up."

"Don't be so foolish, Mary Kate," Aunt Marg protested.

"No, no, no," said Mrs. Sloane, picking up one of the boxes that Dougal had hefted from the truck. "Let me see. This is the pickles. I'll need some little bowls, unless you'd just like to serve them in the jars."

Daddy had hired a fiddler to sit in the corner with a drink at his feet and play mournful Scottish tunes. He had not actually been hired, Daddy had called him up with the request and offered to pay him for it, but because he was an old friend of the family, the fiddler refused. The fiddler was actually a celebrity of sorts and most of the guests considered it something of an event, having him there. He was an old man in a wheelchair, with a sagging pink face and pure white hair and black, fifties-style glasses. He had a deep, resonating voice and was known to be a storyteller. Someone from Ontario had once included him in a book of Maritime folklore, and now he was widely considered a sage. He remembered Bess's father as a little boy, he'd told her once.

Bess was in a state of nervous irritation. She had never seen so many people in the house at once. For the last three days the place was full, morning and night, as many of them were relatives from Boston and Ontario with no other place to stay. The corpse was laid out in the living room, the first thing she saw in the morning when she got up and the last when she went to bed at night. She worried about Dylan, about his psyche and all that, even though he appeared to be having the time of his life, and it was all Bess could do to keep him away from the coffin, from poking philosophically at its contents. It was Cookie, usually, who would intercept him at just the last minute, sweeping him up and away just as the baby was about to experiment with one of Grampa's eyelids. Cookie would take him off into a corner somewhere and bounce him up and down on his knee, singing,

> A deedle deedle dump
> diddle dump diddle dump.
> A deedle deedle dump
> deedle dump dump dump!

And on the last "dump," he would abruptly open his legs, dropping Dylan through the gap. Dylan loved this.

There were relatives like most people had flies in the summer. Cousins and uncles. No aunts except for Marg and a couple of great-ones, arriving with a child or grandchild supporting either arm, wearing black fur coats purchased over forty years ago, and freakish little black hats with veils that had to be pinned into their webby hair if they were to remain in place. The aunts sat in a corner on either side of Gramma's chair, fingering black rosaries, and guiding her through the correct number of Our Fathers and Hail Marys. The procession stopped by her chair to kiss her before heading to the coffin.

"God bless his dear soul, Elizabeth."

"Well, he's in a better place now, God love him."

"Yes, God love his soul."

"He's happy now, dear. No need to cry for poor Iain."

"No, God bless him."

Bess had never in her life heard Gramma so lucid, let alone so gracious. Something had come back to her. The procession moved away from her chair, murmuring, "My God, what a woman."

Daddy and the uncles sat in another corner of the living room, drinking coffee and looking extremely sober. Some were Dad's uncles and some were his bothers. They were all reformed, watching the youngsters soak it up with pity and contempt, the contempt, of course, for the young, and the pity for themselves.

Uncle Roddie's children, for instance, were something of a mess. They had all grown up in Ontario and visited as children in the summers. They were all older than Bess, and she could remember worshipping them with their clothes and cigarettes. They had been young in the sixties, and so the girls were very independent, one wearing a brushcut. They drank beer and were exotic.

Most of Roddie's kids were in the civil service, but one had gone to art school and now worked in the Museum of Civilization. They were still the way they had been, independent and open-minded, arguing with Daddy about the French. Whenever they visited, they would do things like buy a case of Alexander Keith's and go to square dances and Judique on the Floor

Days and all the other festivals. They would come back to the house and sit in the kitchen with their Keith's and start all their sentences with "Jesus, Mary, and Joseph," and "Lord t'undering Jesus." They would play their Rankin Family and Rita MacNeil tapes.

But now they were a mess because Grampa had died and they remembered things about him Bess didn't, or so she supposed. One of them plunked down beside Bess on the couch and asked her how she was holding up and she said fine.

"You were with him right up until the end?"

"Yes."

"Last time I was down was five years ago, I think. God, maybe more. I never had a chance to get down. At home, we always would talk about it, spending maybe a month out of the summer, visiting all the relatives just like we used to. What was he like?"

"He wasn't like much of anything. I mean, he was pretty old."

"Ah, Bessie, you don't remember him like I do. What a man. What a great man. The stories he used to tell. But a simple man, you know?"

But I've lived with him all my life, Bess wished to say. Then she felt she was being callous all of a sudden and got up to get Aunt Marg, very dignified and controlled with her hand around her glass, because she would be able to talk to the cousins the way they wanted to be talked to. Bess penanced herself by fetching drinks for everybody and bringing the more distracted ones plates of food.

"Sit down, sit down, Bessie," said Mary Kate Sloane. "Mary Katherine and the boys are taking care of all that."

"No, no, no," said Bess.

Cookie, in fact, was sitting at the dining-room table with a scotch alongside of him, picking at a tray of squares. "Sit down, for the love of Christ, Bessie. Wait, fix yourself a drink first."

She sat down, feeling a tingling in her legs. He didn't say anything while she took her first sip.

"That's a nice buck your dad's got hanging outside," Cookie finally remarked. "Got it on the weekend, did he?"

"No, just the other day," she said, thinking for the first time about the gutted deer, swinging in the wind upside down from the big, leafless maple, with a red, open gash down its front. Everybody had forgotten about it. She thought that it probably wasn't a thing to have outside a wake, but she wasn't sure. Nobody had said anything until now.

"Season finished Saturday," Cookie pointed out.

"I know," said Bess. "But there was nothing to be done. Daddy looked out into the field early the other morning and it was just standing there."

"No shit!"

"Yes, he nearly killed himself going for the rifle."

"Were you there? Did you see it go down?"

"Oh, yes. Alistair was asleep on the couch because he had passed out the night before and Daddy was hollering for him to get up."

"Did he get up?"

"He got up just in time to see Daddy shoot it."

It had been just like the time with Uncle Remus. Men running to and fro, hollering to each other. Except Uncle Remus had been crazy and the buck just stood there the whole time, in the morning frost.

"Well, I'll be jiggered," said Cookie leaning back.

"Do you think anybody noticed it, Cookie?"

"The deer? Jesus, yes, she looks great."

Daddy wandered in and put his coffee cup down on the table. He examined the trays for something good.

"I was just saying to Bessie that's a hell of a nice deer you got out there," Cookie told him.

"Thank you, Angus," Daddy said, picking up a square. "You tell your mother to sit down and have a bite to eat, now. There's no need for her going to all this trouble."

"She don't mind at all, but I'll see if I can bring her a bite." Cookie got up apologetically and went to find his mother, and Daddy sat down in his spot.

"Glad to see you're enjoying yourself," he said, indicating Bess's drink.

"I'm taking a break, here."

"What's all this with the little Sloane fella?"

"Cookie's nice."

"Cookie's nice, is he? Weird little eyeball bastard. Ruf says you're just as thick as thieves, you and the Sloane boys. I said to him, 'I hope that's not right, Ruf, I honestly do.'"

"What's wrong with the Sloanes?" she said to him pointedly.

He held up his hands. "Mary Kate's a saint and I'd never say a word against her, now."

"Well, what the hell?"

"Don't let me hear about you running all over hell with those boys, that's all I'm saying."

"I don't. I never do anything."

"Drunk till all hours with The Boss on his deathbed."

And what was there to say to that? There was nothing to say. The times when Bess was angriest were always the times when there was nothing to say. When Daddy told an unfair truth and made it so there was nothing to say. She got up and went to find Cookie so that she could make a joke out of it.

Later, she was to feel sorry, getting angry and getting up like that so that she could be away from him. She felt sorry watching him move among all the people that he was so unused to with nothing to defend himself but an empty coffee mug and a napkin with a brownie on it. He wore a grey wool sweater that stretched out over his belly, and a tie stuffed down inside of it, so you could only see the knot. His father was dead. The problem was, Bess kept having to remind herself of that, that today was an especially bad day for him, and that all of his anger was justified today. And it was basically her fault. She knew that he was the angriest man in the world and that it was her fault. That his father had died and that he was poor and then not poor and then poor again, that he had been an alcoholic but then got to a point where he had to quit, and so quit, all by himself, without any help from AA or anyone. It was her fault because she had done nothing the right way. She had done nothing in her life to make any of it worthwhile.

❖

Red Ruf Bank, looking like a large, grey baby in his dark suit and with his combed-down hair, got on well with Leland MacEachern when both of them put in an appearance on the last day of the wake, Leland and his wife and daughter Maureen in tow, Maureen probably having been dragged along because she was closest in his family to Bess's age, and since they had played together on all the camping and fishing trips that their families had gone on all those years ago, both families assumed that they were friends.

It was rather an awesome thing, Leland coming to pay his respects,

118

because he was now an MLA in the Conservative government and you sometimes saw him on television. After he had spoken quietly to Gramma, holding her hand all the while, and knelt down beside the corpse to pay his respects, he stood chatting with Ruf and Daddy and all the men, and his wife and Maureen stood with the women, Bess trying to think of something to say to Maureen, who had grown very sleek and stylish, in a conservative kind of way.

"How's your little boy?" Maureen wanted to know.

"He's very good."

Mrs. MacEachern turned her head and said, "Oh, that reminds me, Ellen. We brought a bag down for those people you used to help, remember?"

"The Sloanes."

"The Sloanes. But I was just thinking that there may be one or two things in there to fit Bess's little one. David's boy, Peter, outgrows things faster than we can buy them, so everything's practically unused!"

And, before Bess had time to think about it, she had answered enthusiastically, that this was great, and she couldn't wait to look through the bag. She was momentarily enchanted by the thought of Dylan in new clothes, which he needed, but after she stood there listening to the women talk for a little while, the feeling wore off. She had just turned to resume her search for Cookie, when she realized that he was approaching with Dylan in one arm and fresh scotch for Bess.

"Do you want to know something funny?" she said to him, relieving him of both Dylan and the drink. "Every now and again I find myself having a good time."

"It's all this free booze," said Cookie. "Do *you* want to know something funny? You know that wire fence in the playground of the Forks school?" Bess shook her head and reminded him that they hadn't gone to school together. "Oh, yeah. Well, there's this fence in behind the school that they put there to keep all the little bastards from running off into the woods at recess. Anyways, every day at recess and lunch, I used to go and talk to the fence."

"Talk to the fence?"

"Yes, that fence was my Jesus best friend. And I gave him a name too. Jaimeson."

"Oh, yeah."

"Maybe if little Dilly here goes to school at the Forks, he'll take to talking to Jaimeson too."

"I hope to God he doesn't."

Maureen MacEachern, Bess saw, was observing them for lack of anything else to do. Bess looked at her and said, "Oh, this is Dylan," jostling the boy in her arms to draw Maureen's attention.

"What a sweetie," said Maureen, "oooh, what a sweetie." She poked at his nose. Cookie stood there, smiling, trying to see through his glasses.

"This here," added Bess, hastily pulling her free arm around Cookie and towering over him, also spilling a little bit of her drink, "is my husband."

"Is that right?"

"His name," said Bess, "is Red Angus John Dougal Sloane McFelly."

"But he doesn't even have red hair!" said Maureen.

"No, I know. They call him that because his great-uncle once had an Irish setter."

Bess put Dylan down and let him run.

A moment, later she explained to Cookie, who hadn't even questioned, "Daddy figures you and me are going to run away together."

"Actually, you can't blame me, most men are afraid of that," he said, looking thoughtful. "Me running off with their women. I'm a known snatch-sniffer."

Bess couldn't believe it, this at the poor old bastard's wake. She had to run to the bathroom, it was so funny.

Big Dog
Rage

EVEN THOUGH I WAS ONLY FIVE or something, I can remember the first time I met him because I was brimming with hatred and rage and despair. Being a child, I'd never felt such things before, not all at once. His dog had killed my dog in front of me, picked her up in his teeth, shook her once, and broke her neck. We'd collided in the woods behind my house and had been having a pretty amiable chat for a couple of kids when his Lab went crazy. It was on a leash — he'd been taking it for a walk. Mine wasn't, because I had just wandered down into the woods to play and she followed me like she always did. I don't remember much about it. I just remember being in the vet's with my mother and his parents and my dead dog having been carted off somewhere and his about to be put to sleep, and he was crying and hating me as much as I was hating him and his dog was wagging its tail and trying to put its nose up my crotch.

We got to be friends after a while because my mother was after his parents for compensation or something and would drag me over to his house and we'd go off and play spaceman while they had it out. Spaceman was his own game and entirely original. He would pull all the pillows off the chesterfield and chairs and we would bounce around on them pretending to be on Mars or somewhere. If a monster came, we would both jump in his father's recliner chair and recline rapidly, launching ourselves out into space. He vowed he would never get another dog, and so did I.

We whined to go over to one another's houses every single day for the next five years. My mother thought I was crazy because she was the kind of person who identified people immediately as being either good people or bad people, no one was in between, and it was always based on how other people's actions affected her. She thought Germans were bad, for example, not because of anything they had done historically, but because some Germans had bought up all the property in Dunvegan that used to belong to her family. The Newhooks had killed our dog, so they were bad also. That was how we met them. It made them our natural enemies, she thought.

And then she would talk about him like he was my boyfriend. He's going to break your heart, she would tell me. He broke your heart once, he'll do it again. She meant because of the dog, but I had gotten over it, and it irritated me that she never would let me forget.

Gerald and I made a game of it. The vet had said *Big dog rage*, and it was three words we never forgot. Big dogs see small dogs and become infuriated by their very presence, the vet told us, their very *being*. Big, friendly dogs, like yellow Labs — a breed I can't see to this day without hyperventilating — dogs who would normally never hurt a fly. Out of the blue they will jump on a little dog and kill them.

Big dog rage! he would suddenly shout in the middle of a cartoon, and lunge at me, teeth and claws.

His mother told me years later that when Gerald was a baby, she had left him with that same Lab, the Yellow Labrador of Death, in the living room while she went into the kitchen for something. She heard the Lab make this gurgly, pleading sort of noise that he'd never made before. She glanced back into the living room and saw that Gerald had stretched out his chubby hand and grabbed hold of the yellow Lab's scrotum, and the Lab was just sitting there, waiting for Gerald's mother to do something about it.

He could stop himself from biting the kid's arm off, she said to me, *but he couldn't stop big dog rage.* Gerald's mother always got weepy when she talked about that dog. I think she actually loved him more than Gerald ever did, more than any of my family ever loved the black poodle. My mother always said it was the *principle* of the thing, referring to all the grief she put Gerald's parents through afterwards, insisting the Lab be put to sleep or else she would call the police and get them to do it. *Imagine what could have happened to the little girl,* she said, meaning me. That's what she told them she was going to say to the police. So in the end Gerald's parents gave in and put the dog to sleep. His name had been Harvey, after the imaginary rabbit. It was Gerald's mother's all-time favourite film.

We played spaceman and big dog rage. We dressed up as Siamese twins at Hallowe'en. We decided we were going to be exactly the same person when we grew up. We would dress alike and have the same haircuts. We would talk at the same time when people asked us questions, and say precisely the same thing. We would be the same person, so we would just be able to talk like that. We would have the same job and live in the same house. Many of our days were spent practising for it, trying to find clothes that looked exactly alike, trying to talk simultaneously to his mother. We played on the same teams, and even though I was better than him at sports, I made it so that I wasn't. He quit Scouts because they wouldn't let me join.

His father made Gerald become an altar boy, however, because Gerald's father had been an altar boy when he was a kid, and my mother would not let me be an altar girl because she thought it was against the Pope. That's how it started. So he was up there serving mass on Saturday evenings and Sunday mornings, and I would watch him, agonized and inwardly raging against the Pope, while Gerald puttered around the altar, ringing the bell and carrying around the host.

"It's stupid," he said.

"But I want to do it because you're doing it."

"I know, but it's better if we figure out a way for me to get out of it, because it's stupid."

"I can write to the Pope." My mother had me believing that writing letters was the best and only way to change anything. I believed I could just write to anyone I wanted and they would read it, because that's what she believed. Even if they never responded, even if nothing ever changed, deep in my mother's heart she trusted that every recipient would be deeply shamed and chastened by her words. She wrote to newspapers, MLAs, businesses, lawyers, all the people who had wronged her over the years, on a regular basis.

"No," he said. "The Pope will never change his mind. I have to get out. I have to show I'm not worthy to serve the mass."

"How?"

"I can sin. " His face lit up, epiphanic. "I'll become a sinner."

"No! Just pretend to be a sinner."

"If I pretend to be a sinner, than I'm still sinning because I'm lying," he insisted.

"But you won't have sinned in your heart."

"But I will have if I lie! There's no escape. I've got to sin."

I floundered. It was a theological quagmire, but Gerald wasn't interested in negotiating it with me. I could tell he was excited about it, about having no choice, about circumstances conspiring against him like this. He had decided on his course of action.

Mass became suspenseful, torturously so. Gerald kept testing his boundaries, and I never knew how far he was willing to push it. He started digging at the interior of his left nostril one day while the priest gave the homily, but this was commonplace boy-behaviour as far as the congregation was concerned, even if it did occur on the holy altar. His father merely smacked him one on the back of the head and told Gerald not to let him catch him at it again. And the priest had had his back turned the entire time anyway.

"It's gotta be the priest," Gerald reflected. "He's the only one who can kick me off the altar. The priest has gotta catch me at something."

The whole thing made me uncomfortable because it looked to me as if Gerald was getting ready to do to the world one of his favourite things to do to everything else: take it all apart. Unscrew all the teensy imperceptible screws, and start tinkering around inside.

Gerald held the round, golden tray underneath the priest's hands as the latter fumbled the host towards the waiting tongues and hands of the congregation. He waited for it to be my turn to receive so that I could get an up-close view of what he was going to do. He simply dropped the tray onto my foot and then picked it up again.

"You old slut," he said to the tray. He breathed on it and then polished it with his sleeve.

If the host had not melted onto the roof of my mouth I would have choked on it. I thought the priest would reach out and knock our heads together — I was certain he would have assumed that I was involved in

Gerald's blasphemy somehow, that the word *guilty* would have appeared on my forehead in blistered, red script.

But the priest was cool. He knew it was important to correct Gerald, but more important was the necessity not to make a scene. So he glowered for only a split second, and waited until after mass to give Gerald a brief, kindly-but-stern talking-to. He told Gerald that God didn't appreciate that kind of language, and that was that. Say an act of contrition and try to be good. Gerald was disgusted.

"It's no use," I told him, hopeful.

"It didn't work because the only people who saw and heard it was you and the priest," said Gerald.

The next Sunday when it was time to ring the bell before communion, Gerald just kept ringing and ringing it until he was sure the priest and everyone else was looking at him and then he did this little dance to the bell-music that he used to do for me which he called the Dirty Boogie, and which basically involved just waving his pelvis around. He made a face at the two other altar boys, and they cracked up, and so did all of the less-pious parishioners, of whom there seemed to be quite a few. But I was frozen in my seat. My mother punched me hard in the arm because she was wiser than the priest — she knew I was, at the very least, guilty by association.

When Gerald was allowed to appear in public again, he was as giddy from the crime as if it had occurred moments ago. He would climb up to the top of the monkey bars and perform the Dirty Boogie for everyone, and everyone on the ground would cheer and do it with him. Then he would leap onto the ground and lead everyone in a Dirty Boogie dance-line. He was the most popular boy in town. Meanwhile, everybody's parents had started making dire predictions about Gerald. To be kicked out of the altar boys apparently did not bode well for a young man's future. It was taken as the worst sort of omen.

I was disturbed for all the obvious reasons. To serve the mass was sacred, but Gerald had acted like it was any other foolish thing your parents would force you to do, like violin lessons. Something to be weaselled out of at all costs. When I was very young, I never suspected it was the altar boys who rang the bells before communion. I always thought it was God. I'd hear the sound of bells suddenly echoing throughout the church and would look around wildly, in a panic. I started to get nervous and fidgety every Sunday before communion, waiting for the disembodied bells to sound, until finally my mother grabbed my swivelling head and forced me to watch the altar boy reach unobtrusively down beside his chair to give the bells a shake. It was one of the first religious anticlimaxes of my life, but I still thought ringing the bells at mass had to be one of the holiest things a kid could ever hope to do, and Gerald treated it like doing the dishes.

And Gerald had committed all these sins to be with me, but now that he was such a big shot he wasn't with me as much any more. Other boys began to take an interest in him because he was bad. Gerald loved it. He waved his pelvis around every chance he got, at teachers, girls, and parents. Boys followed, and imitated him like monkeys. When people got tired of that he had to think of something else to do.

He clamoured to be in the Christmas play. And not just as a haystack or donkey, he wanted to be something right up front, a wise man or an angel, if he couldn't be Joseph. He wanted to be Joseph, but at this point, with his reputation, it was laughable. He managed to get himself positioned as Balthazar, all decked out in a bathrobe and a big bedsheet-turban, and when it came time for him to present the frankincense to the Baby Brenda doll they had sat in a pile of straw, instead he opted to shout, "Go long!" and punt the doll across the stage with his foot, in front of all the parents. One of the shepherds in back instinctively raised his tinfoil-wrapped hockey stick to keep the baby from flying off into the wings, and the effect was as if some kind of spontaneous sporting event had broken out. I was an angel, told to stand at precisely the opposite position on the stage from where Gerald was supposed to present his offering. I'll never forget the floppy, swaddled body of Christ shuttling towards me like that.

So practically overnight Gerald had turned himself into the kind of boy who doesn't get chosen to be in Christmas pageants any more, or any pageants. Who isn't trusted to carry the milk money up to the office and is followed around the schoolyard relentlessly by the recess monitor. My mother was filled with satisfaction. In the later, wet winter months, somebody left a naked Baby Brenda doll with tits drawn on it on my doorstep, like an orphan. I took it in and washed it and dressed it up in clothes and put it to bed, but after a while it started giving me nightmares, so I threw it in the closet. Then all I could think about at night was the doll lying in my closet, so one morning I got up and put it in my mother's closet.

In the wintertime, the backyard of my house, sloping down into the woods, got turned by local kids into the beginning of a long, meandering sled-hill. They would pour buckets and buckets of water all along the whole thing until it was so unbearably slick that the moment you set foot on it, you would find yourself propelled into the woods at breakneck speed and there would be no way on earth you could slow yourself down. You would shoot past trees and bushes and screaming kids until finally you would find yourself rapidly approaching "the hill" — the steepest part of the whole ride, full of bumps and kid-made ramps. This was the climax of the ride, the only problem being that the bottom of the hill gave way to the Trans-Canada Highway, where pulp trucks went barrelling past on their way to and from the mill, making their loud and angry farting noises. There was a pretty deep gully which kept most of the sliders from shooting right out into the highway, but I had seen a couple of the speedier ones come so close my heart jumped. Even so, it didn't stop me, or anyone else, from spending entire twelve-hour days repeatedly hurtling ourselves towards the speeding traffic.

I remember the queer frenzy of those times, the bright snow against the grey sky, how the snow seemed like this cushion that would come between you and any harm, even though we were constantly almost breaking our necks and braining each other with snowballs, and kids would leave crying and dripping and come back in different snowsuits half an hour later, all memory of past offences having dried up as well. Nothing could keep us from the speed.

The only place I saw Gerald on a fairly regular basis then was the hill, shooting past me, loaded up on a sled with five or six other screaming boys. In the summer we used to sit on the top of the hill and watch for a pulp truck to go by and as soon as it made its noise, Gerald would jump up, make a face, and wave his hand in the air — "Oh my God! Hold your breath!" — and I would pretend that it was too late and I was already dead.

I had seen his mother around town and her face would melt like it always did when she saw me, because she associated me with the tragedy of dead dogs and childhood. She would hold my face in her hands, with her eyes all dewy, and ask why I never came to visit, and I would curse Gerald for having the sweet, soft mother that I wanted, and for cutting me off from her. I missed the whole decent normalcy of his entire family — the sweet, soft mother, the remote, joking father, and Gerald completing the triangle. They struck me as being wholesome and complete in a way that me and my suspicious, letter-writing mother could never aspire to. No matter what my mother said about the Newhooks, I always understood that they were better than us in a very fundamental way, and later I grew to understand that this was the reason my mother hated practically everyone.

But I wanted to be with people like that, those my mother said would break my heart. I wanted to be friends with my mother's enemies and prove that I was not like her, but like them.

On the top of the melting hill, I saw Gerald was scarcely two feet away from me, hands on his hips, yelling orders at a bunch of boys sprawled down at the bottom. He was screaming his head off so that they could hear him and his face was red under his blond hair, and I thought he looked like a Viking and I wanted him to belong to me again. I lobbed a lightly packed snowball at him and he spun around as if to say: *Who dares!*

"Nice doll," I told him.

"What?"

"Nice doll."

He cocked his head. "Nice dog?"

"Nice *doll*," I said.

"Nice doggie," Gerald said. "Good doggie." He panted at me and threw himself, stomach first, down the hill. I sat down.

He returned, pulling behind him a very lovely new sled I had seen before in the Christmas Wish-book, black, like his snowsuit, and sort of designed to look like a cross between a speedboat and a motorcycle. He was excited.

"Did you see that?" he said. "I came *this close* to the highway and I was only sliding *on my stomach!*"

"Where'd you get that?"

"Someone gave it to me." He glanced down at the sled. "On this thing I'll overshoot the gully, no problem. I'll be completely killed."

"Let me go on with you," I said like nothing had ever happened. "More weight will make you go faster."

He looked skeptical.

"We'll end up right in the middle of the highway!" I enthused. "Death will be instantaneous! We'll just be one big blot on the road."

"When I come back," he promised, flinging himself down onto it and flying away.

◇

The Devil's
Bo-Peep

◇

WELL, IT BEGAN. The family were given a wheelchair to bring her in with, and Ramona watched from behind the desk as this wild-eyed, rotten apple of a woman was brought into the lobby howling as if her entire family — who were in fact all around her, patting her hand, kissing her cheek, reassuring — had been killed in some kind of big disaster. The kind of all-annihilating disaster Ramona was always dreaming of, which would be, in her imagination, like God blowing a candle out.

"You are going to leave me here to die," the woman was saying. She had a thick near-Scottish accent, like most of the senior citizens of the area, and was winding a clunky set of ancient rosary beads into the flesh of her hands so insistently that soon her hands were actually bound together by the beads, but she didn't notice. The man, the son, was in control and stubborn. The son's wife looked as if she needed to be checked in herself — Ramona guessed that she had been doing most of the work where the old woman was concerned. The daughter, the son's sister, was the most sprightly of the bunch. She must be from away, thought Ramona.

"Nobody's leaving you to die, Mumma."

Ramona had done the intake on the old woman, and she thought the entire situation was foolish. The family merely wanted to go away for a week. A son in a far-off province was getting married, they wanted to attend, but had no one to look after the mother. The senior's home, on the other side of the parking lot, didn't take people as decrepit as this woman was; it was really more of an apartment complex for the elderly but self-sufficient. The woman needed around-the-clock care, however, so dear old Doctor Joey, the administrator and apparently an old friend of the family, took it upon himself to offer up one of the hospital's rarer-than-gold empty beds.

The sprightly daughter smiled at Ramona. "I'll be visiting her every day, making sure she doesn't get too lonely."

"We'll be back in a goddamn week!" the son was hollering at the wailing wheelchair.

"I'm staying up at the house while they're gone," the sister offered. "So I can come every day."

So, thought Ramona. The son's family had been caring for the woman into her extreme dotage, but the daughter wasn't even willing to put up with her for a week. No wonder she looked so fresh. She was about thirty years older than Ramona.

There was a sullen-eyed teenage girl poking around the waiting area, one of the family but trying to pretend she wasn't. Ramona used to have to run home from school every day and take care of her own grandmother, so she allowed herself a trickle of sympathy for the sulky thing, even though she did not approve of her enormous earrings and foolish clothes. If Ramona had a daughter, she would force her not to dress like an idiot until she was nineteen at least — then the girl could walk a tightrope in the town square wearing a G-string, for all Ramona cared.

The old woman was now wailing for the granddaughter, whose unfortunate name was Cassie Ann — "Cassie Ann! Cassie Ann! Where is my Cassie?" — and the girl tugged on her earrings and shuffled over, looking around to see who else might be in the lobby watching. I would teach her not to care what anyone thinks, thought Ramona. Like myself.

"Take off my handcuffs!" the woman begged, holding her hands out pathetically to the granddaughter, finally figuring out that they were inextricably bound.

The old could be dramatic. Ramona had noticed it before. She watched the girl blink three quick times before attempting to unwind the rosary beads. Soon she was yanking. They wouldn't come. The woman started wailing again, as though she took this as some sort of horrible cosmic portent. At last the family stared helplessly at Ramona, the authority figure, who came over to examine the bonds. She'd never seen such a thing before. The old woman shrieked at the sight of Ramona's big body in her white, blank uniform as it advanced.

"What in God's name kind of rosary is this?" Ramona demanded. It was enormous, a caricature of the real thing.

"We got her an extra big set," the wife answered, quiet and guilty.

"She's half blind, so she can't see the beads," the son interjected. "We needed big ones so she could tell the Our Fathers from the Hail Marys!" He glared at Ramona, daring her to question further. Ramona sized him up and decided to back down for the time being.

The mother was thrashing in her chair. "Why am I in chains?" she shrieked at Ramona. "Why have you done this to me?"

Oh, thought Ramona, this is lovely. This is just the cat's tit.

"We'll have to get some scissors," Ramona stated, heading back towards the nurses' station before there could be any argument.

The sullen granddaughter was shocked into speech. "You can't cut up her rosary!" Apparently she did fine wearing some kind of heavy-metal T-shirt with a skull and a 666 plastered across it, but the thought of cutting her grandmother free of the Our Fathers and Hail Marys offended her religious sensibilities. Ramona returned with a big pair of desk scissors and peered at the girl, who was standing protectively in front of her grandmother's chair. The grandmother had somehow deciphered the logistics of the situation and as a result quieted down and began paying attention. She knew only this: Someone she loved was standing between her and the big, unfamiliar person in white. It comforted. And Ramona was going to have to wreck it, having no time for such indulgences.

"I remember you, dear," Ramona said to the girl all of a sudden. And she did. The teenage girl had been brought in at seven in the morning some time last year with a stomach full of pills. Ramona had stuffed the tube down her nose and pumped green and black out of her stomach, barking at her all the while just what kind of foolish nonsense was she trying to perpetuate? Now Ramona smiled, and the girl stepped out of the way.

Perhaps Ramona shouldn't have raised the scissors quite so high as she approached the old woman, brandishing them, really, as it only served to send her into new fits of terror. As the family watched, the wife with her hands together and the son chewing on the inside of his face and the girl with her back to them all, Ramona ignored the wails and thrashing, slashed the rosary to pieces, and got the woman free. Oversized beads with bits of string attached clattered to the floor and rolled crazily off in every direction. Ramona hollered down the hall for an orderly.

"Well!" said the sister, standing apart from them all, a few feet away. "That's done." She wiped her palms on the front of her skirt.

◇

Ramona saw at once that the old woman, whose name, it turned out, was also Cassie Ann, was going to have to be given her own room because she was so disruptive. The waste of hospital resources was appalling, and she thought Doctor Joey a politicking twit. She understood it all. The soft-hearted son could not bear the notion of putting dear Mother in a home, and so, early in her agedness, when she was still dear old Mother and not a gibbering banshee, he committed himself, and his entire unwitting family, to her eternal care in the bosom of home and hearth. Ramona knew the scenario so well because her own goddamn mother had done it to her, although perhaps if they had had more money and a few helpful relatives living nearby, it would not have been such a trial, and Ramona would not have been relegated to primary caregiver from the ages of twelve to eighteen while her mother worked at the fruit stand. She knew she had to have a career because it didn't look as if anyone was going to marry her, and she needed a reason to move the hell out of the house by the time she finished high school. She despised children, so being a teacher was out. The only other possible alternative was to enrol in nursing school, and considering she already had so much hands-on experience emptying bedpans and dispensing pills, it seemed the natural thing to do.

Of course, two months after Ramona had settled into the nursing program at Saint Mary's, her grandmother died. It was typical.

But she continued on with the program anyway and did well, and then eventually moved back home to work in a hospital also named after Saint Mary — the hospital in which she had been born. This was a practical decision, because here she could look after her own mother, who had given

138

birth to Ramona late in life and was getting on. Ramona prided herself on the fact that she did not live with her mother out in the sticks, but had her own little house here in town, the mortgage paid with her own money. And when her mother could not get along on her own any more, Ramona would have no qualms. None. She had enough to do, enough old, sick people to take care of.

It was true that most of the patients in the hospital were old. Not a lot happened on this corner of the planet, so there was usually little to arouse excitement, the only youthful faces appearing whenever some kid flipped over his ATV while tearing around the hills. And sometimes people ran right into stately, immovable moose with their cars. The most exciting thing had been a few years ago when the mine was still operating and one of the shafts gave way. Miraculously, nobody was killed, the shaft was fairly close to the surface, so they were able to haul everyone to safety eventually. For weeks following, the wards were filled up with men of all ages, shapes, and sizes. Ramona tried to treat them with the brisk irritation she displayed towards her regular patients — an attitude that said: Who do you think you are, taking up all my time with your foolish ailments? — but found that she couldn't. The men were so lively and full of jokes. They knew they wouldn't be there for very long, and enjoyed themselves to the fullest. Ramona was so unused to people having fun in the hospital that she was completely disarmed. They shouted at the TV news and ate all the meals with gusto and then complained about them to Ramona with equal vehemence. They talked about the lives they couldn't wait to get back to, their wives and children. At visiting hours the halls were full of wives and children, all young, arms full of flowers. Some of the men even talked about the mine itself as if it were some kind of glorious haven. Indeed some of them loved the mine, the very mine that had dropped tons of rock on top of them only a few days before.

But soon the healthy male bodies knit themselves together, as was only natural, and Ramona was left once again with the old and the sick. All those who kept coming back, the terminally ill, the terminally old, taking up all of her time.

Today was more interesting than most, not because of the shrieking old woman, which was par for the Jesus course, but because Ramona was having lunch with a friend. This was a complete anomaly for Ramona — typically she just strolled down the street to her house, a mere five-minute walk away, and had some soup and a roll by herself. But this was a special occasion because Tamara Rutledge was in town, and she and Tamara had gone to nursing school together and been friends. It was one of those queer situations where they had lived in the same tiny part of the world for years and not said boo to each other, but once they were both alone in the same city, they sought each other out like sisters. Tamara was home to see her parents, because her father was dying of leukemia. Ramona had done his blood count up at the hospital a hundred times, and soon he would check in for good.

Ramona had enjoyed having Tamara as a friend in the last couple of years before graduation, because Tamara was a bit strange, and it was funny to show her to the other friends Ramona eventually made. At one point, Ramona had a good deal of friends. They would go to the Misty Moon and the Palace together on weekends and get drunk and dance with each other. During the week they would study and drink tea in one another's room and look at magazines. The friends were all inevitably from small towns like Ramona, and they banded together.

But Tamara was like someone from away. She sat in her room playing guitar and singing songs she made up in her terrible voice, but if you asked her to play one of the songs for you, she wouldn't do it. She wanted to travel all over the world after graduation, working for free in places like the Philippines, where you could catch a disease, or the Arctic, where you would freeze to death. One of her favourite songs, the only one she would sing out in public, was "Leaving on a Jet Plane." She could play it very well. She had several boyfriends and brought them to her room, which Ramona thought was vulgar, but, as many of the girls had pointed out, she wasn't able to hold on to a single one of them for more than a couple of months, so what was the point.

All those girls were married now, except for Ramona and Tamara. Everyone knew that Tamara couldn't keep a man, and Ramona could care less about them to begin with — she trusted her friends understood that much about her.

"Did you ever see anyone get all tangled up in their own rosary beads?" Ramona said to her friend. They had finished embracing and looking each other up and down.

"Are you speaking euphemistically?" asked Tamara with her bright, open face.

It was an irritating beginning, typical of Tamara. She didn't know enough to answer no, and wait for the story.

"Of course not," said Ramona. Before Tamara could interject any other comment, she launched into the story of the old doll in the wheelchair who checked in that morning, and what a trial it all had been. She embellished with a description of the comically oversized beads, a lament for the well-meaning ineptitudes of Doctor Joey, and finally a description of the sullen teenaged girl with her stomach full of pills last year and her earrings like two daggers.

"So then doesn't the devil's Bo-Peep enter into the fray," she was saying. "She does fine with the six-six-six emblazoned on her chest everywhere she wanders, but, dear God, don't cut up Nana's rosary in front of her!"

Tamara was twiddling her hair like a five-year-old, her mouth slightly open. "The devil's Bo-Peep, my Jesus, I haven't heard that in years."

Ramona was gratified. "I don't know where I heard it, it just came to me out of the blue, thinking of that thing with the Satan-shirt on her."

"My father used to call me that," said Tamara. Leave it to her to turn the conversation back to herself. "When I was a teenager going out with the boys. I think he would have been happy if I stayed a spinster my whole life."

But you *are* a spinster, Ramona stopped herself from pointing out. She was too polite. "What does he think about your travelling all over Kingdom Come?"

"Well," said Tamara, "Kingdom Come is pretty much the only thing on his mind these days as it is, he's not too interested in my goings-on any more."

Ramona was irritated again. "But when you started out on your travels, he wasn't too pleased, as I recall." Ramona knew all this already, but she wanted Tamara to remind her of it.

"Oh, he figured I'd catch some exotic disease." Tamara blew at her bangs with scorn. "Then, when I went up North, every time I called home it would be: 'Now don't you ever show up at this house with some big Eskimo in tow!' *Eskimo*, he calls them."

"Well, what do you call them? Inuit, I suppose."

"Actually, I was working almost exclusively with the Dene."

Tamara looked as if she wanted to talk about the Dene some more, so Ramona said, "And is there a man in the picture these days?"

"Now I'm in Indonesia. Hm? Oh." Tamara smiled and blew at her bangs again and Ramona wondered why she didn't just go for a trim. "Yes, yes, isn't there always a man in the picture."

"A different one every time I talk to you," added Ramona. "You must like the variety."

Tamara's face registered pain, and Ramona was reminded of why she enjoyed spending time with her. Tamara was always blurting things out, leaving herself open, and it confirmed for Ramona how glad she was to know that she was nothing like her friend.

She returned from the luncheon buoyant and revitalized, having not visited with anyone except for her mother in months. She extracted a promise from Tamara to come over and see the house some time during her visit home and Tamara said she would do her best and Ramona replied for her not to put herself out, thus ensuring the visit would take place.

"Bring your guitar and sing "Leaving on a Jet Plane" for me," Ramona called when they parted.

◇

The old woman Cassie Ann had to have her call button taken away, because once she became aware of its function she just sat there pressing it over and over again. This meant that now the nurses had to go out of their way to check on her every half-hour or so, and sometimes she would just wail for no reason, causing whoever was on duty to drop whatever it was she was doing and rush down the hall to find the old doll propped comfortably up on her pillows, gazing around herself like a great lady. The situation offended Ramona. It was a situation where the patient was not even sick, merely old. So old, however, that she might as well be deathly ill, being more trouble in her senility and decrepitude than all of the other patients put together. The woman should have long ago been admitted to a reputable home where she would receive constant care from professionals. That the family had opted to make themselves slaves to her needs for so long was unfathomable to Ramona.

The sister, the old woman's daughter, she disapproved of profoundly — it turned out that she was a nurse! The one person in the entire family who could have provided real aid where it was needed instead had offered to "take care of the house" while they attended their wedding, and "visit Mumma every day." Ramona sized her up as one of those selfish women, not unlike Tamara, who put their own comfort and frivolous desires before everything that matters. Ramona recalled how fresh and lively the sister looked compared to the son's wife, and even the teenaged daughter. She was probably the kind of woman who went to spas and what-have-you on the weekends.

Because she was also a nurse, the sister seemed to feel that she could just call Ramona by her first name, and double-check with her about her mother's dosage and other things that were normally no one's business but the hospital staff. Sometimes when Ramona returned to empty out the bedpan, she found that the sister had already performed this duty, and although, God knows, Ramona didn't begrudge her, she thought it presumptuous, to say the least.

"I just thought I'd make things a little easier for you around here, Ramona," the sister would chirp in her smiley voice.

Ramona had all sorts of comebacks for this that she was too polite to air.

When the sister left, Cassie Ann would cry and ask Ramona, "Why doesn't she stay with me?"

Ramona would say, "Because she's selfish and ignorant." Ramona didn't know why she called the sister "ignorant." She didn't know why she replied to the old woman in that way at all.

"She's my daughter," said Cassie Ann. "She studies the nursing up at Mount Saint Vincent."

Ramona snorted. The Mount. They were all lesbians up there.

"She's getting married in the fall to a tall man. He's too tall. No one will dance with her daughters."

"Isn't she doing well for a woman her age!" muttered Ramona. Time had no meaning for the senile. She remembered her own grandmother describing what her day had been like in school, talking to Ramona like she was her mother. It used to make her feel insane, in that room with her grandmother calling her "Mumma" and asking for treats. A dark, airless room, thick curtains always shut tight because the light made her grandmother depressed. An enormous picture of Humphrey Bogart above her bed the way most old women Ramona knew would have pictures of Jesus or the Pope, but her grandmother had been obsessed with Humphrey Bogart because she had once caught a glimpse of him on the streets of New York City, where she had worked as a much-coveted Nova Scotia nanny. She said she liked Humphrey Bogart because he looked "normal." He didn't look abnormal like the other movie star men. She cited Clark Gable as an example of a movie star who didn't look "normal."

Ramona's grandmother was said to have always acted like a big shot her whole life because she had lived in New York and stood within a few feet of Humphrey Bogart. But didn't she come flying back home at the end of her work period just like everyone did, looking for a long-faced, black-eyed husband, and toting a suitcase full of miniature Statues of Liberty and Empire State buildings to be distributed to family and friends. Ramona now had the largest and best of her grandmother's Statues of Liberty — the one her grandmother had purchased just for herself — on the mantelpiece of her home. The old lady had left it to Ramona in her will along with the china and silverware.

Ramona's grandmother was named Ramona also. Day in and day out Ramona used to come home from school and toil away in Ramona senior's shrine to normal men and darkness.

❖

They had kept Tamara's father at home as long as they could, but later in the week he had to be checked in. Ramona wondered if Tamara would stay until he died. This hadn't been Tamara's plan, as her father had always gone in and out of remission and had days when he was as strong as an ox and his wife would get up to find him pulling weeds in the garden. But now his condition had suddenly deteriorated, almost as if he was attempting to do the polite thing by dying while his daughter was home to see it. Ramona had seen terminal patients do this sort of thing before. It was really quite remarkable.

She was gratified to run into Tamara in the lobby, as they hadn't been in touch about coming to see the house.

"As you can see," explained Tamara, "things have been a little overwhelming at home."

"Well, come down for lunch, it's a five-minute walk!"

Tamara made much of Ramona's Statue of Liberty, which she hadn't seen before. Ramona thought it was foolish, the fuss she made over it.

"It's just so out of place with the rest of your stuff!" Tamara exclaimed. "This majestic, enormous piece of kitsch in the middle of such a tasteful little home. Everything else is so traditional."

Leave it to Tamara to exalt a thing so commonplace. Ramona was irritated at her friend for noticing something about the house that she never had — a paradox, an apparent contradiction in Ramona's well-ordered environment. She commanded Tamara to put the damn thing back on the mantelpiece and come into the kitchen for soup.

After, she served them tea in Ramona senior's delicately flowered china.

"God, I haven't had tea in ages," blurted Tamara.

Ramona put her cup down. "Are you crazy?"

"I mean," she corrected herself, "of course I've had tea ... just not caffeinated. I'll be wired all day."

"You drink *decaffeinated* tea?" Ramona demanded.

"No, no ... of course not...." Tamara's hand suddenly darted forward and she seized a teacake and shoved it in her mouth.

"Well, what in God's name are you drinking?

"Earl ... eee."

"Swallow your food, for Pete's sake, Tamara."

"Herbal tea," Tamara confessed, swallowing.

Ramona shook her head and smiled.

"There's all sorts of lovely teas...." began Tamara.

"I'm sure there are, dear," Ramona soothed. Tamara was two years older than Ramona, but Ramona called everyone "dear."

"I'll bring you some. I've got a wonderful blend from Indonesia —"

"No, no. You keep that for yourself," said Ramona. She changed her tone to indicate the subject closed. "So I imagine you'll be extending your visit for a while now," she began.

"Hm?"

"With your dad's condition."

"Oh." Tamara's honest face folded up into its little expression of pain, again. "Yeah, Dad's gotten worse. There's nothing I can do, though."

"Well, at least you're able to be with him throughout the ordeal."

"Oh — wouldn't I love to."

"Well, what's stopping you?"

Tamara glanced up with a bewildered, irritating smile. "I've got to go back to work."

"My God, Tamara, you're father's dying."

"There's nothing I can do about that, Ramona."

"You can stay with him. For God's sake, it's bad enough you've been gallivanting all these years, never paying your family a second thought —"

"I've been working, Ramona!"

"Working!" Ramona snorted.

Tamara cocked her head. "What do *you* think I've been doing?"

"I think you've been doing exactly what you've pleased your entire life."

The women had been smiling at each other and speaking in pleasant tones the entire time, so it did not sound particularly abrupt when Tamara suggested they tidy up the china and return to the hospital. Ramona told her not to be ridiculous, that she would take care of the dishes when she came home that evening.

While she was gone, Cassie Ann had demonstrated sudden and surprising vigour by throwing a half-filled bedpan at one of the student nurses. It hit her square in the chest and knocked her to the ground, and Ramona discovered the young woman, wet and weeping, in the staffroom cradling her right breast.

"What did you do to her?" Ramona demanded.

"I didn't do anything. She told me to stop singing."

"Why were you singing?"

"I *wasn't* singing!"

"Show me your tit," said Ramona.

146

With the entire bottom half of her face quivering, the student nurse exposed herself. An ugly bruise was forming. The student nurse saw it and cried harder, like a child who suddenly notices she's bleeding.

"It's nasty," admitted Ramona.

"I didn't expect people to hurt me," the student nurse sobbed. "Nobody told me people would be hurting me."

Ramona suggested the student nurse take the afternoon off, more to get rid of her than to be kind. Self-pity turned Ramona's stomach. She went to check on Cassie Ann, in whose room an orderly was mopping up pee.

"Well, my darling, you're turning this place upside down, now, aren't you?"

The orderly looked up to see if she was talking to him. He was an old, feeble-minded man who had worked there for as long as she could remember, perhaps even back when Ramona was born.

"I don't care for people singing. Everybody singing their songs all day long," responded Cassie Ann.

The orderly wrung out his mop and shuffled off down the hall.

Ramona fussed around the room, straightening. "What songs would those be now?"

"La, la, la. Hm, hm, hm," stated Cassie Ann in a monotone. "The same songs over and over again, day in and day out. No one gets tired of them but me."

"I get tired of them as well," said Ramona. "La, la, la, hm, hm, hm."

"Well, this is it," agreed Cassie Ann.

Ramona was tickled with herself for playing along. She didn't often indulge in such foolishness.

❖

She saw Tamara in her father's room a couple of days later, singing to him quietly. Ramona deliberately went on to glance at a few patients down the hall before returning to see if Tamara was still there. She was, and to Ramona's disappointment, she was still singing. "Leaving on a Jet Plane." Ramona loitered in the hall, impatient, because it was time for her break and she wanted to ask Tamara to join her for a cup of tea. Then she realized that she was the nurse, and had every right to barge into people's rooms whenever she liked.

147

"Mr. Rutledge, dear, how are you today?" She picked up his chart and examined it busily. "Tamara."

"Ramona! Why haven't you been to visit me before now?" Tamara's father demanded in his kind, weakened voice.

"Oh, we're awfully busy around here, as you well know, now, Mr. Rutledge."

As soon as decorum allowed, she had disengaged Tamara from her father and brought her to the cafeteria for tea.

"How's he been?" Ramona asked to be polite.

"Well — you saw his chart."

The fact was that Ramona had only pretended to read it, and otherwise had no idea of Mr. Rutledge's condition, as he was not on her ward. She nodded sympathetically. "When do you leave?

"Sunday."

"Oh, you'll have to come for dinner Saturday."

"I really should be spending time with my mother."

"Bring your mother," Ramona decreed magnanimously.

"I've only got two more days home, Ramona, and I don't know when I'll be back again."

The last part of what she said was a line from "Leaving on a Jet Plane." "It will do the two of you good to get out," said Ramona.

Tamara had been twiddling with her hair in her usual, childlike way, but abruptly she raised both hands to either side of her head, taking her hair into handfuls, and yanked. It looked as if she were trying to pull her head open.

"I can't do it," she said.

"Well, then, fine," replied Ramona. "I see," she added.

Ramona waited for Tamara to either change her mind or offer effusive apologies, but Tamara sat yanking at her hair, letting there be silence. "I see," Ramona repeated, to prompt her.

"I don't see the point to this," said Tamara, releasing the hair on one side of her head in order to pick up her teacup, peer into its depths as if to read the future, and put it down again.

"What?" said Ramona.

"I won't be a martyr."

"What?" Ramona almost hooted at the word.

"I can't be the big person any more. It does no good. It changes nothing. I suffer. I suffer along, pointlessly."

"What, in God's name, are you talking about, Tamara, and when have you suffered a day in your life?"

Tamara smiled suddenly, not happily, but she let go of her hair. She leaned over and spoke to Ramona as if the latter were deaf. "I'm very sorry," Tamara articulated, rising.

And she didn't even call her friend to say goodbye before leaving on the jet plane. Ramona felt angry on behalf of poor Mr. and Mrs. Rutledge, having raised a daughter who would not even stay to help them towards death. She went to visit her own mother on Sunday, and yelled at her for keeping the house in such a mess and having the heat turned up so high. She cleaned the house from top to bottom, complaining all the while, as her mother sat in the front room playing hymns on her wheezy old organ and wiping occasionally at her eyes. Then she made them a casserole out of the groceries Ramona had brought from town and they ate it together for supper. She told her mother all about Tamara and how shoddily she treated her family and how she flew all over the world and you never knew where she would end up next.

"Where is Tamara these days?" Ramona's mother asked, once they had eaten dinner and she could speak to her daughter again.

"Indonesia," Ramona spat.

"What is she doing in Indonesia?"

"Who knows," said Ramona. "Getting a tan." She washed the dishes, broke a cup, cleaned it up, and then went home.

◇

"La, la, la. Hm, hm, hm," Ramona announced to Cassie Ann every time she entered the room. Sometimes Cassie Ann responded, and sometimes she did not. One time the daughter was there when she said it, and smiled at Ramona quizzically.

"It's our own private joke," said Ramona, flustered.

The daughter seemed to approve of her mother having a private joke with the nurses. Ramona told her about the bedpan incident with the student nurse, playing up the girl's injury and subsequent trauma. Rather than being alarmed or guilty, Cassie Ann's daughter merely shook her head and related an incident of her own, when she was in her twenties, and a man she was giving mouth-to-mouth resuscitation to threw up. Then and there, three months before graduation, she'd almost quit the nursing program and enrolled in secretarial college, she claimed.

"Now you behave yourself, Mumma." The daughter smoothed Cassie Ann's hair and kissed her tenderly goodbye, but Cassie Ann was gazing out the window and humming, oblivious. The daughter turned to Ramona and smiled again. "It's certainly an improvement over the screaming and crying! I think she's adjusting well. You girls are so good with her." With that, the daughter flounced away, free and pleased.

Of course, not five minutes later, Cassie Ann realized her daughter had gone and began screaming and crying. Ramona watched her for a few moments, considering a sedative, as the old thing raved.

"Why, why, why? I wish, I wish, I wish!" Cassie Ann shrieked. Instead of going to get the sedative, or doing anything at all about it, Ramona sat down on a nearby chair and continued to watch. Everything about Cassie Ann's demeanour screamed impotence. She bashed her crumpled-paper fists against the yielding white bed. She flopped her head back and forth across the soft pillows. She was absolutely like a child throwing a tantrum, but even a child would have been able to do some kind of damage, to produce a result, however mindless. A spilled drink. A broken lamp. A bruised body. Today there wasn't even a bedpan to throw.

After a little while Cassie Ann broke down into weak sobs, and Ramona sat marvelling at herself and all the rare and precious time she was wasting. Nurse's time. Critical to her job was the ongoing awareness of how people depended on her to parcel out these moments of her life in the most useful and efficient way possible.

And yet an hour had passed during which Cassie Ann sobbed herself into exhaustion, not a tear having worked its way down into the innumerable gullies of her face. At last, Ramona witnessed Cassie Ann returning to herself, seeming to take note of her steel and grey surroundings as if she had only just arrived. It was almost a comical contrast to the wild way she had looked around moments before, like the world was on fire — one vast, encircling threat.

Ramona shifted in her chair and felt her back pop, and Cassie Ann, somehow uncommonly alert in her exhaustion, looked right at her.

"The devil has my soul," she sighed, quite matter-of-fact.

Ramona got up from the chair and straightened her skirt, looking around for anything else that might need straightening.

In Disguise
as the Sky

I AM A SADIST FOR DOING IT, but they have to learn. I give them test after test after test every week. They almost weep at the thought. There's no rules. They just have to keep practising, memorizing, testing and re-testing themselves.

I understand how it insults them, how the English language in general is an insult to reason with its *there, their,* and *they're,* its *it's* and *its.* "*I* before *e* except after *c*" and all that pointlessness. *Though* and *through* and *trough.* It's infuriating. They get angry at me. They demand: Why? And I'm a teacher, but because I am a teacher of a very insane and arbitrary science, the only answer I can give them is this — it's a child's answer: *Just because.*

And spoken to like children, they respond like children: Who say?

Who says, I correct. *I don't know. Whoever made it up. Just some guy.* I don't feel like much of a teacher, saying things like that. But it's true. And thus do they come to understand what an embarrassment to English speakers our language really is. All of them leave the class feeling a good degree more contempt for me and my countrymen than they started with. That means I am doing my job.

On the last day of class I usually ask them to tell me a little bit about their own language, not for their own benefit, but because it's fascinating to me how much more rational they all seem. A Japanese student showed me how the characters for things were basically just drawings of them. A Thai student showed me how the little round heads on all the lovely, looping characters where what made up vowel sounds. The one Russian I ever taught merely spat at me: "Russia language make sense."

Russian makes sense, I told him. *You don't have to say 'Russian language,' it's implied.*

He rolled his eyes, as he had been doing all along. Over the semester, it becomes harder and harder for them to believe that this is the language of the most prosperous nation on earth, of the Internet, of the global marketplace. This is the one out of all the others, for all their beauty and simplicity, that's won out.

One, won.

But prepositions makes them angriest. At least for some things you have the handy little rules of thumb. The *i* before *e* stuff. Subject and object. It's "my friend and I" if it's the object, but "my friend and me" if it's the subject. That's a tricky one but you can learn it. You can study it and you can learn it. All I can do with prepositions is give them long, endless lists. *A secret between us. A story about a man.* Is it always a story *about* something? *Yes, that's right.* So then they go and write something like, "This is a story about Ernest Hemingway." *No, it's a story* by *Ernest Hemingway* about *an old man dying with his hat off in the rain.* But you said it was *always* a story *about* something. About *something* but by *someone.* So a book can only be about something or by someone? they ask with so much hope. *A book is an object. It can be* on *something,* off *something,* by *something....* But you said it could only be by *someone!* I don't know how they keep from killing me.

But they don't. They come to feel sorry for me because I am only a dumb representative of my dumb language. A dumb citizen of a dumb English-speaking country that should be clamouring to join up with the wealthy and fearsome realm next door, they think, but remains stubbornly sovereign, middle-income, and weak. They don't get it, because to them we are all the same. It's not like we're a bunch of Latvians on this side of the border, with Ukrainians on the other side. That's precisely how my Russian student put it to me. "You are all mongrels," he said. "You have no culture, why do you care? It is not as if you are a bunch of Latvians or something."

"Not as if you *were,*" I corrected. Eye-roll.

I had taught them the word *mongrel* the week before. They loved it. They used it all the time after that. They loved having a word to express

156

what it was about North Americans that had baffled them for so long. This blandness. This striving towards homogeneity. This relative indifference to immigrants, for example, people of all races and creeds. This relative indifference to our own families and communities. That I had moved across the continent away from mine and not yet dried up from despair.

But I like my country, if not my language. I like that we're not all a bunch of Latvians. They may have simple languages, but their nations are complicated. Indonesia, for example, is complicated. Yugoslavia is complicated. I like simplicity. I like that slogan, "Keep It Simple, Stupid," and would have it posted up in my classroom, if it weren't such an outlandish contradiction to what I teach. *Obscurify, students. Clutter. Complicate.* So I have it pinned up in my kitchen at home instead. In my apartment, I forget about the Byzantine world of English grammar. I get take-out food, everything in medium-sized portions. I watch television shows that were not created to be enjoyed by people with imaginations. I sleep on a futon. I don't dream.

❖

In the office, two male voices are talking about something called "day-cake." One of them is my student, Kunakorn, from Thailand, and the other is someone I don't know, hanging around the desk like he works here. He probably does work here. This is such an irritating place to work that people quit and get hired all the time, so I am always running into people I don't know who are supposedly my co-workers.

Kunakorn says, "My favourite is day-cake," and my new co-worker replies that he is partial to day-cake as well. Then I remember what day-cake is. Kunakorn has a habit of making up his own words for objects when I'm not around to tell him what they are. He has an even worse habit of deciding that the word he makes up is more appropriate and easier to remember than the actual English word, once he's learned what it is. So he'll go for months, for example, refusing to call a basketball net anything other than a "sky-hole."

One of Kunakorn's pet peeves about North America is how much bread we eat. He's had some bad experiences with bread. When he first arrived here, his host-family served him nothing but sandwiches and hamburgers.

Finally he just went out and bought a bag of rice and sat down and ate an entire pot of it himself. He thinks almost all the food we eat is a variation on the loaf of bread. Cinnamon buns, meat loaf, cookies, cake. To him it is all just bread. One time he was rhyming off a litany of such food to me, pretend-bread, he called it, bread products we Westerners irrationally gussy up in order to disguise its fundamental bread-character.

"Biscuits, scones," he said, impressing me with his baked-goods vocabulary. "Cake," he added. "Day-cake," he finished.

I told him there was no such word as *day-cake*, and he got frustrated. Kunakorn always claimed that he preferred to use the words that he made up because they made more sense. This was undeniable, but I insisted on correcting him nonetheless, because that was my job. That's the job of language. To impose arbitrary rules.

"Day. Cake," he repeated impatiently. "You often have in day."

"That's just regular cake!" I said.

"No, no! You don't have day-cake at night, that is difference. You can have regular cake at night."

"It doesn't make sense," I emphasized to him. Usually when his own personal vocabulary made sense, I would acknowledge it. I even praised him for his ingenuity sometimes, because he could come up with some quite reasonable substitutions. He called pillows sleeping bags, and sleeping bags out-blankets. You could not deny the logic.

But day-cake was nonsense, I told him. He gestured and jumped around trying to describe it to me, and finally I asked him to draw a picture on the board, which he did.

"It's a muffin," I said.

"Muh — "

"Muffin."

"Muh-vin."

"Muffin."

"Muffin. What 'muffin' mean?"

"It means that," I said, pointing to the board.

"But what it *mean?*" he repeated. "Day-cake?"

"No," I said. "It doesn't mean anything. It just means that." I pointed again.

Eye-rolls all around. That was their problem with English in a nutshell. It is no wonder Kunakorn refused to give up his own thoughtful creations for something so ridiculous-sounding.

So I come stampeding out from behind the partition where I'm photocopying lists of prepositions, hollering, "Muffin! Muffin! Muffin!" Kunakorn gives me a look as if his suspicion that I just make up all the craziness I drill into him day after day has been vindicated. He points with triumph at the new co-worker.

"He say 'day-cake.'"

"Why are you standing there talking about day-cake?" I say to the new guy.

The new guy is shorter than me, and about ten pounds lighter. He is absurdly overdressed to be sitting at the front desk. He looks like a boy who's been polished up for his first communion and I try not to wince.

But I do wince when I realize I've scared him. It is awful to scare a short man in a communion suit.

"Day-cake," he repeats. "It sounds nice!" He tries to be bright, breezy, the way people he's seen who work in offices in sitcoms always interact. Chipper, sardonic. Not jumpy and horrified at the sudden appearance of a tall woman with large breasts screaming "muffin."

That I know all this about him already is making me depressed and I want to go out and buy a coffee and walk around the block. First I have to make him feel more at ease, and quickly, or I will feel sick to my stomach all day long. I hunch my back so that my breasts won't further unnerve him and wag a finger at Kunakorn.

"This guy thinks he can just make up his own language and get accepted into Harvard Business School saying 'day-cake' for *muffin* and 'out-bed' for *sleeping bag* and God knows what else. It's our job to break him of this terrible habit!"

I make a half-assed gesture as if to chuck the new guy on the shoulder like the buddy I am, and the new guy smiles and lets his breath out. But then something terrible happens. I watch his face as he attempts to make it a perfect imitation of mine — the easy, co-conspirator grin meant to put him at ease. The fakeness on my face when transferred to his own magnifies itself about ten times over and my stomach contracts at the sight. No, I think. This guy cannot be this uncomfortable. I want to give him liquor.

I'm just about to rush hunchbacked out the door like an office Quasimodo when he says something nice, something that relieves me. It's nice because it's honest. He has forgotten himself for a moment.

"It's just so refreshing," he says, "to hear a different version of things every once in a while."

I turn around then because I want to smile at him again and be encouraging of unguarded moments like this, but already he has gone green. He picks up a pen and tries to twiddle it and ends up writing on his face, like the open book that he is. Clearly it's precisely such moments that he's desperate to avoid.

Now I'm going to feel sick to my stomach all day long. I walk around the block and can't drink my coffee. Everything I see exacerbates the situation. There is a man who sits on the corner every day surrounded by pigeons, asking people for change. Usually he is able to put on a brave face, crack jokes, say please and thank you to the passersby so they won't be intimidated or offended by him, but today must not have been a good day. Today he can't quite hold up the façade that he is just a regular Joe, a good, decent guy down on his luck, bearing ill will towards no one. As I'm walking towards him, he's still doing the please-and-thank-you thing, the obligatory have-a-nice-day, but already my antennae is out, he's sort of weaving, chanting the pleaseandthankyous and haveanicedays like cynical prayers, and finally, just as I'm passing, he bashes the back of his head against the building and howls:

"For the love of God and Jesus, people! I'm in pain!"

I am more like one of the pigeons at his feet than a pedestrian. The pedestrians alter their courses slightly, scarcely looking up, but me and the pigeons — the pigeons and me — we fly off in every direction.

⬧

At my apartment I classify this day as having been a Bad Day in my journal, taking note of the events that made it so. I do this every day, examining why it was good or bad and taking note of the events so that in the future I can try to recreate the good events and avoid the bad ones.

But the good days aren't really characterized so much by good events as lack of bad ones. I write that down in my journal. That is a little bit of wisdom for later on. I walk around my apartment for a while and eat some of my medium portions and repeat to myself, *Go to sleep, go to sleep*, which is meant to settle my stomach and calm me enough to sit and watch sitcoms before it's time for bed.

The first step is to remove yourself. I have students who come from, literally, the other side of the planet. If you took a long spike and drove it into the ground here, and it went all the way down the middle of the earth and out the other end, it would come out practically in their own backyard. But these same students, who had all the power to wrench themselves out of their huge families and their tiny communities and sit on a plane for fourteen hours, are the same ones who will sit in class weeping for days on end, and it's usually the same reason: *Because I miss my mother.* They will call their mothers every night, asking for news about their grandparents, siblings, cousins. When they hear that so-and-so has lost a hand in the factory, they cry. When they hear that so-and-so's daughter has ran away again, they cry. They come to class crying about one thing or another happening on the other side of the planet on a regular basis. But mainly their mothers, or lack thereof. My point is, they haven't removed themselves at all.

It is that intimacy that is the problem, I have determined this long ago. The intimacy of little towns and families. You cry because of the intimacy. It may as well have happened to you. The less intimate you are, the less it bothers you. That's what cities are for. That's what I thought cities were supposed to be for. But the city is becoming a disappointment to me.

It is not so much hands being cut off and daughters running away, in the city. It is more like this:

I was sitting in the park reading a book on a beautiful day in the summertime. People walked by me in couples, groups, and families. There was a little canteen close to where I was sitting and all the people stopped to get ice cream and popsicles.

But then a man in a white cap who didn't seem to be enjoying the sun very much came and sat down on the other end of the bench. He was huffing and puffing from his walk and just sat there for a few moments, wiping his face with his cap. He wore a terry-cloth shirt the same colour blue as the sky, and white pants, like his cap. If he had, for whatever reason, started to levitate and float off into the horizon, he would have blended in perfectly with the sky, like Winnie-the-Pooh had hoped to do one time, but failed.

The man kept glancing at the canteen and all the people coming and going to get ice cream and popsicles. He'd stare at the beach for a while, and then glance back at the canteen, as if to see if it were still there. I couldn't read at all at this point. Finally he heaved himself up and tottered over to the canteen to buy himself an ice cream. It was obviously difficult for him to walk, not because he was so fat, but he also had some kind of limp.

So then he sits down beside me again with a rocky-road ice cream and eats it in about five minutes.

Then, the glancing-back started up again. Gazing at the beach, glancing towards the canteen, elaborately casual. After another five minutes of this, he stood up again and staggered back towards the canteen.

And this is what he said then:

"I'll have another rocky-road, please."

And then he came and sat down beside me again, with his second ice-cream cone.

He did this four more times in the space of an hour and a half — gazing and glancing, convincing himself that no one was paying attention, working up his courage — and I remained cemented to the other side of the bench like one of those bronze statues they sometimes install in parks to blend in with the real human beings, not having turned a page since he arrived. My tailbone had started to ache and sweat was trickling down my sides, but I couldn't budge until he left. I couldn't risk giving the slightest hint that I knew exactly what was going on. It was unthinkable. It was unspeakable.

That's the sort of thing I mean.

◇

When I talk to my mother on the phone, we have a very pleasant chat. She tells me about neighbours and relatives I don't even remember any more, but even so it is never anything too lurid or horrifying. There are lots of operations, but most of them are successful. Daughters and sons are always getting married to other people's daughters and sons, and then having babies. It washes over me. Then my father is allowed to speak and asks me how I'm doing and I tell him fine. Then he asks me if I need any money and I make a joke about how if I needed money, I wouldn't say I was fine. We laugh. We hang up. It wasn't always so painless, but over the years we've managed to lay down some unspoken ground rules. It took a while. It used to be like a game where you scored or lost points despite yourself. Now it is more like a little play.

❖

He's dressing in casual wear. Like after the first day on the job he went to the Casual Wear section at Eaton's and announced "office casual" to a salesgirl who decked him out from shoes to shirt. And she made him buy two shirts, three pairs of pants, and a couple of sweaters, all in coordinating colours to be mixed and matched throughout the week. And everything is ironed. And the brown sweater still has the tag. I shadow him around the office making small talk with a pair of scissors behind my back until one of the advisers simply calls out, "Nice tag, Sandy-boy," on her way to the bathroom, turning him green again and making me wish to nestle the scissors into the socket of her eye.

Even his name, Sandy. It's a description, like a dog's name. Scruffy. Fluffy. Makes you want to pet him. Weeks go by, and after Andrea has referred to him as Sandy-boy for the eleventh hundred time, I slam the photocopier and demand to know if he doesn't have any other names.

"Leopold is my second name," he tells me, quivering, because I've frightened him again.

"Jesus! That's it? Isn't Sandy short for anything?"

"Alexander," he shrugs.

"Alexander! You have a name like Alexander and you go around letting people call you Sandy? People could be calling you Alex. 'Alex, what time is the meeting? Phone call, line one.... Oh, thanks, Alex.' Doesn't that sound nice?"

"But my parents call me Sandy," he pleads.

"Your parents named you Alexander Leopold. Clearly they had some big plans. They just started calling you Sandy when you were a baby and couldn't get out of the habit."

"But everybody calls me Sandy. It's on my driver's licence."

I start calling him Alex all the time so he'll get used to it. I even refer to him as Alex when he's not around, and nobody knows who I am talking about. I make a special point of calling him Alex around Andrea.

"His name's Sandy."

"No," I correct. "His name's Alexander. Sandy is just a nickname."

"I asked him what his name was, he told me Sandy."

Andrea is a hard nut. She is one of those disquieting people who gives off an air of knowing how everything should be at all times. She has all the answers. She's an adviser, as I've said, and one of the few people in this place who is qualified for, and good at, her job. She was born to advise.

"Don't you think Alex is a better name?" I beg her.

"Yes. But I don't think it's *his* name. I think his name is Sandy."

Andrea calls things as she sees them. She has no vision.

I have come home from work some days and written in my journal about Andrea that she represents the way the world is. There are all sorts of holes dug into the world in certain shapes and sizes and people are born and shoved into those holes whether they care for them or not. Then they just grow into the shapes and sizes of the holes. And then everybody marvels about how those particular people are perfect for those holes, and isn't it great how perfectly things work out in this world of ours.

You can do the same thing with pumpkins. We had a pumpkin patch in our garden and my little brother used to grow them into whatever shapes he wanted. He'd put a band around the middle and make them grow into figure eights, for example. Later on, he saw in a farming magazine where you could buy little masks to put over the growing pumpkins, and when you took it off the pumpkins would have faces. He would line them up at Hallowe'en and everyone would wonder how he did it. And he'd tell them: *They just grew like that.*

And this being an Andrea kind of world, a lot of people believed him. They thought: If they exist, then that just must be how it is.

It seems a very passive way to live your life, and yet people like Andrea are the most stubborn I've met.

My brother was always doing things like that. How many boys do you know to whom it has occurred to direct the growth of pumpkins? He was a real original, my mother used to say. A genuine authentic, she used to say. She would desperately try to come up with all sorts of upbeat expressions to describe him. He was another one who liked to hear a different version of things every once in a while.

❖

The Thai students have taken to Alex. They sense that he is like them — horrified by everything around him. Kunakorn often tells me of his first night in this country. He was bussed to the university after his sixteen-hour flight and deposited in a dorm room, given instructions in English, and left alone. He could speak not a word of English, of course, and was hungry. He took his key, screwed up his courage, and ventured out into the quad where young, drunken North Americans were celebrating frosh week. He bumped into a few staggering students and nobody was kind to him when they realized he was a foreigner as they were all intoxicated not so much by alcohol but by being together in a group with people exactly like themselves. So he was shoved by some guy in a backwards baseball cap who called him "loser." He remembers this word quite clearly, thinking it was maybe a pejorative North American term for *Asian*, and fell into a girl who shrieked and spilt her beer all down his back.

At long last Kunakorn arrived at some sort of all-night campus convenience store and purchased the largest bag of the most filling-looking food he could find. It was a bag of Wonderbread. He made his way back to his room and padded his stomach with it so he could sleep. He couldn't believe how utterly bland it was. His first taste of North America.

And then it was on to the sandwiches and hamburgers of his home-stay family. Thus was an unhealthy fascination born. He'll come into class every week announcing yet another bread-product he's discovered.

"Cracker."

"Oh, come on, crackers?"

"Yes, cracker. Flour, water. Bake."

"But that's like saying chips are bread."

That gives him pause. "Maybe chip *are* bread!" At lunchtime, he scurries off to investigate.

165

"No," after he returns. "Potato." He crosses his arms triumphantly. Don't even get Kunakorn started on potatoes. The potato is the second bizarre thing we eat in far too many forms, according to him. I have promised to bring in mashed potatoes at the end of the semester to show them all how lovely these grey lumps from underneath the earth can be when properly prepared.

"Comfort food," I teach them. "Food that makes you feel warm and safe. Perhaps your mother gave it to you when you were a child." I make a list on the board of all the foods that do it for me. Mashed potatoes, number one. With cream and butter and garlic, oh my God. The garlic was my brother's idea when he was fourteen and getting more creative with every passing minute. We all thought he was crazy. My father wanted to know if he was turning into some kind of Eye-talian. *Trust me*, he said. *Trust my palate.* My father couldn't stand him using words like *palate*. But no one could deny the potatoes were great that way.

Peanut butter and jelly sandwiches, I write. Kunakorn exhales with disgust. Boiled eggs. They all nod at that one. Pumpkin pie. Blank stares.

Then they all have to make their own lists. Kunakorn writes:

> *rice*
> *rice*
> *rice*
> *rice!*

"Rice is every bit as bland as bread!" I protest, a patriot.

Kunakorn looks at me like my father at my brother saying *palate*. "Noooo! Rice *heaven!*" he croons.

So the Thai students take Alex out for Chinese food all the time. They pay for him, they sort of make a pet of him. There is a syndrome among English as a Second Language teachers that it reminds me of. Some ESL teachers have no life and no friends, just like lots of people in lots of other jobs. And when they start teaching foreign students, they are given the kind of attention and regard that no self-respecting North American would ever deign to lavish upon someone so low on the social scale as a teacher. So their students become their social circle. Suddenly, the teacher finds him or herself popular and beloved in a way he or she has never known. It gets messy, obviously. Students start expecting their marks to reflect the goodwill they've shown. Everyone's around the same age, so teachers start sleeping with students. Lines are crossed.

That's kind of what's happening with the students and Alex except there is no power imbalance at play, so I suppose it is benign. Alex has some friends, friends who aren't instinctively aware of things like his trip to Casual Wear. Friends who don't tack "boy" to the end of his name. Friends who have their own dangling metaphorical price tags. I am happy for him. But I cannot convince them to stop calling him Sandy.

❖

I still have to keep careful watch. His collar is always flipping up and I have to put it down for him. Once when he returned from the bathroom with his fly open, I had to stop myself from going over and doing it up. He's getting used to working around breasts, but the office is still riddled with female landmines, full of grown women who aren't as protective as I am. Andrea came raging towards me one time, demanding to know if I could give her a spare tampon "before I start gushing into my shoes." I tried to cover his ears, but it was too late.

"You're always fussing over that boy," says Andrea to me.

"He's not a boy," I say. "Don't call him 'boy.'"

"People will think you're in love with him." I look up at her and see that she's grinning. Of course she knows that nobody is ever going to think that.

"You need a man," Andrea says. "Why isn't there a man in the picture?"

A man in the picture. She puts it this way every time she asks me about it. Apparently there is a picture, and there is supposed to be a man in it. The hole in the ground that was dug out for me is of such a shape that there is supposed to be a man there as well.

"What would be your perfect man?" Andrea persists.

Well, let's see. I write a pointed response to Andrea in my journal since I'm incapable of doing it in person. My perfect man, Andrea, the man I want, is a character in a story I have been told ever since I was capable of understanding stories. He is big and strong. He is kind and compassionate. He is everywhere and all-powerful. He does not let bad things happen to good people. He is merciful. He is perfect. He can do it all. He takes you in his arms and wipes the tears from your eyes. You forget about everything. It's just a story I was told, and it wasn't fair to me, and it sure isn't fair to men, but this is the man I've been told about my whole life, so this is the man I'm waiting for. In the meantime, someone has to take care of Alexander.

At the end of the semester, everybody brings their favourite food, and we always invite the office staff to come and have some. All the women come trundling in, sampling and exclaiming over the exotic dishes, and I stand there looking around for Alex until I realize they've left him to answer the phones.

"Where's Alex? Where's Alex?" I keep saying. They pretend not to know who I'm talking about.

Another Thai student, Maliwan, comes up to me, taps me on the shoulder, and then takes a huge step back. That is how she asks for my attention, like I'm carrying a two-by-four and could whirl around and catch her on the side of the head. She's one of the most timid people I've ever met. I poke her on her own shoulder a few times to demonstrate how annoying it is.

"Just say my name. Don't poke."

"Sorry. Sorry. You are stress out."

I taught them "stressed out" last week. They liked it. *Stressed out* and *mongrel.*

"No, I'm not. Why don't you go get Alex?"

"Why you call Sandy Alex?"

"Why *do* you —"

"Why *do* you call Sandy Alex?"

"Sandy is his nickname."

Maliwan knows what *nickname* means, because she used to have one too. When she first arrived in Canada, she tried to convince me her nickname was Sharon Stone.

"Ah," says Maliwan, remembering how I refused to call her Sharon Stone. "You don't like nicknames."

I decide to just let her believe I don't like nicknames.

After much prodding, Andrea finally agrees to pile up a plate for herself and go back to the office so that Alex could come and get some food. The greeting that rises up from the Thai students takes me aback. They swarm him. Maliwan takes him from dish to dish, explaining what everything is and what it has in it.

"I usually can only eat shrimp if it's battered," I hear him tell her.

I glower at the office staff before they can react.

"You are allergic," Maliwan prompts.

"That's right!" Alexander replies, beaming.

I'm exhausted after the party, but can't keep myself from following him around trying to make him take the leftovers home. He won't take it. He keeps telling me that he's a meat-and-potatoes man.

"I'm a meat-and-potatoes man," he tells me. "I don't like my meals fancy,"

"Listen," I step in close, fed up. "I know things about you. You are not a meat-and-potatoes man. You eat your mother's cooking, or else you eat an exact replica of your mother's cooking in fast-food form. You're afraid of anything else. You're not some rugged food-individualist. You leave here at night and you go to Burger King. You are destroying yourself."

It's too much. His face like a landslide. I regret it the moment it's out.

"I'm allergic —" he starts to protest, but I smother it with a hug. I long to suffocate us both.

◇

Now I have three weeks off before the semester starts again, the second week of which my mother is coming to visit. In the meantime, the only thing to do is update my journal and go visit the doctor to complain about the awful, hideous, monstrous nightmares I have been having. In fact, I haven't been having nightmares at all, but I have started dreaming from time to time, and that is enough. A pumpkin patch with faces. All sorts of different expressions. She gives me a powerful drug that will blast it from my head.

Usually this time of year I would go to the park with a book but I haven't been able to do that since seeing the man in disguise as the sky.

The school is late with my pay as usual, so it gives me an excuse to drop by the office from time to time and pretend to kick up a fuss about it while making sure everyone is being nice to Alex. Maliwan and Kunakorn are always hanging around, waiting to take him to lunch.

"Is Maliwan your girlfriend?" I ask Kunakorn one day when we're kidding around and feeling chummy. These are the sort of questions I put to students point-blank, as they don't tend to understand our inane North American euphemisms. *Do you two have a thing? Are you guys going out? Are you seeing one another?* But Kunakorn looks at me like I've uttered the most obscure one of all.

"No! I...." he stumbles.

"Boyfriend?"

"No! Not boyfriend! I go ... with Maliwan...."

"You go out?"

"To lunch! I just go with Maliwan and Sandy...."

"You're just friends," I help, thinking I shouldn't have put him on the spot.

"Yes! But what word? Thai friend. There is word...."

"'Friend' is good enough." I try to calm him down, but Kunakorn is not the sort of person who can tolerate knowing he doesn't know something.

"I will find the word and tell you," he promises me.

He calls me at home at three in the afternoon. They know they are not supposed to call me at home unless they are having some sort of grammar crises, but they always do anyway, usually at night, in the middle of their parties, in order to settle bets about the meaning of words and idioms.

It so happens I am still in bed at three in the afternoon, unused to not having to go to work, and unable to muster up enough imagination, thanks to the anti-nightmare pills, to think of anything else worth doing. When the phone rings, it's as if my brains are lightly spread out across the pillow, and I have to mentally gather them up together in my head before I can figure out what the sound means and how I am supposed to respond to it. I pick it up on the seventh or so ring.

"Hello?"

"*Chaperone*," says Kunakorn.

I'm distracted when my mother comes, wanting to check on him. I had taken him to dinner at a steakhouse after talking to Kunakorn and encouraged him to eat as much meat and potatoes as he wanted. I'd talked to him like he was one of my students: *Is Maliwan your girlfriend?* He didn't turn green this time, but baby-girl pink. And he smiled. *Is she your first girlfriend?* A pointless question, as obviously she was. And of course he told me she wasn't and I was so happy I pretended to believe him and apologized for saying he went to Burger King all the time.

"It's true though," he admitted. "That's the kind of food I like, I can't help it."

"No, you can't," I agreed. "You should eat whatever makes you happy." I gave him my home phone number in case he ever needed anything.

It only occurred to me afterwards how painful and nasty and miserable first girlfriends and boyfriends could be and that was why I kept wanting to get rid of my mother and head down to the office with some kind of picnic basket loaded down with pre-emptive comfort.

I had spent a week doing a sort of tailor-made meditation in preparation for my mother's visit. Writing lists in my journal of everything I could think of. Cloud formations, for example. Cumulus, stratus. Berries. That was a good one, I could think of so many different kinds. I got down to Saskatoon berries and salmon berries and then huckleberries, which I wasn't even sure existed, and chokecherries, which I wasn't sure qualified. The berries list was a couple of pages long. Then I tried doing a list about the names of famous dogs, which at first I thought was a great idea — Lassie, Old Yeller, the Littlest Hobo — but of course I inevitably found myself writing the word *Sandy* and realized my brain had ambushed me again.

◇

My mother is concerned that I no longer go to church and feels we should go together, but I tell her I don't know where any churches are, which is a lie. I walk past a Catholic church every day on my way to work, situated right alongside of a Catholic elementary school called Our Lady of Perpetual Help. A big white Mary perches upon the school's rooftop like a slender owl, looking down at all the little children in their uniforms, running back and forth behind the chain-link fence.

My mother says that's fine, she will find a church for us to go to together. I tell her we won't have time. I spread out before my mother catalogues, pamphlets, brochures, and outline for her all the activities I have planned for the week. Walking tours. Suspension bridges. Native art exhibits. High tea. Ferry rides.

Oh, my darling, she says. I just want us to spend some time together.

Very sincere, my mother. Warm, melting eyes. She's not lying, that's really what she wants. She want to get inside my apartment and see me in it. Open up my cutlery drawers, poke around in the cupboards. Cook meals with my pots and pans. Buy me things, to go in the apartment, so she'll always feel she's there, inside my life.

There is no alcohol in my apartment, so she takes it upon herself to empty out a cupboard and stock me a little bar — wine and gin. I don't play along.

"But, Mother. I don't drink."

"Everybody should have a little wine and gin on hand, my darling!" Festive. Trying to get that festive feeling in the air. Get things uncorked.

This is her plan: To get inside my apartment and get me drunk. To get me talking.

I wake every morning at six and drag her off my futon and out into the city. We ride the trolley around the park and go on a bird tour and listen to a lecture about soapstone carving. Lunches and dinners are tricky. She'll go for the wine every time. After she finishes the first glass, it's: "Oh, may as well get a half-litre. What do you say, my darling?"

"None for me, thanks, Mother."

"But it's your holiday! Live a little!"

"We've got the suspension bridge next. You don't want to be falling off."

Next tactic: melting eyes, trembling lips. "Let me do something nice for you, you work so hard, I see you so rarely."

"I'm having a wonderful time, Mother." Thoughtful pause. "Aren't you?" Searching look, borderline hurt. Two can play at this game.

The day is mine. By nightfall, she is so wiped out her bedtime belt of gin knocks her off her feet. I open up my journal to gloat over the victory and strategize for tomorrow. Walk on the beach in the morning followed by a lunchtime concert at the university. Then a sudden wave comes over me, my eyes glaze. Exhaustion, from keeping my guard up all day. I'll use the concert time to think about how to spend the afternoon and evening.

I dream about scooping the guts out of a jack-o'-lantern with my hands and wake up and vomit all over the couch. My mother comes rapidly tip-toeing

172

out of the bedroom, face slick with Mary Kay night cream. It shimmers in the grey, pre-dawn light. She says, "Oh! My darling!"

I'm lying on my back shuddering and start to say, "Isn't it supposed to absorb into your skin?" before turning my head and vomiting again. My mother goes to wipe off her face and put on some clothes and take care of me.

Stomach flu, like when I was a child. I vomit throughout the day. My mother goes out and buys consommé, crackers, and rum and honey. To make me hot toddies, she says, when I'm better.

"I knew we were pushing ourselves too hard," she mutters loudly to herself in the kitchen. "I'm an old homebody anyway. I'm happy to just hang around the house and spend time together!"

She is in heaven. Myself, on the couch with ginger ale and Mr. Dress-up on television, appalled by what my body has done to me. It was on her side all along. Nausea keeps me prone. My mother can sit and talk to me, her hand around a cool glass of gin, for hours on end.

It is so good, to have this time with me. How lucky for this to have happened while she was here! What would I have done if she hadn't been? No, really, what would I have done? Did I have someone to call? Didn't I get nervous, living all by myself? A young women in the city? It would make her nervous. Oh yes, it seems like a very secure building. I don't go out by myself at night, do I? Oh, my darling, I really shouldn't. Of course, I must have friends I can always call. Not that I've introduced her to any of them. Haven't I met any men? Great big city like this? Still no man in the picture?

Glass of gin number two: It is hard, having me so far away, for both her and my father. They feel so removed from my life. They want to be of support to me, but how is it possible, my being so far away? If I moved back home, they could be of so much more help. There is lots of work back home these days, the economy has picked up quite a bit, had I heard? She could help me find an apartment, we could shop together for things. It would mean so much to them, now that they are getting on. The years just seem to fly by. The house so big and empty. Nothing left but memories. Not all good. And after all, I am all they have left in the world now that....

"This isn't fair," I manage to gasp, gripping the empty ice-cream bucket she's given me in case I can't make it to the toilet. "This isn't fair, Mother."

"I'm sorry, my darling," she murmurs, adjusting the cloth on my head. "You're sick. We can talk about these things later." And she wobbles off into the kitchen for gin number three, having granted me a temporary reprieve.

By evening, I'm finally able to sip some consommé and sit up to watch a weepy women's movie with Bette Midler that she's rented for us. We've both lost count of the glasses of gin and my mother sits with a roll of toilet paper on her lap, snuffling. Every now and then she pats a spot beside the toilet paper, inviting me to put my head there like when I was a girl. I ignore her. I have spent the entire day at her mercy and have dropped all pretence of civility.

Weirdly, the phone rings, the first time since she's been here. She jumps up and runs all around the apartment trying to find it, which I allow. Finally she discovers it in the bedroom, alongside of the futon she's been sleeping on, and drags it out to me on the couch.

"It's a boy!" she declares, like someone has just given birth. "He says his name is Sandy! What a nice name!"

"Hi, Alex," I say into the phone, glaring at her. She pretends to have gone back to Bette Midler, a huge mound of tissue pressed against her nose.

He is confused about Maliwan, and keeps telling me he doesn't understand her culture. It is such a different culture, he says, I don't know what's going on half the time. I don't understand her way ... the ways of her culture. After listening to him ramble for a few minutes, I figure out what he means by culture and take over.

"First of all, Alexander, calm down."

"I'm calm!" he protests.

"Calm down!"

"What's wrong? I'm very calm." I can picture his face arranging itself into a look of sitcom tranquillity. Convincing himself.

"I'm sick," I fret.

"Oh, I'm sorry ...."

"No, I just mean ... I want to help. I'm just really sick."

"I should go." He sounds as if he's getting farther and farther away. He sounds as if he's standing in front of a well into which he plans on doing a forward roll as soon as he gets off the phone.

"Alex, Alex? Come and see me tomorrow, okay?"

"You're sick," he despairs.

"I'll be better tomorrow. Come and see me at around eleven."

"I'm sorry to —"

"Shut up! Come!" I give him my address. I hang up the phone and close my eyes. My stomach gurgles a warning.

My mother shifts on her side of the couch. "Visitors at last?"

"Tomorrow's Sunday," I inform her, eyes closed, seeking strength. "You won't want to miss church."

On the Lord's own day the nausea has subsided somewhat, but I'm weak like I've never been. I'm able to put on clothes for Alex's visit, but can't abide the thought of a bath or shower. My mother offers to help with a sponge bath, going as far as to try and ease me off the couch, and I flail my arms at her, grunting.

"You're a regular bear," she observes, snapping open a pink Mary Kay compact to touch up her eyes. "I'll say a prayer for you." I've scarcely spoken to her all morning. Conserving energy.

Alex shows up at eleven on the dot, toting a box of Dunkin' Donuts that I can't even look at. Oblivious, he starts shoving a Boston cream into his mouth, explaining that he hasn't had breakfast yet. I try to be indulgent. He is a man in pain. I avert my head while he finishes the doughnut, but as soon as the last blob of cream disappears, he goes to work on another one. I look up at the ceiling while he talks and chews and swallows. He has a large cup of coffee as well. He keeps forgetting it is too hot to drink and takes one searing, painful sip after another. I envision clouds and berries as he talks.

Maliwan is seeing an *old man*, he says. Some disgusting, probably married, businessman who saw her looking at sunglasses in the mall and bought her a pair. She goes with him to clubs and restaurants. He buys her dresses. She just told Alex this, one day. They were sitting on the beach with Kunakorn and she looked at her watch and said: Now I must visit Andrew.

"Now I must visit Andrew!" he repeats. "And Kunakorn just sits there with me! Why does she need a chaperone with me and not with Andrew?"

"Did you ask?"

"Yes. That's how I found out he was *old*. Kunakorn just waves his hand and goes, 'He old man.'"

"He didn't use a verb?"

"What?"

"Kunakorn. He's always dropping his to-be verbs. He told me he'd prac-tise. Did you ask Maliwan about it?"

"She says she doesn't need a chaperone with Andrew because he doesn't count. He's too old to count as a boyfriend. She says he's more like an uncle."

"But you count as a boyfriend?"

"Yeah."

"Well, that's good."

"Yeah, but it's crazy!"

"Have you told Maliwan how you feel?"

"I don't know what to say! Maybe it's a Thai thing."

"I don't think it's exactly a Thai thing." I don't really know what kind of thing it is. I decide that it's beside the point.

"How do you feel about Maliwan?" I ask. He looks up at me in sudden fear. It's as if I've inquired: How would you like a punch in the face? Then the ersatz, sitcom casualness settles over his pasty features and he leans back and takes a wincing sip of coffee.

"You know," he says, draping his arms across the back of the couch, pretending like his mouth isn't full of blisters, "she's nice. I like her."

I know all right.

In the twenty-five minutes before my mother gets back, I develop and outline a plan. First, he has to find out how Maliwan feels about him. Is she just playing around or what?

"Because, if you're serious, Alex — *if*— then you have to let her know. Are you serious?"

"I don't know."

"Well, if you don't know, then you can't expect her to know. And there's no reason for her not to go out with as many old men as she likes."

"But —"

"There's this thing called commitment, Alex, and it sounds to me like that's what you're looking for."

"I don't know! It's all so serious!"

"This is grown-up stuff. You can't just ask a woman to stop seeing whoever she wants to see and not give her a good reason."

"But I don't know if I have a good reason. I just don't want her to."

"Then you have to think up a better reason than that."

"Like what?"

"Tell her you want to *explore* a commitment."

"Explore —"

"A commitment."

"You mean, go steady?"

From what era is this child? "Yes, yes, for God's sake, just tell her you want to go steady and see what she says."

"But what if she says no?"

"It's better to know that now before you get too involved." Listen to me. The endless thumbings-through of waiting-room women's magazines over the years has really paid off. I am some kind of relationship-savant.

"But I don't want her to say no," he sulks.

The front door rattles. My mother is home. My instinct is to leap off the couch and hurl my body against the door to keep her from Alex, but the attempt amounts merely to my standing up, experiencing a whirling head-rush, and collapsing back down onto the couch.

"You have to go now, Alex," I hiss.

Alex looks around. It's like a bedroom farce all of a sudden, my burly husband about to burst in and catch us.

"Oh, hello!" chirps my mother.

"Alex has to go now," I say, shoving him off the couch with my foot.

"I'm the mother!" says my mother, holding out her hand. Alex wipes the icing sugar off one of his and shakes it for her.

Beads of sweat bloom across my back and between my shoulder blades at the sight of them touching. "Leave him alone!" I bark, enraged and panicked.

"She hasn't been well," confides my mother, lightly placing her hand on his shoulder to torment me further. I can see Alex responding already to her sweetness, her innocent dusting of Mary Kay, her prim, motherly scarf tucked into her collar. Red Riding Hood and the Wolf, decked out like Grandma. I breathe through the knot in my chest.

"Alex," I say. "I'm going to throw up all over the place in a minute. Give me a call in a few days, okay?"

"I'll leave you the doughnuts," he says generously, bidding a hasty retreat.

My mother picks up the box after he's gone. "There aren't any dough-nuts left," she sniffs.

◇

One more day until she goes home. I am still very weak. The hour with Alex and the handful of horrific moments he spent in the company of my mother have sent me into a relapse. The fever returns and my mother has to wrap me in towels to keep the couch from wringing with sweat. I sleep until dinnertime and dream of the fat man floating up into the sky with his ice-cream cone, blending right in. I wake to the deceptively comfort-ing smell of consommé. My mother sashays into the living room, working on a glass of wine, one in a series of who knows how many. My suspicion is a few, because she starts in immediately.

"What a nice boy, that Sandy boy was."

"His name is Alex. Didn't you hear me calling him Alex the whole time he was here?"

"He's very young."

"Yeah, he's like twenty." I speak rapidly, trying to put the topic to rest. "I work with him. He's going through everything at once. First job, first girlfriend. I'm trying to help him manoeuvre his way through."

"He's the sort of boy you want to help," she agrees. "I just took one look at him and I wanted to take him in my arms." The sheen of her eyes starts to wobble a bit. Brimming. She must be close to polishing off the bottle. "You know who he reminds me of —"

"Stop," I say.

"Well, you do, though. Don't tell me you haven't noticed."

"Stop. Off limits."

"But then, I get so lonesome for him — I think I see him everywhere —"

"Stop! Out of bounds!"

She keeps talking and I keep hollering sports expressions at her: "Foul! Penalty! You're out!" But she keeps on and I run out of sports words. The next thing I know, I'm hollering my lists.

"It's been five years and you never want to — "

"Cumulus!"

"The priest says that after a loss families need to —"

178

"Boisenberry! Saskatoon!"

"I know that you blame —"

"Pineapple! I bet you didn't know that was a berry, did you? Famous dogs! Benji! The one on 'The Little Rascals'! Sandy!"

"I haven't seen you in over a—"

"Sandy!"

"Why don't you ever let me *talk?*" she shrieks, and throws down her drink. I cross my arms. She jumps up to get a towel, ashamed of herself. She's been both wasteful and sloppy. Failing to live up to her own standards of motherhood. Shamed into silence. Victory.

◇

The next week is spent recovering from my holiday. It's slow going. I remain on the couch, absorbing televised reality, where nothing too evil happens to anybody and everyone is both cool and lovable. Alex calls to give me updates. Maliwan was pleased with the idea of going steady. At first she didn't believe him, that he would want to explore a commitment "with Thai girl," but somehow he convinced her of his sincerity. The old man with the money is now out of the picture. I tell him I am happy for him. I have dreams of Alex wafting slowly, safely up into the sky, waving bye-bye to me as he disappears into the blue. I sleep and sleep. The whole ordeal has left me spent.

My mother leaves without trying to make me talk any more, but she isn't quite able to keep herself in check at all times. So I have to show her something, to make her stop. I have to give her a small taste of what it would be like if I did start talking. She strides about the apartment, gathering up her belongings, mumbling, clucking, shaking her head from time to time.

"What are you saying, Mother? Say it out loud and strong, belt it out, Mother."

"I'm just sorry to have to tell your father we haven't made any progress," she clucks, sad-chicken-like.

"What makes you think I want to make any progress?"

She stops to shoot me a pious look that outrages me so much I sit up. "It's a terrible thing to hold a grudge," she intones.

"A beautiful boy," I say.

"What?"

"A beautiful, blue-eyed boy who liked pumpkins."

Her mouth falls open, thinking the walls are coming down at last.

"A beautiful boy who liked to hear a different version of things once in a while."

"Yes?"

"A genuine authentic."

Her bottom lip starts to work.

"A real original."

"Stop, now."

"Only one thing to do with a boy like that."

"All right."

"Pull his wings off." I make a gesture like I am plucking the petals from a flower. With each pluck I enunciate one word. "Tear. Him. Limb. From. Limb."

"That's enough," she says behind her hands.

"I agree," I agree.

With that, the last of my energy is spent. Pushing my mother all the way back to the other side of the continent. She kisses my cheek when the taxi comes.

"I hope you feel better, my darling. It was a lovely visit."

I've won. I'm beat.

❖

That's an expression it took a long time for my students to understand. *I'm beat.* You're what? *Beat. Like when someone beats you at a game.* Beat by who? *Beat by whom.*

Beat by whom? *Nobody. Just beat. Whipped. Tired.* Shouldn't it be beaten? *The expression is "I'm beat."* But nobody has beaten you? *Not necessarily.*

Back at work, the beat feeling doesn't go away. I tell everyone I've been sick. The students bring me a variety of home remedies. Andrea prescribes a man. Put some colour in your cheeks. Good for what ails ya, she says, yukking it up, embarrassing Alex. Maliwan comes for Alex every day at lunch, Kunakorn not always in tow. Apparently Alex has proven himself a gentleman. They stand at the elevator holding hands. They are like kittens.

Andrea extends a long finger down towards the back of her throat whenever they leave the room.

"Don't you think they're sweet?" I demand. Andrea has two of those "Love Is ..." posters hanging in her office, for God's sake. You'd think she'd eat it up. Instead she pronounces, "Too sweet." Grimly, a hard-nosed realist.

"They're happy!" I argue.

"They're not happy," Andrea contends. "They're blissed-out."

"Well, so *what?*"

"Icarus," she answers to my surprise, tossing her head towards the sky like he's actually up there waving a red flag.

◇

Things get back to normal and I'm grateful. I work, come home, eat medium portions, watch television. Take notes in my journal about what is easy and what is hard. Take care the next day to avoid whatever was hard. The bus was hard one day because I saw the fat man from the park in his white cap struggling to climb the steps and making everybody wait and feel resentful of him. He was sweaty, too, and you could see the loathing on people's faces. So I leave the apartment an hour early and walk to work for the rest of the week.

I have to be easy on myself. I exchange pleasantries with Alex and avoid Andrea. I get engrossed in genuinely fascinating conversations about the future-possible with Kunakorn. He is in the highest level now and prides himself on his knowledge. Kunakorn is like a grammar textbook — he can rhyme off all the rules, do all the exercises flawlessly, but he still walks around dropping his to-be verbs all over the place and using "in" for "on" and "beside" for "under." He brings muffins in the morning, for a joke, knowing I will get agitated by his conversational sloppiness at some point. Then he'll hold out a muffin to me.

"Comfort food," he'll say.

Maliwan is in the same class and would be failing dramatically if it wasn't for Kunakorn's ongoing tutelage, and perhaps a bit of cheating, which I overlook. Maliwan is basically on holiday, sent over by her family to obtain the fastest, cheapest ESL certificate going before returning to Thailand to help run their factory. It is odd to think of how much more money than I — the privileged North American — Maliwan must have. She lives with two other girls in a $15,000 apartment and goes shopping for clothes every day at lunchtime and skiing on the weekend. But she shows up dutifully for class every day because she knows if she misses more than two she's out of the program and her parents will yank her back home to the other side of the world.

So it's odd when she misses one class in the middle of the semester, but downright troublesome when she misses a second. Kunakorn promises me he'll check in with her after class.

"Tell her, if she's sick, it's no big deal — she just needs a doctor's certificate," I say.

The next day Alex calls in sick and Kunakorn shows up with extra muffins.

"How is Maliwan?" I ask.

"Thai," he says, picking walnuts off the tops.

"What?"

"Thailand," he corrects himself, using the English term. He hadn't heard me properly. He thought I said "where," not "how."

The way Kunakorn tells it, one of Maliwan's roommates, a friend of the family's, called them up and told them Maliwan was planning to marry a Canadian. Apparently, the roommate had the idea that "going steady," which Maliwan constantly bragged about, meant the same thing as being engaged, or else she just decided one thing would lead to the next. To make matters worse, she got Alex mixed up somehow with Andrew, the rich old man, and told them Maliwan's paramour was in his sixties. The parents believed the roommate and told Maliwan to come home. It sounded to me like the roommate, who worked for her visa as a hostess in a restaurant, had merely tired of watching wealthy, twenty-year-old Maliwan having the time of her life.

"So she's just gone?"

Kunakorn looks at his watch. "Bangkok, now." He leans on his hands and puffs out his cheeks. "Sandy," he remarks, not bothering to try and find the words.

◇

Sandy takes the whole week off. I am grateful. So grateful I actually find myself talking to God again from time to time, muttering quiet words of appreciation in the bathroom or waiting in line for a coffee. It is such a peaceful week as we prepare for mid-terms and I walk to work with my eyes straight ahead, focused on large, blank buildings in the distance with windows like mirrors. Even the bum who cried out on the corner last semester is nowhere in sight these days. It's quiet and warm, the weather patchy, a little bit cloudy, a little bit sunny, not too much of either. Even. It is a good week. One of the best weeks I've had.

Another week goes by. Sandy, I tell myself, is licking his wounds. Taking some time off. Coming to terms with his emotions. All these inane, comforting euphemisms I come up with. I realize I don't brace myself when I push open the door to the office any more, expecting to see him doing battle with the photocopier or barely defending himself from Andrea or turning green at the sight of someone's exposed bra strap. The ease of knowing I won't be called upon to extinguish any flare-ups of mortification.

My parents haven't called since my mother's visit so I call them. "I'm so glad you called!" says my mother. "I meant to tell you. Your grade three teacher died last week. Remember? She had cancer for years. It was just a matter of time. Everybody was expecting it. She went peacefully. It was a relief."

"It was so nice having you here, Mother," I tell her.

"Oh, my darling," she says, voice a-tremble. "I had a lovely time."

I eat well. One day when the weather is mild, I return to the park with a book. The sky is clear. There is no one else in sight. The ice-cream stand hasn't even been set up yet because it's too early in the season.

◈

Run
Every Day

◈

ONE OF THE THINGS ABOUT CHILDREN that not too many people talk about is their instinctive fascination with power and pain almost as soon as they become aware such a thing exists. It comes before they can walk properly, before speech, before "mama," practically. I once witnessed a two-and-a-half-year-old pick up a block, look at it, look at her little friend sitting nearby, look at the block once more, and then hit. Apropos of nothing, as they say. Just a block, a fellow human being nearby, and a vague germination taking place in the brain.

Another one of the things not too many people talk about is the terror of childhood, and it is a terror that starts when you develop a peer group, once you are permitted to roam. You aren't allowed to roam far, but you're allowed to roam as long as you're with them. It's as if parents believe that children are going to take care of one another, like it's instinctual or something. In my town, kids ganged together and hid in the woods and waited for other kids, alone or in pairs, to ramble into pouncing distance. That sounds more like an instinct to me. I did it. I threw crab apples at a boy one time until he threw up. I felt horrible afterwards. But I didn't feel horrible when I was doing it.

For a while, the worst possible thing that could happen to you if you were a kid in my town would be to run into Gerald in the woods. He was around twelve then, and no friend of mine, although we were almost inseparable when we were little. But when we were twelve, it was like we had never met.

He was a legend and I was a nobody. I was one of the endless gaggle of kids who scurried to get out of his way, but also drank up the tales of his horrific doings like he was a character in a comic book — the kind your parents never let you read. Gerald and his disciples would stomp off into the woods after school and on weekends, take off their shirts and booby-trap every inch of the area surrounding their fort. The whole woods, really. Often they would just lie in wait. People in school whispered to each other about the wild and obscene things Gerald would do to you if he caught you in the woods. I never went in. I used to spend my whole life there, but I never went in once Gerald took over. I knew boys who went in armed with sticks and crab apples, hoping to siege the fort, and I knew girls who went in on dares, just to be brave, or because deep down inside they just wanted to see what he would do. I understood that. But I never went in.

There was a time, not long after we stopped being friends, when myself and a bunch of stupid girls were coming back after a birthday party. It had been stupid because Sharon Crisp had gotten in a fight with Madonna MacLeod's older sister. Madonna was the birthday girl, and friends with Sharon, but Sharon and Madonna's sister had never gotten along. We were playing kick the can and Madonna's sister kicked the can directly at Sharon's head. There was a huge fight and everybody started taking sides and I got depressed and ran into the woods. This was back before Gerald had made it the incontestable property of himself and his gang, and it was still the most peaceful place I knew to be. I was a morose kid and hated conflict ever since I had made the boy throw up with the crab apples during a war over somebody's tree fort. Also I think I must have known that once everybody realized I was gone they would get worried and come looking for me.

That's what happened. They split up into two groups and went in at either end of the woods, playing search party. I could see what they were doing because I was sitting up in a tree on a plank someone had nailed across the highest branches, so I climbed down and found a clearing and pretended to be dead. Then Sharon's search party found me and gave me mouth-to-mouth resuscitation and CPR and electric shock therapy and everything they could think to revive me and finally I leapt to my feet and said I was cured. Then we all went looking for Madonna's search party, which took forever because it turned out they were hiding on us, watching and laughing behind a tuft of bushes the whole time. By that time it was getting late and we were all friends again, and just as we were heading home, Gerald and his disciples came out of nowhere. Gerald was holding a rusty coat-hanger out in front of him like a divining rod.

"If anyone moves," he said, "I'll electrocute you."

I just bolted. I think all the other girls took their cues from me and ran away too, squealing, like it was another game. If I hadn't gone first, though, they might have stayed. Madonna's sister, who was big, might have tried to out-tough Gerald or something. But they saw me fly, and thought that I had named the game: Chase Through the Woods. That's not what I was doing at all, though. I was just going the hell home as fast as I could.

Somebody chased me partway. It might have been Gerald, but it could have been any of them. It seems characteristic that he would launch himself after the first person to bolt, sort of to teach them a lesson, but I don't know. The person behind me didn't say anything, but I could hear him panting and breaking twigs beneath his feet and slender branches with his face. There was a moment when I'm sure I felt fingertips brush my back. I kept my eyes straight ahead. The edge of the woods, down Cosgrove Street, past the playground, down the steep hill practically head over heels, across the church parking lot and, by the time I hit Harbour Street, I was alone. Maybe even well before then, I don't know. I didn't care. I kept running anyway, all the way to my house.

And this was before he had even really established himself as the genuine holy terror he eventually became. A year or so later, Madonna MacLeod was telling me a story I had already heard twice that day about how Gerald's gang nabbed a girl called Kerrie Retard (she wasn't really retarded, just despised) and her brother, tied them to trees for a while, and then made them kiss each other on the mouth. And that was just for starters. Right in the middle of the story, though, Madonna thought of something and her eyes went wide and glittery. "Holy cats!" she whispered. "It's a good thing we ran that day!"

He was kind of like a god, but a bad god. Since the only theology I knew back then was Catholic, the only god I could compare him to at the time was Jesus. I thought about how all Jesus' friends must've felt when they realized he was actually kind of a superhero. When my mother started referring to Gerald as that Antichrist, it struck me as being the most perfectly apt thing I had heard in my life.

But now I realize Gerald fit in better with the pagans. The original gods were all bullies, too.

That's how he was for a couple of years, and then something happened. To tie other kids to trees and menace them is one thing when you're twelve, something else entirely when you are suddenly well over five feet and can palm a basketball. All that stuff stopped. Maybe because there were one too many phone calls from parents, but probably he just decided it was stupid after a while. He was still bad but somehow not as powerful — because he had grown up. Here's what I think: Everybody loves a bad little boy. The very phrase is adorable. But how about a bad, big fifteen-year-old. Not much encouragement there. The word that people started using was as follows. *Thug*. Gerald sort of went underground for a while and then he emerged, a fledgling thug. He skulked, he smoked. He wore a jean jacket with the names of bands written on it in magic marker. He talked back to adults. He was nowhere near as popular as he used to be.

◇

This, the memory-flotsam that comes bobbing to the surface at the prospect of going home to help my mother pack. Nobody wants to buy the house but she doesn't care, she is moving. Somehow, in the past five years, it has become her dream to sell the quaint little two-storey structure built by shippers at the turn of the century, and move into a mature person's apartment complex on the outskirts of Halifax. Over the past five years she has started talking about the house like it is her own personal nemesis, like it's out to get her. Like the house harangues her to clean it day in and day out. It points a gun to her head and tells her to shake out the rugs. It holds its breath until she Windexes the smudges from every single window. It's too big and empty, she says, even though it's small and crammed full of her and my father's stuff. All my stuff, too, from day one of my being. She never used to like to get rid of anything. Not like now.

You can hear the excitement in her voice over the phone. She says, *One big purge*. The idea of getting rid of practically everything in one fell swoop seems downright sensual to her. She enumerates to me in shameless detail all the stuff she's going to give away. For example, she doesn't say, *All the furniture*, she says, *Your dad's old chair with the rip. The blue loveseat the dog used to climb up on. Those two end tables my grandmother gave me — they're history. I don't care, dear, I'm sick of the sight of them. If you want them, you come and get them, because they're going to Goodwill or on the junk heap, either one.*

Normally, I wouldn't go. My mother threatened to kill herself one time, and I didn't go. She threatened to set the house on fire and jump in the strait, and I didn't go. But that was because I knew she was full of shit. She was angry and sad and at the end of her rope, but ultimately she was full of shit and I could hear it in her voice. She had always felt that way, and she always tried to get me to do something about it instead of doing something about it herself. So I didn't go and I never went. But what's happening now is something else. She sounds neither sad, angry, nor at the end of her rope. She sounds, in fact, ecstatic, and because I've never had occasion to detect that particular note in her voice, I'm assuming my mother is going crazy. So I go.

It is not that I walk around thinking about Gerald all the time at the age of thirty living hundreds of miles away; that would be ridiculous. It is that every time I talk to my mother, she pictures a girl of seventeen. Everything she knows about me beginning from my birth and ending there is all that she knows about me, so she pretends there isn't anything else. Gerald is the biggest, most dramatic presence from this period. He had the starring role in my youth, and since my mother doesn't acknowledge any other aspect of my existence, Gerald is still her number-one reference point.

So rather than asking me about Dave, the man I've lived with for the past three years, she'll say, "I saw your honey-pie at the Sobey's the other day buying a can of poutine sauce," and I'll know exactly who she means. "He has a shaved head and two earrings in both ears. Just imagine! One week it's the hair down to his arse and the next it's no hair at all. I certainly don't know what the attraction is, my dear, but I can't say I share your taste in men."

At which point I will remind her that it has been thirteen years since I professed myself attracted to Gerald. One decade plus three years, during which time I've acquired two university degrees and held exactly eight different jobs. I've lived in six different cities and towns and had four serious relationships with men. If she pushes it, I will go on to reveal to my mother how many different people I've had sex with since then.

And then she'll sigh and say something like, "Well, I guess love is blind."

Because Gerald was such an enormous mistake, maybe she assumes that the rest of my life all just went irrevocably wrong as a result. Maybe she thinks that anyone who could be so catastrophically dumb as to get involved with Gerald Newhook can't be doing so well in the real world. Maybe she thinks she is being kind by not inquiring into what kind of sad semblance of a life I've managed to piece together since then. Maybe she gave up on me at that very moment.

◇

We always pretended like we had just met when we were sixteen. Like we'd never been best friends in our lives. It was embarrassing to have been children together, and we were such complete strangers by that time that it was easy to get romantic about one another all of a sudden. Of course our parents would never let us forget, so we stayed far away from them. My mother figured things out pretty quickly, though. In fact, she had never forgotten Gerald since the first time he and I met, walking our dogs in the woods, not much more than five years of age. His dog attacked my dog and killed her, and somehow after that we were always together. My mother considered this the first incontrovertible evidence of my self-destructive streak. Even when he was twelve, and bad, and thoughts of meeting up with him in the woods gave me nightmares, my mother would report to me on his doings as if I were always some kind of silent partner, an accessory after the fact. She'd always say it like this: "See what your *boyfriend's* done now? You're to stop wasting your time with that christer." But neither of us had spoken in years.

She was psychic, really. When we started sneaking around together in high school, it was as if nothing had changed for my mother. In her mind, things kept on as they always had: me making the same old screw-up.

◇

She's changed in almost every respect except that. Otherwise, I'd be talking to a stranger. The house is stripped except for a few functional items of furniture. Afghans that have languished on couches and armchairs for so long I had thought them indistinguishable from the upholstery have been snatched up, shaken out, and, in my mother's word, "tossed." The set of encyclopedias purchased in 1978 for my betterment "tossed." My father's collection of *National Geographic* and *Horizon* "tossed." The interior of the house looks freakishly modern because already my mother has "tossed" all the old furniture, heirlooms and all, and replaced it with Swedish-style "apartment furniture," in anticipation of her move. We sit at the stark, square wooden table that has replaced the seventies' pedestal and I sit there expecting to be given a cup of boiled black tea in my grandmother's china. Instead, she takes down a sleek, white ceramic pot from K-Mart which she says she got for five bucks. She liked how it matched the table in its complete lack of interesting detail. She shows me a sugar bowl that also matches. Plain and white. "Two-fifty," she tells me. "Cheap, cheap, cheap!" she chirps.

"You never used to care about cheap," I say.

"I know," she agrees. "For some reason, I always wanted everything to last."

She drinks only green tea now and offers me some because she says it's good for the blood. I am too disoriented to make conversation. After some silence, she remembers our only common ground and actually relieves me by starting in on Gerald. For a moment, things come into focus.

"You two were an awful pair of tea grannies, weren't you?" she remarks.

"Who?" But I know immediately.

"You and that boy. I remember the two of you, three bags a pot, boiling the piss out of it."

If the script had been playing itself out normally, this would be the point when I would launch into my elaborate reminder that the incident, or incidents, she was describing took place more than thirteen years ago, that I am now thirty, with two degrees, eight jobs, and so on and et cetera. But at present I am so unnerved that I find myself actually playing up to the old script, the one I always despised. Come back, Mother. Walk towards the light.

"Yes, we were, weren't we?" I agree.

"So you could walk on it," she mutters, her old self.

"What?"

"The tea. So strong you could walk on it. Foolishness."

193

"Yes, it was foolishness, wasn't it?" I encourage. "I guess we didn't have anything better to do."

She shakes her head, the old look settling into the spot between her eyebrows. Contempt, and disdain and disbelief. Ah. I sit back and wait for the "What in God's name did you ever see in that little christer" tirade. But then she shakes her head again, shakes the lines right off her brow. "Oh, well!" she chirps.

She tells me about the mature person's apartment complex. It has a big elevator so she won't have to climb a lot of stairs. It has a courtyard with a fountain that all the rooms look out over, and a gas fireplace. She starts referring to it as her "bachelor pad" as I chew on my the nail of my right thumb. She says she has already met some of the women who live there, and they can't speak highly enough of the place. She and the women are going to have "wild parties," she says. In her bachelor pad.

I stand up and start poking at the buttons on the dishwasher. "Where did you meet these women?"

To my surprise, the dishwasher starts up. It hasn't worked since I was thirteen. The lines come back to my mother's forehead and she hurries over, batting me out of the way.

"For Christ's sake, dear, don't go fiddling with that, I just got that fixed, now."

"You got it fixed?" I repeat. She always used to store my grandmother's dishes in there because it seemed like the safest place and because we never owned a china cabinet.

"Yes, I got it fixed." A hint of the old tone returns. Dolt, the tone says.

"What about the good china?"

She straightens up and smiles. Gone again are the peekaboo lines, gone is the tone.

We say it together: "Tossed."

I stop asking questions by dinnertime. It ends when she tells me about having met the apartment building ladies at her craft co-op. I ask her what a craft co-op is, and she says all these ladies get together and make quilts, hook rugs, weave baskets, crochet pillowcases, and then peddle their wares to some of the tourist shops around town. "It's more of a social thing than a business endeavour," she assures me. "But we make a little here, a little there. Sometimes somebody will bring in a new pattern we've never tried before."

It's all so outlandish I lean over and stare into her face. "You hate crafts," I say, holding up one finger. "You hate ladies." That's another finger. Then I just give up and spread my hands wide. "A social thing?" My mother's hobby used to be writing letters. She would simply write letters about how stupid everybody was and send them to magazines and newspapers to make herself feel better. The provincial paper used to be her own personal Wailing Wall. She sent them a letter a month, usually having nothing to do with what was in the news, but personal slights that she had suffered throughout the course of her days. But she was clever about it, she couched her complaints in terms of society's widespread moral malaise. If somebody cut her off in traffic, it would be "What has happened to common courtesy?" When I started talking back, it was "Why are today's teenagers so disrespectful?" When the bank teller closed his wicket after she called him a tit-head, she lamented "the shameful decline in standards of service." The newspaper printed every letter faithfully. They thought my mother was the Common Man. Sometimes her heartfelt moral concerns even sparked the occasional editorial response. That was my mother's social life. For years.

I'm reliving all this when she blows at her hair and sort of slouches backward like an impatient teenager. "My dear, my dear," she sighs. "You don't know what I hate. You don't know what I like. You don't know a darn thing about your old mother."

Your old mother. And then she tops herself.

"Tell me about your friend, Dave."

❖

Dave thought it was funny I was taking my running shoes because I'm an awful runner. I'm sporadic, I have no discipline. I can go maybe fifteen minutes without stopping, but that's all I've been able to do for years. I haven't improved at all. I can't force myself to go every day. My back gets sore and I feel sorry for myself. But I take the shoes wherever I go with the best of intentions. I want to be the kind of person who just goes out and flies.

"What are you planning on doing with those?" he asked me. Dave is the kind of person who goes out and flies, for hours sometimes. Through parks, along the beach, into the woods, and all the way back. Everyone in the neighbourhood knows him.

"These will be my sanity-makers while I am home," I told him.

"I think you have to put them on your feet and run around for them to work," he said. "To derive the specific sanity-making benefits, that is."

Ha ha. Twenty km weekend marathon fun-run freak.

"Every day," I vowed.

"Don't go every day," he said seriously. "You'll kill your back and your knees."

"All day, every day," I prayed into the suitcase. He left me alone to pack after that.

◇

My mother asking me about Dave reminds me of my shoes, once the shock has worn off. This being the first time ever. There have been days when I've deliberately spoken about him to her on the phone for over ten minutes — how he was feeling, his job, how somebody gave him this video game and he stayed up until four in the morning playing it three nights in a row. And she would wait for me to finish, sighing and huffing into the phone the entire time, and then she would say something like, "Well, that arse of a doctor up the street still doesn't know what he's talking about. First he says it's my thyroid, then he says it's my diet." She'd say something like that or she'd say something about Gerald. That's as close as she ever got to acknowledging what I was talking about. "Well — you and men, that's something I've never been able to figure out, going around with that lovely fellow you managed to hook up with." She never called him by name. "The Antichrist" or "that young bastard," "that christer," "the little creep," or when she was being sarcastic it was "that lovely fellow." "The beautiful young specimen that he is."

I go over to my suitcase, still on the porch where I dropped it upon arrival, and dig around for my shoes.

"I'm going for a run," I tell my mother.

"Are you running these days?"

"I've been running for years," I say. She has no way of knowing otherwise.

"Your Dave is a big runner, isn't he?"

Another shockwave. "Yes. Yes, he is. He's the one who got me into it. When we first moved in together. Three years ago, that is."

She just gazes out the window, seeing nothing, because it's dark outside and it's basically a mirror. "I think that's great," she murmurs.

God almighty, my mother thinks something is great. "What?" I demand. "What's great?" I'm just waiting, waiting for the jab, the barb, the dripping, festering, fetid spew of sarcasm.

"That you're taking such good care of yourself. I've been getting more exercise these days too. Some nights the ladies come by after dinner and we'll all go for a walk along the water."

◇

It doesn't seem fair that my mother is just allowed to turn herself into a nice person all of a sudden. It seems like the kind of thing that should only have come about after a period of prolonged suffering. Like Saint Paul on the road to Damascus, she should have been struck blind and given a good greasing out by God first, it seems to me. She could be as kind and decent and laid-back as she liked, after that. It shouldn't have all been on my part. The suffering, I mean. I suffer for my mother's sins, and now she is redeemed. She goes tottering off to her ladies and her bachelor pad and her embroidered pillowcases while I pack up thirty years of shit.

On the other hand, of course, I should be happy.

The running is terrible, painful from the first step. I haven't been out in a while. My lungs burn. I have to stop three times, and every time I stop, I think I might die because I can feel my heart and my blood speed up in a really alarming way. When I was a kid there was a rumour about this woman on TV, that her heart exploded from doing aerobics all the time. It feels like that, like it's a possibility.

At one point I find that I am standing at the bottom of the steep hill beside the church parking lot, the same place I almost broke my neck running from Gerald, or somebody. Blood like a washing machine inside my head. I stand there with my hands on my hips for a moment and a perverse, masochistic part of me wants to try and run up that hill. When we were kids, even, we couldn't. We had to claw with our hands, because it's practically vertical. I just remember hurtling down it, scarcely able to keep my feet beneath me, and something in me wants to try and run back up again. One of those strange impulses you get when your pulse is going a hundred miles an hour. A car pulls into the parking lot, high beams hitting me like a prison searchlight. The person in the car honks and waves and I am about to bolt away from this friendly weirdo when I remember that this is a small town, where everyone assumes they know everybody else, even women standing alone in parking lots at night. I wave to be polite but the person doesn't acknowledge me further. He or she has recognized that I am a stranger. He or she pulls into the church, maybe it's the priest or the janitor or a member of the Ladies Auxiliary. He or she turns off the engine and headlights but doesn't get out of the car. I do a token stretch and then jog casually away, a fraud in every respect. Not only am I stranger, but I'm not even a real runner.

And even my identity as a stranger isn't quite the truth. "Well, the town is abuzz," says my mother the next day. She is returning home from the craft store and I am going through boxes that have already been packed on my mother's instruction, seeing if there's anything I might want. I've spent the morning sitting in the same position on the floor, transfixed by the contents of the boxes. In one I discovered piles and piles of those Mad-lib books I used to buy when I was a kid. Books full of stories with all the nouns and verbs and exclamations taken out. You were supposed to do them with friends, ask your friends to supply vowels and nouns and exclamations and fill in the blanks. Then you would read the stories to each other and get a big laugh out of them. For some reason, though, I preferred doing the stories by myself. There was no element of surprise involved or even comedy, I would just read the stories and fill in the blanks with whatever words seemed most appropriate. I filled pages and pages with this sort of banality.

"Why is the town abuzz?" I ask. The page in front of me says: *When I grow up I would like to be a* <u>dog</u>. *Then I could* <u>bark</u> *all the time. People would* <u>hear</u> *me and exclaim, "*<u>Be quiet</u>*!" I would also* <u>sniff</u> *and* <u>dig.</u> Just mind-numbingly boring.

"Well, the craft store is abuzz, anyway," my mother amends. "That's the only place I've been so far today."

"Abuzz with what?"

"Everybody has heard that you're home. Someone saw you out running around last night."

I am aghast. And the phone rings then and it's Madonna MacLeod. "Weren't even gonna call me," she says.

Of course I wasn't going to call you.

"My God," I say. "How the hell have you been?" I exaggerate the amazement in my voice in order to counteract the familiarity in hers.

"The same," she says. "So are you coming over for a drunk?"

"I could come over for a drink," I reply slowly. She snorts.

"Guess what?"

"What?"

"You know how Peter Pecker Jessop was living with Therese" — she pronounces it "Traz" — "Cormier?"

"No."

"Wanda Cormier's sister?"

"Okay."

"They split up because she spit on his dad the one time."

"Huh."

"Ten years!"

"Tch."

"Oh, fuck off!" She barks impatiently. "I know you weren't gonna call me."

"I was so. How is your mum?"

I promise Madonna I'll drop by later on, although probably I won't, and she should know that. She should know there's no reason why I would drop by. Madonna calls me, no matter where I am in the world, a couple of times a year, with all "the news." I never call her and ask for the news. And she never asks me for any of my own news, either. It's like I'm an astronaut, floating around all by myself up in space, and Madonna's down on the ground in Houston, my only link to the rest of the world.

"I got all the news for ya," she'll say. And it's always a different version of Traz Cormier and Peter Pecker Jessop. A litany of names, all familiar and meaningless, one name doing something to another name. Oh, you don't remember that name? You know, the name who's related to this other name. Her name's cousin was my dad's friend's brother's name.

Worse are the times when I'll know the names. I'll know every other one. It will leap out at me like a fish from an otherwise undifferentiated stream and land in my lap. It will feel like a pinch on an unexpected part of my body. Shane, who I kissed at the dance, even though I was supposed to be going out with Gerald at the time. Vesta, with whom I shoplifted condoms and nail polish at Shoppers — because if you get caught, you don't want them thinking you were shoplifting *exclusively* for condoms — and who is Gerald's second cousin. Sharon, who got along all right with Madonna but hated Madonna's sister. All three of whom I left behind me in a cloud of dust the day Gerald came upon us in the woods.

Like Kafka, Madonna is a memory come alive. She'll talk about that birthday party like it was a day ago. She'll talk about how much she enjoyed the cake. Not just how it tasted, but the way it was decorated. She is in league with my mother, or how my mother used to be, in that she doesn't particularly bother to acknowledge the passage of time or, at least, the occurrence of change. There is no change. There's only "news." In Madonna's world, it is everybody's desire and responsibility to make sure they are as caught up on "all the news" as they can possibly be at all times. I can only assume that's why she always sounds so disappointed in me.

◇

But with the next run, I can feel the change already. My thighs have braced themselves, and my lung capacity seems to have expanded. I do about ten minutes, stop, and immediately realize I don't need to, so I keep going for another five. I stop again, look around for the ghostly fireflies that appeared in front of my eyes last time, but they are nowhere to be seen. I'm getting better. I walk for a couple of minutes, deeply impressed with myself. A car heading in the opposite direction slows down to get a good look at me. An old person with a helmet of close, white curls peeps over the steering wheel, and I wave. The old person raises an index finger carefully. I can't tell if it's a man or a woman. I can't see if he or she is smiling or frowning, because the bottom half of its face is hidden by the steering wheel.

This time I'm running in broad daylight, and all sorts of people can see me. Cars honk, people nod from their porches, kids follow me a couple of blocks on their tricycles. I'm considering heading off towards the highway for less conspicuousness, but it's quite a few blocks away. It would be easy to run into Madonna, Shane, Sharon, Vesta, Madonna's sister, the kid I made throw up with the crab apples, whose name was either Earl or Wayne.

Or Gerald, anyone, on these bustling streets. My mother runs into Gerald all the time, the way she tells it. In the store, at the crosswalk. He never says anything to her, she brags. He wouldn't dare. He knows her feelings all too well. I used to imagine my mother giving him the evil eye and scuttling away, cackling to herself like some kind of medieval crone. Gerald actually used to do some pretty funny impressions of the look that would settle over my mother's face whenever he caught her eye. Like she had just been getting ready to sit down to dinner with the Queen at one end of the table and the Pope on the other, he used to say. When what do they set down before her, but a silver-gilded tray laden with the finest Parisian turds.

I'm at the highway, I must have been running for thirty minutes now, and it is probably too much. Dave always warns against pushing myself too far early on, but I'm feeling great. I congratulate myself on having thoughts about Gerald that are grown-up and very nearly fond. Untainted by cringing memories of the past. I could run into Gerald, I think. And that would be fine. He would see that I am a runner, that I live a healthy, productive lifestyle. You see, Gerald, I had to take some time off from my fulfilling job as a cataloguer at a museum where I work while I'm finishing up my Master's thesis. Yes, that's right, another Master's. I had to come back and help my mother pack up thirty years, something I did not dread doing in the least, seeing as how she and I have such a close, caring relationship based upon mutual respect. Now that I have come to terms with all my past issues and what have you. Oh, yes, completely to terms. Yes, Gerald, I really can't tell you how gratifying it is. To bestride the earth, fully in command of yourself, utterly at ease. Healthy, of sound mind and body. Secure with your place in the world.

A pulp truck comes up from behind and *blats* me awake, passing within inches. I'm enveloped in a harrowingly warm cloud, the truck's own breath. Splinters and the smell of bleeding lumber, but also sheer nearness and speed. I turn around and teeter home, fireflies dancing in front of my eyes, legs of brine.

◇

There is truth in the observation that we always seemed to come together whenever nobody else was interested in hanging around with him. Who do you think had the kindness to point that out to me if not my own dear mother? When we were children, he had just moved into town and was regarded with the suspicion of anyone with a weird last name and no identifiable relatives in the community. That's one of the reasons I liked him so much. To me, he was exotic. Like in kindergarten, there was a boy named Simon from Quebec who could scarcely speak a word of English, and he fascinated me. He was bad-tempered and potato-faced and boys and girls alike would torment him quite successfully, but I alone would fight them off and follow him from place to place like my old dead dog used to follow me. I always wanted to kiss him and take hold of his bulging cheeks and after a while he would run if he saw me coming, so that was that. But then there was Gerald, who was more fun than pudgy Simon had ever been.

And then we were older, and his popularity waned again and he seemed angry and disturbed about everything, going around with this slouching demeanour as if he wanted to pull in his lanky limbs and regenerate into a fetus and disappear. His blond head dulled to mousy brown and black sporadic hairs began sprouting on the most unlikely parts of his face and his eyebrows grew rapidly together and sometimes he'd just be walking along and he'd trip for no apparent reason. When we were little, I had always thought he looked like a Viking. He didn't look like a Viking any more.

And so I loved him.

It seemed to help. Sometimes we'd be watching videos in his basement after his parents had gone to bed and he'd jump up and point at the television and yell, "That's just like me!" even though it was usually nothing like him. But I understood what he meant. It was just like the way that he was in his head. I understood how difficult it was to show people how you really were in your head. Sometimes, even, he'd yell that the TV was just like "us," and I'd be thrilled.

◇

My mother steps into the dining room and freaks, a good old-fashioned mother-freak-out, fond memories rushing back. She storms from one pile of mildewed history to the next, ranting about the boxes.

"My nice boxes!" she keeps shrieking. "My nice, good boxes!"

The nostalgia wears off and I hear myself snap: "What?" A good old-fashioned, sullen, teenage-me snap. I am a memory come alive.

"What are you yelling about?"

"My nice neat boxes!"

I look at the boxes to determine what's so special about them. They are brown, cardboard, mainly from the liquor store. This End Up.

"What about the goddamn boxes?"

She kicks over one of the piles I've made, causing me to stand up and my hands to jerk in an involuntary anticipation of throttling.

"Do you know how long it took me to *pack* all this stuff?" she shrieks.

I look around at my piles. It's true, all the nice, good, neat boxes have been laid bare.

"But," I say, "you told me to go through them."

"I didn't tell you to unpack every goddamn one!"

Okay, she didn't. And I, being the grown-up, I, the evolved one, will deign to admit my part in the disagreement. I have practised this sort of thing innumerable times, writing out imaginary dialogues on the backs of envelopes and napkins. *Mother, I apologize for having upset you. Clearly there was a miscommunication between us, and I'm sorry for that. On the other hand, I want you to be aware that when you use that kind of tone with me, when you come in here kicking and screaming and accusing, it just isn't helpful to either one of us. I become defensive and resentful and lash back at you, and then we have a big blow-up that serves only to alienate the both of us.*

I take a deep breath and get my bearings. This is good, I'm thinking, this is the first time I've kept my temper enough to really lay it on her. Won't she be ashamed when she hears how rational I can be in the face of her own childish rantings.

"Mother," I begin. "I apologize —"

She plops down in a chair and starts laughing.

"Just *listen* to me," she says. "Getting myself all worked up like that." She blows at her hair in that new, strange young way she has while I stand there tingling with self-righteousness.

"Clearly there was a miscommunication —"

"I guess to God there was." She stands up again and looks around, hands on hips. "Don't tell me you want all this crap?"

I look around with her. "No...." I try to remember what I was thinking when I emptied the boxes. I don't recall thinking anything.

"Well, you'll put it all back nice and neat, won't you, dear?"

"Of course!" I snap. Defensive, teenage snap. It's a new dance craze. Everybody do the Teenage Snap. I collect myself and resume. "When you use that tone —"

She starts laughing again. "You mean this tone?" Then she does an imitation of herself, high-pitched and incoherent. "*Rar rar rar rar rar!* You mean that tone?"

Speechless.

"I know, dear, it's sickening, a woman my age. I just need to take my pill." She pats me on the bum and hops away up the stairs. I crouch among the piles.

That's gotta be some pill.

◇

Later, when she's out with her ladies crocheting "God Bless Our Happy Home" onto various objects, it occurs to me. It's so obvious I practically slap my forehead and take the stairs two at a time to see if I'm right. There sits the box in her medicine cabinet alongside of all the medicinal artifacts of my family. This seems to be the one corner of the house she has yet to purge. My dad's ear medicine is still in there. My Kermit the Frog toothbrush. False eyelashes from the seventies that she only wore once, and then I wore at Hallowe'en. In the middle of it all, the box. The ultra-modern box with its sleek, proud lettering, cradling its ultra-modern cure within. The miracle cure of the twentieth century. Of course. My mother's harassed doctor must have wept with relief the moment it hit the market. I open the box and shake out its contents — there's still quite a few left. She must have just got her prescription filled. I carry the pills into my room and tuck them away underneath the balls of clothing that sit unpacked in my suitcase. Then I return the empty box to its place of honour beside the eyelashes. There is approximately nothing going on in my head as I perform these actions, and yet for some reason I bounce down the stairs giggling like a teeny-bopper on her way to the formal.

Seeing as how she won't be home for a couple of hours at least, there doesn't seem to be much else to do except wander into the living room and start emptying out a few *other* boxes.

◇

Madonna happens to be standing outside the bank when I run by, lighting a smoke and retrieving a ratty little dog that she must have tied to a nearby hydro pole while she went in. It is not necessarily the case that I spotted and then ignored her. I am at the height of my run, blood churning in my head, and to see Madonna leaning against a pole inhaling smoke seems at once unreal and at the same time utterly expected. It's as if everything around me is wallpaper — the bank, the trees, the water, the crumbling street, Madonna, and the dog. To acknowledge her seems to make as much sense as saying hello to a picture on the wall.

Of course there's no way Madonna's going to let me get away with it. She barks, "Hey!" and the dog barks also, as if agreeing. I turn around but don't feel like I can just stop. Madonna pushes up her sleeves, holds the cigarette more securely, and runs to catch up with me, dragging the rat along behind her.

"Will you slow the frig down a minute?"

"I'm sorry!" I jog in place, pumping my knees, aware of how I look.

"What's the matter with ya?" To her I appear to be having some kind of fit.

"It's just ... my heart rate ... it's way up there. I shouldn't stop."

"You don't have to stop, I'll keep up."

I take her at her word, but adjust my pace. Madonna trundles along beside me, smoking.

"Looked right at me, didn't stop. I thought you must be going retarded."

"I was —" The only thing I can think to say is that I was "in the zone." Madonna will laugh to puke if I tell her I was "in the zone."

"I was spaced out," I say.

"I guess you were."

The dog whines, its tiny toenails clicking rapidly along the pavement. Madonna glances down. "Dora doesn't care too much for this."

"That's not the same dog," I say, squinting down at the thing. It's one of those infinitesimal terriers exactly like Madonna's mother had when we were teenagers.

"That's Dora," Madonna confirms.

"Jesus Christ, we better stop!" I am rapidly doing calculations in my head, trying to recall Dora's puppyhood. The dog stands trembling, a pink tongue the size of my baby fingernail protruding from her scraggily muzzle. Madonna picks her up with one hand and gives her a kiss on the face. I get a violent head rush from the sudden inertia and have to lean over.

"You're killing yourself with that there," my childhood friend observes. She drops her cigarette on the ground directly in front of my eyes without even bothering to step on it and make sure it goes out.

"I'm still getting used to it," I explain.

I straighten up and witness Madonna sort of adjusting herself mentally. She considers the sky and pushes down her sleeves again. "So Gerald Newhook's getting married," she says.

"I thought he already was married."

"No, no, he was just living with somebody for a few years, someone Beaton."

"What happened to her?"

"Oh, you know. He was always screwing around. But so was she."

"So who's this new one?"

"From out Mabou way."

"What's her story?" I hear myself saying. But there's no other way to talk.

"Oh, you know."

"Is he working?"

"On and off at the mill. Laid off last year, sold hash for a while. Plays with the band at the tavern."

"Well, I think that's wonderful," I say, finding my breath and trying to shake off the whole girls'-bathroom feel of the conversation. Madonna smiles.

"Well," she says, "you know Gerald."

"Actually, I *don't*," I point out. "It's been ... what?" I pretend to be casually racking my brain. "Thirteen years?"

Madonna shrugs and the dog pants and trembles against her chest. She holds it up to her face, puckering her lips and talking baby talk. "Is that how long it's been?" she asks it. "Is dat how wong it's been, Dora-Dora?" The dog wriggles and flicks its tongue towards her in adoration. I start pumping my knees again while Madonna looks me up and down.

"I gotta keep going, I'm right in the middle," I plead.

"You're heart's gonna explode like that one on television."

"That was an urban myth."

"No, I heard it from someone," she murmurs, bored already with the subject, casting her mind into the past like a fisherman's net. Then her eyes light up. I get a seasick conviction she's about to exclaim "Holy cats!"

Instead she says, "Remember that time in the woods? We were running then, boy. Scary."

What infuriates me is that I know precisely what she is talking about, the very day, the very occasion, eighteen years ago on her twelfth birthday. Because any normal human being with a normal memory span wouldn't, I pretend that I don't and fly away.

⟡

Only one time, I remember, did we ever talk about being kids together, he and I. It was when we were having a fight. The beginning of the end. I got pissed off finally, and yanked myself away from him, and he followed me down the street. Hey! he kept yelling. Hey you!

Remember when our dogs killed each other? Remember that?

I thought he was trying to be gross and cruel, and I stopped.

You mean your dog killed my dog.

And then mine had to be put to sleep, he said.

So what? I said.

So your dog killed my dog indirectly.

I remember I stared at him with my mouth open. By being killed, by *your* dog?

That's right! he said.

So?

So, he said, everything is your fault.

⟡

"Don't go into the woods!" Madonna calls after me, laughing.

So despite her, I do, I head straight there, ploughing through twigs. Bushes I remember barely being able to conceal myself behind have eaten up entire clearings. It's no place to run. All the old paths are so overgrown I can hardly make my way through, a gauntlet of thorns and whiplash branches. The kids must not even bother coming down here any more. On the street, someone in a car sees me stagger out from behind the wall of trees, legs and face ruddy with welts, and stops to ask if I need any help.

◇

Nice Place
to Visit

◇

MOUNT BAKER ROSE LIKE AN ICEBERG up from the centre of the August haze, and Bess was feeling guilt again, because it was all so beautiful. Below her, green islands dotted the blue sea and Meghan was pointing out whales and screaming to be heard over the engine. In the seats ahead of them were three fat rich people, packed together like marshmallows while she and Meg luxuriated in all their space at the back. On Saturna, when the three fat rich people were boarding, Bess's instinct had been that she and Meg should offer up their seats, but she glanced over at Meg and saw she was pretending to be asleep. As the three fat rich people crammed in, she heard graceful, subtle mutterings about the thin young girls in the back. "Perhaps those lovely, thin young girls ..." and so on. Certainly unassertive, but insistent all the same. Bess felt guilt the entire half-hour flight. It was that, and having left her son at home, who had begged and screamed to come.

The plane lowered itself towards the island and skipped across the harbour like a pebble and Bess was reminded of the opening credits of "The Beachcombers."

"They were fat, they were rich," Meg rationalized on the dock. "Here's what would have happened. You and I would have been uncomfortable the whole trip because *they* can't get off their big arses and lose a few pounds! So *we're* supposed to be inconvenienced."

The pilot heard their accents and asked where they were from. When Meg said, "East Coast," he thought they meant Toronto, so Meg stood there and explained that Toronto was not on a coast, and then went on to detail every pertinent aspect of Atlantic Canadian geography so that he would know in the future. She was very sweet about it, and the pilot unloaded their knapsacks, listening patiently.

Bess thought the West Coast had done wonders for Meg — she had somehow wriggled out from underneath a houseful of backwoods brothers and made her way here, where she had blossomed, apparently. She wore the kind of bright clothing that would never be seen in a tavern back home because people would think you were showing off, she wore hiking boots with dresses, and she didn't wear make-up. She was strong and assertive in a way that was still quite alien to Bess, and her boyfriend lived on a houseboat. Bess used to think that they had nothing in common, and she still thought she and her cousin had nothing in common, but somehow, out here in the alien beauty, she was finding she liked Meg better than she had at home.

But it was awkward. Bess had never been anywhere and felt as if she didn't know how to talk to people. She knew that Meg had stopped drinking as of two years ago, and couldn't imagine how they were going to have a conversation. Did it mean that Bess wouldn't be allowed to drink? Would it be insensitive? Was Bess expected to adopt the lifestyle while she was here and have to hike and swim and cycle all the time? She especially hoped no one would ask her to ski as she knew that she would break her own neck. Then Bess felt disgust for herself. The big adventurer, whining for a beer, needing to sit down and smoke every half-hour.

The boyfriend handed her a beer the moment she walked in the door, as he had just finished opening it for himself, and a few moments later he offered Bess a cigarette as well. At first she declined, because she was trying to train herself to smoke only in the evenings, but once finding herself with a beer in her hand, she realized how unnatural it was not to have a smoke in the other. Glancing at Meg, who was standing in the open doorway, but not complaining, Bess asked if she might have one after all. The boyfriend, whose name was Lyle, grinned and bobbed his head. "It was a valiant effort," he told her.

Lyle looked like what her father would describe, with his ancient frame of reference, as a beatnik. Bess had learned to understand that by this he meant people who did not iron their clothes or cut their hair when it needed to be cut, so almost anyone young, who wasn't in the military, was a beatnik by her father's standards. Still, Bess was surprised, because Meg had described him as a businessman. Standing out on deck, surrounded by water and mountains and sailboats, Lyle explained that he was an independent consultant.

"Oh!" went Bess.

"Well, it's great because I get to work out of my home and, you know, home is here." He swept his arm at the mountains and water possessively.

"You never have to *go* anywhere?" marvelled Bess. Her father's voice: *What in Christ's name kind of job is that?* The longer she had lived away from him, the more she came to realize that this voice had, at some point, usurped the position of her conscience. She was constantly beating it back. Her son running about the apartment in a makeshift Peter Pan costume — she had plastered her hands to her mouth, scarcely before hollering at him to stop flouncing around the place like a big fruit.

After the single beer, the jet lag caught up to Bess and made her wobbly, so Meg suggested they go into town for coffee and groceries and allow Lyle to get a little bit of work done.

"How will we get into town?"

"We'll walk, Bess," said Meg.

Bess hadn't walked anywhere in ages. She was mad at herself for allowing this to be known. But where was there to walk, and what point was there to walking, where she was from? The streets were ugly and adversarial and there were days when she could not bring herself to contemplate moving around on them.

She felt her jeans were too tight to walk in, so she went into Lyle's room with her knapsack to put on shorts. There were clothes heaped on Lyle's bed and the curtains had not been opened, so the room was dark and smelled of sleep and sweat and stale breath. When she emerged, Lyle and Meg were standing close together, Meg with her hands on her hips and with her head down.

"Sorry the room was such a fucking mess," Meg spat when they were out in the open air.

Bess was marvelling at the size of the trees. "God, no problem." The truth was Lyle's slovenly houseboat put Bess far more at ease than Meg's assiduously scrubbed apartment in the city the night before.

"It's really inconsiderate," said Meg.

"No, no."

"It makes me sick," said Meg.

Bess remembered Meg's parents' house, Bess's Uncle Alistair's, where Meg had lived right up until she was twenty-two with four of her seven brothers. It was a house of men, there could be little doubt. It was painted a greenish black colour and there was a shaving mirror above the sink in the kitchen. One time Bess dropped by to find a pile of freshly caught fish on the coffee table in the living room, and young Alistair with his boots propped up alongside of it, watching "The Price Is Right" and flicking cigarette ash into a bowl of tomato soup. Meg used to shriek at her brothers all the time and they would laugh at her. Findlay had once gone into her room and taken her birth control pills in order to give to his girlfriend, who couldn't afford them. At Meg's small, bright apartment the night before, she had done impressions of her brothers for Bess, who was punchy from her all-night flight and laughed until her ribs ached. Meg stuck out her front teeth and crossed her eyes and pulled her jeans down so that her stomach would hang over the waistband and the crack of her ass could be seen, and then she walked around bow-legged.

Meg was cosmopolitan now. She got them both iced cappuccinos and biscotti at the coffee shop, and Bess drank the cappuccino down like a milk shake and wanted another one. The jet lag lifted immediately and she looked around herself with renewed disbelief at the painful, vivid sky with the clouds hugging up against the mountains. Meg had purchased wild rice, salmon, and rapini, among other exotic items at the market, because Lyle was going to cook for them that night.

"You live here," Bess kept repeating.

"You could live here," said Meg. "Why don't you look for work?"

"Oh, Jesus Murphy," said Bess. It was inconceivable. "Dylan."

"Dylan would love it!"

"Of course he would love it," said Bess, not optimistically. That he would love it was not the point.

"You're thinking how hard it would be," intuited Meg. "Listen — it's not hard. I'm here. It seems so hard and then you get out here and wonder how in the name of God you were able to tolerate that hell-hole you were in for so many years. It changes everything."

Bess was offended. What had been hard was getting out of her parents' house and into the little apartment with Dylan in the city. Meg had no idea what a triumph this dingy one-bedroom on a grey, violent street represented to Bess. Meg had never been there, and therefore had no way of knowing whether or not it was a hell-hole.

"I'm not saying you live in a hell-hole," amended Meg the moment Bess was thinking it. "I'm just remembering my own situation. You think you're stuck and you think you can do no better. Then you come out here, and the whole world opens up."

Meg spread her arms. Bess looked around.

❖

On the weekend, Lyle's friend was supposed to take them out on his sailboat. He was called Wills, instead of Will, because he was from England, and Bess was obsessed with the idea that they were going to try and set her up with him. As pleased as she was about the sailboat, she could not bear the notion of being paired up with a stranger, and thought she might plead sick. The idea of sex had been a horror to Bess ever since the trauma giving birth to Dylan. She'd had a couple of passive relationships since then, but as soon as anyone tried to touch her, even made any careful suggestions, her gorge would rise and once she had actually thrown up in the fellow's presence. The guy had abruptly said, "Shall we go to 'er?" and Bess ralphed. After that, she decided not to bother herself with such things any more. It was embarrassing. Just something else to make her stand out from the rest of the world.

She phoned her parents' house that night and they told her that Dylan had refused to get out of bed the first day and ever since had been dragging himself around the house like a ghoul. Her father had taken him to buy a couple of new hens and that had cheered him up somewhat, but for the most part he was like "a little lost soul," as Bess's mother put it.

Bess winced at hearing what she had known was an inevitability, considering his behaviour before she left. As Bess was a freak, so was her son a freak. It was not healthy for two people to be so bound up with each other.

"When are you coming home?" was the first thing he said to her.

"It's really nice out here!" she said brightly. "Maybe we'll both come out here some time."

"Why didn't we both go out there this time?"

"Because I'm not a gazillionaire, I told you," she said.

"Kids *don't* cost twice as much to fly," Dylan stated for the hundredth time since Bess had announced her travel plans. He had taken it upon himself to find out about this at school, after Bess had tried to convince him otherwise.

"It's still more than I have right now, Dylan."

"Me and Pop bought some chickens, and I named one of them Ted. Do you want to talk to him?"

"No, I don't want to talk to the Jesus chicken."

"I'm going to go get him."

"I will kill you if you go and get the chicken."

"Talk to Nan." He was gone.

"He's running outside to get the chicken now," Bess's mother tittered on the other end of the line.

"For Christ's sake, Mother, don't let him bring that thing inside!"

"Oh, he just loves that bird."

Bess could hear the screen door slamming shut a second time.

"Here's Ted," said Dylan. "I'll hold him up to the phone."

"Do you know how much this is costing?" No answer. She was screaming at Ted. After a few moments, Dylan came back on the line.

"Did you talk to him?"

"I phoned to talk to you," Bess said sweetly, having used her time with the bird to take a couple of breaths.

"You can talk to me all you want when you come home," he reasoned.

"Sometimes moms need vacations."

"Sometimes kids need vacations too," her son rejoined.

Bess thought, *You little fucker*, blowing kisses into the phone.

◇

She imagined Meg's life, tanned and healthy, independent with her own nice, woman's apartment full of brightly coloured woman things, partaking of grown-up, normal sex with her boyfriend on a houseboat. On an island on a houseboat. Without even a hint of nausea, Bess could only assume. Meg had wrenched herself from the family of boys, flown across the continent,

216

and opened herself up like a flower, somehow. That was how. Merely by going away. Bess and Meg had used to go to the dances and the tavern together back home, resenting one another because they didn't have anyone else. Meg would pay Bess grim visits in the afternoons to break up the monotony of their endless, aimless days in their respective parent's homes. Whenever one of them was working, she would treat the other to booze and vice versa. It never occurred to them to do anything with their money except drink, there was so little of it. Bess was itching to interrogate her cousin as to the hows and the whys of her giving up drinking. It would have been inconceivable to Bess a couple of days ago, but as the clean, wet air and looming monster-trees and sun and clouds and water worked on her being, she could almost imagine forgetting she needed a drink some evening.

"But there's sun and water and trees back home," Meg observed as they struggled their way up a hill to see the view.

"But where?" panted Bess.

"All around!" said Meg.

"But where?"

If Bess ever forgot about drinking, Lyle was always there to remind her. He was an aficionado of all sorts of fine and tasty booze. He had a liquor cabinet right there on the houseboat just like somebody's dad, and every night brought out a different bottle for them to sample, saying what a pleasure it was to have another drinker on board to keep him company. They drank Jamaican rum and thirty-year-old scotch and Benedictine. Bess always drank too much of everything and felt embarrassed the next day, thinking if she had wanted to get drunk, there was always plenty of beer in the fridge — she should not have guzzled Lyle's good stuff. But Lyle was gracious and told her not to be ridiculous whenever she balked. Meg would sit nearby smiling at Lyle's stories and drinking Italian sodas to stay awake.

It turned out the friend with the sailboat, Wills, was gay, although Bess would never have figured it out for herself, and had to be told. He was a member of Lyle's book club, and a doctor who merely sailed from one coastal town to another doing locums at the various hospitals, occasionally docking his boat and flying inland for brief stints. (*What in Christ's name kind of doctor is that*, the father who owned Bess's conscience demanded.) Wills was one of the best-looking men she had ever seen, and Bess felt dowdy alongside of him. Meg and Bess sat up in front (bow? stern?) tanning themselves while Lyle and Wills stayed at the helm. Bess felt like she was rich, and felt guilty. The father inside her head wanted to know who she thought she was. All I ever do, Bess explained to the father, is go to work and eat food and talk to Dylan and go to bed at night. Goddamn lucky to have a job, grunted the father, especially in this economy. I am not saying that I'm not grateful to have a job, explained Bess. When you have responsibilities, interrupted the father, when you've got a small boy depending on you, sometimes your own goddamn pleasures have to take a back seat. Always, they do, Bess argued, helplessly getting angry. Well, who held a gun to your head and told you to have a baby all those years ago? Nobody did. Well? It's not just that my goddamn pleasures are supposed to take a back seat. It's that there are no pleasures. There aren't even supposed to be any.

"Isn't this beautiful?" said Meg.

Bess opened her eyes. The sea was the mountains and sky in reverse. A heron launched itself from a nearby crag of an island. She wanted to scream and pull at her own hair.

"Horrible," she grunted.

Meg glanced at her, not particularly surprised.

Meg hugged her knees. "Lyle's so hungover."

"Really?" Bess glanced back to see Lyle at the wheel, gazing steadily at the horizon as Wills leaned back, talking and gesturing with a beer can.

"Oh, come on, he looks like shit," said Meg, but the truth was he looked no different than since Bess had arrived. "He always drinks too much when there's other people around."

Guilt again for Bess. "I'm sorry."

"Jesus, it's not your fault!"

Bess felt like apologizing again, simply on instinct because Meg had yelled at her, but stopped herself.

"It reminds me of my father," said Meg. "Just sitting and drinking and sitting and drinking. Finding himself more and more fascinating the more he drinks. Assuming there's nothing on earth you would enjoy more than to sit there and listen to him explaining himself to you, endlessly, on and on, over and over again."

"Huh," said Bess.

"It made me crazy," said Meg. "He'd make you sit there and he wouldn't let you get up. 'Listen to me, I've got somethin' important to say to ya,' but it was always the same thing over and over again, and it didn't have anything to do with me. I might as well have been a doll, or a mirror."

Bess didn't know what to say, as she had never liked Meg's father to begin with.

"Lyle is nice," she offered.

"I know," said Meg. "He's a great guy. He is a wonderful, caring man." She leaned back and closed her eyes again.

They ate dinner on the sailboat, Wills making pasta for everyone, but once the red wine was gone, they headed over to Lyle's place to "unearth" another bottle of Jamaican rum. Wills told them hilarious stories about trying to teach Lyle how to sail when they first met, and thinking that Lyle was gay and trying to put the moves on him and Lyle being too drunk and obtuse the whole time to know what was going on. Almost all of Wills stories were about Lyle doing something foolish.

"He's just a tiny little boy," Wills told them, "underneath that *übermensch* exterior of his. Just a wee naive little boy at heart." Lyle was smiling and swirling the ice cubes around in his drink. Bess was relaxed when the men started asking about her own little boy, which, she understood, was perhaps the only thing about herself that made her interesting to them.

"He's a big bastard," she reflected sloppily. "Likes hockey and trucks. He'll probably be the kind of kid who spends entire afternoons lighting farts with his friends in the backyard."

Lyle looked alarmed. "You must do something."

"He sounds perfect," corrected Wills.

In the middle of all the hilarity, Meg had gone into the bedroom for some unstated reason and, after a few moments, called for Lyle to join her. Wills looked at Bess and clenched his teeth.

"So it begins," he said.

Bess leaned forward. "What?"

"You might want to sleep over at my place tonight."

"Why?"

Wills inclined his head towards the bedroom and Bess listened. Meg was crying. Lyle was speaking very low and Meg was shouting in whispers, and then she would cry again.

"What the hell's going on?" Bess hissed.

Wills rose. Bess couldn't believe the party was to end so abruptly. "I'm out of here. You should come. They'll be at it all night."

"No, no," Bess laughed. "They'll stop."

"They won't stop," said Wills.

◇

They stopped at five in the morning, an hour and a half of silence went by, and then they started again, but only for fifteen minutes or so. Lyle came out of the bedroom and went into the bathroom and then he came out of the bathroom and walked out the front door. Bess finally went to sleep after that, and five hours later she sat up and saw Meg at the kitchen table with a cup of coffee and the newspaper in front of her.

"Today we should swim."

"How long have you been up?"

"I didn't sleep," said Meg.

"Jesus, go to sleep, Meg."

"No," said Meg. "There's no point now. I can't sleep in the day."

They were going to rent mopeds in order to drive up to the lake, but it turned out they needed a credit card number to give, and neither of them had a credit card, and Meg could not remember Lyle's number. They turned around and walked back towards the bike shop, to rent bikes. They hadn't wanted to do this at first because the ride was all uphill and neither of them were feeling particularly athletic.

"We are slaves to our credit rating," said Meg. "We are the outcasts of society."

Bess thought it was strange Meg wouldn't have a credit card, being gain-fully employed, but it turned out she had screwed up in the past with an Irving Big Stop card in her early twenties. Bess had done the same with a Zellers card during quite a bleak time in her life. Feeding Dylan Zellers macaroni every day, Zellers chips, dressing him in Zellers jeans and Zellers shoes, taking him for sundaes at the Zellers restaurant. She told the story to Meg to cheer her up. Meg laughed and laughed and related a time when the only way she could get a drink was to order a complete meal along with the two or three beer she actually wanted at the Big Stop.

"Sitting there shaking with the DTs," she gasped. "Food growing legs, crawling around on my plate."

The lake was a blessing when they reached it, the two of them soaked in sweat, Jamaican rum seeming to ooze out of Bess's every pore. There was hardly anyone else around, and they waded in easily, as into a cool bath. Water got into Bess's mouth, and she gulped it in, it tasted so fresh. They floated on their backs and saw three eagles fighting over a fish.

At the houseboat, Lyle was still not there, and Meg made more coffee to drink and started looking around for food to cook for dinner.

"Lyle, Lyle, Lyle," she said as she paced around the kitchen. "Lyle is probably using his credit card to purchase something big and fancy right now."

"For you, maybe," said Bess. Meg made a barking noise at this. "Maybe he's with Wills," she suggested.

"Maybe he's getting his cock sucked," said Meg, "Now that the workers are on strike."

Bess had no idea what to say.

"That is terrible," Meg scolded herself. "What a terrible thing for me to say about Lyle."

Just as Bess and her cousin had finished a meal of cheese and grapes and apples and bread, Lyle and Wills came in with two bottles of wine and an armful of take-out food from the nicest restaurant on the island. They were in high spirits after spending the day sailing — "at sea," as Lyle put it.

"Alas, we were merely *at lake*," joked Meg. Lyle complained how could they have gone up to the lake without him, and Meg told him he hadn't been there to ask. Lyle said that he had been there at around noon to see if they wanted to go sailing, but the two of them were gone, and Meg said that they had left at 12:30, so he couldn't have been there at noon at all.

"So I'm just lying," said Lyle.

"I don't know," replied Meg, bland.

Wills gathered Bess into his arms, retrieving one of the bags of take-out at the same time, and waltzed her out the door. "Plenty of booze on the boat," he told her outside.

For the next few hours they sat drinking on his sailboat, Wills very decently pretending to flirt with Bess and find her attractive. He was the consummate host.

"I'd be happy to have sex with you," he was saying. "I mean, I'm a flamer, I do *flame*, as it were, but I'm not always averse to sleeping with women."

Bess doubled over at this and said that she didn't think she wanted the first person she'd slept with in years to be someone who claimed he "wasn't averse" to it. Then she put her head in her hands and reflected how pathetic this must sound. There was no nausea because the subject was so clearly academic. Wills was interested in the fact that she'd been celibate for years and tried to get her to confide in him, but Bess felt resentful all of a sudden and wouldn't do it. She was thinking about Lyle and Meg and wondering if it was not somehow all her fault. In the middle of the night, she had distinctly heard Lyle muttering something about his booze, and Meg's hiss had pierced through the wall: "Then why do you keep offering it?" At the same time, she was afraid they would leave her for Wills to look after the rest of the week, and she was unequal to the idea of becoming a favour someone was doing for his friends. Especially a man so lovely and legitimate as Wills the sailing doctor, to whom she also felt unequal, kind as he was.

Meg came wandering out of the dark a few hours later. "Came to get you," she said. "You guys didn't have to leave."

"How's everything?" Wills inquired.

"Fine, fine. He's gone to the mainland on business."

"He's gone to the mainland on business," said Wills. "You can't fly out at night."

"I know," said Meg. "But that's where he said he was going, and who am I to question?"

"There's late ferries," remembered Bess.

"Of course," agreed Meg. "There's late ferries. Why wait until morning when you can sit alone on a ferry for seven hours?"

Meg kept staggering on the way back to the houseboat, unable to find her footing on the dark path, where enormous tree roots snaked and crossed each other above the earth, forming natural human booby traps. "Look at me, I'm drunk," she kept saying. "Drunk on love." Clear-headed and brave, Bess found it in herself to ask if Lyle was mad at her for drinking all his booze.

"Number One," said Meg. "If somebody doesn't want you to drink all his booze, the sane and normal thing to do is to stop insisting they have more of your booze all the time. Clearly we all haven't been so meticulously brought up as to comprehend the gentle art of lying. Some of us have not had the privilege of such training, and can't be expected to understand the game, let alone win."

Bess waited for Number Two, but Meg was apparently finished. "Tell him I'm sorry," Bess said.

"I always tell him, over and over again," answered Meg.

At the houseboat, Meg got out the Jamaican rum and tried to make Bess have some more, but Bess only wanted to sleep. "This is what happens to those who love to offer, but hate to give," said Meg. "Their rum gets all drunk. It's a metaphor."

"No, I don't want to drink any more of his rum," Bess protested. "I'll buy him another bottle and I'll drink beer the rest of the time I'm here."

"It's the only way he'll learn!" Meg declared, shoving the bottle towards her. Bess crawled away from her, onto the couch, and pulled the blanket up.

Her stomach was shaky the next day. She had been dreaming about living in her parents' house again. She dreamt about her parents' house the way most people dream about high school and writing exams. Someone was supposed to pick her up and drive her to the airport for an important meeting, and Bess spent the whole dream getting ready for it — selecting the right clothes, putting on make-up, trying to find her shoes — and once everything was ready, her ride still hadn't come. In the dream, Dylan was a baby again and her grandparents were going to look after him for her, but she was vaguely worried about that because she knew her grandparents could die any moment, they were so old. In real life, they were both dead. Her parents' house had actually been their house, and she didn't know who in the family had lived in it before them.

It was a boring, useless anxiety dream and she woke up earlier than she wanted to, with a headache. Meg was sitting against the fridge with her eyes closed, and Bess almost booted her when she went to get cream for her coffee.

Meg opened her eyes and to Bess she looked as if she had spent the night smoking and drinking. She had deep and hungry lines around her mouth as though having used it to consume a multitude of poisons over the years. She looked like she had looked back home, only worse.

"What are you doing?"

"Meditating," said Meg. "When you haven't slept, meditation is like an acid trip. All these characters come and talk to you."

"You still haven't slept?"

"No, I can't sleep. Today we have to do lots and lots of fun things."

"I feel like shit."

"I know, but the only way to get through the day is to keep busy."

Bess didn't agree. She thought it might be nice to spend at least one day lounging around the houseboat, maybe strolling into town to drink more cappuccino and buy one of those enormous women's magazines that allow hours to pass effortlessly as page after page of unreality moves through your mind, catching on nothing. It might be nice to sit on the deck of the houseboat doing that, Bess thought. Meanwhile Meg was combing the phone book trying to find out about kayaking and whale watching. It was all expensive so they agreed to pack a picnic lunch and instead take the bicycles out to some sort of strange park that Meg had found a brochure for, the Castleman Family Farm, it was called.

It took an hour to bike to the Castleman Family Farm, and they were disappointed. Suddenly the road opened up into a great expanse of field, backdropped with woods, and tiny, empty buildings grew up from the tall, yellow grass. A plaque in front of one of the buildings stated that this, indeed, was the Castleman Family Farm. The Castlemans were one of the island's founding families, and had worked the farm for over a hundred years. They kept dairy cows. They were gone, now, though, the Castlemans and the cows. Bess and Meg moved from one empty building to the other, and peered in through the cloudy windows. In the cowshed there sat archaic milking equipment. In the building that was identified as having been the family homestead, there was nothing.

Both of them were thinking that it was exactly like back home, but nobody had made home into a park for people to come and wonder at. Nobody had ever biked out to their parents' hundred-year-old houses for curiosity's sake and peered in the windows. And the reason was that there were people still living in them, which didn't make things as quaint as when they were long abandoned. Anyone who might have lived there in the past was a safe and distant figure, about whom anything might be surmised. Meg stomped from one building to the next, pissed off, pronouncing the Castleman Family Farm to be the most depressing place she'd ever seen. A bunch of tourists drove up in a sport utility vehicle and let their children run around, snapping one picture after another of the crumbling cowsheds. One little boy tore through the grass, screaming, "I'm a farmer! I'm a farmer!" over and over again.

"I'm never having kids," gloomed Meg. Only five days ago, Meg had been outlining her plans to have no less than six kids, and she claimed she was going to give them names like Sunshine and Waterfall, and their nicknames would be Shiny and Fally. She had bombarded Bess with questions about Dylan her first night there until Bess thought she would scream, so hungover with guilt was she.

The flesh on one side of Bess's body began to tingle. She absently rubbed at it, and then it began to sting. "Something strange is happening to my body," she stated to Meg, who gaped at her.

"Are you turning into the Incredible Hulk?" asked Meg.

"Look," said Bess, holding out her arm, now red. "Ow."

"Ooh," said Meg. "Poison ivy? Is it itchy?"

"No, it fucking hurts," said Bess. She examined her leg, also burning, and saw it was covered with the infinitesimal red pinpricks as well.

The boy who had been screaming about being a farmer, now merely screamed and ran headlong at one of the sport utility vehicle women, jumping up and down before her and waving his arms. He was one of those ugly, orange-haired children with blotchy freckles whose faces turn violently red when they get angry or cry.

"It's nettles," said Meg, having examined Bess's skin. "It's nettles!" she called to the horrified grown-ups, gathering around their screaming boy.

"Nettles?" repeated Bess.

"Yeah, you know, nettles. We have them back home, I think."

"We do?"

"Yeah ... somewhere."

"I've never seen them before."

"Well ..." Meg murmured, doubtful. "They're around somewhere." The tourists from the sport utility vehicle were looking at Meg, seeing her as an authority of some kind, hoping she would come over and explain what was happening. Apparently they had never experienced nettles either. Meg just stood watching the red-haired boy throw his continued fits of agony.

"Be honest with me. It can't possibly hurt as much as that little bastard is pretending."

"No," said Bess. "It just kind of ... surprises you by how it feels."

"Little snot-nose attention-seeking self-centred little rich *brat*," spat Meg with quick hate. Bess wanted something all of a sudden, but couldn't pin it down. It irritated her, combined with the pain in her skin. She wanted to get out of the sun. Have a cool drink somewhere and wait for her flesh to become her own again. She wanted to be somewhere else besides the dead Castleman Family Farm, surrounded by the ghosts of cows. She wanted to get off the island and go to Meg's small, bright apartment in the city and imagine it was actually hers. Wanted to be Meg as she was in the city. She did not want to be Meg as she was on the island. She was starting to realize, in fact, that she did not want to be *with* Meg as she was on the island. Then she thought of Dylan, and knew she wanted to be there instead, in their apartment on the grey street, sitting on the second-hand couch with the enormous faded afghan on it, knitted seventy-odd years ago by Bess's father's mother. Dylan on her lap, the two of them watching "Star Trek" repeats after supper, smell of toast and macaroni all around.

Meg broke down after dinner, having checked the answering machine as soon as they returned, getting only business messages for Lyle, nothing from Lyle himself. She went to the phone and dialled his cell, and then his pager, and then she made a salad and grilled some chicken for their dinner and did not eat it, crying instead. After dinner she phoned her own answering machine in the city to see if any messages were left on it, and after that was when she began to pace and talk and rage in such a way as to make Bess despair of their getting any sleep again that night. In the middle of her rage, she stopped and dialled Wills and asked him to come over, and Bess wanted to know what in the name of God she did that for.

"He explains things to me and he helps," said Meg. "He likes to talk about Lyle."

"Have they been friends for a long time?"

A pall dropped over Meg's face. "The only reason Lyle is friends with Wills is that Wills is in love with him," she brooded. "Lyle needs to be around as many people who are in love with him as possible."

Bess decided that she hated Lyle and a few hours later she had decided that she hated Meg and hated Wills as well. The two of them sat all night, speculating endlessly upon the secret thoughts and motivations of Lyle. Wills indulged her, feeding her obsession. Meg had been right: Wills liked to talk about Lyle. Neither of them wanted the drama to wind itself down.

Meg was reduced to clichés. "He thinks he's the centre of the universe!"

"Yes," said Wills.

"But he's not!"

"No," said Wills. "But he thinks he is."

"Forget about Lyle!" Bess shouted in exasperation, and Meg glared as if the words had been in cruel, bad taste.

"My God, Bess, this is my relationship we're talking about. This is my long-term partner we're talking about."

Bess felt guilty, like she didn't understand such things and had spoken presumptuously. Meg turned back to Wills.

"No man is perfect," she said.

"No."

"You have to accept your partner for who he is. I have to show him that I do that."

"Yes."

"But I can't do that if he's not here!"

"I know, love."

"Goddamnit!" Meg went to the bathroom and threw up.

"She hasn't slept for two nights," Bess told Wills.

"That's nothing. The record is a week and a half."

"Well, we should do something."

"Lyle is the only one who can do anything," Wills sighed. "It is for the rest of us to await his whim — to sit and suffer in communion." He poured himself some more wine and settled into the couch. Meg came out of the bathroom, red-faced and teary-eyed, and curled herself up in the crook of Wills's arm. He cooed at her uselessly. The two of them looked comfortable together and nearly content. Tomorrow was Friday, Bess thought, and the day after that was therefore Saturday, and then it would be Sunday, the day before which Bess could fly home. Three long days of the vigil remained. She had planned for herself a lengthy vacation, knowing there might never come another chance for such ease, and escape.

About the Author

Raised in Cape Breton, Nova Scotia, 29-year-old Vancouver resident Lynn Coady was nominated for the 1998 Governor General's Award for Fiction and the Thomas Raddall Atlantic Fiction Award for her first novel *Strange Heaven*. She received the Canadian Author's Association/Air Canada Award for the best writer under thirty and the Dartmouth Book and Writing Award for fiction. Coady has published a number of short stories. Her articles and reviews have appeared in several publications including *Saturday Night*, *This Magazine*, and *Chatelaine*. She has also written award-winning plays and a screenplay.

Acknowledgements

God bless Charles for always being interested enough to peek at the stories before they were finished, and Christy Ann Conlin for her ongoing and supportive nebulous kinship.

CEASE FIRE

Other books by this author:

The Mustard Seed Conspiracy
The Church in Response to Human Need (ed.)
Taking Discipleship Seriously
Why Settle for More and Miss the Best?
Wild Hope
Live It Up! How to Create a Life You Can Love

CEASE FIRE

Searching for Sanity in America's Culture Wars

▼ ▼ ▼

Tom Sine

William B. Eerdmans Publishing Company
Grand Rapids, Michigan

© 1995 Wm. B. Eerdmans Publishing Co.

255 Jefferson Ave. S.E., Grand Rapids, Michigan 49503

Printed in the United States of America

00 99 98 97 96 95   7 6 5 4 3 2 1

Library of Congress Cataloging-in-Publication Data

Sine, Tom.

Cease fire: searching for sanity in America's culture wars / Tom Sine.

p.   cm.

Includes bibliographical references and index.

ISBN 0-8028-3799-9 (alk. paper)

1. United States — Church history — 20th century.

2. United States — Civilization — 1970-

3. Christianity and culture — History — 20th century.

4. Christianity and politics — History — 20th century.

5. Culture conflict — United States — History — 20th century.

6. Evangelicalism — United States — History — 20th century.

I. Title.

BR526.S577   1995

261'.0973 — dc20   95-11722

CIP

This book is dedicated to my friends in the Evangelical Alliance in Great Britain for their single-minded commitment to the gospel of Jesus Christ, their participation in a faith that is both spiritually vital and intellectually reflective, their passion to see God's love extended into a world through both word and deed, and their determination to define their public policy positions from the study of Scripture instead of partisan political ideologies of the right or left.

CONTENTS

▼ ▼ ▼

ACKNOWLEDGMENTS

▼ ▼ ▼

This book would not have become a reality without the kind assistance of friends and associates. My wife, Christine, has given her tireless support and assistance in editing.

I am particularly indebted for the enormous amount of time David Virtue and Greg Cowley have invested in both researching and giving me feedback on the manuscript. James Skillen, Rodney Clapp, Robert Webber, Robert Clouse, Stan Grenz, Dale Soden, and Richard Pierard provided important guidance for the project. Richard Pierard also provided invaluable assistance in giving me feedback on the manuscript.

I also want to give special thanks to a group of readers, including Steve Hayner, Martyn Eden, Earl Palmer, Terry McGonegal, Jack Tench, Cliff Benzel, John Paarlberg, Karen Latea, Mark Cerbone, Gary Fenton, and Carol Luden, whose insights were essential to the final manuscript. And finally, warm thanks to my two sons and my mother for their understanding and support during this difficult project and to my friends in Alta Vista for their steady encouragement.

CHAPTER 1

▼ ▼ ▼

Searching for Sanity in America's Culture Wars

THREE ABORTION DOCTORS and eight aides are gunned down, and six are killed. More than 150 abortion clinics are firebombed. A church is vandalized by gay prostitutes. A pro-choice group calls for "massive militant action" against anti-abortionists. And a small but growing number of those on the religious right condone the shooting of abortion doctors as justifiable homicide. These in-your-face, take-no-prisoners confrontations have already led to bloodshed in our streets. The growing polarization, animosity, and violence in our society make Lily Tomlin's question chillingly pointed: "Is there intelligent life in America?"

A False Choice

"Culture wars always precede shooting wars," warns University of Virginia sociologist James Davison Hunter.[1] He's right. In any culture, increasingly shrill rhetoric, name-calling, and volatile confrontations always presage a growing level of violence — as

---

1. Hunter, quoted by Joe Loconte in "The Battle to Define America Turns Violent," *Christianity Today*, 25 October 1993, p. 76.

they have in Northern Ireland, the former Yugoslavia, Israel, Rwanda, and the horrific bombing in Oklahoma City.

We could be seeing the beginning of the same depth of divisiveness in our own society. We have a disturbing example in the abortion "debate." For years, both sides in the abortion controversy have been confronting each other face to face, sometimes trading punches. But now the moral contest has escalated to a new level of madness: activists are gunning down doctors who perform abortions.

Culture wars not only precede shooting wars but also provoke them. Growing polarization inevitably raises the stakes, first producing increasingly fiery rhetoric and then inducing violence. Extreme speech is inextricably bound up with extreme acts. Remember the massacre that took place in a mosque in Hebron in February of 1994, in which Jewish extremist Baruch Goldstein shot and killed twenty-nine Arabs before he was killed himself? One of those delivering the eulogy for Goldstein reflected the profound racial animosity that led to this brutal act by declaring, "One million Arabs are not worth a Jewish fingernail."[2]

After millennia of human experience — including the horrifying example of the Holocaust and other genocide in our own century — why haven't we learned that inflamed speech and the demonizing of enemies will inevitably lead to the shedding of blood? When culture wars proceed unchecked they do indeed become shooting wars. And Christians who buy into the inflamed rhetoric of either side might find their own fingers on the trigger. Apparently, a growing number on the right are actually arming themselves and joining the paramilitary movement.

On the one hand, many evangelicals, fundamentalists, and conservative Catholics are frightened by the rapid changes going on in society. They are alarmed by the breakup of the American family, declining moral values, and a growing disregard for human life. Many feel alienated and powerless either to voice their urgent concerns or to stem the menacing tide of change. It should not be surprising that many conservative Christians who

2. Rabbi Yaacov Perrin, quoted by Henry Louis Gates Jr. in "No Love for the Other Side," *Seattle Post Intelligencer,* 3 April 1994, Focus section, p. 1.

feel left out are attracted to Rush Limbaugh to be their loud voice of discontent.

Conservative Christians are feeling growing pressure to sign up with the religious right in order to resist unwelcome change. But they really seem to have very little awareness of how far those on the right have departed in both their agenda and their tactics from the biblical faith that the leaders on the right claim as the basis for their activism.

On the other hand, more "progressive," mainline Protestants and Roman Catholics are also concerned about change in society. But their greatest concerns are the escalating intolerance, violence, and injustice sweeping through American culture. Growing numbers of progressive Christians feel compelled to join the politically correct on the left in order to address more effectively the issues they care about. Many of them seem as blind as their counterparts on the right to the fact that much of the agenda and tactics of their accepted leaders contradicts the principles of the Christian faith they claim.

Choosing up Sides in the Shooting Wars

Protesters jumped out of the way as two middle-aged men scuffled past them on the lawn of a Wichita abortion clinic. The men held each other in a furious embrace, half of a pro-life poster wedged between them. Sweating and yelling at one another, they fell to the ground and rolled into freshly distributed manure beneath a laurel hedge.

Leonard Massey had lost his teenage daughter Brenda three years earlier after she had made a desperate attempt to end her own pregnancy. Traumatized by the loss, Leonard joined a pro-choice group connected to the United Church of Christ he and his wife attended. They wanted to see abortion made safe and legal so that other young women wouldn't lose their lives as their daughter had. The demonstration at the Wichita clinic was the first that Leonard had ever participated in.

Kurt Billings had spent three nights painting a sign for the pro-life demonstration at the clinic: "For God's Sake STOP 'Safe and Legal' Abortions." He had no sooner started walking in front of the abortion clinic with a group from his Assembly of God church than a man in a blue coat dashed out from among the pro-choice protesters and tore his sign in half.

Kurt grabbed his assailant with one hand and slugged him with the other, and they both went down into the laurel hedge. Someone alerted the police. Twenty minutes later, Leonard and Kurt were both having a new experience — being booked at the police station for assault and battery!

Christians of All Stripes in Search of a Third Way

As I travel the country working with evangelical, Roman Catholic, and mainline Protestant churches, I am finding that more and more people are feeling a mounting pressure to choose sides as the culture war heats up. The American church is becoming increasingly polarized — not by theology but by political ideology.

I am also discovering growing numbers of Christians from all backgrounds who are bone weary of the inflamed speech and polarizing ideologies of both the left and the right. They have no desire to side with either of the extremes or to get caught up in the unholy name-calling and mayhem that is terrorizing the public square. These self-directed Christians, from a broad spectrum of Christian traditions, choose to read their newspapers and their Bibles for themselves and to do their own thinking.

They are seeking a third way, looking for another place to stand and a new reason for being that more authentically reflect a biblical faith instead of a political ideology, right or left. Unfortunately, there is currently little available in print that enables people either to make sense of America's culture wars or to find an alternative to its polar extremes.

This Journey . . . Should You Decide to Take It

This book is written for those who are sincerely seeking an alternative to the extremes, some of whom are already caught up in the culture wars and want out. This is an invitation to both conservative and progressive Christians to discover a new biblical place to stand, one that rejects the political agendas of right and left and promotes responsible Christian engagement as we approach a new millennium.

Cease Fire is also written for those outside the church who are trying to understand this troubling culture war and the assumptions on which those in both camps are operating. Political commentators and the popular media alike have a disturbingly superficial understanding of the troubling assumptions from which the religious right is operating. Perhaps an "insider's" look might be of some help to these readers.

In this journey we will begin by looking at how both the far left and the far right have seriously misdiagnosed what's wrong and who the enemy is. And we will see how their misdiagnosis is directly responsible for their polarized political positions. Then we will briefly look at the future to which those at the extremes would transport us — and the tactics they are using to take us there. We will also predict who is likely to get the upper hand in this culture war and how the result is likely to shape our common future.

Finally, this book is a serious quest for a third way. We will offer an alternative critique of what has gone wrong and an alternative biblical vision for the future that has the potential to draw together Christians from many traditions. I will also propose some strategies for creative engagement that would, I believe, both honor Jesus Christ and make a bit of difference in our world.

Confessions of a Frustrated Evangelical

My own roots are deeply imbedded in evangelicalism, and it has been especially difficult for me to see the American evangelical movement slowly being politicized and co-opted by the religious right. One of the reasons I am writing this book is that I would like to make a small contribution to an effort to challenge this takeover and call other evangelicals to recover their heritage of genuine biblical faith.

Therefore, you will find in this book that I tend to be much harder on the evangelical right than I am on the progressive left. That's because evangelicals are family. I feel both a greater stake in their pilgrimage and a greater latitude for criticism, since it is in a sense self-criticism. And as a consequence I will devote considerably more space to the religious right than to the Christian left in each section.

A group of evangelical leaders shares my keen sense of frustration at the co-opting of American evangelicalism. Several prominent evangelical leaders, including Tony Campolo, have recently issued a call to those from all Christian traditions who are looking for a biblical alternative to the adversarial extremes of this culture war. This group is calling Christians to a third way.

Cease Fire is my own call to evangelicals across this country who are fed up with America's culture wars and the politicization of the church to join these leaders and speak out. We need to work together for the spiritual revitalization of American evangelicalism, for a reunification of the American church, for the spiritual renewal of America, and for the elaboration of a new biblical basis for engagement.

Before we speak out, we need to do our homework, to examine Scripture prayerfully and be very clear about the vision we believe the Bible calls us to. *Cease Fire* is the effort of one struggling Christian who, with much prayer, is keenly aware that he sees through a glass darkly. I don't presume that I'll be able to persuade everyone to embrace my viewpoint; my goal is simply to spark a discussion of how Christians of different views can come together around both the Table of God and the Word of God to discover jointly a new place to stand and a new basis for both hope and action.

A Word of Affirmation for Both Sides

Let me make it clear from the beginning that I wholeheartedly share the concerns of the Christian right about the disturbing rise in the number of out-of-wedlock births among teenagers, the growing pressures on family life, and the pervasive moral decline and secularization of American culture. Further, I applaud the efforts of the leaders on the right to bring issues of moral values, family life, and a sense of the sacred back into the public square.

I also share the concerns of progressive mainline Protestants and Roman Catholics about the alarming growth of the underclass in America, the pervasive racial and sexual discrimination in our society, and the mounting violence in our cities. And I support the efforts of progressive Christian leaders to call for a more just and tolerant society that works to prevent crime and increase opportunity for the marginalized.

So while I want to challenge what I believe are some very questionable assumptions of those on both the left and the right, I do not mean to question for a moment the integrity, motivation, or commitment of leaders on either side. My intent is simply to try to discover why each side is so adversarial by taking a good hard look at their largely unstated assumptions.

A Church and a Society Divided

As I have already suggested, I believe that most of the views and values currently dividing American Christians are rooted not in our faith or in Scripture but in secular culture and politics. These views, I would argue, have grown not out of our Christian heritage but out of the European Enlightenment, and over time they have hardened into narrow political ideologies. Mainline Protestants have often allowed the political left to define their agenda, as evangelical Christians have often allowed the political right to define theirs.

"It is unacceptable to expect the church to do more to address the escalating urban needs in our cities," insisted a denominational executive at a forum in which I had challenged mainline Protestant churches to get out of their buildings and join others in the streets working to empower the urban poor. "Our only hope is to see the Reagan administration adopt much more liberal social policy regarding the poor and the homeless."

Apart from the fact that this executive's response was out of touch with political reality (no one was going to persuade the Reagan administration to adopt more progressive urban policies), it betrayed a very troubling assumption — namely, that a liberal political agenda and the agenda of mainline churches were one and the same. The denominational executive strongly believed that it was the responsibility of the state rather than the church to address the growing human needs of our cities and hence that it was inappropriate to expect the church to be significantly involved in direct action.

My wife and I are evangelicals who also happen to worship in a mainline Episcopal church. I am very frustrated by the fact that many in leadership in oldline denominations seem to equate the most left-leaning agendas of the Democratic Party with the agendas of the kingdom of God.

When speaking in mainline settings, I often note that it seems as though some mainline Christians have an almost congenital need to be on the forefront of whatever cause is seen as socially progressive at any given moment — without regard to biblical mandate. And now some progressive Christians are moving beyond unquestioning support of liberal politics to an unexamined embrace of the ideologies of political correctness. This is likely to produce an even more profound polarization both within their denominations and within the American church as a whole.

On the other hand, just as many mainline Christians uncritically subscribe to a liberal political agenda and conform to the norms of the politically correct left, many evangelical Christians have uncritically bought into the ideological agendas of the secular right. Of course they are concerned about specific faith-related moral issues, too, but often these concerns are shaped more by apocalyptic fears about American culture than by Christian faith.

To understand the Christian right you need to understand not what they think or even what they believe. You need to begin by discovering what they are afraid of. Those on the religious right live in genuine terror of a liberal humanist elite who they believe are intent on laying siege to their families, undermining their faith, and collectivizing America for a one-world takeover by the Antichrist.

These deeply rooted fears motivate true believers on the

right to embrace right-wing political ideology with a passion seldom found on the left. Bombarded by propaganda, many have come to believe that the only way to save their families from the "sinister elite," to protect their faith, and to save America is to mount a militant political counterattack on their liberal foes.

Leaders on the right, for example, often speak as though abortion is the only pro-life issue. Pro-life activists seldom mention the fact that thirteen million children die from malnutrition every year. Some of them may consciously recognize that if they were to endorse a consistent pro-life ethic, as many Catholics do, and speak out on pro-life issues like world hunger, they couldn't blame feminists, liberals, and abortionists for the deaths of these children. It would become immediately apparent that it is political conservatives, not liberals, who consistently cut back humanitarian aid to help the poor help themselves. And it would also become apparent that the affluent lifestyles and indifference of Americans (including pro-life Christians) contribute to the tragic deaths of millions of children every year.

Part of the problem, frankly, is that many American evangelicals don't do their own thinking. Many of us seem to be content to simply follow our leaders. No questions asked.

Carl F. H. Henry, one of the most prominent scholars in the American evangelical movement, has stated, "We are in desperate need of a renewal of evangelical intellectual life."[3] Mark Noll, in his provocative book *The Scandal of the Evangelical Mind,* also decries the growing anti-intellectualism in American evangelicalism, quoting Canadian scholar N. K. Clifford: "The Evangelical Protestant mind has never relished complexity. Indeed its crusading genius, whether in religion or politics, has always tended toward an over-simplification of issues and the substitution of inspiration and zeal for critical analysis and serious reflection."[4]

3. Henry, *The Christian Mindset in a Secular Society: Promoting Evangelical Renewal and National Righteousness* (Portland, Ore.: Multnomah Press, 1984), p. 24.

4. Clifford, "His Dominion: A Vision in Crisis," *Sciences Religieuses/Studies in Religion* 2 (1973): 323; cited by Noll in *The Scandal of the Evangelical Mind* (Grand Rapids: William B. Eerdmans, 1994), p. 12.

Part of the reason for this pervasive and growing anti-intellectualism is that virtually all evangelical electronic media have settled for airing viewpoints that all too often reflect a superficial and culturally co-opted view of life and faith. The brightest and most thoughtful representatives of evangelical faith are rarely given access to popular media. Therefore, Christian radio and television tend to reinforce this anti-intellectualism instead of countering it.

The problem is particularly acute because the religious right has a virtual lock on popular Christian media. And they use it very effectively to reinforce a simple black-and-white view of the world, to play on people's fears, and to promote a very narrow political ideology which holds that to be a born-again Christian one must be a conservative Republican.

Many Christians have told me how upset they are that people immediately assume they are a part of the religious right when they identify themselves as evangelical believers. Billy Graham is reportedly finding it increasingly difficult to secure cooperation from mainline churches in his crusades because he is avowedly an evangelical. And in a growing number of instances evangelicals are finding it difficult to share their witness of Jesus Christ because it has all gotten tangled up in the politicized agendas of the Christian right. Somehow the call to a biblical faith has gotten lost in this contentious culture war.

An Aberration in World Evangelicalism

This politicized evangelicalism that is so serious an obstacle to the gospel witness in America is also an aberration in the larger international evangelical community. In Canada, Australia, New Zealand, Britain, Holland, or Germany you don't have to be politically conservative to be considered a born-again Christian. As we will see later in this book, evangelicals in these other countries are all over the map politically and yet manage to be quite unified in their common commitment to Jesus Christ.

While I was traveling in Australia recently, an evangelical pastor confronted me and asked, "Why do you Yanks seem to think the United States of America and the kingdom of God are one and the same, the flag and the cross indistinguishable? Do you really believe your country is God's special nation?"

Stuart McAllister, general secretary for the European Evangelical Alliance, expressed his concern regarding American evangelicalism in a letter: "My fear in the U.S. scene is the Christianization of America and the politicization of the church. There is a marked intolerance from those on the right, and a certain naivety regarding the role of the market to solve all ills and an uncritical acceptance of the consumer society. I also fear the power agenda and the message that seems to come over at times that righteousness can be imposed by state power. I am grieved that winning the lost and building credibility is not higher on the agenda."

Clive Calver, the president of the Evangelical Alliance in Britain, wrote that "the rise of the religious right . . . has caused a grave concern here in the U.K. We have long sought to develop a partnership between those on the right and left of evangelicals. . . . In fact our Chancellor of the Exchequer Rt. Hon. Kenneth Clarks once commented to me — 'Clive, one minute you are talking to me about social issues, the next moment on moral ones. What are you evangelicals? Are you right wing or left wing?' My answer was that we are both! It is the perspective that we need to see highlighted here in the U.K."

Brian Hathaway, one of the leading evangelicals in New Zealand, stated, "One of my observations of the U.S.A. religious scene is that the fences are very high between the various Christian streams. . . . This is not true in smaller countries like New Zealand, Australia or the United Kingdom where there is much greater cooperation across the Body of Christ. There is a tendency within the U.S.A. to think all good ideas originate from within the country, that the U.S.A. has little to learn from the rest of the world. . . ."

Hathaway is right. We American evangelicals have much to learn from Christians in other parts of the world who haven't been co-opted by political ideologies of either the right or the left. I have found evangelicals in other countries to be more reflective, more committed to the importance of Scripture, and more determined to work with the whole church.

Before we look further at the political ideologies of the left and right, I think it might help to reflect briefly on the recent history of the growing polarization in the American church. What has transpired in recent decades to draw so many evangelical and progressive Christians into these two divergent ideological camps?

Looking Backward — Evangelicals and Billy Graham

I jumped to my feet, dropping my magazine, portfolio, and schedule book on the floor as Billy Graham walked in. I had just completed a presentation at the Murdock Charitable Trust in Vancouver, Washington, and was in the waiting room when Graham and his son Franklin unexpectedly arrived. Falteringly I approached them, introducing myself. Before me stood the legendary evangelist whom I had first heard speak in Portland in 1954. Dr. Graham was very cordial as I tried to gather my wits. It was a very important moment for me because of the esteem in which I hold Dr. Graham and the honor I felt in meeting him. Billy Graham represents what is best about American evangelicalism, and he has been the de facto leader of the movement for over forty years.

In the early seventies, Billy Graham, Wheaton College, and *Christianity Today* were at the forefront of the evangelical parade. In those days, following Jesus meant focusing almost exclusively on personal piety and private morality. Most evangelicals probably held conservative to moderate views on political issues, but political activism of any kind was for the most part considered beyond the scope of legitimate Christian concern. Some evangelicals were beginning to allow their faith to inform public as well as private morality, but, generally speaking, both American Catholics and mainline Protestants awakened to a broader sense of social responsibility before American evangelicals.

Catholics, Vatican II, and Social Activism

Catholic political opinion after World War II had a strong conservative bias. Francis Cardinal Spellman, the "American Pope," was intensely anti-Communist and suspicious of both the labor and civil rights movements. He was successful in rallying strong Catholic support for the U.S. war in Vietnam. During the sixties the notorious right-wing John Birch society reportedly received more support from Roman Catholics than from any other religious group.

In 1962, Pope John XXIII convened the Second Vatican Council, calling for the renewal of the Church in all its aspects. Out of strong Christian compassion for the marginalized and the poor, the pope challenged Catholics throughout the world to adopt a new level of social responsibility. "In documents condemning the sinfulness of poverty, war, injustice, and other social ills, the church puts its authority squarely behind the worldwide movement for social change."[5] It also called for the liturgical renewal of the church and the rediscovery of the church as the community of the people of God.

After John F. Kennedy became the thirty-fifth president of the United States, the climate in American Catholicism began to change. Many young priests and nuns joined the civil rights and antipoverty movements. They did so often without the approval of older, more conservative leaders. After Vatican II, a new generation of American Catholic bishops began to speak out on a broad range of social, economic, and political issues.

In 1986 the bishops' pastoral letter *Economic Justice for All: Catholic Social Teaching and the U.S. Economy* introduced a fresh perspective and set the bishops on the way to bringing Scripture to bear on a number of other social issues, including public morality and the value of human life.[6] They remain very actively involved in the pro-life movement today, but they are now challenging conservative Protestants to join them in adopting a consistent pro-life ethic, speaking out for human life imperiled by hunger, violence, and unjust economic policies as well as by abortion.

A strong conservative element within American Catholicism endorses the Church's pro-life and pro-morality positions but

5. Kenneth D. Wald, *Religion and Politics in the United States*, 2d ed. (Washington: CQ Press, 1992), p. 285.
6. See Wald, *Religion and Politics in the United States*, pp. 292-93.

adamantly opposes some of its other political and economic agendas. This group includes such people as Richard Neuhaus, Pat Buchanan, and William Bennett, who are trying to establish a broader coalition with the Protestant right on the basis of shared civic rather than spiritual concerns.

Nevertheless, the dominant view of American Catholicism since Vatican II, while embracing concerns for pro-life, family, and moral issues, is generally more progressive. As a consequence, and doubtless partially in reaction to the new activism of conservative Catholics, many progressive Catholics have begun to associate themselves with the agendas and advocacy of the political correctness agenda.

Mainliners, Social Activism, and Political Liberalism

During the fifties, mainline Protestants got so caught up in constructing churches for their burgeoning memberships that they gave little thought to social issues or political activism. Many oldline Protestants benefited directly from the postwar economic boom, and they tended to be relatively conservative in their political outlook.

When the civil rights movement fired up in the sixties, however, it stirred the consciences of many mainliners, particularly clergy. A number of pastors and some laity got involved in fighting racism, protesting against the Vietnam war, and launching urban ministries to assist the poor. They were determined to give their faith compassionate expression, and many did.

In the eighties there was a resurgence of interest by denominational leaders in a broad spectrum of economic and political issues. This time their activism was expressed less on the streets than through a number of denominational resolutions, including the United Church of Christ's 1987 "Christian Faith and Economic Life" statement, the Presbyterian Church (USA)'s 1984 "Christian Faith and Economic Justice" statement, and the United Methodists' 1988 "Resolution on Economic Justice."

These documents reflect a growing inclination on the part of the mainline churches to seek to secure the ends of biblical justice through liberal political strategies. In fact, it is becoming increasingly difficult to distinguish the political agenda of many mainline Protestants from the political agenda of the liberal edge of the Democratic Party. Many of their views are hardening into the sort of doctrinaire political correctness that can only perpetuate and escalate the culture wars.

Evangelicals Wake Up to Social Responsibility

In the early seventies, evangelicals finally woke up to the urgent social issues that mainline Protestants and Catholics had begun responding to in the sixties. In 1973 a group of evangelical leaders convened in Chicago to reawaken in evangelicals the sort of social responsibility that had been common among their predecessors in pre–Civil War America.

Out of this convention came the "Chicago Declaration of Evangelical Social Concern," which sounded a call for repentance: "We acknowledge that God requires justice. But we have not proclaimed or demonstrated his justice to an unjust American society. Although the Lord calls us to defend the social and economic rights of the poor and the oppressed, we have mostly remained silent." The statement goes on to deplore the complicity of evangelical Christians in racism, militarism, and sexism. It not only stirred a vigorous discussion among evangelicals but also opened a new dialogue with ecumenical church leaders.[7]

For virtually the first time, American evangelicals joined Roman Catholics and mainline Protestants in discussing how our Christian faith can enable us to engage the issues of our times responsibly. In the seventies, evangelicals began examining a broad range of issues from the nuclear arms race and the civil rights movement, abortion, and urban poverty.

Billy Graham was one of a number of evangelical leaders who began reevaluating his political views. During this period of ferment, he came out forthrightly against the nuclear arms race

7. See Ronald J. Sider, *One-Sided Christianity? Uniting the Church to Heal a Lost and Broken World* (Grand Rapids: Zondervan, 1993), p. 19.

and he conducted preaching tours inside the Soviet Union, both at the expense of the support of many of his more conservative backers.

Then, seemingly out of nowhere, in the late seventies the religious right appeared and hijacked the evangelical movement. Jerry Falwell, Jimmy Swaggart, Pat Robertson, Tim La Haye, the Moral Majority, the Religious Roundtable, and a host of others took over the evangelical parade and detoured it sharply to the right. It was an intellectual takeover from which American evangelicalism has never recovered.

Initially, in spite of repeated warnings from Charles Colson, a former member of the Nixon White House, the leaders of the religious right sought to court those with political power. They won the full attention of the Reagan and Bush administrations, which warmly welcomed their support. In retrospect, most analysts concur that the new relationship was largely one-sided: while the religious right did much good for the Republican cause, they actually received very little in return in the form of the advancement of their central political concerns, including the restriction of abortion rights and the promotion of school prayer.

During the same time that the religious right was having its way with American evangelicalism and the Republican Party was having its way with the religious right, there were signals of problems on the liberal left. In contradiction to the claims of the political right, I believe we are seeing today the eclipse of political liberalism and the resurgence of an angry political conservatism.

But the left has not disappeared. The growing activism of a more radical feminist movement, the emergence of an active gay and lesbian coalition, the promotion of racial separatism on our campuses, and even the appearance of militant animal rights activists are all evidences of a new generation of radicals who are intent on promoting dramatic change in American culture.

Not surprisingly, a few of those committed to radical political change have moved into strategic positions in some of the mainline Protestant and Catholic churches. While their numbers are few, a growing emphasis on their brand of political activism and sensibilities is spreading though many of the more progressive Protestant and Catholic churches.

Toward the end of the eighties, the unexpected end of the cold war brought an immediate and dramatic drop in support and interest in conservative causes. Without the threat of the "Evil Empire," the conservative mission began to lose some urgency.

"We seem to be embarking on a new era," I wrote in 1990. "Ronald Reagan is back on the ranch. The Moral Majority has quietly folded its tents and slipped away. Falwell has gone back to preaching at Liberty Baptist, and Pat Robertson has his old job back on *The 700 Club* T.V. show." But, I added, "it would be a mistake to assume that the influence of the religious right is behind us."[8]

Indeed, the election of Bill Clinton gave dramatic new life to the conservative movement. By unintentionally pushing the religious right's hot buttons on such issues as abortion and gays in the military, President Clinton gave the movement exactly what it needed: a new enemy. Once again there is furious propagandizing on the Christian right about a liberal elite that wants to socialize America.

The most visible part of this reborn conservative movement is Pat Robertson's Christian Coalition. Since it was founded in October 1989, this organization dedicated to conservative political action has reportedly garnered a mailing list of over 30 million and an active membership of over 1.5 million and is growing rapidly. Having learned from the failure of the religious right during the eighties to shape national policy from Washington, D.C., the Christian Coalition shifted its focus to influencing politics on the local level. "Ralph Reed, the executive director of the Christian Coalition, has talked of 'shimmying along on our bellies' to get votes at the grass-roots. Randall Terry, the leader of Operation Rescue, stages holy mayhem outside abortion clinics. Both agree that their best policy is to struggle at street level, and leave national politics to look after itself" — at least until after the 1994 Republican takeover of Congress.[9]

The methods by which the Coalition has sought to extend

8. Sine, *Wild Hope* (Dallas: Word Books, 1991), p. 130.
9. "The Godly Right Gears Up," *The Economist*, 5 December 1992, p. 25.

 17

its influence have been controversial, especially its efforts to elect candidates to local political office. The *New York Times* calls the Coalition a "Christian stealth movement" because its candidates for elective office often don't reveal the real nature of their political agenda until after they are elected. Not surprisingly, this tactic is causing serious polarization in local communities, on school boards, and within local precincts of the Republican Party.

For example, the Coalition recently captured a majority presence on a five-seat school board in Vista, California, by securing the election of three candidates. Once in office, the Coalition-aligned officers split the board and caused a furor in the community. For one thing, they made it clear that they viewed the other board members to be part of a liberal conspiracy. "I know they don't look kindly on me," said liberal trustee Sandee Carter. "In fact, they think I am Satan's messenger."[10]

On July 14, 1994, a group of progressive religious leaders from mainline Protestant, Catholic, and Jewish backgrounds announced the formation of the Interfaith Alliance "to combat . . . the intolerant view of the religious radical right."[11] The next day, in a joint interview with Ralph Reed on CNN, Joan Campbell, a spokesperson for the Interfaith Alliance, strongly denounced the extremism of the religious right.

"I have no idea of who Rev. Campbell is talking about," Reed responded calmly. "The Christian Coalition is a mainstream political organization that is simply speaking out for those issues that most Americans genuinely care about."

Obviously unprepared for the Coalition's claim to be a moderate organization and Reed's professionally smooth manner, Campbell was left speechless. She abandoned her offensive against the religious right's agenda and tactics and fell back to a defense of the values that the Interfaith Alliance stood for — "inclusivity and diversity." Round one went to Reed and the Christian Coalition, hands down. The new Interfaith Alliance was

10. Carter, quoted by Stryker McGuire in "When Fundamentalists Run the Schools," *Newsweek*, 8 November 1993, p. 46.
11. "Clerics Form Anti-Rightist Coalition," *Seattle Post-Intelligencer*, 15 July 1994, p. A3.

clearly outmatched. I seriously doubt that the religious right can most effectively be challenged by frontal assaults from the progressive left.

Introducing the Contenders

As we stand at the threshold of the twenty-first century, we are confronted with two stridently ideological movements in the American church, each claiming that it correctly defines the ills of society and that it alone can offer the only remedy for our full restoration. I want to give you a brief snapshot of what political correctness looks like to those on both ends of the spectrum before we proceed to examine their assumptions and agendas in more depth.

James Davison Hunter tends to see those on the politically correct left as a relatively monolithic group, all working very much for the same cause. Many on the religious right go even further than this, viewing their opponents on the left as a tightly organized conspiratorial elite working for a clearly defined Satanic mission.

But in fact the various identifiable segments of the left — including radical feminists, the most committed defenders of multiculturalism, radical ecologists, and the gay and lesbian coalition — have never been able to agree on a common agenda. Even within these segments there is often a lack of consensus. The feminist movement, for instance, has become badly splintered over the past decade, and its leaders have gone off in many different directions.

The only things that groups on the left seem to have in common are that they value progressive change that will benefit their particular constituencies (often at some cost to others). And they tend to disparage those who do not agree with them as "neanderthals of insensitivity." But even if these groups are wide ranging and uncohesive, for the purposes of this discussion we will refer to them collectively as the left. And I will use terms like "the p.c. left" and "the radical left" interchangeably.

While there are some differences among various groups on

the religious right, they tend to be much more homogeneous in both their critique and their agenda than the activists on the left. In describing them, I use such terms as "the religious right," "Christian right," and "ideological conservatives" interchangeably.

In This Corner: Political Correctness on the Left

Over the past decade, many of the new groups on the left have come to define themselves not only as outsiders but also as the victims of a male-dominated, Eurocentric, heterosexual, and even anthropocentric world. Like the religious right, they find it useful to stress their status as victims.

Many of those in the splintered groups on the left took up their cause as advocates of diversity on our campuses and inclusivity in our society because they felt that these issues represented the highest principles of a democratic society. Inspired by their principles, they wanted to get in the ball game to promote their viewpoint. Ironically, once they were in the game and had garnered a little influence, many of them became vocal opponents of diversity. Some fear that free and open discussion of some topics can itself become a tool of oppression, further victimizing already exploited groups and individuals. So they seek to police the speech and the actions of everyone in society — thereby producing the stereotype of suffocating political correctness.

When confronted by the charge that they are not open to analytical thinking and the free debate of issues, they respond that those advocating analysis and discussion are inherently oppressive, patriarchal, and "logocentric." As Henry Louis Gates, a black professor of English at Duke, has suggested, "Today routinized righteous indignation has been substituted for rigorous criticism."[12]

Among the chief demons cited by the politically correct on

12. Gates, quoted by Francis J. Beckwith and Michael E. Bauman in *Are You Politically Correct? Debating America's Cultural Standards* (New York: Prometheus Books, 1993), pp. 29-30.

the left are dead white European males (DWEMS), whom they accuse of having passed on a cultural, political, and economic heritage that is inherently oppressive. Western culture bears the responsibility, they charge, for having historically oppressed women, plundered the environment, promoted the genocide of indigenous peoples, and systematically dismissed the art, literature, and music created by women and people of color.

In one sense, of course, many of the *isms* opposed by the left deserve to be challenged. Christians and nonbelievers alike have a moral obligation to oppose racism, sexism, ageism, and other forms of bigotry and discrimination. But the radical left goes beyond such opposition to advocacy of special consideration for groups who have been victimized in the past — thereby effectively establishing a new form of politically correct bigotry and discrimination. Some even oppose "speciesism" — that being the presumption that human beings have a privileged place in the biosphere; they contend that the human species has no right to dominate, oppress, slaughter, or eat other species.

The politically correct left would include groups like the ACLU, Planned Parenthood, NOW, and ACT UP. They all seek not only to sensitize the rest of society but to promote progressive social change that would benefit their respective constituencies.

Quite apart from seeking to promote politically correct speech and attitudes, members of some of the groups on the left have taken to promoting their causes in violent ways, too. Pro-choice advocates have subjected Joseph Scheidler, the founder of the Pro-life Action League in Chicago, to a beating and have shot his office windows out.[13] The Animal Liberation Front has claimed responsibility for planting a series of fire-starting devices in stores in New York City that sell furs. Various "eco-terrorist" groups have committed vandalism and provoked violent confrontations around the country. And ACT UP has taken the cause of AIDS research into noisy and sometimes violent protests in the streets.

Ideological proponents of the left have crossed the line in

13. See "Pro-Life Movement Struggles for Viability," *Christianity Today,* 8 November 1993, p. 42.

other ways, too. One of the most influential groups among progressive Christians is made up of feminists. Many feminists have worked long and courageously to educate the Christian community about the tragic effects of a politics of oppression. And let me be very clear at this point that I am a strong advocate of the full participation of women in all roles of church and society. I applaud the initiative taken by many in mainline Protestant denominations to open clergy positions and all areas of church leadership to women. But there are some expressions of feminism that raise concern even within the women's movement.

For example, some leaders within the movement assert that the oppression of women is inexorably linked with certain essential elements of the historic faith. They have in effect declared war on the historic Christian faith and come to view feminism as a kind of religion in its own right. Of course the Judeo-Christian faith originated in a male-dominated culture. But for many, even in the women's movement, this does not require the wholesale repudiation of historic faith. They recognize that all of our histories are less than ideal, and they therefore choose to build on the themes of liberation and transformation that are inherent in the Christian faith.

Christina Hoff Sommers has made an important distinction between two very different kinds of feminism, which she refers to as "equity feminism" and "gender feminism." The former, "equity feminism," remembers the gains that have been made by women in the past. "American women owe an incalculable debt to classically liberal feminists who came before us and fought long and hard, and ultimately with spectacular success, to gain for women the rights that men of this country had taken for granted for over two hundred years." Equity feminists essentially seek basic human rights for women and men alike — fair treatment, an end to discrimination, and equality of opportunity.[14]

On the other hand, the movement that Sommers calls "gender feminism" is preoccupied with a vision of the victimization of women and the domination of males. Sommers states

14. See Sommers, *Who Stole Feminism? How Women Have Betrayed Women* (New York: Simon & Schuster, 1994), pp. 17-24.

that gender feminists promote the conspiratorial view that males are consciously at work in America "to keep women cowering and submissive."

> The feminists who hold this divisive view of our social and political reality believe we are in a gender war, and they are eager to disseminate stories of atrocity that are designed to alert women to their plight. . . . [They] believe that all our institutions, from the state to the family to the grade schools, perpetuate male dominance. Believing women are virtually under siege, gender feminists naturally seek recruits to their side of the gender war.[15]

One of the major training grounds for gender feminists is women's studies programs in colleges and universities, says Sommers, and "all indications are that a new crop of young feminist ideologues coming out of our nation's colleges are even angrier, more resentful and more indifferent to the truth than their mentors."[16]

While I was writing this book I spoke at a major ecumenical gathering in Minnesota's Twin Cities. During a break, I struck up a conversation with an older Presbyterian layperson who seemed a little down in the dumps. In the course of our conversation I mentioned the subject of this book. He slowly began to open up. He shared his story with me haltingly, his eyes downcast. Six years before, his daughter had graduated from an Ivy League college. She had majored in women's studies, and she was radicalized by the feminist ideology there. One of the outcomes was that she hadn't spoken with him since. She still maintained contact with her mother, he said. But she had essentially severed all communication with him — simply because he is a member of the oppressive dominant male gender.

A small but vocal group of these gender feminists have become very influential in a number of Christian organizations and mainline seminaries. They are not only seeking to radicalize the church to support their feminist ideology but, as I will show,

15. Sommers, *Who Stole Feminism?* pp. 15-16.
16. Sommers, *Who Stole Feminism?* p. 18.

 23

are also laboring to fundamentally replace historic Christian faith with feminist alternatives.

The Response from the Right

Those on the right have those on the left clearly in their sights as their new enemy. Listen to Pat Robertson's characterization of the p.c. left:

> The tactics of these politically correct brainwashers are the tactics of the Gulag, of Auschwitz, and of the Chinese Communist labor camps. The propagators of political correctness (PC) may be Americans driving BMWs and living in five-bedroom homes, but they are idealistic totalitarians dressed up in academic robes. There is virtually no freedom of expression left on the campuses of our great universities today, thanks to the architects of PC.[17]

As we will see, both the polarities are given to this kind of overstatement when describing the other.

And in This Corner: Political Correctness on the Right

Michael Kinsley, a contributing editor for *Time* magazine, has provided one of the most incisive definitions of political correctness and has pointed out that it applies to those at both extremes: " 'Political correctness' . . . has degenerated into an all-purpose term of political abuse that means little more than 'a view I disagree with.' But it is meant to suggest a stifling orthodoxy, an intolerance of opposing views that verges on censorship, victimization chic and a stagy oversensitivity to robust remarks."[18]

Putting the best light on it, political correctness affirms our

17. Robertson, *The Turning Tide* (Dallas: Word Publishing, 1993), p. 154.
18. Kinsley, "Right-Wing P.C. Is Still P.C.," *Time*, 9 August 1993, p. 66.

obligation to be civil with one another in our personal exchanges and to oppose intimidation and harassment. Unfortunately, in the hands of ideologues, political correctness is used less as a shield to protect civility than as a weapon to strike down the free exchange of ideas.

Those on the right are as concerned about politically correct speech as those on the left. Borrowing from the horrific images of ethnic cleansing in the Balkans, the American Center for Law and Justice declares that "advocates of 'religious cleansing' will not rest until every vestige of religion is erased from the public arena."[19] This kind of overstated rhetoric is calculated to reinforce the belief that conservative Christians are the victims of a liberal conspiracy to silence them.

The p.c. right, like the p.c. left, are very noisy in their claims to be the chief victim in society. The religious right claims that it is routinely persecuted and excluded from the public square because of its faith. The leaders of the religious right work very aggressively to convince conservative Protestants that they are being victimized by the very elite who are trying to lay siege to "Christian America."

Furthermore, there is a stifling movement in the religious right not only to determine politically correct speech but also to exact politically correct behavior. A leading Christian radio spokesperson recently called an evangelical seminary president a "traitor" for his politically incorrect behavior. The traitorous act? The seminary president was one of the "Gang of Twelve" who had the temerity to meet with President Clinton to share their concerns and their ideas.

Rush Limbaugh calls his followers "Dittoheads" with good reason. He promises that he will take on the responsibility of doing their thinking for them.

On Fridays, I remind my audience that the weekend is coming. "The weekend is upon us, folks, so head on into it with aban-

19. The quoted text appears in an advertisement on p. 32 of the October 1993 issue of *Christian America*, which is published by Pat Robertson's Christian Coalition.

don. Relax and forget everything and have a great time. I will stay informed for you. I will devote my weekend to keeping track of all relevant events so that you won't have to. On Monday, if you're here, I'll tell you not only what happened over the weekend that was of any importance but, as an added bonus, I'll tell you what to think about it as well."[20]

Limbaugh dismisses this as a "parody of what elite liberals in the media do," arguing that his listeners are not robots, that they are able to think for themselves. But he clearly sets the agenda of what he considers it important for them to think about.

Leaders on the religious right do essentially the same sort of thing. They do not invite their followers to study the issues, search the Scriptures, and develop reasoned Christian positions. Rather they seek to influence them by distributing one-sided "fact sheets," presenting narrow lines of argument, and doing what they can to corral their people into their ideological camp. Leaders on the far right, like some leaders on the far left, are taking it upon themselves to decide what the important issues are and what everyone should think about them.

The p.c. right includes groups like the Christian Coalition, Operation Rescue, Concerned Women for America, the Family Research Council, and the American Center for Law and Justice. They all seem to be working from pretty much the same conclusions about who the enemy is, what's wrong, and how it can best be fixed. They all promote the notion that a small "cultural elite" composed of liberals, feminists, gay activists, and environmentalists is intent on destroying our families and undermining our faith.

The Response from the Left

In 1992 a group of gay radicals responded to the charge from the religious right that they are part of a cultural elite secretly running America:

20. Limbaugh, *The Way Things Ought to Be* (New York: Pocket Books, 1992), p. 24.

Although we would be the first to accept the mantle of the "cultural elite," we fail to see any of the alleged "benefits" that the traditional family values set seem to think go along with the title. Destabilizing the nuclear family, infecting the minds of impressionable youth with subversive thoughts, and influencing the course of western civilization through OUR stranglehold on all forms of media is a full-time job, and WE're not being paid nearly enough. First of all, WE'd like a better health plan, damn it. And how about that mansion in Beverly Hills, complete with hot and cold running surf punks and punkettes?

Come on. If WE were really running things the way they say WE are, the evening news and Sunday papers would be full of images of Rush Limbaugh and John Leo's heads on pikes. Jesse Helms and Bill Dannemooer in full Minnie Pearl drag doing the pistol dance. King George being force-fed broccoli. 24 hours a day, 7 days a week.

The idea of a queer takeover of the country's values is obviously a religious right smokescreen — so what are they really afraid of? A good time? Loosening up? Having a little fun, some self-respect. . . . Well, Pat [Robertson], WE're waiting.[21]

A Tidal Wave Coming Our Way

It's a fair question. What are those on the religious right afraid of? I doubt that most of those on the progressive left have any idea of the apprehensions, real and imagined, that stalk America's conservative Protestants. Like fundamentalists all over the world, many are terrified by the engulfing, unstoppable tidal waves of social change, modernity, and secularization. Not surprisingly, fundamentalists in traditional religions everywhere are trying to hold back the waves. And of course they are failing.

Fundamentalists in America are moderns, but they aren't modernists. Progressives on the left are really the modernists. They aren't trying to resist the wave of dramatic social change. They are attempting to catch it and ride it into the future. According to Marshall Berman,

21. "A Word From US," *ECCE Queer* 2 (Fall 1992): 1.

to be a modern . . . is to experience personal and social life as a maelstrom, to find one's world and oneself in perpetual disintegration and renewal, trouble and anguish, ambiguity and contradiction: to be part of a universe in which all that is solid melts into air. To be a modern*ist* is to make oneself somehow at home in the maelstrom, to make its rhythms one's own, to move within its currents in search of the form of reality, of beauty, of freedom, of justice, that its fervid and perilous flow allows.[22]

I don't believe the progressives are going to be any more successful in riding the waves than the fundamentalists are in resisting them. But I do believe that looking at the way the two view change does help us to understand a foundational difference between those on the p.c. left and the p.c. right. Those on the right are afraid of change and are desperately trying to find ways to turn the clock back. Many evangelicals undoubtedly join the religious right because they are afraid of dramatic societal change. Their concerns are certainly legitimate. As we will explain, there are other ways in which we as evangelicals can address troubling challenges, ways that are more consistent with the biblical faith that we claim.

And I am confident that the Christian left can find ways to work for social change that are fully congruent with their Christian faith, without uncritically embracing all agendas of the radical left.

In this book I have chosen a style that is both direct and somewhat personal and anecdotal. But I believe it is possible to be direct about issues without resorting to name-calling or invective. And I think it is even possible to have a bit of fun with the issues without demeaning those at either polarity.

In the first part of the book, we will look at the diagnoses offered by the ideological left and right as to what has gone wrong and who the enemy is. If we are to understand the two polarities and their impassioned advocacy, we must first be clear as to what

22. Berman, *All That Is Solid Melts into Air: The Experience of Modernity* (New York: Simon & Schuster, 1982), pp. 345-46.

their diagnoses are and what problems they are trying to solve. Then in the second part of the book we will visit the future to which both groups would transport us, to see if the destination is worth the trip.

SECTION I

▼ ▼ ▼

Demonizing, Polarizing, and Defining What's Wrong

"TIME IS SHORT! We must take immediate steps to abort a Soviet conquest of the United States! Write your congressman today and demand we dramatically increase the supply of weapons to the democratic forces of El Salvador," Pat Robertson urged the audience of the *700 Club* in 1984.

I listened, somewhat uncomfortably, backstage. The Christian Broadcasting Network had flown me to Virginia Beach to share some of my projections for the future of the church as we approached the nineties.

As I came on the set across from Pat Robertson, the lights came up and the cameras framed us together. Pat turned toward me, and, instead of asking me about my forecasts for the future as planned, he asked, in somewhat urgent tones, "Don't you think that's right, Tom? Don't you feel we need to immediately increase the U.S. supply of weapons to the Salvadoran military to head off a Soviet takeover of the hemisphere?"

I took a deep breath. "Absolutely not. Pat, I think that's the worst thing we can do. Frankly, I believe Pope John Paul has a better idea. He is calling for a total arms moratorium in Central America, asking all sides to stop sending in weapons so that we can work for a negotiated settlement."

Robertson blanched at my unexpected response and immediately changed the subject. Not surprisingly, I have never been invited back to the *700 Club*.

Robertson was passionate in his opposition to the Nicaraguan forces and his advocacy of aid for the Contras in the eighties because he was confident in his diagnosis of what was wrong in that section of the world and who the enemy was. In this part of the book, we will look at the assumptions of the religious right and progressive left concerning what's wrong in the world and who the enemy is. This is in an attempt to understand what lies behind the increasingly adversarial contention between these two competing viewpoints. I will try to show how flawed assumptions on both sides raise serious doubts about the validity of their respective agendas for societal change.

In this opening section we will attempt to understand how both the religious right and the politically correct left have defined what is wrong and who the enemy is. First, in Chapter 2, we will examine the power critique of the left. Then, in Chapters 3 and 4, we will return to analyze the apocalyptic critique of Pat Robertson and those on the Christian right. In the process, I think, we will discover why both sides have adopted such adversarial, polarized viewpoints.

CHAPTER 2

▼ ▼ ▼

The White Heterosexual European Male Conspiracy

"MALE AND VIOLENCE! Male and violence! Male and violence!" boomed the speaker system immediately in front of me on the grass. A lesbian activist was at the mike chanting her propaganda in a proto-rap style. I was in Vancouver, British Columbia, on a warm spring day in 1985, watching the final "performance" in the city's annual folk-life festival.

The woman on the platform went on to explain that the terms "male" and "violence" are virtually synonymous. She made abundantly clear her belief that all violence, human suffering, and wanton abuse on the planet can be traced back to testosterone-crazed males. Her message to all the men in the audience couldn't have been more clear: "Get off the planet, leave a donation at your local sperm bank, and don't bother to leave a forwarding address."

In his book *The True Believer,* philosopher Eric Hoffer insightfully points out that "mass movements can rise and spread without belief in God, but never without belief in a devil. Usually the strength of a mass movement is proportionate to the vividness and tangibility of its devil. When Hitler was asked whether he thought the Jew must be destroyed, he answered: 'No. . . . We should then have to invent him. It is essential to have a tangible enemy, not merely an abstract one.'"[1]

1. Hoffer, *The True Believer: Thoughts on the Nature of Mass Movements* (New York: Harper & Row, 1951), pp. 89-90.

Devils. The ideological left clearly understands the importance of devils. Despite their differences, the various groups on the left largely agree in their analysis of what's wrong. The problem is that power is not distributed equally, and those with more power tend to victimize those with less power. Specifically, people of color, women, gays and lesbians, the poor, and the nonhuman species with whom we share planet earth have been victimized by white heterosexual European meat-eating male capitalists. Whoever wields the power is viewed as a devil.

This can make things a little dicey, because we have all directly or indirectly been involved in the oppression of others with whom we share the planet. None of us is exempt.

Confessions of a LWEM

President Franklin D. Roosevelt began an address to the Daughters of the American Revolution with the words "Fellow immigrants." As Alan Bloom explains it, "Roosevelt was gently ridiculing those ladies for believing that in America old stock constituted any title whatsoever to privilege."[2]

But with title or without, the D.A.R. are among the most privileged people in our country, not principally because of their ancestry but because they are wealthy WASPs in a dominantly WASP society. Indeed, most whites have an automatic advantage over those in our country and our world who are not white solely on the grounds of the color of their skin. And LWEMs (living white European males) like me are a particularly privileged lot.

Having grown up white, male, heterosexual, and European in America, I find it very difficult to write this chapter. Like the Daughters of the American Revolution, my origins apparently go back to the earliest days of our country's founding. John Cribbs,

2. Bloom, "Western Civ — and Me: An Address at Harvard University," in *Are You Politically Correct? Debating America's Cultural Standards,* ed. Francis J. Beckwith and Michael E. Bauman (New York: Prometheus Books, 1993), p. 147.

one of my forebears, fought in the Revolutionary War and continued to serve in the military afterward. He was involved in what were euphemistically called "Indian clearing operations." On November 4, 1791, the tables were turned. In a camp pitched south of the Maumee River in the Ohio Territory, Cribbs met his end along with six hundred other militiamen in an Indian counterattack that has come to be known as St. Clair's Defeat, in honor of the unfortunate leader of the white troops, Gen. Arthur St. Clair.

My ancestors settled in Virginia. It is almost certain that they participated in the institution of slavery. I do not believe that I am responsible for the acts of my forebears, although I do assent to the truth of Jim Wallis's assertion that "the United States of America was established as a white society, founded upon the near genocide of another race and then the enslavement of yet another."[3]

Even if I am not personally responsible for my ancestors' behavior, I am nonetheless a beneficiary of it, whether I like it or not. Virtually every living American has benefited in some way from the land confiscated from native peoples and from labor derived from enslaved and marginalized peoples in different periods of our country's history.

While writing this chapter I visited the Civil Rights Museum in Birmingham. As I walked among the displays and viewed the video screens, I was plunged back into the savagery of white racism that was exposed during the civil rights struggle and the determined resistance of those who had been excluded. I was overcome as I viewed again the images of the snarling police dogs, the water cannons, the unarmed people being brutally clubbed and in some cases killed.

I was reminded again of how people who have a privileged position in society (whatever their racial or cultural background) will go to virtually any lengths to preserve their dominant position. And I was reminded again that white racism is still resisting movement toward a society in which all Americans enjoy equality of opportunity.

3. Wallis, "The Legacy of White Racism," in *America's Original Sin: A Study Guide in White Racism* (Washington: Sojourners, 1994), p. 8.

Growing up male in America, I nevertheless early developed a very high regard for the women in my family. My grandmother and mother were strong, loving, creative individuals who had an enormous capacity for both caring and hard work. Still, as I look back I realize that their options were severely circumscribed because of the times in which they were raised. My mother has mentioned many times that she would have liked to have been a doctor. My wife, a generation later, was able to realize that dream and become a doctor. That simply wasn't an option for my mom when she was beginning her life.

Many women in our society have suffered much more than limited options. They have been abused, raped, and brutalized. Liane Rozzell tells what it was like to grow up under the double burden of being both black and female in America during my mother's generation. In many parts of our country, women of color were not protected by law in those days. White employers could take advantage of black female employees with impunity.[4]

Today the legal protections may be stronger, but they do not suffice to provide an environment in which women can feel free from harassment or threats to their physical safety, much less access to a genuine equality of opportunities for employment and advancement. It is not yet an easy time to be female in America.

Other groups are also having a difficult time. Most of my generation took heterosexuality for granted. Sure, we had heard of homosexuality, and we shared off-color stories growing up. But for most of us it simply wasn't a part of our experience. In school it was rumored that a small group of guys on the football team spent a lot of time together, but I don't remember knowing anyone who had come out in those days.

In later years I have gotten to know a few people of gay and lesbian orientations. One of my most vivid memories is of a singles conference I spoke at in 1988, at a Lutheran camp called Holden Village. One evening in the main lodge, a group gathered around a fire raging in the fireplace began to share very openly

4. See Rozzell, "Double Jeopardy," in *America's Original Sin*, pp. 25-27.

and spontaneously the struggles they experienced with their sexuality. I would estimate that about a third of those who shared
were gay or lesbian.

It was remarkable how candid they were in talking about
such private matters with strangers. I still remember one twenty-
two-year-old gay man telling us that because of his Christian
commitment he had chosen a lifestyle of abstinence. "I have a
desire to be in a mutually caring relationship," he added, "but I
have no idea if that is a possibility for my future." No one
responded.

Most heterosexuals have little appreciation of the sort of
harassment that homosexuals commonly experience. One warm
spring evening in Seattle my son Clint and I decided to take in
a film. Clint was nineteen at the time and a student at Seattle
Pacific University. The film we wanted to see was playing at a
theater in the Broadway district, a neighborhood that is home to
a relatively large gay and lesbian community. As Clint and I were
crossing the street in the middle of the block, a huge four-by-four
pickup with a roll bar and oversized tires came whipping around
us. It stopped abruptly at an angle in the middle of the intersec-
tion. A couple of young skinheads jumped out of the truck and
headed toward us.

"You fags want to fight?" one shouted, fists already clenched
and ready.

"You stupid idiots," Clint shouted back, "this is my father!"

The two skinheads showed no sign of having heard him.
They kept taunting us, inviting a fight, and Clint, who had done
some boxing, was ready to go for them. I pulled him away, and
we managed to get into the theater without trading any punches.
But we were both pumped with adrenalin and livid at the outrageous encounter and the attitude that had precipitated it. It
was a brief taste of the sorts of situations that gays and lesbians
have to contend with all the time.

The privileges I have enjoyed growing up white, male, and
heterosexual have not entirely insulated me from the realities of
hardship around me. In recent years, I have been exposed to even
greater hardships in the world that lies beyond the borders of
America. I still remember my first trip to Haiti in 1976 — the

unbelievable poverty of Port au Prince, a mother with a child, clearly suffering from malnutrition, begging for coins.

On many occasions since I have been forcibly reminded that I live in a very privileged part of the world. *All* Americans, men and women, gay and straight, black and white, benefit from a privileged way of life that is unknown to most of those with whom we share the world today.

What's the point of this personal journey? I want to establish the point that I do understand something of the realities that have given rise to the social critique of the ideological left. I acknowledge that people who grow up white, male, and heterosexual in America as I have are among the world's most privileged, and that privilege has come at a very high cost to people of color, women, and homosexuals. But I am troubled that some of the most vocal activists on the left fail to recognize their own privileged status.

I am hardly alone in noticing this contradiction. Many people of color have rejected alliances with proponents of traditional liberal proposals on the grounds that the leftist ideologues and their proposals are sometimes themselves essentially racist and classist. Many women theologians refuse to call themselves feminist because they believe the movement has become elitist, principally concerned with issues related to middle- and upper-middle-class American women. And the residents of the slums of Haiti and the back streets of Calcutta doubtless find it difficult to give much credence to arguments focused on the plight of oppressed segments of American society.

But this, I believe, is one of the essential flaws in the critique of the ideological left. One cannot adequately explain what is wrong in our society solely in terms of who has privilege and power and who doesn't, because the calculus of power is always relative. Any given group will be able to cite another group more powerful than itself. Wealthy, educated, white American women who are vastly more empowered than most inhabitants of this planet can still rightly point to men as a class of oppressors, for example.

Therefore I don't believe the leftist critique is adequate. We simply can't explain all that is wrong in society in political terms of who has the privilege and power and who doesn't. While those on the left sometimes incorporate a cultural critique, too, the primary diagnosis is essentially Marxist. It revolves around the issues of power — who's got it, how they have abused it, and who needs it.

John Taylor has called the ideologues of the left the new fundamentalists. He describes them as an eclectic group including "multiculturalists, feminists, radical homosexuals, marxists, new historicists. What unites them — as firmly as the Christian fundamentalists are united in the belief that the Bible is the revealed word of God — is their conviction that Western culture and American society are thoroughly and hopelessly racist, sexist, oppressive."[5]

Historian Robert Hughes, writing about radical feminists, stated that "the Pope is only infallible part of the time, when he speaks *ex cathedra* on matters of faith and morals. The radical performance artist, in her full status as victim, is infallible all the time."[6] The same can be said of the radical feminist and other "oppressed" individuals. Those on the left take it as axiomatic that oppression confers validation. Ironically, the fact of being a victim grants one a special kind of power and status.

Leftists who buy into a critique that focuses solely on issues of power are seldom willing to entertain other moral questions, questions that relate to personal responsibility. Nor are they willing to consider a spiritual or religious critique of society. In fact, those on the secular left are often outraged by the assertion of the religious right that we are all accountable to the God who created us for our personal and moral behavior.

Like their counterparts on the right, however, the ideologues on the left have often demonstrated a susceptibility to conspiracy theories. Some radical African American leaders have attributed the incredible rise in suffering in the black community from drugs, AIDS, violence, and imprisonment to the machinations of

5. Taylor, "Are You Politically Correct?" in *Are You Politically Correct?* p. 17.

6. Hughes, *Culture of Complaint: The Fraying of America* (New York: Oxford University Press, 1993), p. 187.

a powerful white elite dedicated to the destruction of the black race in America. Some blacks have pointed to the Jews as the architects of this genocidal conspiracy. There are those in the gay community who believe that the AIDS virus was created and released as part of a heterosexual plot to wipe them out. And so on.

While the constellation of the left's devils includes white males, heterosexuals, Eurocentrists, biocentrists, and the like, the radical left seems, by common consent, to have fixed on the religious right as the archdevil. They have variously described their conservative foes as "Antiabortion Terrorists," "Homophobic Fascists," "Religious Coercionists," and "Right-Wing Hatemongers."

Of course part of the reason for the growing animosity is the recent increase in the religious right's use of confrontational tactics and aggressive legislative initiatives directed against gay and pro-life groups. But another reason for the hostility is the antipathy of the left toward religion generally. Many on the far left contend that religion has no place in the public square and are working through the American Civil Liberties Union and other groups to create a religion-free political environment in the United States.

As Stephen Carter, professor of law at Yale, points out in his watershed work *The Culture of Disbelief*, these efforts by the left are seriously endangering the constitutional guarantee of the free exercise of religion.

> When citizens do act in their public selves as though their faith matters, they risk not only ridicule, but actual punishment. In Colorado, a public school teacher was ordered by his superiors, on pain of disciplinary action, to remove his personal Bible from his desk where students might see it. . . . He was also told to take away books on Christianity he had added to the classroom library, although books on native American religious traditions, as well as on the occult, were allowed to remain.[7]

7. Carter, *The Culture of Disbelief: How American Law and Politics Trivialize Religious Devotion* (New York: Basic Books, 1993), pp. 11-12.

In other words, a number on the radical left tend to see religion generally and Christianity specifically as a part of what's wrong. Many view Christianity as a part of the patriarchal power structure that has marginalized those they speak for. But in their militancy they fail to recognize that they are in serious danger of undermining the free constitutional exercise of religion and that their increasingly contentious battles with those on the right threaten the very fabric of public discourse.

Progressive Christian Buy-In

In spite of the fact that there are those on the left who have no use for religion and would like to see it banished from the public square, many mainline Protestants and Catholics continue to feel duty bound to align themselves with any cause labeled "progressive." I have the sense, for example, that growing numbers of progressive Christians are buying into the radical feminist critique of what is wrong with society.

"All the baggage of patriarchal society will have to be thrown overboard," insists radical feminist Germaine Greer. "Women must explore the dark without any guide."[8] In their efforts to throw all the patriarchal baggage overboard, radical feminists within the church have embarked on the ambitious task of redefining the nature of God and the nature of the church. The most extreme of their efforts are threatening the very core of a historic understanding of Christian faith.

On November 6 and 7, 1993, over two thousand ecumenical Christians attended a conference entitled "Re-imagining: God, the Community, the Church," provoking a nationwide firestorm of controversy. Individual congregations of the Presbyterian Church (USA) all over the country collectively withheld millions of dollars in support in outrage over the denomination's partial sponsorship of the conference. This issue has largely been resolved, but the debate goes on.

8. Greer, quoted by Katherine Kersten in "How the Feminist Establishment Hurts Women," *Christianity Today*, 20 June 1994, p. 23.

The basic controversy stemmed from the fact that some radical feminists and lesbians within mainline churches provided the primary leadership for the conference and used it to promote an alternative view of the divine and of Christian faith. Participants were invited to re-imagine God as Sophia, a feminine name derived from the Greek word for wisdom. A follow-up report by the Presbyterian Church (USA) said the conference had used this term and other language "in ways that imply worship of a divine manifestation distinctly different" from a Christian view of the Godhead.[9]

In a celebration modeled after the Eucharist, milk and honey were substituted for the elements. "Sophia was blessed, thanked and celebrated and praised in language appropriately reserved for expressing the grace of our Lord Jesus Christ, the love of God and the communion of the Holy Spirit."[10] Evangelical church historian Richard Lovelace reports that one presenter at the conference "offered three goddesses for worship including Kali, the Hindu goddess of revenge. . . . Speakers denied the incarnation of Jesus Christ as a Savior 'from top down,' and recommended instead female human saviors who have worked their way up to godhead 'from the bottom up.'"[11]

At the heart of the radical feminist critique of the Christian faith is the assertion that the Bible is a patriarchal and anthropocentric book written by and overwhelmingly interpreted by men. Many contend that Scripture has served historically as yet another tool of a patriarchal church to suppress the aspirations of women. On that basis they categorically reject its authority. Freed from the constraints of Scripture, their re-imagining of God has extended from traditional theism to various forms of pantheism and polytheism.

Some have endorsed worship of Gaia, the great matrix, the mother goddess. Others have proposed worship of a variety of

9. Peter Steinfels, "Presbyterians Try to Resolve Long Dispute," *New York Times*, 17 June 1994, p. A24.

10. Joseph D. Small, "Re-imagining: A Theological Appraisal," Christian Faith and Life Program Area, Congregational Ministries Division, Presbyterian Church (USA), p. 3.

11. Lovelace, "Theology, Economics and the Future of the Church," *The Presbyterian Layman,* May/June 1994, p. 11.

fertility deities with whom they believe women can more closely identify. And yet, although these more radical feminists have clearly abandoned traditional Christian beliefs, they still want to promote their pluralism of deities under the banner of Christian faith. For many of us such a viewpoint borders on the incomprehensible.

I want to emphasize again that I accept the validity of at least some elements of the feminist critique. The Christian church has indeed long been a male-dominated hierarchical structure that has consciously excluded both the insights and the gifts of women. I am happy to see that this situation is now changing in most mainline Protestant denominations: women are being ordained and are moving into leadership positions. Growing numbers of women are moving into professional leadership positions in the Catholic Church as well.

But I seriously question the radical feminist belief that the cause of equality and the health of the church will be advanced by abandoning the church's historic commitment to the authority of Scripture to direct our lives and define our faith. When we reject Scripture as a basis for our faith, we cut ourselves off from any hope for consensus about who God is or what God's purposes are for the world. When we abandon all external authority, we are left to define reality solely on the basis of our own subjective experience. I would further argue that when we abandon Scripture, we abandon our best hope for finding a bridge that might unite the polarities and provide us a new place to stand.

Of course, while affirming our confidence in the authority of Scripture for all life and faith, we need to recognize the important challenge by some feminist, black, and Third-World theologians to do a serious critique of our hermeneutic. In many cases, that hermeneutic does uncritically reinforce the status quo instead of working for that transformation of culture we are called to by the gospel of Jesus Christ.

Increasingly the critique in more progressive churches of what is wrong with society and the church is also being defined by those who consider themselves politically correct. If this trend continues, the views of progressive Protestants and Catholics could be indistinguishable from the critique and agendas of the secular ideological left; any evidence of their unique Christian identity could also be lost. Moreover, as progressive Christians mute their Christian identity in an effort to be more inclusive and accommodating to their compatriots on the left, they inevitably bolster the accusations of the religious right that they are abandoning historic faith. In this way they contribute to the growing polarization and deepening split in the American church.

What's Wrong with the Critique of the Left

I believe that any objective look at American society will confirm at least in part the charge of those on the radical left that our society is indeed racist, sexist, and homophobic. On the other hand, I believe that any objective examination of history and culture will show that the abuse of power is not the special province of any particular group.

During the eighties, the Sandinistas righteously promoted their revolution in Nicaragua as a movement for the poor. They forcefully denounced the rich and powerful as the source of all evil. And of course they did make some progress in ameliorating the plight of the impoverished in Nicaragua. Today, however, many of the Sandinista leaders show signs of having succumbed to the greed they once denounced. Some have become both wealthy and preoccupied with protecting their wealth in ways that directly contradict the principles of their revolution.

The black-and-white worldview of the ideologue has difficulty accommodating this sort of problematic human behavior. Sometimes disenfranchised people wind up oppressing other people. And sometimes white heterosexual males wind up using the power they have to empower the weak. Those of us in the offending groups are far from the hopeless lot that some left-leaning ideologues assume us to be.

Taking initiative to get to know our ostensible foes personally often breaks down the easy stereotypes — on both sides. It might also help to deflate the sorts of conspiracy theories that seem to spring in quantity out of ignorance and suspicion. The world just isn't that simple or the power of a few that great.

The left's critique is also hobbled by its failure to take into account the transcendent and spiritual dimensions of human life. Marxist criticism pointedly omits such considerations as a matter of principle. And this rejection of the transcendent persists to a considerable extent even among post-Marxist progressives. But we are spiritual beings, and I contend that no critique can fully succeed that overlooks this reality.

Finally, many on the politically correct left have become so committed to a doctrinaire defense of their beliefs that they have unwittingly begun to subvert them. They are so fierce in championing inclusiveness and tolerance that they demonize all those whom they view as threats to those virtues. From Planned Parenthood to the ACLU, many of these groups on the left can't find harsh enough terms with which to decry their foes — particularly those on the Christian right.

Regrettably, this tendency is increasingly evident among progressive Christians as well. The newly formed Interfaith Alliance began its crusade for "inclusivity and diversity" not by seeking to build bridges to people on the religious right but rather by denouncing them as "radical right-wing extremists [who] have declared a holy war in America promoting an agenda of hate and intolerance."[12]

Isn't it time for more progressive Christians to set aside the highly politicized critique of the secular left? Isn't it time for progressive Protestants and Catholics who care very genuinely about others and their world to do their own analysis of what's wrong? Isn't it time that they draw on their own faith tradition and follow Christ's injunction to love their enemies? Isn't it time for those who are advocates of a more inclusive, tolerant society to reach out to more conservative Christians with whom they may disagree on political issues? Isn't it time for progressive Christians to sit down at table with their more conservative sisters and brothers and rediscover the faith that unites them?

12. This phrase appears on p. 2 of the initial brochure published by the Interfaith Alliance Brochure, 1501 K Street N.W., Suite 738, Washington, D.C. 20005.

CHAPTER 3

▼ ▼ ▼

"Late Great" One-World Takeover

"DON'T YOU REALIZE that if we start feeding hungry people, things won't get worse," the earnest young woman chided me. "And if things don't get worse, then Jesus won't come!" She was taking part in the question and answer period that followed a lecture on world hunger and Christian responsibility I had just delivered at a Christian college out West. I stood there, mouth open, flabbergasted, not knowing how to respond to this kind of twisted end-times logic. Over the years I have become increasingly disturbed at how widespread this particular viewpoint has become among conservative Christians in America.

In this chapter we will examine the religious right's notion of what's wrong and who the enemy is. We will see that their views are significantly influenced by this sort of apocalyptic filter. In Chapter 4 we will then explore how the religious right applies its end-times critique to our contemporary world.

While those on the left tend to base their critique on a sense of the past (histories of oppression and domination), those on the religious right tend to base their critique on their confident belief that they know how the world will end. Many on the religious right firmly believe with the same conviction that Jesus is the Son of God, that the Bible is the Word of God, and that the destination of the "late great planet earth" is a one-world Antichrist takeover. The beginnings of this profoundly influential end-times perspective lie in nineteenth-century England.

The Beginning of the End

From the earliest days of the Christian movement there has been speculation about the return of Christ and the end of the world. This ongoing conversation received a unique twist in the writings of Edward Irving, Henry Drummond, and John Nelson Darby in Britain during the 1820s.

John Nelson Darby left the established Protestant Church of Ireland in 1828 to join a new sect called the Brethren (which later came to be known as the Plymouth Brethren). Drawing on the writings of others, he produced a new theory encompassing the whole of human history from creation to the end of the world called *dispensationalism*. According to his reading of Scripture, God has related to humanity in different ways during different periods of history, or "dispensations." The chief inspiration for Darby's theory was Daniel 9:24-27, though working from that starting point he proceeded to find additional support for his views throughout Scripture. He taught that we live in the "church age," a "great parenthesis" between the first and second coming of Jesus Christ.

> One cycle of prophesied events ended with Jesus' crucifixion; the next will begin with the *Rapture* — the moment when all believers will rise to meet Christ in the air. Once the prophetic clock starts ticking again with the Rapture, the final sequence of events will unfold with dismaying rapidity for those left behind, beginning with the seven-year rule of Antichrist and the Apostate Church, the so-called *Tribulation* (Matt. 24:21), of which the second half will be sheer hell. . . . The Tribulation will end with the *Battle of Armageddon,* when Christ, the saints, and the heavenly host return to earth and defeat Antichrist and his army. Next will come the *Millennium,* Christ's thou-

sand-year rule on earth; a final, doomed uprising by Satan; the resurrection of the dead; and history's final event, the Last Judgment.[1]

Darby made several trips to the United States popularizing his theology of premillennial dispensationalism. He found many converts among Baptists and Presbyterians, and their numbers continued to grow through the early years of the twentieth century. As Paul Boyer notes in his insightful book *When Time Shall Be No More,*

> The premillennial message of inevitable decline seemed frighteningly apt after 1914. . . . [World War I] appeared to hasten the end-time geopolitical alignment prophecy writers had long anticipated. If a defeated Germany lost its lands west of the Rhine, and the Allied alliance continued in peacetime, wrote Arno Gaebelein in 1914, the latter could lead to "the predicted revival of the great confederacy of Europe" — the ten-nation revived Roman Empire ruled by Antichrist supposedly foretold in the Book of Daniel.[2]

Popularizing the End Times

After World War I, premillennial dispensationalism rapidly spread through the American evangelical community, arguably becoming the dominant view, at least among those who were aware of the distinctions among the various views concerning the second coming of Christ and the consummation of history. It remains a potent view in the evangelical and charismatic communities today, although it has virtually no adherents beyond those groups. Indeed, many American Christians of many traditions, including evangelicals, look forward with eager anticipation to the return of Christ without giving any credence to the dispensationalist interpretation of how the world will end.

1. Paul Boyer, *When Time Shall Be No More: Prophecy Belief in Modern American Culture* (Cambridge: Harvard University Press, 1992), p. 88.
2. Boyer, *When Time Shall Be No More,* p. 101.

Among those who accept this view, a considerable number of variations have arisen since the end of World War I. Hundreds of popular authors have spun out sensational predictions about the end times. By far the most successful entry in this genre is Hal Lindsey's *Late Great Planet Earth,* over nineteen million copies of which have reportedly been sold. As we approach a new millennium, there is a "doom boom" in Christian bookstores as prophecy pundits try to outguess one another regarding the timetable "of these last days."

Millions of predominantly evangelical and charismatic Christians not only buy these books but often uncritically buy into the highly speculative projections that they propound. We will show that many leaders on the Christian right are massively involved in this kind of end-times speculation. In fact, we will demonstrate how their entire analysis of what is wrong and who the enemy is is based on some very shaky assumptions about how the world will end.

Conservative Protestants got caught up in this great end-times guessing game because they haven't paid attention to what the Bible has to say about the return of Jesus Christ. The Bible teaches that there are only two reasons why we are told about the end times and "wars and rumors of wars." It isn't so that we can figure out the timetable of the last days. The reasons Scripture offers are (1) so that we will be ready and (2) so that we will be serving. That's it.

The last question the disciples asked the resurrected Christ in Acts 1:6-8 was the timetable question: "Lord, are you at this time going to restore the kingdom to Israel?" Jesus' response? That's none of your business. That's God's business. Your business is Jerusalem, Judea, and Samaria — the world. If we want to understand what our responsibility is for the world, then we shouldn't waste our time fiddling around with prophecy charts. We must ask a different question of Scripture: "What are God's purposes for the human future?" We will seek to answer this question in Chapter 9. In this chapter, however, I will seek to explain the potentially negative consequences of trying to figure out the events of these "last days" and of applying these speculations to contemporary political issues.

Politicizing the End Times

Virtually all the leaders on the religious right are absolutely certain they know how the world is going to end. Jerry Falwell, Tim La Haye, Charles Stanley, and Pat Robertson are all convinced that Scripture plainly teaches that the human race is destined for a terrifying collectivist future. Absolutely confident of their forecast, they believe they have the inside track on understanding world events. As a consequence, their one-world takeover scenario becomes their master grid for interpreting all contemporary political issues — often with dismaying and tragic results.

For example, Pat Robertson was keen to rush more arms to the Salvadoran military in the mid-eighties not merely because he feared for the future of El Salvador but because he was convinced that the entire Western hemisphere and indeed the whole planet faced a dire threat. He sincerely believed that the guerrilla war in El Salvador and the revolution in Nicaragua were parts of a Satanic socialist plot to collectivize the planet for a coming takeover by the Antichrist. Many of the other leaders on the Christian right have similarly interpreted world events in terms of this very limited end-times model of our human future.

Consider, for example, the perspective of the Christian right on the struggle of American blacks against segregation during the civil rights movement of the sixties and the struggle of South African blacks against apartheid during the eighties. In both cases a number of leaders of the Christian right characterized the struggling blacks not as victims of social injustice but as pawns that were being manipulated by sinister forces intent on collectivizing the American and South African populations for a one-world socialist conquest.

I am sure these conservative Christians would profess their belief that God's unconditional love was extended to all peoples. And I am sure they would affirm their instrinsic worth as image bearers of God and support their democratic rights as citizens to participate in their own societies.

Nevertheless, their apocalyptic presuppositions have so affected their vision that they are not able to see the legitimacy of the efforts of these peoples to secure official acknowledgment of that intrinsic human worth. And this despite the fact that the pleas for equal treatment were often made with specifically biblical argumentation by representatives of Christian communities. To the extent that the apocalyptic presuppositions of the religious right made them indifferent or antipathetic to the plight of their black neighbors in these two cases, I would argue that these presuppositions caused them to work against the purposes of God.

It is my contention that the Christian right's historical critique is largely determined by its view of the end times. And this view is in turn based on a questionable interpretation of a handful of verses in Daniel and Revelation. Let's take a closer look at those passages to see how secure a foundation they provide for this key element of the religious right's worldview.

The Foundation of Apocalyptic Presumptions

One cannot read Timothy Weber's *Living in the Shadow of the Second Coming* without being impressed by the many positive contributions that premillennial dispensationalists have made in the context of American Christianity. Dispensationalist leaders have challenged their disciples to take their faith more seriously and to become significantly involved in world mission.

My quarrel in this chapter is really not with dispensationalism. My quarrel is with the popular end-times speculators who insist on using their theories to explain contemporary political events and define Christian political advocacy.

With their popular writings, end-times speculators have reinforced the belief of many Christians, including most of those on the evangelical right, that the Bible speaks about the ultimate destiny of the human race with total clarity. They are persuaded that it unambiguously tells us that we are headed toward a one-world conquest by the Antichrist. In fact, a number of biblical scholars, including evangelicals, find little support in the handful of passages in Daniel and Revelation cited by the end-times speculators to support the one-world takeover theory.

The book of Daniel, written in the second century B.C.E., offers up a highly symbolic vision of four kingdoms. End-times theorists choose to read these passages in apocalyptic terms. Following John Nelson Darby, they believe that the author of the book of Daniel is providing a vision of the end times, describing the consummation of human history. This is decidedly a minority view among biblical scholars, however. Outside this camp there is a consensus that the author is in fact providing a symbolic rehearsal of events that occurred within his own historical time period.

Let's look at one of the key passages from Daniel:

> The fourth beast is a fourth kingdom that will appear on earth. It will be different from all the other kingdoms and will devour the whole earth, trampling it down and crushing it. The ten horns are ten kings who will come from this kingdom. After them another king will arise, different from the earlier ones; he will subdue three kings. He will speak against the Most High and oppress his saints and try to change the set times and the laws. (7:23-25)

Popular end-times buffs such as Hal Lindsey argue, with no substantial supporting evidence, that the fourth beast described in this passage is a fourth and final world-encompassing kingdom — a "revived Roman Empire" — that has not yet appeared on the world stage even in our day. But the end-times popularizers maintain that the arrival of this oppressive kingdom is imminent, and they eagerly look for signs of its coming.

Lindsey, for example, believes that the formation of the European Common Market and other efforts toward economic and political cooperation among European states may well be preludes to the arrival of the ten-nation confederacy that he says is predicted by Daniel and the book of Revelation — the vanguard of a new world order that will be headed by the Antichrist.[3]

Commentators from other traditions find no reason to impose an end-times reading on this passage from Daniel, however. In his commentary on Daniel, Robert A. Anderson maintains that it is most natural to read the passage not as a description of a

3. See Lindsey, *The Late Great Planet Earth* (Grand Rapids: Zondervan, 1970), pp. 92-105.

revived Roman Empire in the distant future but rather as a political entity contemporary with the author of the text. "The fourth kingdom (v. 23) is . . . that of Macedonia (Greece). At its height under Alexander the Great, and certainly from the point of view of a writer living in the small 2nd-cent. B.C.E. province of Judea, it did indeed 'devour the whole earth.' "[4] Norman W. Porteous asserts the same thing in his commentary on Daniel.

Nor does either of these commentators find evidence in the text to suggest that the evil king signifies some all-powerful Antichrist figure brutally ruling over the world at the end of history. According to Porteous, Daniel is describing Antiochus Epiphanes, a particularly blasphemous ruler from his own time.[5]

The other primary passage used to support the one-world takeover scenario is found in Revelation 17. Drawing on some of the imagery of Daniel, John, writing at the end of the first century C.E., paints a similarly symbolic picture, presenting fantastic images including that of a beast with seven heads and ten horns. Lindsey identifies this beast with the Antichrist and the ten horns with the ten-nation confederacy that he believes will take over the planet under the rule of the Antichrist.[6]

Nonapocalyptic readings of this passage vary, but few approach the level of specificity or certitude evidenced by Lindsey and his compatriots. Some scholars have identified the beast with Nero, who ruled Rome during John's time. Conservative scholar George Eldon Ladd identifies the beast with the Antichrist but describes its multiple heads as "successive manifestations of the worldly kingdoms at enmity with God through all the changes of history," including the consummation of the world.

As for the association of the ten horns of the beast with ten temporal kings, Ladd writes, "It is idle to speculate as to the identity of these kings, or to understand them, as some do, as ten European kingdoms or a revived Roman Empire. . . . It is very possible that the

4. Anderson, *Daniel: Signs and Wonders,* International Theological Commentary (Grand Rapids: William B. Eerdmans, 1984), pp. 88-89.

5. Porteous, *Daniel: A Commentary* (Philadelphia: Westminster Press, 1965), pp. 105-6.

6. See Lindsey, *The Late Great Planet Earth,* pp. 104-5.

number ten is meant to be symbolic designating the fullness of the Antichrist's powers and is not intended to be taken literally."[7]

Most of us who grew up evangelical in America after World War II were exposed to the dispensational worldview and never seriously questioned it. Much of our evangelical community simply had no contact with responsible alternative scholarship. We took it as gospel that our world was destined for a totalitarian takeover by the Antichrist. And we were assured by our leaders that we wouldn't have to worry, because God would rapture us out of this world just before the collectivist conquest becomes a reality.

> Garrison Keillor tells the story of a prophecy teacher who came every year to Lake Wobegon and explained the whole Bible to the "Sanctified Brethren" with the help of an elaborate chart called "The Course of Time from Eternity to Eternity."
> · "When I was a kid," Keillor explains, "I could look at that chart and feel that I understood all of human history. There on the chart it was perfectly explained and simplified. This wasn't anything I could have explained to anybody else. It was simply a feeling of utter certainty."[8]

I no longer enjoy that feeling of "utter certainty" when I see the prophecy charts. How about you? I look forward with a growing sense of anticipation to the second coming of Christ and the inbreaking of God's new order. But I am much less confident than I was at eighteen that I know precisely how the final chapter will be written.

But many of those on the religious right feel that they can't afford to be uncertain. From their perspective, they're betting their lives that they have it right. And they are absolutely confident that this is a trustworthy grid through which they can accurately analyze and understand political issues in our world.

They are constantly on the lookout for signs of oncoming socialist, Satanic, one-world government, for the arrival of the

7. Ladd, *A Commentary on the Revelation of John* (Grand Rapids: William B. Eerdmans, 1972), pp. 230, 231.

8. J. Ramsey Michaels, *Interpreting the Book of Revelation* (Grand Rapids: Baker Book House, 1992), pp. 146-47. Michaels is quoting from "The Wobegon Preacher: An Interview with Garrison Keillor," *Leadership* 10 (Fall 1991): 58-59.

Antichrist. In the context of this sort of vigilance and suspicion, it's easy to jump to conclusions about the significance of events — and to demonize those whom you perceive as enemies. But the track record of those who have sought to identify the "real Antichrist" is not impressive.

Will the Real Antichrist Please Stand Up

The apocalyptic biblical literature in Ezekiel, Daniel, and Revelation has fascinated and puzzled Christians throughout the history of the church. Many have seen clear links between the symbols in these passages and events and personages in their own day — links that have typically proved dubious to Christians of later periods.

One of the favorite guessing games during the past two millennia has involved the attempt to identify the real Antichrist. Many early Christians identified the Roman emperors (especially Nero) with this consummately evil figure. During the period of the Crusades, many nominated Saladin, the head of the Muslim forces at this time. Other Crusaders identified the Jewish people as a whole with the Antichrist and, with that justification, slaughtered thousands of them as they made their way out of Europe to the Holy Land to battle Saladin and his "demonic" forces.

Martin Luther publicly denounced the pope as Antichrist, and many Protestants followed his example in subsequent years, demonizing all Catholics. The Reformation period was also marked by several bloody peasant revolts against aristocratic political leaders who were identified with the Antichrist. Thousands died in these efforts convinced that they were fighting to defeat evil and advance God's cause in the world.

The early American colonists threw accusations in several directions. Some propounded the theory that Native Americans were in league with the pope in some kind of global Satanic conspiracy. During the French and Indian War, the French were nominated, and during the Revolutionary War, Britain's King George was often accused. For their part, many Russians were convinced that Napoleon was the Antichrist as his forces invaded their homeland.

During our own century, many have labeled Hitler the Antichrist. Some viewed his invasion of Poland as the first step toward the creation of the ten-nation European confederation. During the early years of World War II, virtually all radio evangelists were convinced that Mussolini was the real Antichrist. Who would make a better candidate? Who was better placed than a Roman to revive the ancient Roman confederacy?

Following the war, the establishment of the nation of Israel in 1948 gave birth to a vastly expanded body of speculation about the approach of the end times. Anti-Catholic conspiracy theories got new life with the election of John Kennedy as president. The evangelist Jack Van Impe confidently predicted that the Soviet flag would be flying over Independence Hall in Philadelphia by 1976, setting the stage for the arrival of the Antichrist.[9]

One author, Mary Relfe, undertook an extensive investigation of the "number of the beast," 666, mentioned in Revelation 13:18. She located the dreaded number everywhere from product codes in Sears catalogues to shirt collars imported from China. In the end, she reached the conclusion that the real "Mr. 666 is Anwar Sadat." The book in which she revealed the results of her investigation came off the presses just three months before Sadat was brutally assassinated (and book sales plummeted after that).

Another theorist noted that each of Ronald Wilson Reagan's three names contained six letters — 6•6•6 — but there was never much chance that the religious right would endorse the assertion that one of their own was in any way complicit.

Pat Robertson "guaranteed" that there would be a 1982 tribulation "sparked by a Russian invasion of Israel," preparing the way for the Antichrist.[10] Interestingly enough, Jerry Falwell also cited a prediction that the struggle between the Soviet Union and the United States would come to a cataclysmic crisis as early as 1982.[11]

9. See Russ Chandler, *Doomsday: The End of the World — A View through Time* (Ann Arbor: Servant, 1993), p. 255.

10. See Chandler, *Doomsday,* p. 257.

11. See Falwell, *Listen, America!* (Garden City, N.Y.: Doubleday, 1980), p. 104. Falwell cited the prediction of former Air Force Secretary Thomas C.

Even as the cold war wound down, the religious right remained suspicious of the Evil Empire, and for a time Mikhail Gorbachev's name was placed in consideration. As soon as the U.S. entered the Gulf War with Iraq, however, many leaders on the right switched their choice from Gorbachev to Saddam Hussein. Recently Jack Van Impe has suggested that the real Antichrist is Juan Carlos, king of Spain.

Reading the history of religious speculations about the end times leads one to ask, "Will the real Antichrist please stand up?" How in the world could religious leaders have missed the mark so many times and leaders on the Christian right still be so outrageously confident that this time they have it right? Particularly when these very leaders have been dead wrong in some of their own end-times speculations?

The covers on the early printings of *The Late Great Planet Earth* used to warn readers not to make plans for 1985. Elsewhere Lindsey was widely understood to be teaching that the world was due to come to a violent end within forty years of the restoration of the state of Israel in 1948.[12] After 1988 had come and gone, Lindsey extended the deadline to the year 2007 — forty years after the Israeli Six-Day War in 1967. As we have seen, other leaders on the Christian right have been guilty of the same revisionism when their speculations as to when the world would end proved to be in error.

This great end-times guessing game has become a major preoccupation of conservative Protestants. There is a huge promised ego payoff for the person who finally gets it right. *88 Reasons Why the Rapture Will Be in 1988* was a two-million-copy best-seller. I wonder how many of those who purchased the book asked for a refund in 1989. I suspect that, like those who play the lotteries, they are addicted to trying to win the big one. As soon as the next end-times salesman comes along selling his wares, they will be willing to part with their money to play the big end-times lottery game — just one more time.

Reed that the Soviet Union would run out of oil and push the world to the brink of war by the spring of 1982.

12. See Chandler, *Doomsday*, p. 251.

The Dark Side of the
Great End-Times Guessing Game

There are those who dismiss the great fascination with the end times as so much harmless self-deception. It's my contention, though, that it is often far from harmless. Historically, when Christians have taken the step of identifying some individual or group that they hate or fear as the Antichrist, this identification has often served as a sanction for escalating hostility and blood violence. So it was that the Crusaders in good conscience set out to do God's will by slaughtering Jews and Moslems. So it was that European Protestants came to persecute Catholics.

And the beat goes on. This ongoing attempt to identify the real Antichrist is still spawning racism, polarization, and conflict. In a chapter of *The Late Great Planet Earth* entitled "The Yellow Peril," Lindsey describes how "vast hordes of the Orient" are likely to threaten our future. In *Whatever Happened to Heaven?* David Hunt predicts that the Antichrist's apostate order will be based in the Vatican.[13]

I am convinced that the relentless and impassioned search for the Antichrist through the years has produced a tragic amount of racism, religious hatred, and violence. It both nourishes and feeds off the illusion that the world can best be understood in simple black-and-white apocalyptic terms — the powers of the Antichrist versus the powers of God.

A World on the Skids

Many sincere conservative Christians steeped in popular end-times fables genuinely believe that the world is getting worse and worse and that nothing of any significance can be done to make it better. Facing the problem of poverty around the globe, for instance, they are inclined to throw up their hands and quote — inappropriately — Jesus' statement, "The poor you will always

13. Hunt, *Whatever Happened to Heaven?* (Eugene, Ore.: Harvest House, 1988), pp. 174-75.

have with you" (Matt. 26:11). But Jesus was of course not counseling callous fatalism concerning the poor here. He was simply pointing out that the needs of the poor would outlast his brief time on earth. Because of their confident read on how the world is going to end, many conservative believers are convinced that this world is going to hell in a handcart, and no one, including the Creator God, can do much about it.

I sincerely doubt that many of these good people ever prayed that the Berlin wall might come down, that Soviet communism might collapse, or that South African apartheid might end. It is impossible for many of them to ever conceive of anything on that scale getting better. Their only hope for the future is simply to get a few more people into the lifeboat while there is still time.

What many evangelicals have done is to unquestioningly buy into this degenerative view of history and this fatalistic view of the future. I believe those who have succumbed to this brand of pessimistic determinism have little motivation to work for constructive social change.

In fact, in an article I published in *Sojourners,* I pointed out that for many of these folks, to work for peace and justice might actually be seen as working against the "destructive designs" of God. "Those who subscribe to this latter-day fatalism conclude that nothing can be done to alter the growing plight of the world's poor, change unjust economic structures, or advance the cause of God's kingdom here on earth."[14]

Even their comrades in arms in promoting right-wing political causes, the Christian Reconstructionists, strongly denounce this fatalistic aspect of premillennial eschatology. Gary North calls them "pessimillennialists." And R. J. Rushdoony, the patriarch of Reconstructionists, declares, "The rapture generation is the useless generation."[15] Frankly, much of the new vision for change on the religious right comes, as we will see, from the

14. Sine, "Bringing Down the Final Curtain," *Sojourners,* June/July 1984, p. 14.

15. Rushdoony, *God's Plan for Victory: The Meaning of Post Millennialism* (Fairfax, Va.: Thoburn Press, 1977), p. 51.

postmillennial vision and optimism of the Reconstructionists and directly contradicts this kind of end-times pessimism.

What I believe has happened is that the powers of darkness have actually worked through these end-times musings to convince tens of thousands of committed, educated, resourceful American Christians that they can't make any real difference in the world. In this view, even the Creator God is really impotent to effect any significant change on this side of the millennium. All God is allowed to do is bring down the curtain at the end of history.

Beware International Cooperation

One of the most disturbing side effects of this kind of end-times hysteria is the apprehension it evokes among adherents regarding any form of international cooperation. The founding of the United Nations in 1945 sent a number of these end-times pundits into an absolute feeding frenzy. They have described the U.N. building as the headquarters for world humanism, the center for a pluralist spirituality, and "the home of Antichrist himself." Charles Stanley maintains that the United Nations is proof of the Revelation prophecy "that the anti-christ will come upon the scene, there will be an attempt to have one world government."[16]

Given their eschatological certitude about how the world is going to end, these true believers are typically suspicious of anything international. In Jack Van Impe's book, *11:54 and Counting,* he lists three pages of international agencies including the World Bank, the International Monetary Fund, and the Council on Foreign Relations to demonstrate that a "new world order is on the horizon." He and his end-times colleagues are particularly fearful that these organizations will assume totalitarian control of the entire global economy for the Antichrist.

The Trilateral Commission is a particular favorite of the international conspiracy theorists on the right. The commission is a private organization of about 300 business and labor leaders,

16. Stanley, *Stand Up, America!* (Atlanta: In Touch Ministries, 1980), p. 138.

scholars, and political figures from the world's three major economically developed areas — North America, Japan, and Western Europe. Founded in 1973 partially through the efforts of David Rockefeller of Chase Manhattan Bank, the commission is dedicated to devising strategies for resolving problems facing the First World countries and for fostering better economic and political ties with the Third World. Among the Americans who are or have been members of the organization are former presidents Jimmy Carter and George Bush, former secretary of state Cyrus Vance, and former secretary of defense Caspar Weinberger!

Whatever the stated aims of the commission, the fact that it has brought together a powerful international elite to work for global cooperation has elicited the darkest suspicions of the far right. Hal Lindsey contends that the Trilateralists indoctrinated Jimmy Carter and then used their influence to propel him into the White House. In 1974 Lawrence Patterson started a monthly magazine to expose the Trilateral conspirators, and the publication uncovered the influence of "Zionist-Trilats" everywhere it looked. A sample accusation: "David Rockefeller and his friends . . . run the drug cartel from their luxury suites in mid-Manhattan."

President Bush was characterized as the "puppet of the international bankers" and of such "Zionists" as Alan Greenspan of the U.S. Federal Reserve Board and South African diamond magnate Harry Oppenheimer.[17] A disturbing number of those who subscribe to these end-times theories seem attracted to blatantly anti-Semitic explanations of what's gone wrong with our world. Recent trade pacts such as the North American Free Trade Agreement (NAFTA) and the General Agreement on Tariffs and Trade (GATT) and the associated formation of the World Trade Organization are being viewed as fresh evidence of the sinister global conspiracy.

Recently, speaking at an evangelical church in Oregon, I urged Christians to become more involved in supporting responsible international organizations that are working for the protection and restoration of the rain forests. Members of the audience responded in immediate horror. They were very

17. See Boyer, *When Time Shall Be No More*, p. 266.

sincerely concerned that participation in any kind of international effort to care for the created order would be a first step
down the slippery slope to a one-world takeover by the Antichrist.

As we enter a future in which the many peoples and nations
of the world are increasingly restive and in which all people face
increasing threats from disease, hunger, dwindling natural resources, and environmental pollution, the church of Jesus Christ
should be in the forefront of those seeking to promote international cooperation, democratization, movement toward the
rule of law, advocacy of social justice for the poor, and care for
God's creation.

But I am afraid many American evangelicals will continue
to actively oppose virtually any form of international cooperation
and indict Christians who do — because of their unexamined
commitments to these kinds of end-times phobias.

What's Wrong with This Picture?

Since leaders of the religious right have based much of their
critique of what has gone wrong on this end-times speculation,
it is time to check the foundations for rot and general structural
soundness. Indeed, not only their critique but their political
advocacy as well is erected on their confident assertion that they,
and they alone, know how the world is going to end. Let's check
it out.

I want to emphasize again that virtually all Christians —
Eastern Orthodox, Roman Catholics, mainline Protestants, evangelicals, and Pentecostals alike — look forward to the second
coming of Christ. Most Christians believe that Scripture points
to some kind of judgment at the return of Christ and a traumatic
birth process associated with the coming of God's kingdom. But,
unlike many conservative Protestants, most of these believers
make no attempts to figure out what the highly symbolic apocalyptic biblical literature means regarding the timing of Christ's
return. Concerning the end of time, they accept Christ's assertion
that "No one knows about that day or hour, not even the angels
in heaven, nor the Son, but only the Father" (Mark 13:32). They

are content to leave such matters to God. And they focus their energies on seeking to live out their lives with faithfulness and hope, ever watchful for Christ's appearing.

The dismal record of conservative Christians trying to puzzle out the events of the end times has led historian Mark Noll to comment that their efforts have "inspired the witticism known as 'Murphy's Armageddon Observation: Those who don't learn from the past are condemned to write end-times books. *Corollary:* God doesn't read prophecy books.' The sad fact remains that an awful lot of evangelicals still do."[18] Even more troubling is the fact that they insist on trying to use their end-times theories to understand political and cultural changes in our world and to chart a course for political action based on those end-times assumptions.

You see, the religious right has erected not only its entire critique of what is wrong but its agenda for setting things right on this apocalyptic scenario of a one-world Antichrist takeover. And, as we have seen, this scenario is based entirely on some very speculative interpretations of a handful of passages from Daniel and Revelation. What would happen to the Christian right's entire house of cards if this foundational assumption about how the world is going to end was found to be without support?

As we have seen, this particular end-times interpretation of these passages from Daniel and Revelation is disputed by a broad range of biblical scholars and commentators. We have also seen that predictions of specific dates and events based on an end-times reading of Scripture have been uniformly wrong in the past. What, then, are the prospects that the end-times theorists will be any more accurate about the future? Let's consider the real-world prospects for a one-world socialist government takeover.

Most political scientists today would argue that we are rapidly moving away from the likelihood of any one-world government. Growing tribalism, ethnic unrest, and civil strife are not only tearing the former Yugoslavia apart and devastating Rwanda, they are even driving many of the states within the

18. Noll, *The Scandal of the Evangelical Mind* (Grand Rapids: William B. Eerdmans, 1994), p. 174.

former Soviet Union to break away from any sort of confederacy. Communism is no longer a significant threat as a collectivizing force in our world. And in general the economic and technological empowerment of ethnic, racial, religious, and ideological groups is generating much more geopolitical fragmentation than unification.

It is true that new international networks, coalitions, and alliances are being forged as we become a more global society. We are seeing the formation of an international electronic network and an increasingly global consumer society. But Arab nations can't even work together. How in the world could all of our diverse nations be persuaded to cave in to a totalitarian, one-world takeover? Such an assertion is, in my opinion, neither based on Scripture nor in touch with the real world. I am much more concerned about the threats that are within our culture than those imagined threats from without.

I think it's patently evident that both the critique and the agenda of the religious right are built on a very shaky foundation. Jesus warned us never to build anything we want to last on shifting sand.

Can't we as evangelicals affirm that Scripture is indeed inspired yet admit, with a little humility, that our various end-times theories may not be? Can't we evangelicals enthusiastically look forward to the return of Jesus Christ while honestly confessing that we really don't have a clue as to how the Creator is going to play out the end game? And while Scripture makes it clear that God's creation is headed toward a traumatic birth episode and judgment at some point in the future, can't we celebrate the positive change taking place in the world today that bears the signature of the Creator God? Looking to the creating and redeeming God who promises to make all things new, can't we seek to become people of hope and compassion rather than people of fear, reaction, and invective?

CHAPTER 4

▼ ▼ ▼

The Russians Are Coming, The Russians Are Coming

"SEE, BY WIRING my sawed-off shotgun inside the door of my pickup truck, I can open the door and fire in one smooth motion," the old Texas rancher explained.

"Why do you want to do that?" I asked, bewildered.

"When the commies come," he responded in a hushed voice, "I'm gonna be ready for 'em!"

During the entire cold war, since the end of World War II, American foreign policy and our national consciousness were singularly preoccupied with getting ready for the commies. The Soviet threat stirred the deepest fears of the American people and largely defined both our view of the world and our sense of national mission.

Now, with the unexpected end of the cold war, many Americans have lost not only their enemy, but also their sense of national identity and mission. For over forty years the moral calculus had been simple and straightforward. The Russians were godless, and we were God-fearing. The Russians imposed a command economy, and we enjoyed a free-market economy. The Russians had Marxist-Leninist totalitarianism, and we had democratic freedoms. In the wake of the cold war, the United States has been struggling to redefine its identity and its mission in the new world order — with only limited success.

But I believe the leaders of the Christian right have lost far more. Not only have they lost their cosmic antagonist, the "Evil Empire," but they have also lost their entire explanation of what is wrong and how the world will end. This is a major loss, since the Christian right's entire agenda for societal change is based on its confident analysis of what is wrong and who the global conspirator is.

We have already noted that the leaders of the religious right are absolutely unanimous in their contention of how the world is going to end — a global takeover by the Antichrist. Most of them have associated the nations of Gog and Magog described in Ezekiel 38 and 39 with modern Russia. And they are sure that the way that history will end will be a Russian invasion of Israel. This will set the stage for the Battle of Armageddon. Following this great battle, the Antichrist will conduct a seven-year reign of terror, followed by the consummation of history.

Hal Lindsey is one of many who have specifically identified Gog with Russia. "We have seen that Russia will arm and equip a vast confederacy," he writes. "This powerful group of allies will lead an attack on restored Israel. However, Russia and her confederates will be destroyed completely."[1]

Jerry Falwell adds, "It is at that time when all hell will break out. . . . I believe there will be some nuclear holocaust on this earth, because it says [in Ezekiel 39] that blood shall flow in the streets up to the bridle of the horses in the Valley of Esdraelon for some 200 miles."[2]

Tim La Haye concurs: "Almighty God is going to destroy Russia's mighty armies by his supernatural power. Furthermore, he will send a fire on the homeland of Magog or Russia. . . . Russia will be almost entirely destroyed."[3]

1. Lindsey, *The Late Great Planet Earth* (Grand Rapids: Zondervan, 1970), p. 71.
2. Falwell, in an interview with Robert Scheer for the 4 March 1981 edition of the *Los Angeles Times,* as cited by Grace Halsell in *Prophecy and Politics: Militant Evangelists on the Road to Nuclear War* (Westport, Conn.: Lawrence Hill, 1986), p. 34.
3. La Haye, *The Beginning of the End* (Wheaton, Ill.: Tyndale House, 1972), p. 77.

Significantly influenced by the apocalyptic vision of the religious right, Ronald Reagan observed in 1971 that the leftist coup in Libya was "a sign that the day of Armageddon isn't far off. . . . Everything is falling into place. It can't be long now. Ezekiel says that fire and brimstone will be rained upon the enemies of God's people. That means they will be destroyed by nuclear weapons."[4]

Paul Boyer has persuasively explained why leaders of the religious right have long been stridently opposed to any efforts to work for a peaceful resolution of our differences with the Soviets and so unanimously in favor of escalating the race toward a global holocaust: they are convinced that we are in an "inexorable march to Armageddon" and that it is God's will that we continue moving in this direction. As television preacher James Robison put it, "Any teaching of peace prior to [Christ's] return is heresy. . . . It's against the word of God, it's anti-Christ."[5]

During the years of the Reagan presidency, the Moral Majority included as one of its primary points of "Christian" advocacy a massive military buildup to be ready for the Soviets. During this time, many leaders on the religious right characterized Catholics, mainline Protestants, and other evangelicals who were working for peace as examples of "Soviet subversion."

"The Russians are coming, the Russians are coming" for leaders on the Christian right reflected more than the conviction that history will be consummated with the Russian invasion of Israel. In this cosmic end-times drama, the Soviets were also assigned to play an even more sinister role — as Satanic agents working to subvert and collectivize the planet for the Antichrist.

Prophecy author John Walvoord, for instance, argued that "the ultimate Soviet threat" had less to do with military power than ideological subversion. Communism, says Walvoord, is "a

4. Reagan, quoted by Paul Boyer in *When Time Shall Be No More: Prophecy Belief in Modern American Culture* (Cambridge: Harvard University Press, 1992), p. 142.

5. Robison, quoted by Boyer in *When Time Shall Be No More*, p. 145.

movement based upon blasphemy against God" that anticipates the demonic one-world religion of the Antichrist.[6]

As Michael Lienesch has suggested, the religious right has long believed that "communism must be fought on every front. Given its dedication to world domination, its expansion must be checked constantly and in every part of the world. Moreover, containment is not enough; because communism is an ideology, it respects no boundaries and must be confronted and defeated both politically and philosophically."[7]

In other words, leaders on the religious right were convinced that the Evil Empire was the agent that Satan planned to use to collectivize the planet for the reign of the Antichrist. And these leaders, over the years, have convinced their followers that this was indeed the way the world would end. As a consequence, it would be difficult to exaggerate the feeling of fear, antagonism, and loathing that many conservative Protestants developed toward the Soviet Union.

Given the cosmic Satanic role assigned to the former U.S.S.R., it isn't difficult to understand why leaders of the religious right have been so totally confounded by the unexpected end of the cold war. They were so sure they had it right. For years they have been able to rally support for most any right-wing cause simply by riding through the streets shouting "The Russians are coming, the Russians are coming!"

It is incomprehensible to many leaders on the Christian right that they could have been so wrong about (1) who their global enemy was — the "Evil Empire," (2) what was wrong — the Marxist-Leninist plan to collectivize the planet for the Antichrist, and (3) how the world would end — with a Russian invasion of Israel, to set the stage for the end of history and the reign of God.

I suspect that Hal Lindsey might have an extremely difficult time persuading Boris Yeltsin or his successor to invade Israel to set the stage for Armageddon and the end of the world. Regardless

6. Walvoord, quoted by Boyer in *When Time Shall Be No More*, p. 165.
7. Lienesch, *Redeeming America: Piety and Politics in the New Christian Right* (Chapel Hill, N.C.: University of North Carolina Press, 1993), p. 215.

of who rules Russia, you don't have to be a political scientist to realize that it simply wouldn't be in Russia's self-interest to pursue such an insane course of action.

Instead of coming to terms with the stark reality that those on the right were dead wrong about the Soviet role in their end-times scenario, a number have chosen the course of massive denial.

For example, in the last months preceding the breakup of the Soviet Union, long after a consensus had emerged among Western political analysts that the reform process there was irreversible, I heard Pat Robertson tell his *700 Club* audience that *glasnost* and *perestroika* were in fact parts of a KGB plot to take over America. In his 1990 book *The New Millennium,* after dutifully reporting changes in Russia, Robertson asks his readers, "Could the entire scenario be nothing but a KGB ruse conceived by the master, Yuri Andropov?"[8]

The cover of the magazine of the John Hagee ministries for March/April 1994 has the headline "Red Star over Bethlehem." Inside, Hagee suggests that the real Antichrist may very well be Russia's right-wing nationalist leader Vladimir Zhirinovsky. Hanging on tenaciously to the old end-times script, Hagee insists that

> Russia will lead five armies in a massive attack against the nation of Israel. . . . I believe that in the near future, and I mean near future, there is going to be a surprise attack on the nation of Israel launched from Russia. . . . The attack will come after Israel signs a seven-year peace treaty sponsored by the West. . . . After this Russian led battle in Israel, the anti-Christ, sponsored by the European Common Market, will rush into the political vacuum and become a worldwide dictator.[9]

Hagee is not about to let Russia off the hook. The Russians have to play their assigned role in this apocalyptic scenario regardless of whether it is in Russia's game book or the national interest.

As we have seen, the religious right's entire critique of what's

8. Robertson, *The New Millennium: Ten Trends That Will Impact You and Your Family by the Year 2000* (Dallas: Word Publishing, 1990), p. 33.

9. Hagee, "Red Star over Bethlehem," *John Hagee Ministries,* March/April 1994, pp. 1-3.

wrong and who the enemy is are based not only on some very questionable interpretations of apocalyptic literature but also on a view of Russia as the cosmic protagonist that has been totally swept away by the collapse of the Soviet Union.

Will the Real Global Conspirators Please Stand Up!

A few on the religious right are beginning to grapple with the enormously unsettling possibility that they had it wrong. They realize that they must find a new global conspirator that they can clearly demonstrate is laboring to collectivize the planet for the Antichrist or their entire critique could come unravelled.

Conspiracy theories that provide simple black-and-white answers to complex world events have long been popular with American fundamentalists. A conspiratorial view of history is, for many on the religious right, an essential ingredient in understanding what's wrong and who the enemy is. While not all on the Christian right embrace a conspiratorial view of history, such a view permeates the entire movement. Historian Richard Hofstadter argues that there is something inherently paranoid about all of American politics.

> The distinguishing thing about the paranoid style is not that its exponents see conspiracies or plots here and there in history, but that they regard a "vast" or "gigantic" conspiracy as *the motive force* in historical events. History *is* a conspiracy, set in motion by demonic forces of almost transcendent power, and what is felt to be needed to defeat it is not the usual methods of political give-and-take, but an all-out crusade. The paranoid spokesman sees the fate of this conspiracy in apocalyptic terms — he traffics in the birth and death of whole worlds, whole political orders, whole systems of human values. . . . He constantly lives at a turning point: it is now or never in organizing resistance to conspiracy. Time is forever just running out.[10]

10. Hofstadter, *The Paranoid Style in American Politics and Other Essays* (New York: Alfred A. Knopf, 1965), pp. 29-30.

And while time is forever running out for those on the religious right who embrace a conspiratorial view of history, they have a more serious problem. They are locked in a cosmic global struggle, but they are no longer certain about who the global conspirators are. Fortunately, as in attempts to identify the Antichrist, there is no shortage of candidates. And leaders on the right are leaving no possibilities unexamined and no stone unturned.

I have an acquaintance who is absolutely convinced that a group of Zionist bankers are the real leaders of this global conspiracy. Back before the end of the cold war, I asked him if he really believed Zionist bankers were running the entire world.

"Certainly," he said.

"Then how do you explain the persecution of Jews in the Soviet Union?" I asked.

"It's a part of the Zionist cover-up," he responded confidently.

Once you have chosen your pet conspiracy theory, it provides a ready simple explanation for any and all serendipitous happenings in our complex world.

One of the top nominees for global conspirator as the cold war came to an end and the conflict in the Persian Gulf started heating up was Iraq. Prophecy hobbyists began linking Iraq, ancient Babylon, and Middle Eastern "hordes" with the new agent that Satan will use to collectivize the planet. Many of these speculations were as strongly anti-Arab in flavor as the Zionist banker theories are anti-Jewish.

Pat Robertson draws up his own list of global conspirators in his 1990 book *The New Millennium*. While still railing against Marxists, humanists, and liberals, he speculates that the real global conspirator may be the New Age movement. He even suggests that the Antichrist might well emerge from this movement.[11]

A few pages later, he proposes that the conspiratorial elite may really be environmentalists. "Their real agenda is not the environment: the movements they cluster around are never more

11. See Robertson, *The New Millennium*, pp. 74-75.

than a cover for their hidden agenda. Their agenda is control, and it is almost always anti-business and anti-growth."[12]

The global environmentalist conspiracy theory is also a big favorite with Larry Burkett, author of *The Coming Financial Crash*. According to Paul English, "Burkett says that environmentalism is the next method to total control." Burkett explains what the environmental movement is *really* all about:

> The agenda is central government control, more power, and lots of money pouring through the environmental movement. It has nothing to do with the environment. Communism didn't establish a central control. Socialism didn't. Environmentalism is the method. . . . This whole thing is about global control. And when your economy collapses . . . Americans will accept whatever they have to at that point. And that means global control of their economy and total control, absolute control of this country.[13]

How about it — are the environmentalists the real global conspirators? Some on the right would have us believe environmentalists are seriously subversive watermelons — green on the outside, pink in the middle.

In the end, though, a green conspiracy proves less compelling than a red conspiracy for Robertson. Before the end of *The New Millennium,* he returns to his all-time favorite global conspirator, the Evil Empire. He paints a picture of the Russians taking over Middle Eastern oil fields in a desperate attempt to re-establish Soviet hegemony and reverse the dissolution of the Empire. And of course in this scenario the restored Soviet Empire would be in an ideal position to invade Israel and set the stage for the final apocalyptic confrontation.

But if Robertson is a little uncertain about who the real global conspirators are, he seems to be much more certain about the timetable of the last days. He predicts that Christ will come

12. Robertson, *The New Millennium,* p. 226.
13. Paul English, "Burkett Predicts Hard Times," *Christian American,* January 1994, p. 9.

again on the four hundredth anniversary of the founding of America, which by his calculations will come in the year 2007, when he turns 77:

> History tells us that the first official act of the first permanent English settlers at the beginning of America took place on April 29, 1607 when the settlers planted a seven-foot oak cross in the sand, then knelt in prayer and claimed this nation for the glory of God and His Son Jesus Christ. In God's eyes the United States of America did not begin on July 4, 1776, but on April 29, 1607.
>
> Four hundred years from the beginning of America — ten full biblical generations — takes place on April 29, 2007.[14]

Obviously not content with his efforts to identify the real global conspirators in *The New Millennium,* Robertson gave it another try in a book published a year later. What triggered this newest round of nominees for global conspirator was a phrase coined by then President George Bush. Describing the remarkable new opportunity for international cooperation, democratization, and freedom at the end of the cold war, Bush called for a "new world order." I am sure that as an Episcopalian he had no idea of the sorts of apocalyptic hot buttons that phrase was going to push among his supporters on the religious right.

Robertson immediately appropriated the phrase for the title of a new book. At the beginning of this work, he spells it out in italics, lest anyone overlook its significance: "From the podium of the legislative chamber of the United States House of Representatives, the elected president of the United States of America has announced the beginning of a *New World Order.*" He proceeds to explain that "A single thread runs from the White House to the State Department to the Council on Foreign Relations to the Trilateral Commission to secret societies to extreme New Agers. There must be a new world order. It must eliminate national sovereignty. There must be world government, a world police

14. Robertson, *The New Millennium,* p. 313.

force, world courts, world banking and currency, and a world elite in charge of it all."[15]

While Robertson doesn't clearly identify all the conspiratorial forces operating out of the White House specifically and the U.S. government generally, he is very clear about what their interests are: "To some there must be a complete redistribution of wealth; to others there must be an elimination of Christianity; to some extreme New Agers there must be the deaths of two or three billion people in the Third World by the end of this decade."[16]

The conspiracy is wide-ranging according to Robertson, involving not only the office of the president and the highest levels of the U.S. government but the Trilateral Commission, members of the New Age movement, and the Masons: "The New Age religions, the beliefs of the Illuminati, and Illuminated Free Masonry all seem to move along parallel tracks with world communism and world finance. Their appeals vary somewhat, but essentially they are striving for the same very frightening vision."[17]

Of course, that's where Robertson and many on the right are dead wrong. If the New Agers are the "real" global conspirators, then the restored Soviet Empire, a subversive Trilateral Commission, out-of-control environmentalists, or Shriners on a power trip can't be. These are mutually exclusive options.

Pat Robertson's book *The New World Order* was published immediately prior to the 1992 presidential elections. One has to wonder how this book, which clearly linked President Bush and his administration to the terrors of global collectivism, affected Bush's conservative Protestant constituency. I suspect that Bill Clinton is indebted in part for his narrow victory over Bush to Robertson's tireless efforts to find the real global conspirators.

15. Robertson, *The New World Order* (Dallas: Word Publishing, 1991), pp. 3, 6.

16. Robertson, *The New World Order*, pp. 6-7.

17. Robertson, *The New World Order*, p. 185.

The Humanists Are Coming,
the Humanists Are Coming

While leaders on the politically correct right are in serious confusion about who the real global conspirators are, there is no such confusion about who the real conspiratorial elite is in the United States. Those on the religious right are absolutely certain that they have correctly defined what has gone wrong in America and who the enemy is. The only problem, as we will see, is that their entire analysis of what is wrong in America is directly based on their failed global apocalyptic conspiratorial analysis. For example, their analysis of who the conspirators are in America is directly based on their failed contention that the Evil Empire is trying to create a global socialist collective to help establish the reign of the Antichrist.

"The humanists are coming, the humanists are coming!" has been the rallying cry for the religious right for two decades. Leaders on the Christian right have convinced themselves that a liberal humanist elite is intent on destroying the family, undermining Christian faith, and collectivizing America to participate in a one-world gulag.

One of the most recent books in this hysterical genre, designed to terrorize conservative Christian families, is *The Family Under Siege: What the New Social Engineers Have in Mind for You and Your Family*. In this book, George Grant argues that a group of "social engineers" has an "insidious plan" to destroy our families and subvert our children and that we must fight back.

It is disheartening to me as a Christian that the only operative critique from the religious right of what's wrong in America is the secular humanist critique. The secular humanist critique is simply not valid either biblically or historically. It is based on the confused and discredited conspiracy theories we have already discussed. And this seriously flawed notion of secularism directly contributes to the inflamed rhetoric and polarization that threaten the very stability of our common life in both the American church and our larger society.

The term "secular humanism" was given to us by Francis Schaeffer, who was genuinely and thoughtfully concerned about the growing secularism of American society. It was Tim La Haye who gave us the conspiratorial definition. Schaeffer correctly pointed out that during the Renaissance "man became the measure of all things." But, as I will explain later, the secularism that really bedevils us doesn't have its origins principally in our humanistic past but rather in the Enlightenment.

The Battle for the Mind (1980) is still the authoritative book for many leaders on the right to understand the nature of the humanist "conspiracy" that allegedly threatens America. In this best-seller, Tim La Haye explains, in great detail, how a humanist elite has already taken over America and is intent on a single mission — to draw America into a one-world socialist collective. La Haye's whole humanist conspiracy theory is based on the confident conviction that the Soviet Union is the real global conspirator working through humanists and liberals in the United States to subvert and collectivize America.

In this book, La Haye alleges that a group of aging humanists who signed something called the Humanist Manifesto have already taken control of American society. La Haye charges, without a shred of documentation, that somehow this conspiratorial elite and its liberal allies have already taken control of all public schools, state universities, newspapers, radio, television, and of course labor unions and liberal organizations such as the NAACP and the ACLU.

"It is all very simple," La Haye explains, "if you face the fact we are being controlled by a small but very influential cadre of committed humanists, who are determined to turn traditionally moral-minded America into an amoral, humanist country. Oh, they don't call it humanist. They label it *democracy,* but they mean humanism, in all its atheistic, amoral depravity."[18]

La Haye goes on to make perfectly clear that the ultimate goal of this humanist cadre is not simply to humanize America. The ultimate goal is to systematically break down all moral and religious resistance in America until we capitulate and become a part of a new godless world order.[19] Sound familiar?

18. La Haye, *The Battle for the Mind* (Old Tappan, N.J.: Fleming H. Revell, 1980), p. 142.
19. See La Haye, *The Battle for the Mind,* p. 116.

Of course, not all those Protestants on the right who genuinely believe that what's wrong with America is secular humanism believe it is a part of a global conspiracy. However, I have never heard evangelicals talk about secular humanism without describing it in terms of a group of liberals and humanists who are intent on undermining the things they value — family, Christian faith, and the American way of life. And I am disappointed that there has been so little effort by evangelical scholars or anyone else to develop a more biblically based, historically accurate view of secularism.

Popularly understood, "secular humanists" are those persons who are for abortion rights, gay rights, and a liberal political agenda. Most evangelicals, not finding themselves anywhere on that list, mistakenly assume they are pure as the driven snow. Of course, nothing could be further from the truth. All of us, including those on the religious right, have been eaten alive by a secularism we haven't named. As we will see, it has little to do with anything resembling humanism but everything to do with the individualistic, consumer-driven values flowing out of American culture and Enlightenment values.

By misdefining secularism as something called "secular humanism," the religious right has not only misdefined what's wrong, they have misunderstood who the enemy is. Having essentially politicized their view of secularism, they genuinely believe that evil is singularly resident in those on the other end of the political spectrum. As a consequence, those on the right often have a very difficult time recognizing their own brokenness and often become at least as arrogantly self-righteous as those on the left. I suspect that when we discover that we are all profoundly secularized individuals who need a little mercy and grace, we might treat those with whom we differ with a little more mercy and grace as well.

Secularism is real. It has the ability to undermine our Christian values and short-circuit our faith. But it isn't synonymous with a particular political ideology being engineered by an imagined conspiratorial elite who are out to destroy everything we value. Those conspiratorial fictions have their origins, as we have seen, in our highly questionable end-times theories. But they also bear a disturbing similarity to the conspiracy theories that have been rampant among the most ultra-right reactionary groups in America for the last fifty years.

For example, the John Birch Society's extremist political agenda was based entirely on a conspiratorial view of history. In his classic *None Dare Call It Conspiracy,* Gary Allen charges that a conspiratorial elite is on the verge of bringing down America. He outlines in great detail how this elite will take over America. "After insiders have established the United Socialist States of America . . . the next step is the great merger of all nations of the world into a dictatorial world government. . . . The radicals make a commotion in the streets while the limousine liberals at the top in New York and Washington are socializing us. We are going to have a dictatorship of the elite disguised as a dictatorship of the proletariat."[20]

It is essential to point out that the similarities between right-wing political extremists and the religious right don't end with their conspiratorial view of history. In spite of the religious right's insistence that its political agenda comes out of moral and biblical concerns, any close scrutiny will reveal that it is almost identical to that of right-wing extremists, from banning all gun control to supporting all programs to cut taxes, regardless of the impact on the poor in our communities. How in the world can the religious right claim that its agenda for political action comes from Scripture when both its analysis of what's wrong and its agenda for political action are virtually indistinguishable from the agenda of the secular right and some of the most reactionary groups on the right, like the John Birch Society?

Will the Real American Conspiratorial Elite Please Stand Up!

Those on the right certainly understand the importance of making their devils tangible too. One cannot listen to Rush Limbaugh for long without hearing him make his devils very real, from "femi-Nazis" to "environmental wackos." What has hap-

20. Gary Allen and Larry Abraham, *None Dare Call It Conspiracy* (Seal Beach, Calif.: Concord Press, 1972), pp. 121-27.

pened is that those on the religious right have not only made their devils tangible but, because of their flawed view of what is wrong, they have also made them cosmic.

A number of leaders on the right are convinced that a global conspiracy is indeed afoot and a liberal humanist elite in the United States is running the conspiracy here. Therefore, their foes are not just people with whom they have ideological differences. They often view their opponents as agents of Satan. It simply isn't possible for those who view their opponents as agents of the Antichrist to participate in reasoned, civil discourse with those people. The polarization that is tearing our society apart is a direct product of this kind of conspiratorial worldview and the linking of foes with cosmic powers.

According to Pat Robertson, "Secular humanists are atheists with a well-defined and dangerous agenda. The essential core of this liberal philosophy is hatred of God and religion. Its adherents also hate our Western civilization, which is based on Christianity, and they want to tear it down." And again, "Those who are working for the dissolution of our society have a spiritual agenda. They are not merely attempting to dismantle the historic cultural values of this nation and move us toward a homogenized world. They also want to destroy Christianity and Bible-based religion. It is a clear part of their agenda, and they have already moved a long way in that direction."[21]

No single issue has invoked more name-calling and demonizing of the enemy than abortion. While most conservative Christians oppose abortion in most cases, I believe that there is growing evidence that our name-calling and confrontational rhetoric actually works against a consistent pro-life witness. Referring to pro-choice advocates as "fetal assassins" and "mass murderers" and displaying bumper stickers that read "EXECUTE MURDERERS AND ABORTIONISTS" itself evidences a diminished respect for life and encourages the sort of mind-set that can consider the execution of one's enemies to be a kind of virtuous act.

On August 19, 1993, Shelly Shannon fired a .32-caliber gun

21. Robertson, *The Turning Tide* (Dallas: Word Publishing, 1993), pp. 151, 144-45.

at Dr. George Tiller outside an abortion clinic in Wichita, Kansas, wounding him in both arms. "Is it really so bad?" Mrs. Shannon asked a friend after the killing of an abortion doctor last March outside his clinic in Pensacola, Florida. "People cheered when Hitler was killed. And this abortionist was a mass murderer."[22]

More recently, when Paul Hill gunned down an abortionist and his aide, he justified his act using the same sort of reasoning. And even more recently, five people were wounded and two killed in a tragic shooting spree in the Boston area. Again there are those on the radical right who are justifying these brutal acts. Most pro-life leaders have denounced this kind of violence, and yet few show signs of curbing the sort of extremist pro-life rhetoric that helps promote it.

Looking back, I believe the single most important factor to coalesce conservative resistance to the agenda of "the American conspiratorial elite" was the election of Bill Clinton as president of the United States. Shortly after the election, *Economist* magazine reported, "The religious right, barely able to contain its excitement at the election of a pro-abortion, pro-homosexual, 'five-star liberal' Democrat, anticipates 'hand-to-hand combat' for the next four years."[23]

Never in my lifetime have Christians dedicated themselves with such rancor to the demonizing of a president of the United States. For example, James Dobson, who has been of significant help to millions on issues of family life through his various "Focus on the Family" ministries, has increasingly joined the political fray. When he does, he virtually always espouses a very conservative and adversarial point of view. And when it comes to President Clinton, Dobson has very little to offer but censure. The first issue of Dobson's regular newsletter to appear after the 1992 election contained a long list of highly critical indictments, without a single word of encouragement or a suggestion that readers pray for the new president.

22. Shannon, quoted by Dirk Johnson in "Abortions, Bibles and Bullets, and the Making of a Militant," *New York Times,* 28 August 1993, p. 1.
23. "The Godly Right Gears Up," *The Economist,* 5 December 1992, p. 25.

Like a number of other evangelicals troubled by the very hostile tone of this newsletter, I wrote to Dr. Dobson:

Dear James,

I read your post-election letter with disbelief. Not *one* word of reconciliation or affirmation for our new president, Bill Clinton. I share some of your reservations, but can't you find a single area of praise for him as he seeks to address a number of issues that impact the family from jobs to health care? Frankly, a number of us who are evangelicals and communicators are very weary of the politics of polarization that has come to characterize the religious right. Isn't it possible for "Focus on the Family" to find ways to support their concern for Christian families that has something of the reconciling spirit of Christ about your advocacy?

Dobson didn't respond, but one of his aides did. Essentially, he explained that Dobson believes, as do many on the religious right, that the sole defining issue of our time is abortion. And of course President Clinton holds a view on abortion that a number of us disagree with.

The aide granted that Clinton might undertake welcome economic initiatives or promote needed improvements in the health care system. We must not forget, however, that "even Hitler gave the German economy a boost — but only at great cost in terms of human life and dignity. Perhaps there are times when you don't have the leisure to be as affirming and positive as we might like to be. You don't stop to compliment a man on his hairstyle or tie when he's in the act of murdering your children."[24] But, one must ask in Christian conscience, does this kind of reasoning and inflamed rhetoric genuinely exhibit Christian charity and advance the gospel of Jesus Christ?

The Christian Coalition's publication *Christian American* recently ran an advertisement for Texe Marrs's book *Big Sister Is Watching You*. It read in part,

24. Letter to the author dated 22 January 1993.

They're ruthless, shrewd, and calculating — and they've got a *stranglehold* on the White House. Recruited and empowered by their boss, Hillary, these are the women who tell Bill Clinton what to do. . . .

Big Sister is Watching You unmasks the coven of brutally correct women who now rule over us. Militant feminists, these women possess awesome Gestapo powers. One heads the FBI, another the IRS. Five are members of the Trilateral Commission and the Council on Foreign Relations — subversive organizations whose goal is to end American sovereignty and bring about a global Marxist paradise.

Then there's Hillary Rodham Clinton. What dark powers does she exercise over her husband, Bill? What's her real goal? Is she plotting behind the scenes to become President of the United States? Will she then go on to usher in a frightening New Millennium?[25]

Can Ralph Reed really be serious in his assertion that the Christian Coalition is a moderate mainstream organization when it sanctions the promotion of this sort of over-the-top material in its periodical?

A similarly troubling example of this kind of demonization of the enemy is Jerry Falwell's endorsement and promotion of an independently produced videotape presenting a host of unsubstantiated accusations against Clinton, including charges that he engaged in cocaine trafficking and was involved in the murder of White House deputy counsel Vince Foster and several others. Even some of Falwell's closest supporters are disturbed by the content and tone of this video.

Tony Campolo challenged Jerry Falwell either to substantiate the charges in this vicious video attack on the president or to withdraw the tape and apologize to President Clinton. Falwell refused to do either. Instead, he began directing his accusations at Campolo, too.[26]

I remember that when I was growing up, my father, a con-

25. *Christian American,* January 1994, p. 13.
26. See Laurie Goodstein, "Evangelical Leader Petitions to Rebut Anti-Clinton Tapes," *Washington Post,* 27 January 1995.

servative Republican, disagreed with almost every liberal policy Franklin Delano Roosevelt ever proposed. But it would never have occurred to him to express his disagreement using the kinds of vicious personal attacks on the president and his family that have come to characterize much of the public discourse of the Christian right today. He had too much respect for the office of president to indulge in such ugly vilification and name-calling.

I am deeply concerned that the vicious personal attacks we are hearing today could not only permanently demean the office of the president, but could provoke increasing incidents of violence toward those in national leadership — particularly the president. The recent series of attacks on the White House suggests this may be a very reasonable concern.

In light of this discussion, I predict that the 1996 presidential race will be one of the nastiest in recent history. And I am very apprehensive that the mudslinging on both sides will further discredit the office of the president of the United States.

Frankly, I will be very surprised if the Republicans don't continue their winning ways and take back the White House in 1996 unless there is a viable third-party candidate. But if they do, how is the office of the president likely to be diminished or the person of the president endangered by the vitriolic attacks of conservatives, talk radio, and the religious right?

Can't we evangelical Christians find ways to express our concerns without participating in the rage of talk radio and the viciousness of attacks like Jerry Falwell's? Can't we find ways to demonstrate genuine love and concern for those with whom we differ politically instead of adopting attack-dog-style adversarial politics? Didn't Christ command us to love our enemies and bless them?

Can't we evangelicals admit that we may be not only mistaken about our end-times theories but also dead wrong about the Evil Empire being Satan's agent to collectivize the planet? Can't we face up to the reality that our world is vastly too complex to be explained with simplistic conspiracy theories? Isn't it possible that our real foe is not a liberal-humanist elite but our own embracing of twisted political and cultural values? Isn't it evident that we have totally misdefined what's wrong, what secularism is, and who our enemies are?

Looking Back at What's Gone Wrong

Only as we correctly define what is wrong and who the enemy is do we have any possibility of finding a way to responsibly engage the challenges of our world. As I have tried to show, I believe that both the politically correct left and the Christian right have misdiagnosed what has gone wrong. And this serious misdiagnosis is directly contributing to the inflamed rhetoric and name-calling that are in turn leading to polarization, conflict, and violence.

In July of 1994, my wife and I were invited to speak at Corrymeela Community in Northern Ireland, a group of Christians seeking to extend reconciliation between Catholics and Protestants in that troubled land. Ninety-five people were killed by terrorists during the month we were there, the highest monthly toll in twenty-five years. Since 1967, more than three thousand people have been killed in this bitter civil conflict. The history of Northern Ireland is the history of a culture war that has become a shooting war. We are praying with all the people of Northern Ireland that the movement toward peace in that land will be successful.

Dr. Vamik Volkan is a psychiatrist who has specialized in the study of ethnic hatred and the increasingly frequent conflicts between ethnic groups, including those in Northern Ireland. His research underscores the fact that the distorted characterizations of one group fostered by the leaders of the other group lead directly to conflict and violence. Another specialist in ethnic conflict, Dr. Robert J. Lifton, argues that one of the few hopes for slowing the momentum toward conflict between two groups lies in members of those groups challenging the demonizing rhetoric of their leaders.[27]

I believe this advice applies equally to the growing conflicts between the cultural polarities in American society and in the church. Progressive Christians committed to the gospel of peace and reconciliation routinely speak out against marginalizing

27. See Daniel Goleman, "Amid Ethnic Wars, Psychiatrists Seek Roots of Conflict," *New York Times,* 2 August 1994, pp. C1, C13.

people on the basis of their gender, ethnicity, or cultural background. They must broaden their inclusivity to reach out in a spirit of reconciling love to those with whom they disagree on the religious right as well. This must include calling their leaders to task when they vilify conservative Christians.

I urge all progressive Christians, including those in the Interfaith Alliance, to reach out to their conservative sisters and brothers in Christ and attempt to understand their fears, concerns, and values. I would also urge progressive Christians to set aside the highly politicized, ideological analysis of the extreme left and do their own analysis, working from biblical and faith perspectives.

Similarly, I would urge evangelicals, charismatics, and Pentecostals to take a new look at their political alliances and reconsider their allegiance to conspiratorial analyses and the negative characterizations of progressive Christians. I would also urge them to encourage their leaders to tone down the rhetoric and reach out in the name of the reconciling Christ to those with whom they disagree.

Isn't it time we all called for a cease fire in America's culture war? Isn't it time that Christians on all sides set aside our political ideologies and our polarized analyses, abandon the politics of fear and hostility, and return to Christ's gospel of reconciliation and love? Isn't it time for us to find a new basis as sisters and brothers together to address the urgent challenges that face us as we enter a new century?

SECTION II

▼ ▼ ▼

Earth Mother, Adam Smith, and the Promised Land

THOUSANDS OF BALLOONS raced wildly toward the ceiling as confetti and streamers came cascading down on the jubilant crowd. A field of American flags waved furiously over the throng. More than two thousand people were on their feet shouting and applauding as Col. Oliver North approached the red, white, and blue podium.

This was the Christian Coalition's Third Annual National Road to Victory Conference. It was held at the Washington Hilton — the hotel where John Hinckley Jr. shot President Ronald Reagan and his press secretary James Brady back in 1981. Gun control legislation was not on the night's agenda for this group, however.

Middle-class and predominantly middle-aged white Americans from conservative Protestant churches all over the country made up the bulk of the audience. They were smiling, hugging each other, and waving their flags furiously in the air. An uninformed observer would doubtless have thought that it looked a lot more like a political convention than a religious gathering.

As North stepped up to the rostrum, the crowd hushed. He spoke with passion, challenging the audience to fight for conservative candidates, to pray and to work to take back America for God. He concluded his address with a call to oust liberal foes from every level of government and with the triumphalistic proclamation, "Be of good cheer, my friends, because our day is coming!"

Participants exploded to their feet and gave him a wild standing ovation. Suddenly the room was filled with hundreds of placards dancing above the crowd reading "NORTH & LIMBAUGH IN '96."

Of course North's defeat in the Virginia Senate race in 1994 was a setback for his high aspirations. He has chosen to spend a season working on talk radio — just like Rush. But you can be sure we haven't seen the last of Oliver North, because he is convinced that his day is coming, too!

The American religious right has its own clear vision of where it thinks the country should be headed. The politically correct left has its vision, too. Both factions are doing what they can to set the nation's agenda, marshal forces, and begin the march to a better tomorrow.

Given their radically different ideas of what has gone wrong, it shouldn't be surprising that they have two very different visions for the American future. In this section we will look at their respective visions for what is right and the way things ought to be.

We will first take a look in Chapter 5 at the brave new future to which our friends on the left would take us if we gave them half a chance. Then in Chapter 6 we will examine the future to which our flag-waving friends on the right would transport us if we let them. In the final section, we will consider a third way, a biblical vision that is an alternative to the dreams of both the radical left and the Christian right.

CHAPTER 5

▼ ▼ ▼

Love Mother, Celebrate Diversity, and Welcome a Brave New Future

WATER SLOWLY POURED from the pitcher over the hands of the eight ecumenical leaders standing in a solemn circle. The sun arched high in the spring sky as this group of Catholics and Protestants participated in an ancient Native American water ceremony. Long eagle feathers were drawn slowly over the hands of each of the celebrants at the conclusion of the ceremony.

The group had spent three days with Thomas Berry, a religious ecologist, who had invited the participants to come and share his vision for a new ecological future in which we are reunited with our sacred mother, the earth.

Though trained as a Catholic theologian, Berry has relinquished the biblical vision of God's redemption of people and creation in favor of an essentially ecological hope for our future that draws heavily on Hindu, Buddhist, and animistic teachings.[1]

1. For his description of this vision, see Thomas Berry and Thomas Clarke, *Befriending the Earth: A Theology of Reconciliation between Humans and the Earth* (Mystic, Conn.: Twenty-third Publications, 1991).

Berry urged these Christian leaders to relinquish a historic view of Christian redemption and in its place substitute an essentially Eastern ecological vision.

"Put the Bible on the shelf for at least 20 years," Berry urged. "Nature needs to become our sole authority because nature is the only text without a context."

Berry is one of many on the left whose vision for the better future begins with a return to "mother." Some join him in viewing the cosmos as an amorphous spiritual realm. Others more specifically view the universe or at least our planet as a single living organism, known as Gaia. Overall, those on the left who nurture a sense of the sacred tend to be most heavily influenced by Hindu philosophy, Buddhist ethics, and animistic rituals. Judeo-Christian presumptions of a Creator God who encounters us personally and to whom we are all ultimately accountable are not in vogue for these folks.

Of course, many on the left have no religious inclinations at all. They either pointedly repudiate religion or elevate their political ideology to the level of faith. Some use a rhetoric of spirituality to paper over what is essentially a materialistic worldview. Some, for example, have narrowed their vision of the future to a matter of care for mother earth as an ecological system totally void of any kind of transcendent reality. There are even a few very vocal advocates for a new ecological future minus the troubling human presence.

> If you haven't given voluntary human extinction much thought before, the idea of a world with no people may seem strange. But, if you give the idea a chance I think you might agree that the extinction of Homo sapiens would mean survival for millions, if not billions, of other Earth-dwelling species. . . . Phasing out the human race will solve every problem on earth, social and environmental.[2]

This is, of course, a decidedly minority view. As I have already suggested, there is a good deal less agreement on the left than on the right concerning not only what's wrong but also the

2. "Voluntary Human Extinction," *Wild Earth,* Summer 1991, p. 12.

destination to which they would take us. As we will see, multi-culturalists, radical feminists, and the gay and lesbian lobby would be no more keen on working for a planet "cleansed" of the human presence that would those on the religious right.

Celebrating a Spicy Tossed Salad

In fact, multiculturalists are not advocating human extinction but rather are celebrating the emergence of indigenous peoples all over the planet. For them the better future is a populated world in which indigenous people are empowered to regain title to native lands and run their own lives. They point to Aboriginals in Australia winning the Mabo land rights that recognize their land claims and other native peoples struggling in Canada and Hawaii to gain similar recognition. Christians of all traditions who take the biblical call to social justice seriously believe that we should support the legitimate aspirations of native peoples.

The global rise of indigenous peoples almost seems to be the foreshadowing of an "old" world coming — an "old" multi-cultural future in which traditional peoples are reasserting themselves.

Before we look briefly at something of the myriad of other futures that those on the politically correct left are envisioning, I believe it is important to struggle a bit with the issue of a multiculturalism as it relates to all of our futures.

Fertility rates of whites are down throughout nearly all Western countries, while immigrant populations are consistently showing more rapid growth. This means that the influence of peoples from Asia, Africa, and Latin America is likely to grow as we enter the twenty-first century, while European influence is likely to diminish.

For example, whites will be a minority in California by the year 2010. If present immigration rates continue, people with European roots will be a minority in the United States by 2060. The United States is becoming a predominately Hispanic American, African American, Asian American society. We need to celebrate the gifts we have to offer one another from our diverse cultural and racial backgrounds. But just the opposite is happening. Racism is alive and growing at a disturbing rate. I believe racism is increasing in part because white Americans are fearful of a future in which we are not the dominant group. That is particularly true of those on the conservative side of the ledger.

People everywhere are building more walls. Skinheads are holding more rallies. Californians passed Proposition 187, denying welfare, public education, and nonemergency medical care to illegal aliens. White Howard Beach teenagers used baseball bats on black teenagers who made the mistake of wandering into their neighborhood.

Twenty years ago Fresno, California, was a dominantly white, conservative middle-class community. Virtually overnight it has become a community of surprising diversity. Not only has there been a dramatic increase in Latinos and African Americans, but Fresno now boasts the largest settlement of Hmong peoples outside of Laos.

Recently, when I worked with some churches in Fresno, I discovered many white members living in total denial. These folks seem to be intent on living as though their community has not changed. They attend all-white churches, refuse to learn Spanish or get acquainted with their new neighbors, and chronically complain about the "lousy service" in stores they have shopped in for years that now have owners of non-European ethnic backgrounds.

I have glimpsed the future, and, like it or not, it looks very much like Fresno, California. America is well on the way to becoming what author Ben J. Wattenberg has labeled "The First Universal Nation," a country of unparalleled diversity. And I am convinced that many from white conservative backgrounds will resist the coming diversity with their dying breath.

While many multiculturalists celebrate this world of diversity that is coming, these good people in Fresno and many others like them are not willing to relinquish their melting-pot vision for America's future. White Americans have always been willing to put up with a little diversity as long as the newcomers adopted our customs, values, and language — as long as they became "real Americans."

Never in their most disturbing nightmares did whites in Fresno or the rest of the United States ever imagine that their assimilationist vision for America would break down. Back in the nineteenth century, for example, white Anglo-Saxon Protestants were alarmed at the growing number of immigrants arriving from southern and eastern Europe. We welcomed their labor but not their "alien" values. Concerned, policymakers went to work to ensure that the melting pot did its job. They hit on the idea of promoting universal education as a way to "Americanize" the children of these immigrants in the politically correct values and views of the dominant culture. By 1918 the assimilators succeeded in seeing mandatory school attendance laws instituted from coast to coast. And the public schools did an effective job of anglicizing the children of these new immigrant groups.

As we welcome a new future of rich diversity, the melting pot is experiencing a massive meltdown. It is being replaced by the imagery of what some describe as a very rich ethnic stew in which growing numbers of immigrants choose to retain some of their own culture, customs, values, and language. But I recently came across a new image for America's multicultural future that is even more compelling than an "ethnic stew."

At a Catholic forum on multiculturalism, one speaker characterized this new multicultural society as a huge tossed salad. He pictured a gigantic tossed salad containing artichoke hearts, beets, onions, pasta, greens, Chinese noodles, mandarin oranges, curried seafood, black beans, and feta cheese topped with salsa and just a hint of fish sauce.

This rapid movement from a melting pot to a very diverse multicultural tossed salad is not simply the result of demographic change. It is happening because many new immigrant groups are simply not willing to trade in their ethnic cultural values for those offered by the dominant American culture. And we WASPs are no longer the singular role model for people who choose to share this continent with us.

For fifteen-year-old Guillienne Andelin, a Haitian-American, *assimilation* is a dirty word. She attends a largely black high school in Miami. She does not want to turn her back on her parents' culture or aspirations. She will not accept being labeled alien or inferior by a society that she believes does not look beyond color. "Nothing could stop me from trying to have a better life than we have now," she said.[3] Andelin is representative of millions of new Americans who find strength and support in the diversity of cultures in America's spicy tossed salad.

But many established Americans are not welcoming this growing diversity or the new arrivals. In 1985, 67 percent of Americans responding to a survey expressed a desire to limit immigration significantly. In 1993, the figure climbed to 73 percent.[4] The Fresno reaction appears to be growing.

There are those who view America as a "propositional country" unique among nations. They believe it was founded on principles and values that cannot be significantly enhanced by those late arrivals coming from non-WASP backgrounds. Some believe that uncontrolled immigration can threaten the nation's future. For example, Lawrence Auster has argued that the only way to preserve the integrity of America is to slow down the flow of immigrants dramatically. We must, he says, "exercise great caution before introducing ethnoculturally distinct populations into an established society in such numbers that they cannot easily be assimilated."[5]

Many on the religious right have passionately expressed their opposition to any emphasis on multiculturalism or bilingualism in schools or society. Some are opposed because they view such advocacy as one more aspect of the global conspiracy to prepare Americans for a dreaded one-world takeover.

Most are opposed because they strongly believe that American culture and middle-class white values are the best expression of God's vision of how human beings should live. In Lake County, Florida, shortly after "stealth candidates" backed by the Christian Coalition secured a majority presence, the board voted to demand

3. Andelin, quoted by Deborah Sontag in "A Fervent 'No' to Assimilation in New America," *New York Times,* 24 June 1993, p. A6.

4. See Bruce W. Nelan, "Not Quite So Welcome Anymore," *Time* special edition, Fall 1993.

5. Auster, "Avoiding the Issue," *National Review,* 21 February 1994, p. 54.

that teachers in the district henceforth instruct their students that America culture and institutions are "superior to other foreign or historic cultures."[6]

Pat Robertson has expressed his belief in the superiority of American culture over traditional cultures in very explicit terms:

> I watched an environmental special on television not long ago, the purpose of which was to exalt a tribe of primitive Indians as if they were the ultimate example of virtue and wisdom. The whole idea of this kind of humanist thinking is preposterous. Is this what rational people believe? Do they want to live like jungle dwellers? Is this what mankind has been aspiring to for the past six thousand years?
>
> The common-sense reaction would be to see these primitive tribes in South America, the Philippines, and New Guinea and recognize what we all might be like in our natural state — naked, unlettered primitives. These tribes are not ahead of anybody; they are centuries behind. They are in an arrested state of social development. They are not less valuable as human beings because of that, but they offer scant wisdom or learning or philosophical vision to a culture that can feed the entire population of the planet in a single harvest and send spacecraft to the moon.[7]

Similar attitudes of cultural superiority and a consequent disinclination to entertain the validity or worth of different cultural values is at the heart of the battle that is heating up in our schools over the issue of cultural diversity.

In 1993, after extensive debate, the Accrediting Commission for Senior Colleges and Universities decided that every accredited school should set itself the goal of becoming a multicultural, multiracial institution. Many secondary and elementary schools are also experimenting with curricula that enable students to learn not only about American culture but also about the cultures of the many other peoples who are part of American

6. See Steven V. Roberts, "Onward Christian Soldiers — Their Targets: School Boards, State Gods," *U.S. News and World Report*, 6 June 1994, p. 43.
7. Robertson, *The Turning Tide* (Dallas: Word Publishing, 1993), pp. 151-52.

society.[8] We have already noted the opposition of those on the extreme right to this sort of multicultural approach to education. But resistance is also mounting among those on the extreme left.

A new crop of ethnic separatists has arisen who resist as strongly as Pat Robertson the contention that there is anything of value to be learned from other cultures. Like their counterparts on the right, they are seeking to promote the idea that their culture is superior to all others.

Diane Ravitch speaks out against the new cultural elitism of the left in the course of arguing for more inclusive education. She points out that textbooks in American schools and colleges have, over the years, routinely offered a very culturally limited view of our American past.

> Race, religion, and ethnicity were presented as minor elements in the American saga; slavery was treated as an episode, immigration as a sidebar, and women were largely absent. The textbooks concentrated on presidents, wars, national politics, and issues of state. An occasional "great black" or "great woman" received mention, but the main narrative paid little attention to minority groups and women. . . .
>
> Our schools and our institutions of higher learning have in recent years begun to embrace what Catherine R. Stimpson of Rutgers University has called "cultural democracy," a recognition that we must listen to a "diversity of voices" in order to understand our culture, past and present. . . . The new history is — indeed, must be — a warts-and-all history; it demands an unflinching examination of racism and discrimination in our history.[9]

Of course, those on the p.c. left have no problem being candid about the sins of the American past. But they have a very

8. See Steven S. Weiner, "Accrediting Bodies Must Require a Commitment to Diversity," in *Are You Politically Correct? Debating America's Cultural Standards,* ed. Francis J. Beckwith and Michael E. Bauman (New York: Prometheus Books, 1994), p. 219.

9. Diane Ravitch, "Multiculturalism: E Pluribus Plures," *American Scholar* 59 (Summer 1990): 338, 339, 340.

difficult time finding anything positive to say about our Euro-centric culture, its literature or achievements. On the other hand, the religious right is not only in total denial that there is any underside to America's past, but they are also actively involved in rewriting America's history to convince themselves and every-one else that the U.S. is God's unique creation. And that's the message they want taught in America's schools.

But most Americans and Christians of all ethnic and cultural backgrounds have little interest in the polarized debates regarding multicultural education, bilingualism, and defending America's past. And we don't have space here to discuss in detail the pros and cons of these issues. But there is a general consensus in both society and church that we must prepare the next generation to become a part of a very spicy multicultural salad.

A New Fundamentalism —
Separatism, Tribalism, and Exclusionism

A recent Doonesbury cartoon portrayed an embattled university president saying to a group of protesting black students, "Look, I let you have your own African-American studies program and your own black student union, but I draw the line at letting you have your own drinking fountain."

There is an extreme edge on the p.c. left that has actually rejected the ideals of multiculturalism and inclusivity and seems intent on attempting to establish a new fundamentalism, a new elitism, a new separatism. Most proponents of this sort of cultural balkanization derive their views through an extension of the basic cultural critique of the left. They view society in terms of oppres-sors and victims, and they assert that it is now time to turn the tide, to remove power from the historical oppressor and give it to the historical victim.

In essence, they advocate replacing one kind of radical cul-tural discrimination with another in order to balance the histori-cal inequity. Let's look at the ways this new fundamentalism is expressed on the radical edge of African American, feminist, and lesbian and gay communities.

Afrocentric Separatism

Frustrated by entrenched racism, some African Americans are now arguing that the strategies used to secure victories during the civil rights era are no longer practical or effective. In order to make a true future for themselves, say these critics, African Americans must stop trying to define themselves in the context of a racist culture. They have to focus on their past, their rich African heritage, and work to create their own separate Afrocentric culture.

"While there have been African American scholars in every era," says Molefi Kete Asante, "the European Hegemony since the 1480s in knowledge about the world, including Africa, was fairly complete. The domination of information, the naming of things, the propagation of concepts, and the dissemination of interpretations were and still are in most cases in the West a Eurocentric Hegemony."[10] To the extent that African Americans fall prey to this Eurocentric hegemony, he argues, they are cheated of their self-respect.

In their efforts to overturn Eurocentrism, some Afrocentrists contend that all the triumphs of the West are in fact rooted in ancient African wisdom and culture. They argue that the most important aspects of Western civilization are more significantly grounded in ancient Egyptian culture than in Greek or Roman culture. Further, they insist that Egyptians were all actually black Africans. They attribute any confusion on this point to a long history of European efforts to deny Africans their rightful place in history.

Some contend that Napoleon's soldiers shot the nose and lips off the Sphinx in a deliberate effort to destroy its negroid features.[11] In one of the more influential handbooks of the Afrocentrist movement, *What They Never Told You in History Class*, Indus Khamat Kush claims that Moses, Jesus, Buddha, Mo-

10. Asante, "Multiculturalism: Without Hierarchy — An Afrocentric Reply to Dang Ravach," in *Are You Politically Correct?* p. 187.
11. See John Taylor, "Are You Politically Correct?" in *Are You Politically Correct?* pp. 28-31.

hammed, and Vishnu were in fact all Africans, as were the first Chinese, Indians, Hebrews, Greeks, Romans, Britons, and Americans. In other words, according to this theory, all racial groups have their origins in Africa.

Diane Ravitch condemns this kind of racial particularism as "a bad idea whose time has come. It is also a fashion spreading like wildfire through the educational system, actively promoted by organizations and individuals with a political and professional interest in strengthening ethnic power bases in the university, in the educational profession, and in society itself." It is ironic that it should be thriving in academic settings. The traditional stronghold of the open exchange of ideas should be the last place for exclusivism. "History gives no grounds for race pride," says Ravitch.

> No race has a monopoly on virtue. If anything, a study of history should inspire humility, rather than pride. People of every racial group have committed terrible crimes, often against others of the same group. Whether one looks at the history of Europe or Africa or Latin America or Asia, every continent offers examples of inhumanity. . . . If we teach children this, they might recognize how absurd both racial hatred and racial chauvinism are.[12]

Among the better-known proponents of Afrocentric separatism outside the academy is the Nation of Islam. Long a significant force in the African American community, the organization has been reinvigorated in recent years by the leadership of Minister Louis Farrakhan. The organization's excesses include a thoroughgoing demonization of all whites, claims of a global Zionist conspiracy against blacks, and advocacy of violence. These excesses have prevented it from ever making much headway among middle- and upper-class African Americans. But its sustained repudiation of white culture and advocacy of black separatism (even the formation of a separate black state in North America) has won it a following in a new generation of angry young African Americans. Minister Farrakhan has been invited

12. Ravitch, "Multiculturalism," pp. 343, 353.

to present the case for black supremacy across the nation, from Harvard University to the University of California at Riverside.

Older black leaders are increasingly speaking out to challenge black separatism. The following letter to the editor of the *San Francisco Chronicle* is typical of the growing African American reaction against this kind of black separatism.

> As an African American, a history professor and one who participated in the civil rights movement, I am finally compelled to speak out about the recent events at U C Riverside and repeated statements by blacks claiming to be holy men.
>
> It is a source of deep anguish to blacks who marched at Selma with Jewish men and women — some who lost their lives in our struggle for equality — to hear their motives vilified by the chosen leaders of the Nation of Islam.
>
> The preoccupation with Jews as the source of our collective misery has reached the level of absurdity. At no time in recorded history have Jews accounted for more than 3 percent of the world's population. At the time of slavery, their situation in America was economically, socially and demographically marginal by any standards.
>
> What will be the outcome of this irrational hatred by members of the Nation of Islam for American blacks themselves? No movement based on black separatism has succeeded in the United States, nor will this one. It is time for African Americans to speak out against this anti-intellectual, hate filled platform delivered by the self-aggrandizing leaders of the Nation of Islam. All that we have fought for and won is at stake.[13]

Much is at stake for all Americans if the spirit of divisiveness that has given rise to black separatism spreads further. And, indeed, as I have suggested, it can be found elsewhere on edges of the political correctness movement.

13. Ralph Emerson-Jackson, letter to the editor of the *San Francisco Chronicle*, 9 June 1994, p. A24.

Feminist, Lesbian, and Gay Exclusionism

There are signs of a growing movement toward the politics of exclusionism among radical feminists, lesbians, and gays as well. While still using the language of diversity and inclusivity to promote their cause, a number really would like to see the creation of a more exclusive future in which they are calling the shots. Some radical feminists and lesbians would like to see the emergence of a new matriarchal society in which male participation is very tightly circumscribed.

Radical feminist Alison Jaggars advocates a future in which the family as we know it is abolished altogether. She would like to create a society where, with the aid of technology, "One woman could inseminate another . . . men . . . could lactate . . . and fertilized ova could be transferred into women's or even men's bodies."[14]

All that is preventing the realization of this brave new future, she insists, is the phallocentric and androcentric prejudices of our society. "What we feminists are doing," philosopher Elizabeth Minnich stated, "is comparable to Copernicus shattering our geocentricity, Darwin shattering our species-centricity. We are shattering androcentricity, and the change is as fundamental, as dangerous, as exciting."[15]

New medical technologies are making it possible for increasing numbers of single women, including lesbians, to have children without the direct involvement of men. Some feminists and lesbians believe that these sorts of reproductive techniques hold the promise of freedom for oppressed women. They advocate moving toward a future in which males no longer play an essential role as either sexual partners or parents. This sort of thinking is pointedly exclusionary.

A *New York Times* story reports that a precocious three-year-old asked her single mother whether she had a daddy. "No, you

14. Jaggars, quoted by John Taylor in "Are You Politically Correct?" p. 25.

15. Minnich, quoted by John Taylor in "Are You Politically Correct?" p. 26.

don't have a daddy," her mother replied. "But there was a man who provided the seed I needed to make a baby."[16] There are those who would like to remove even the need for an anonymous donor of the seed. There have been discussions in some feminist circles of tinkering with the reproductive process to make male sperm unnecessary for the ongoing propagation of the species.

Other feminists envision a future in which men are not excluded but male and female characteristics are blended so as to produce androgynous individuals and a gender-neutral society. "With the elimination of sex roles, and the disappearance, in an overpopulated world, of any biological need for sex to be associated with procreation," says feminist philosopher Ann Ferguson, "there would be no reason why such a society could not transcend sexual gender. It would no longer matter what biological sex individuals had. Love relationships, and the sexual relationships developing out of them, would be based on individual meshing together of androgynous human beings."[17]

In one way or another, the feminist solution to the problem they identify as gender oppression lies in the overthrow of our society's entrenched patriarchalism. Some feminists would be satisfied to replace the current oppression of females with a system of gender equality. Other feminists would like to transfer the imbalance of power from men to women, because they are convinced that women are better suited to set economic, political, and environmental agendas. They would argue that a woman-directed history would not be marred by war, the ghettoization of Third World populations, or the ecological rape of the planet.

The homosexual critique of what is wrong with our society is also rooted in a sense of oppression. Gays and lesbians have long experienced marginalization in American society. But during the past decade, the disproportionate toll that the AIDS virus has taken on the gay community has radicalized many to a new kind of activism. For some, this activism is based on belief in anti-gay

16. Carol Lawson, "Single but Mothers by Choice: 'Who Is My Daddy' Can Be Answered in Different Ways," *New York Times,* 5 August 1993, p. C1.
17. Ferguson, *Sexual Democracy: Women, Oppression and Revolution* (Boulder: Westview Press, 1991), p. 207.

conspiracies. The gay activist group ACT UP, for example, has declared that "every death related to HIV/AIDS complications is an act of racist, sexist and homophobic violence,"[18] and some writers have speculated that the HIV virus was created by genetic engineers and unleashed on the public by the CIA or some other government agency with the specific intent of wiping out gays.

Needless to say, the final conquest of AIDS is at the center of the gay vision of the future. Much of the movement's energy and resources may currently be directed toward achieving an AIDS-free future.

At the same time, some more radical leaders have sketched out a larger view of where they would like to see America moving in the future. Several homosexual writers have suggested that we are at a moment in America's ideological history when "queer love" could become the force to transform and "save" the entire society.[19] In an article about the politics of homosexuality in the *New Republic,* Andrew Sullivan says that it "is as open-ended as the conservatives' politics is closed-minded. It seeks an end to all restrictions on homosexuality, but also the subversion of hetero-sexual norms, as taught in schools or the media."[20]

Feminist Barbara Smith has suggested that the homosexual critique may prove valuable in the context of the feminist struggle: "I think that homosexuality embodies an innately radi-cal critique of the traditional nuclear family, whose political func-tion has been to constrict the sexual expression and gender roles of all its members, especially women, lesbians and gays." Smith argues for a multi-issue agenda for revolution in which gays, lesbians, and feminists band together to exert more power. After all, she says, "This is not about political correctness, it's about winning."[21]

Smith is right at least in her assessment that no one group

18. Catherine Saalfield and Ray Navarro, "Shocking Pink Praxis: Race and Gender on the Frontlines," in *Inside/Out: Lesbian Theories, Gay Theories,* ed. Diana Fuss (New York: Routledge, 1991), p. 351.

19. See Caleb Crain, "Gay Glue," *New Republic,* 10 May 1993, p. 16.

20. Sullivan, "The Politics of Homosexuality," *New Republic,* 10 May 1993, p. 26.

21. Smith, "Where's the Revolution?" *The Nation,* 5 July 1993, p. 16.

on the radical left has much of a chance of achieving its revolutionary aspirations for the future on its own. And yet, contrary to the conspiratorial suspicions of some on the religious right, the factions of the radical left show no signs of uniting to work for any common vision for the future.

It's important to point out that many gays and lesbians have no interest in a homosexual takeover of schools, media, and societal norms. They simply want to integrate and be accepted by the middle-class heterosexual society. Like other Americans, including those on the religious right, their vision for the better future is largely defined by the consumer-driven aspirations of the American dream, not the ideological politics of the left.

A Brave New Future:
Christians at the Progressive Edge

Progressive mainline Protestants and Roman Catholics have committed themselves to working for a future born of both their Christian faith and their progressive social concerns. The major areas where a positive merging of these two currents is taking place include

▶ care for the environment as an aspect of our call to be good stewards of God's creation;
▶ efforts to ensure a future of justice and peace for all peoples;
▶ affirmation and utilization of the gifts of all members of the church, including women, ethnic minorities, and the disabled.

However, a number of progressive Christians have totally bought into the analysis of the p.c. left of what has gone wrong. This has decisively altered their vision for the future. Like the leaders of the political correctness movement, they represent "evil" as resident in particular groups: males and heterosexuals. They reject the biblical contention that all are sinners in need of help, including feminists, lesbians, gays, and people of color. They insist that the victims of male, heterosexual domination are by virtue of their victimization the new righteous in the land. As a consequence, this virtuous victim class essentially has no need of being redeemed.

I am particularly concerned that a growing number of progressive Christians have repudiated the historical biblical vision of the Creator God who is redeeming a people and is re-creating a world. Since they don't believe that anything is broken, ruptured, or fallen in a biblical sense, there is no need for redemption, atonement, or a redeemer.

For example, Delores Williams, a feminist spokesperson speaking at the Imagining Conference, stated, "I don't think we need a theory of atonement at all. . . . I don't think we need folks hanging on crosses and blood dripping and weird stuff."[22]

When progressive Christians throw overboard the scriptural vision of God acting in history through Jesus Christ to redeem a world, they end up substituting other visions. Some, highly involved in care for creation and creational spirituality, have, like Thomas Berry, substituted a Hindu understanding that emphasizes the unity of all life but fails to deal with the reality of evil in our world.

Others, like their secular p.c. counterparts, focus exclusively on concern for the world here and now. They have neither a transcendent nor a spiritual vision for our common future.

Still others, those who are strongly influenced by feminist and lesbian writers, have made feminism into both their new religious faith and their answer to the ultimate questions of human destiny. They have replaced "Sky Father" with "Earth mother" and introduced a pantheon of fertility goddesses and pagan practices into what should be a theistic faith. In a pluralistic society, people are free to worship any deity they choose. But I have a serious problem with bringing such pagan practices into the church and sanctioning them as "legitimate" in our Judeo-Christian tradition.

In other words I believe a growing number of progressive Christians are looking to the political correctness movement

22. Williams, quoted in *Presbyterians for Renewal*, February 1994, pp. 10-11.

generally and feminism particularly to define their sense of the ultimate. "The metamorphosis of feminism from a campaign for equal rights to an existential crusade has had a curious result," observes Katherine Kersten. "Too often contemporary feminism holds itself out as a source of ultimate meaning for women. It claims to answer the fundamental theological question: 'Why do we suffer?' For many it has become a religion. . . . But feminism in its religious guise — the sort of feminism that seeks to find ultimate meaning in the self — is fundamentally incompatible with Christianity, and it exerts an increasingly destructive influence in the church world."[23]

As some radical feminists in the church seek to fashion a new vision for our common future, they begin predictably with reimagining both God and all human relationships. For example, Mary Hunt proposes redefining the family in a way that emphasizes "inclusivity and diversity" and the total autonomy of the self. "I have far more hope in substituting 'friendship' as a metaphor for family . . . imaging valuing genital sexual interaction in terms of whether and how it fosters friendship and pleasure."[24]

One has to ask how in the world any progressive Christian can justify totally repudiating the biblical vision of a Creator God who redeems both a people and a world and embracing a politically correct vision that has nothing to do with the Christian faith that they claim. What will be the long-term consequence for the church of this desertion of the scriptural view of God and God's purpose for humanity and creation?

Given the religious right's disturbingly polarized view of what's wrong and who the enemy is, what is the future to which they would transport us? And how is their vision different from those on the Christian left?

23. Kersten, "How the Feminist Establishment Hurts Women," *Christianity Today,* 20 June 1994, pp. 23, 24.
24. *Presbyterians for Renewal News Insert,* February, 1994, pp. 10-11.

CHAPTER 6

▼　▼　▼

Saving God's Bacon, Taking Back America, and Retreating to the Nifty Fifties

A HUSH FELL OVER the huge congregation at the Community Chapel as the seven candidates for baptism slowly descended into the baptismal tank. It was located on an elevated platform in the center of the sanctuary and was framed by the American flag on one side and the Christian flag on the other.

Pastor Bill Ingraham helped each person down into the warm tank. As the candidates stepped down, they struggled to keep their baptismal gowns from ballooning up around their necks. One at a time, they briefly shared how they had committed their lives to Jesus Christ. You could see members of the congregation straining forward on their pews to hear the more timid ones.

Pastor Bill then prayed ardently that God would seal in the waters of baptism the commitment that these seven had made to God. Then he systematically plunged each person backward under the water, and each came up sputtering and beaming.

After the last person emerged from the water, Pastor Ingraham was obviously very moved. He stammered, trying to find a song to express the praise he felt in his heart toward God. Suddenly, with arms and face extended toward heaven, he boomed, "God bless America, land that I love, stand beside her, and guide her . . ."

Clearly confused, the newly baptized and the congregation haltingly followed their pastor's lead, and then joined into singing the patriotic song.

The names have been changed, but this event actually happened. The pastor really did choose an anthem of adoration for a nation instead of a hymn of praise to God at this baptismal ceremony for new believers. And regrettably this occurrence reflects more than a one-time pastoral slipup. It reveals a deep flaw in the American church generally and the religious right specifically.

This event explains in part why the annual meeting of the Christian Coalition seemed like a bizarre combination of a political convention and a camp meeting. And the spontaneous nomination of Colonel Oliver North and Rush Limbaugh for president and vice president at that conference reflected how quickly they fuse religion and politics.

In this chapter we will explore how the religious right fuses their religion and their politics together, how they actually encourage their followers to embrace two very different religions and pay homage to two very different deities, all in the name of Jesus Christ. I can't stress strongly enough that this confusion of Christian faith with a political ideology is unique to American evangelicalism. It simply isn't a part of evangelical Christianity in any of the other Western countries I have visited.

At the very center of this confusion of nationalism and Christianity is a vision for America's future. To be sure, the leaders of the Christian right have a dream for America's future very different from any of those on the p.c. left. Moreover, this vision is drawn from the remembrance of a mythic past and designed to foil a collectivist future. Stay with me and see if this is a future you would choose to inhabit. Before we explore the vision for America's future to which the religious right would transport us, I would like to invite you to join me on a brief personal trip into a recent chapter in our nation's past.

A Personal Look Backwards

I bounded eagerly up the metal steps of the train on a warm August morning in 1942 in Pocatello, Idaho. My parents had moved to San Francisco three months earlier so my dad could take a new job in Alameda helping build troop ships, and I was looking forward to joining them there.

My folks had arranged for an older woman, Mrs. Emma Johnson, to accompany me on this trip. We found our seats, and I quickly settled in for the new adventure — the longest train trip of my young life. But I wasn't ready for what would happen to me on that trip.

As I looked around our passenger car, I realized that Mrs. Johnson and I were virtually the only civilians. The train was loaded to the luggage racks with soldiers, most of whom were probably leaving home for the first time to defend their country.

No sooner had the train begun to inch forward than a soldier sitting across the aisle from us asked me if I wanted to go to the snack car with him and get a soda. Of course I was flattered and went willingly. Over the next many hours, I made the trip to the snack car with dozens of soldiers, returning with comic books, candy, and sodas.

Even though I was only six, I fully understood what was going on. I knew the attention wasn't for me. I was a stand-in for kids that many of these soldiers would never see again. And I was deeply moved.

The point is that one couldn't grow up in the forties and not care very deeply about our country. Too many young men and women gave their lives to defend our freedom. But as grateful as I am for my country's constitutional government and the opportunities it has afforded me, I serve a God whose concerns range far beyond America and its future. I hold to a faith that transcends narrow national self-interest and embraces a world.

Saving God's Bacon

Where many on the right get off the track, not surprisingly, is where they get on . . . in their definition of what's gone wrong. Sincerely believing we are destined for a one-world Antichrist takeover, they are highly motivated to try to save God's bacon.

They seem to believe that if somehow they can take back America politically, they can forestall the liberals and humanists from destroying our families, undermining our faith, and further socializing America. And then perhaps God can use America to head off the collectivization of the planet.

But for years most conservative Christians, nurtured on a diet of dispensationalism, have been convinced that everything is getting worse and nothing can be done about it. So they couldn't even imagine taking action to try to save God's bacon. In addition, they had been heavily indoctrinated to believe that political action was well beyond the pale of an acceptable Christian response to the issues filling their world.

One of the earliest signals that a change was taking place among conservative Protestants was the publication of Jerry Falwell's book *Listen, America!* in 1980. While strongly supporting the end-times contention that everything is getting worse, Falwell did a remarkable turnabout in this book. Jerry Falwell, a convinced premillennial dispensationalist, presents a vision for the American future that is much more postmillennial than premillennial in character. He describes in very optimistic terms how conservative Christians can actually be a part of a right-wing political initiative to take America back. Neither Falwell nor his followers seem to have noticed the inherent contradiction between an end-times view that insists everything is getting worse and a vision for taking back America where we can allegedly make everything better.

Perhaps one of the most telling impacts of *Listen, America!* was not just its optimistic vision for the future but the way this book sanctioned political activism for conservative Protestants. Falwell insisted that now political involvement was not only kosher for conservative Christians but obligatory! God was counting on Christians to take America back politically by way of a right-wing ideological agenda with a few selected moral issues added to the package.

For years people like Robert Ringer, the author of *Restoring the American Dream,* had called on fellow secular conservatives to take America back. But it took Jerry Falwell to dress that vision up in Sunday go-to-meeting clothes and sell it to conservative Christians.

Jerry Falwell declared, "Americans must no longer linger in ignorance and apathy. We cannot be silent about the sins that are destroying this nation. The choice is ours. We must turn America around or prepare for inevitable destruction."[1] *Listen, America!* struck a responsive note with millions of fundamentalists and evangelicals who weren't content to sit back any longer and let the liberals and humanists undermine America's morality, threaten our faith, and soften up our nation for a Soviet takeover.

It is difficult to exaggerate the importance of this vision for the remarkable growth of the religious right. It directly contributed to the mobilization of the Moral Majority and the politicization of millions of fundamentalists and evangelicals. And the public square will never be the same again.

Even though the Moral Majority has gone out of business, the religious right's vision for America's future has not. In fact, it has actually grown in influence and power among conservative Protestants. There is a growing conviction among many in this population that their primary mission as Christians is no longer to share God's love with the world but to try and save God's bacon and take back America.

Nearly a decade later, a new spokesperson has emerged for the reborn right and given birth to the functional equivalent of the Moral Majority. That spokesperson is Pat Robertson, and the new organization is the Christian Coalition. Though he was very active in the eighties, Robertson became the new leader of the Christian right in the nineties.

Falwell came out of a fundamentalist background and drew fundamentalists and evangelicals into the slipstream of his right-

1. Jerry Falwell, *Listen, America!* (Garden City, N.Y.: Doubleday, 1980), pp. 22-23.

wing Christian activism. Pat Robertson, a charismatic, has been very successful in also drawing hundreds of thousands of Pentecostals and charismatics into this new right-wing political crusade. As a consequence, over the past two decades, a dramatically expanding number of conservative Protestants have been recruited and radicalized to serve in the militant army of the Christian right.

Pat Robertson, like Falwell, was reared on a heavy diet of dispensationalism, and, as we have seen, he has a tremendous preoccupation with the end times. However, Robertson has not only been very powerfully influenced by Falwell's optimistic political vision for America's future but has also had his vision dramatically shaped by influential Christian Reconstructionists who have unofficially joined forces with the Coalition.

During the first incarnation of the religious right in the eighties, they worked for a limited legislative agenda in Washington, D.C. (which got little support from the Reagan White House). And they essentially labored to hold back the tide of unwanted social change. Frankly, their end-times fatalism had the upper hand, and they didn't seem to believe they could do much to slow the inevitable decline or defeat of America being engineered by the humanist/liberal elite.

In the most recent reincarnation of the religious right, there has been a complete mood swing. They are no longer content to simply jam their big toe in the dike and pray that they will survive this time of the demonic decline of America.

Today they can be found storming the barricades of secular culture, intent on actually taking over. Driven by a swelling new optimism, many seem almost intoxicated by a belief that it is in their power to take over and take America back. And the Republican landslide in 1994 certainly has fueled their optimism.

While many still cling tenaciously to their various end-times conspiracy theories, they have dumped their dispensational pessimism to embrace the new "take power" optimism of the postmillennial Reconstructionists. More and more leaders on the religious right are heard trumpeting triumphalistically not only about "saving" America but about conservative Christians taking power and taking over.

Again, these conservative Christians don't seem to recognize that they are embracing two contradictory visions of the future at the same time. Many of these good people still cling tenaciously to a premillennial dispensationalism in which they really believe everything is getting worse and nothing can get better until Jesus returns. At the same time, influenced by the postmillennial optimism of the Christian Reconstructionists, they believe they can take over and make things better right now.

This triumphalistic tone clearly dominated at the Christian Coalition's 1994 Road to Victory National Conference in Washington. Robertson declared at the Coalition banquet that the Democratic "extremists" and "radicals" who are intent on destroying everything Christians care about are not going to win. "You don't own our children," Robertson told his adversaries, "and you don't own our country, and we're going to take it back from the likes of you!"

This sort of aggressive confidence in large part reflects the influence of the vision of the Christian Reconstructionists, which grants no place to end-times fatalism or premillennial pessimism. Reconstructionists are convinced that it lies within the power of the church to create the kingdom of God on earth in our time.

"Our goal is world dominion under Christ's lordship, a 'world takeover' if you will," declared David Chilton, one of the leading spokespersons for Reconstructionism. "We are shapers of history." R. J. Rushdoony and Gary North are two of the other leading spokespersons for this "kingdom now" theology. And as Chilton indicates, their agenda isn't limited to taking back America: they are intent on working for a world takeover.

The Reconstructionist vision for a political takeover in the name of God bears a striking resemblance to the political vision of the Islamic extremists. Christian Reconstructionists advocate the abandonment of democracy in order to create a theocracy in which the men of God rule. The new world order they envision includes not only a Levitical theocracy but a libertarian economic system, in which no one gets in the way of the operation of the free market. They seek to realize their utopia by reinstituting Old Testament laws and regulations and imposing contemporary right-wing political ideology.

Pat Robertson shows no signs of having bought into the larger

Reconstructionist vision, but he has clearly integrated some elements of Reconstructionism in his vision of America's future. While he continues to indulge in elaborate end-times conspiratorial speculations about the decline of American society, he also promotes triumphalist strategies for a return to a Christian America.

He has done a remarkable turnabout and doesn't seem to recognize any contradiction between his end-times fatalism and his postmillennial optimism. His books are filled with terrifying descriptions of America's inevitable slide toward a one-world Antichrist collective. And in the very next breath he describes exuberantly how Christians have the power to take back America for God.

Not surprisingly, the Christian Coalition tends to focus much more on Robertson's essentially postmillennial vision for America than on his end-times fatalism. And the Coalition also reflects the Reconstructionist intention of taking dominion in all arenas of society.

In a critique of Reconstructionism, Bruce Barron observes that Robertson is one of a growing number of evangelicals who, "no longer satisfied with seeking legislative change on a handful of issues, are setting out to reconstruct America. They may not be theonomists, but many of them have moved beyond selective lobbying and adopted the patient, long-term, bottom-up, all encompassing approach to change the Reconstructionists have been advocating all along."[2]

What is the future to which the reborn religious right would transport us if we gave our consent? Evangelical historian Richard V. Pierard contends that the political agenda of the religious right is virtually indistinguishable from that of the secular right except for its added stress on a handful of moral issues.[3] My reading of the literature of the Christian right certainly seems to bear out Pierard's assertion.

Both the religious right and the secular right favor building up American military strength to promote American national su-

2. Barron, *Heaven on Earth? The Social and Political Agendas of Dominion Theology* (Grand Rapids: Zondervan, 1992), pp. 100-101.
3. See Pierard, "The Religious Right in America: Where Is It Going?" *Baptist Quarterly* 35 (October 1993).

premacy in the world. Both strongly favor cutting back American foreign aid except in those specific situations that clearly advance America's national interests, regardless of humanitarian consequences. Both are very suspicious of any forms of international cooperation for fear it could undermine national sovereignty. Both are strongly opposed to the liberal policies of governments they deem "socialistic." Both have a supreme confidence in the magic of the marketplace to transport us to an economic utopia beyond our wildest imaginings. Both the secular right and the Christian right tend to deny that we have any serious environmental problems. Both want to see immigration significantly reduced. Both are opposed to multiculturalism and bilingual education and affirmative-action hiring policies. Both are passionate advocates for limited government and cutbacks in domestic programs for the poor. Both groups have a record of opposing virtually all forms of gun control. Both groups typically favor harsher sentencing of criminals, expansion of the prison system, and capital punishment for a larger range of crimes. And, during the debate on Clinton's 1994 crime bill, both groups labeled preventive efforts to reach "at risk" kids before they get involved in crime as wasteful pork-barrel spending.

How is it possible that the political agenda of the religious right looks so much like that of the secular right, when the leaders of the religious right contend that their views come directly from the Bible? There are two possible responses. Either the secular right has been divinely inspired all along and no one noticed. Or the religious right has allowed their agenda for social change to be determined by right-wing political ideology instead of Scripture. Let me explain how I believe conservative Protestants have been co-opted.

Harvey Cox observes that "American Fundamentalism is at once theology, subculture, and ideology, but not all components have equal weight. 'When I was a boy in Virginia,' says Jerry Falwell, 'in a redneck society, patriotism was just a part of life.'"[4]

Americans reared in conservative American culture take in

4. Cox, "Fundamentalism as an Ideology," in *Piety and Politics: Evangelicals and Fundamentalists Confront the World*, ed. Richard John Neuhaus and Michael Cromartie (Washington: Ethics and Public Policy Center, 1987), p. 291.

their right-wing political ideology and conspiracy theories with their mother's milk. For those who grew up with this type of worldview and also happened to become Christians, nothing has changed. Their particular brand of Christian faith doesn't challenge their right-wing political worldview: it accommodates it. And, of course, in addition to all the political agendas that the secular right and the religious right share in common, the religious right adds to the list their selected "moral" issues.

The Christian Coalition has replaced the Moral Majority as the flagship of the Christian right in the nineties. Like the Moral Majority, it strongly advocates "traditional family values," opposes "special rights" for gays and lesbians, and rejects abortion as a way to resolve an unwanted pregnancy.

Many Christians of all traditions can enthusiastically support those concerns that are clearly biblical — encouraging the integrity of family life, sexual abstinence for the young, and concern for human life. But there is a growing concern among many that legislative action may not be the best way to address these concerns.

Similarly, as I outline the political and moral agendas of the Christian right with evangelical leaders in other countries, they share some of their moral concerns. But they would rather see change come from personal transformation than from political action. And they are consistently appalled by the nationalistic focus of the political agenda and see many of the points of advocacy working in direct contradiction to God's purposes reflected in Scripture to work for justice and peace.

This narrow nationalistic view is evident in much of the literature produced by the Christian Coalition. Consider this passage from an essay by Ralph Reed, CEO of the Christian Coalition:

> What would the world look like if Christian conservatives won? . . . What most religious conservatives really want is to reclaim some strengths of the America that most of us grew up in, the post–World War II America that was proud, militarily strong, morally sound, and looked up to by the rest of the world. This America existed until the nation's cultural fabric was torn apart by a combination of the sexual revolution, the war in Vietnam,

Watergate, the rise of the drug culture, and the explosive growth of the welfare state.[5]

Reed's vision for the future confirms the analysis of this chapter. There is none of the imagery of the in-breaking of God's kingdom here. This is a singularly nationalistic vision that any secular right-winger could enthusiastically embrace. I have yet to find a single evangelical leader in another country who would condone this merging of American nationalism and Christian faith.

You see, in spite of claims to the contrary, the vision for the Christian right doesn't really come from Scripture. Obviously there is nothing in the Bible about working for a future in which America is "proud, militarily strong, morally sound, and looked up to by the world." Nor does Scripture call us to equate any of the nations of this world with the kingdom of God. The special status accorded America by the members of the religious right derives not from Scripture but from a particularly creative remembering of America's past.

A Revisionist History, a Mythic Past, and a Nationalistic Crusade

As the lights dimmed in the ballroom of the Washington Hilton, David Barton stepped into the spotlight. "Tonight we are going to present a very exciting slide show on America's godly heritage," he announced. The audience at the Christian Coalition's national gathering quickly settled down and turned to view the screen. Barton told them the "unique" story of America's godly past. His presentation stressed how our nation had been founded by God on biblical principles, and the clear message was that only if America returns to its godly heritage can it fulfill its providential

5. Ralph E. Reed Jr., "What Do Religious Conservatives Really Want?" in *Disciples and Democracy: Religious Conservatives and the Future of American Politics,* ed. Michael Cromartie (Grand Rapids: William B. Eerdmans, 1994), p. 3.

destiny. Barton particularly stressed the importance of raising up a new generation of Christian leaders who honor and support America's Christian heritage.

The Christian right's hope for the future finds its origin not in Scripture but in calling us back to America's godly past, a mythic Golden Age. The problem is that they continually call us back to a past that never existed, at least not as they remember it. As a historian I am deeply distressed at how often those on the right have attempted to rewrite our nation's story to make it say what they want instead of dealing fairly with the facts of history.

Central to this retelling of America's story is the contention by a number on the religious right that the United States is God's new chosen nation, unique in the community of nations, the best thing God ever created. This claim of uniqueness is based on the historical assertion that the United States was founded on biblical principles by godly men. Jerry Falwell's ringing declaration in this regard is representative: "I believe America has reached the pinnacle of greatness unlike any nation in human history because our Founding Fathers established America's laws and precepts on the principles recorded in the laws of God, including the Ten Commandments. God has blessed this nation because in its early days she sought to honor God and the Bible, the inerrant Word of the living God."[6]

Is this claim true? Has America really reached a "pinnacle of greatness unlike any nation in human history because our Founding Fathers established America's laws and precepts on the principles recorded in the laws of God"? Listen to the response of three leading evangelical historians, Mark Noll, Nathan Hatch, and George Marsden: "A careful study of the facts of history shows that early America does not deserve to be considered uniquely, distinctively or even predominately Christian, if we mean by the word 'Christian' a state of society reflecting the ideals presented in Scripture. There is no golden age to which Christians may return."[7]

Regrettably, many evangelicals aren't reading their own his-

6. Falwell, *Listen, America!* p. 29.
7. Noll, Hatch, and Marsden, *The Search for Christian America* (Westchester, Ill.: Crossway Books, 1983), p. 17.

torians. Large numbers of them are listening to the proponents of the apparently more beguiling vision of the United States as God's new chosen nation, God's new Israel. Pat Robertson asserts,

> As we review the history of the United States, it is clear that every one of those promises made to ancient Israel has come true here as well. There has never been in the history of the world any nation more powerful, more free, or more generously endowed with physical possessions. . . .
> We have had more wealth than the richest of all empires. We have had more military might than any colossus. We have risen above all the nations of the world. . . .
> But these things did not happen by accident, nor did they happen somehow because the citizens of America are smarter or more worthy than the citizens of any other country. It happened because those men and women who founded this land made a solemn covenant that they would be the people of God and that this would be a Christian nation.[8]

Robertson is not even close on this reading of history. Our nation's founders never entered into a covenant with God that "this would be a Christian nation." As we will see, most of our nation's founders weren't even Christians themselves. So they really had no basis on which to enter into a covenant with God.

Perhaps Robertson is thinking of the covenant sealed by John Winthrop and the small band of Puritans that entered Massachusetts Bay in 1630, the memorable pronouncement of their belief that they had been called by God to be a city set on a hill for all the world to see.[9] But the Puritans' covenant with God was not about founding a new nation. They were expressing their commitment to set an example of how to purify the church in this "new land" in order to hasten the return of Christ and the establishment of God's kingdom.[10]

8. Robertson, *The Turning Tide* (Dallas: Word Publishing, 1993), pp. 293-94.
9. See Edmund S. Morgan, *The Puritan Dilemma: The Story of John Winthrop* (Boston: Little, Brown, 1958), p. 70.
10. See Perry Miller, *Errand into the Wilderness* (Cambridge: Harvard University Press, 1956).

Thousands of people came to this continent during those early years for all kinds of reasons. Many came seeking their fortune as well as seeking religious freedom. Very few, like the Puritans, made any effort to enter into a covenant with God, and there is no evidence I am aware of that our forefathers sought to enter into a formal covenant with God to establish a Christian nation.

Even without supporting evidence, however, the myth that America was chosen by God to replace God's covenant relationship with Israel remains compelling among conservative Christians today. Perhaps the single most popular book propounding this myth is *The Light and the Glory.* This book was written not by historians but rather by a preacher, Peter Marshall, and a freelance writer, David Manuel. It offers a romanticized and in some aspects fictionalized account of the founding of America on the way to making a case for America's special status as God's chosen nation. "In the virgin wilderness of America, God was making His most significant attempt since ancient Israel to create a new Israel."[11] The authors offer no documentation to support their grand contention.

Reviewing the book for *Christianity Today,* evangelical historian Richard V. Pierard wasted no words in pointing out the book's deficiencies: "What exists here is a naive providential post-millennialism that identifies America as the kingdom of God. . . . Both historically and theologically, this work extolling an evangelical form of American civil religion is so defective as not to warrant serious attention by either scholars or laypeople."[12]

But despite such warnings about the book's inadequate scholarship, it has become the primary source many evangelicals turn to in order to understand the American past. Marshall and Manuel recently authored a new book entitled *From Sea to Shining Sea.* It continues to enjoy a largely undiminished popularity with

11. Marshall and Manuel, *The Light and the Glory* (Old Tappan, N.J.: Fleming H. Revell, 1977), pp. 22-23.
12. Richard V. Pierard, "God's Chosen People," *Christianity Today* 22 (24 March 1978).

the same audience. Apparently the myth that we are God's chosen people is something these folks choose to believe so devoutly that they don't want to have their beliefs shaken by the facts of history.

Other nations have made similar claims to be God's chosen people. And their cases should alert us to the serious dangers that often accompany this claim. Canadian historian Donald Akenson has produced a study of three such countries — the Republic of South Africa, modern-day Israel, and Northern Ireland — in which he does a comparative historical analysis of the covenantal thinking that shaped these three countries.

His findings should be particularly sobering for conservative Christians who believe America enjoys a unique covenant relationship with God. When people believe they are God's chosen nation, then they can readily justify punitive or retributive behavior toward those who are outsiders. The three nations in Akenson's study have each adopted an us-versus-them mentality. Those who view themselves as the "chosen" have rationalized all manner of inhumane treatment of those whom they view as the "Canaanites."[13]

We have already seen this sort of demonization of the "Canaanites" in the religious right's characterization of the former Soviet Union as the Evil Empire. I would suggest that the powerful us/them way of thinking has filtered down to affect the group's relationships with other elements within American society as well. In fact, they have declared a full-scale war on those they would characterize as the "Canaanites" within — feminists, gays, liberals, and humanists, who are viewed as threatening the true and rightful character of God's chosen nation.

Theologian Gabriel Fackre has suggested that in claiming a special status for America as God's chosen nation, the religious right has created a new form of messianic nationalism and, in effect, rewritten the doctrines of creation, fall, and redemption. This revisionist history begins with a second creation — the founding of America. It contains a second fall — America's de-

13. See Akenson, *God's Peoples: Covenant and Land in South Africa, Israel and Ulster* (Ithaca, N.Y.: Cornell University Press, 1992).

parture from the biblical principles on which they believe it was founded. And it proposes a new method of redemption by contending that God has chosen to use the United States of America instead of the church to redeem the world.

"Perhaps the greatest departure from Christian doctrine by the Religious Right is its transfer of the status of special covenant from the elect of God in the particular history of Israel to another people," says Fackre. "The functional elevation of America to the place of a chosen nation adds to the Christian story a chapter which is not in the Book."[14] Fackre is absolutely right. There is no support in Scripture for this kind of messianic nationalism. And neither is there any historical support for the religious right's contention that America is God's chosen nation.

Those on the right base their claim of American exceptionalism on two main assertions: (1) America's founding fathers were godly men, and (2) America is a uniquely Christian nation founded on biblical principles. Falwell reflects both of these claims when he urges Americans "to come back to the faith of our fathers, to the Bible of our fathers, and to the biblical principles that our fathers used as a premise for this nation's establishment."[15]

Let's look at the first assertion, that the founders of America were godly men. What exactly was "the faith of our fathers" that Falwell refers to? It varied from one individual to another. Of course, there was a small group of convinced Christians among the founding fathers including Patrick Henry, John Witherspoon, and John Jay. But they were the exceptions. The rest evidenced no belief in such things as the deity and resurrection of Christ, the doctrine of the Trinity, and the divine inspiration of Scripture.

Listen to Noll, Hatch, and Marsden's description of the kind of religious faith our nation's founders professed and the kind of God they served.

These brilliant leaders . . . were at once genuinely religious but not specifically Christian. Virtually all these great men had a

14. Fackre, *The Religious Right and the Christian Faith* (Grand Rapids: William B. Eerdmans, 1982), p. 62.
15. Falwell, *Listen, America!* p. 50.

profound belief in "the Supreme Judge of the world" and in "the protection of Divine Providence," to use the words of the Declaration of Independence. Yet only a few believed in the orthodox teachings of traditional Christianity — that, for example, Christ's death atoned for sin, that the Bible was a unique revelation from God, or that the miracles recorded in Scripture actually happened. . . .

The God of the founding fathers was a benevolent deity, not far removed from the God of eighteenth-century Deists or nineteenth-century Unitarians. This God had made the world an orderly and understandable place. He had created mankind with great skill and imbued him with nearly infinite potential. The men who put the nation together were sincere moralists and great humanitarians. They were utterly convinced that human exertion and goodwill could make America a nearly ideal place. They were not, in any traditional sense, Christian.[16]

It is true that the founding fathers often raised their voices in prayer to God. But their prayers were not addressed to the God revealed in Jesus Christ. They were praying to the impersonal, rational god of nature. This was a god who had little ability to intervene in history, little interest in redeeming the world, and little inclination to have an intimate union with his adherents.

Some of these men not only rejected some of the tenets of orthodox Christian faith but actually opposed the activities and teachings of the historic Christian church. In his youth, Benjamin Franklin worked to undermine Puritan influence and beliefs in Philadelphia. Thomas Jefferson succeeded in removing all the courses on Christian faith from the curriculum at the University of Virginia. And he predicted approvingly that the historic Christian faith would disappear from America and be replaced within a generation by a more rational religion that would conform to Enlightenment principles.

Jefferson also did the first cut-and-paste job on the New Testament in America. He cut out every single reference in the

16. Noll, Hatch, and Marsden, *The Search for Christian America*, pp. 72, 73-74.

New Testament to miracles. And Jefferson's New Testament ended where his faith did — with a sealed tomb. Check it out in your local library.

Perhaps the confusion over the specific content of the faith of the founding fathers stems from the fact that they often used the rhetoric of traditional Christianity, but they didn't invest it with its traditional meanings. For example, Jefferson spoke of Americans as "a chosen people." But his understanding of chosenness had nothing to do with redemption in Jesus Christ. He was simply redefining the term to mean those who had the good fortune to be born in America.

However, while the nation's founders were not committed to the historic Christian faith, they did understand the importance of religion. They realized that if they were to successfully midwife a new political experiment, they would certainly need the assistance of religion. So they invoked the assistance of nature's god and borrowed Christian terms and symbols and created a new civil religion that they hoped would be adequate for the challenge of nation building.

This brings us to the second claim of the religious right, that America is special in God's eyes because it was founded on biblical principles. To what extent is this actually the case? Before we can attempt any definitive answer, we will have to settle the issue of what these "biblical principles" are. But there is a fairly direct refutation of this claim recorded in one of the official documents of the young republic, a treaty with the nation of Tripoli that was negotiated during Washington's term as president and signed by President John Adams in 1797. In the context of assuring the leaders of that Islamic nation that religious opinions would never lead to disharmony between the two states, the treaty specified that "the government of the United States of America is not in any sense founded on the Christian religion."[17]

Certainly this supports the assertion of Noll, Hatch, and Marsden that "it is historically incorrect to regard the founding of America and the formulation of the founding documents as

17. *Treaties and Other International Acts of the United States,* vol. 2, ed. Hunter Miller (Washington: U.S. Government Printing Office, 1930), p. 365.

being Christian in their origins."[18] It is a serious error, they argue, to call Christians to "restore" the Bible as the sole basis for American law and government.

Let me be clear at this point that I am not denying the reality of Christian influence in the founding of America. Nor am I suggesting that the founding fathers were insincere in their religious beliefs. Rather, I am suggesting that they did not directly use biblical principles in composing those documents. Their principle allegiance was not to the Bible or traditional Christian doctrines but rather to Enlightenment principles of human autonomy and reason. The Declaration of Independence appeals to "self-evident" truths, not biblical truths. It appeals to the laws of nature, not the revelation of God in Christ.

Was God involved in the founding of America? Absolutely! The Bible insists that the Creator God is involved in all human activity. Tito Paredes, an anthropologist and an evangelical believer from Peru, said something in this regard that has helped my thinking about it: "God is in all cultures and nations both affirming and judging." Our task, then, is to identify and celebrate the ways in which the Creator has indeed been involved in America's history as well as in the history of every nation and people. That obligates us to consider the ways in which our history comes under the judgment of God as well.

It is clear, therefore, that there is nothing in either Scripture or history to support the contention that America is God's new chosen nation, God's special agent to save the world. That is the role of the church. Regrettably, some leaders of the religious right do history the way cult leaders do theology: they select bits and pieces of history and arrange them in ways that support the positions they want to prove. The result is no longer history but mythology. Perhaps the most troubling aspect of this mythmaking is that it has drawn many sincere Christians to unwittingly embrace another faith and serve another god.

18. Noll, Hatch, and Marsden, *The Search for Christian America*, p. 130.

Will the Real Christian Religion Please Stand Up

The Bible repeatedly warns of the serious danger that even the elect can be deceived and led astray to embrace faiths other than the gospel of Jesus Christ. Frankly, I believe that is exactly what has happened to many sincere believers who have bought into the religious right's myth of a Christian America. While still confessing their loyalty to the gospel of Christ, they have been seduced to embrace another faith — the civil religion of America.

Henry Steele Commager, one of America's leading historians, has argued that "the new nation began with two religions, one secular and one spiritual. Almost all Americans acknowledged themselves as Christians," but in fact they "generally shared what has been called 'a civil religion' . . . a secular faith in America herself, in democracy, equality and freedom which were equated with America in the American mission and the American destiny."[19] Because most of the European immigrants were familiar with the symbols and language of the Christian faith, these symbols and language were naturally incorporated into the evolving civil religion. But while the trappings seemed familiarly Christian, the essential values and purposes of the civil religion were quite different from those of the Christian faith. Robert Bellah, one of the leading authorities on civil religion, explains:

> The words and acts of the founding fathers, especially the first few presidents, shaped the form and tone of the civil religion as it has been maintained ever since. Though much is selectively derived from Christianity, this religion is clearly not itself Christianity. For one thing, neither Washington nor Adams nor Jefferson mentions Christ in his inaugural address; nor do any of the subsequent presidents, although not one fails to mention God. The God of the civil religion is not only rather "unitarian," he is also on the austere side, much more related to order, law, and right than to salvation and love.[20]

19. Commager, *Jefferson, Nationalism, and the Enlightenment* (New York: George Braziller, 1975), pp. 189-90.
20. Bellah, *Beyond Belief: Essays on Religion in a Post-Traditional World* (New York: Harper and Row, 1970), p. 175.

A remarkable coincidence accompanied the fifty-year celebration of the signing of the Declaration of Independence that was used very deliberately to garrison national support for America's emerging civil religion. On July 4, 1826, Thomas Jefferson and John Adams both died. Americans, strongly believing in providence, tried to discern the meaning of this unusual coincidence.

Then President John Quincy Adams went on national T.V. (or its equivalent) and said in effect, I will tell you what these events mean. "In this most singular coincidence, the finger of Providence is plainly visible! It hallows the Declaration of Independence as the Word of God, and is the bow in the Heavens, that promises its principles shall be eternal, and their dissemination universal over the Earth." The president went on to declare that this event signaled "the auspicious commencement of the political salvation of the world."[21]

The blatant claim that this remarkable coincidence somehow sanctioned the Declaration of Independence as the Word of God and America as God's agent of salvation in the world must be for those Christians who take Scripture seriously nothing less than heresy. But this kind of civil religion and its heretical assumptions have permeated American culture and the American church since our nation's founding. And the religious right has embraced much of the imagery of this civil faith apparently without noticing that it bears very little resemblance to their Christian faith.

Because the founding fathers were seeking to appeal to as many people as possible in the already comparatively pluralistic society of a young America, they sought to purge their civil religion of as much sectarian specificity as possible. Most significantly, they spoke not of the God revealed in Jesus Christ but rather of the rational god of the Enlightenment, nature's god. In essence, they turned around Pascal's dictum: Not the God of Abraham, Isaac, and Jacob but the god of the philosophers and scholars. In practice, American civil religion has made of this god a tribal deity or a national mascot singularly concerned about the protection and advancement of one nation, the United States of America.

21. Adams, quoted by Merrill D. Peterson in *The Jefferson Image in the American Mind* (New York: Oxford University Press, 1960), p. 6.

And now America's religious right is following the lead of the nation's founding fathers. In their own efforts to attract the largest possible number of people to support their causes in our yet more pluralistic culture, the leaders of the religious right have taken to promoting a similarly indistinct, generic god and a civil faith that bears little similarity to Christian faith. As their agenda has shifted from the realm of faith to that of politics, they have had to make the shift in various ways from orthodox Christianity to the more accommodating civil religion. They do not seem to appreciate the fact that these are two profoundly different religions committed to two very different deities.

"Do You Still Pledge Your Allegiance?" is the title of an ad for Pat Robertson's Regent University. The ad reads,

> The United States was founded on enduring principles, drawn from the "laws of nature and of nature's god." Today, these same principles are stoking the fires of freedom in emerging democracies around the world. In this world of revolutionary turmoil, your allegiance to eternal truths counts more than ever. The graduate School of Public Policy at Regent University aims to equip those called to restore the qualities that made America great and good, and to renew the Christian witness in public affairs.[22]

This call to bend the knee to nature's god and the laws of nature is a call to civil religion. It is not a call to pledge allegiance to the God revealed in Jesus Christ and God's principles that are directing our world and determining our future. And the goal of this faith is not to see the love of God extended to a world but to see the greatness of America restored.

Don't take my word for it. Attend meetings of the Christian Coalition. Their overarching goal is that of a religion of America, to see American greatness restored and the promotion of a morality that is drawn more from American culture than from biblical principles.

A friend of mine attended the latest national conference

---

22. The advertisement appeared on p. 8 of the July/August 1992 issue of *Christian American*.

of the Christian Coalition in Washington, D.C. Something was missing and he couldn't put his finger on it. Toward the end of the conference, he identified what it was. The name of Jesus Christ had scarcely been mentioned during the entire conference. I suspect the reason is that there is little basis in Scripture for connecting Jesus to the cause of promoting American nationalism. You need the rational god of the founding fathers for that task, the god of "Law and Right." And undoubtedly they don't want to offend those who are not of the Christian faith.

At the center of this religion of America is a repudiation of the fall. Like some progressive Christians, the proponents of American civil religion reject the biblical claim that anything is broken, ruptured, or fallen. Therefore, there is no need to work for a vision of human redemption. I am not sure evangelical Christians who believe very strongly in both the fall and God's intentions to redeem a people realize that this is a missing component in America's civil religion.

> One of the most powerful aspects of the Enlightenment was its leaders' rejection of the Christian vision of sin and redemption. This rejection was linked with the positive vision of a society based on the inherent goodness of human persons and the possibility of human redemption. The principle set forth by Jean-Jacques Rousseau is that people are good and all evil is resident in society, not in people. Since society is the agent of evil, it follows that society can be reformed by exercising the good within humans until society, by becoming good, becomes the agent for salvation. . . . Humankind alone must answer to itself and create its own future.[23]

Our founding fathers, who bowed their knee to "nature's god," were not working from a biblical view of redemption through the crucifixion and resurrection of Jesus Christ. They believed that individuals were basically good and could live moral lives and enter into beneficial associations with one another

---

23. Robert Webber, *The Church in the World: Opposition, Tension, or Transformation?* (Grand Rapids: Zondervan, 1986), pp. 170-71.

through their own initiative. And so they promoted a civic morality as an integral part of a civil religion.

Today those on the religious right are doing exactly the same thing. They are promoting and seeking to legislate a morality that is drawn from American culture, not biblical faith. They are still calling people to return to "traditional moral values," and the future they are working for is not the in-breaking of God's transnational kingdom. They are calling Christians to labor for the nationalistic vision of taking America back and restoring its "greatness and goodness."

In this civil religion, the best thing God ever created was America. The entire focus of this civil faith is the United States of America, its power and prominence. You cannot read the literature of the Christian right without getting the clear message that our "Christian" agenda is to restore America's status, power, and influence in the world. This certainly is Ralph Reed's call to American evangelicals.

Will Herberg describes American culture-religion as "a kind of super-religion." He goes on to state that "civic religion has always meant the sanctification of the society and culture of which it is the reflection, and that is one of the reasons why Jewish-Christian faith has always regarded it as incurably idolatrous."[24] Pledging allegiance to this "super-religion" of America is "incurably idolatrous." And those who pledge their allegiance to this nationalistic idolatry do indeed tend to sanction everything about America from its cultural values and political policies to its economic system.

Free-Market Economics: A Gift from on High

If many on the right are convinced that America is the greatest thing God ever created, they are equally convinced that the second greatest thing is the free-market economic system. I have found in my visits to conservative churches that speakers can say something

24. Herberg, *Protestant — Catholic — Jew: An Essay in American Religious Sociology* (Garden City, N.Y.: Doubleday, 1955), p. 279.

a little off the mark theologically and get away with it. But if anyone says anything critical of the free-enterprise system, he is likely to be stoned on the spot with hymn books. For those on the religious right, the free-market system is not just an economic theory; it's a central pillar supporting the edifice of their civil religion. On the basis of some acrobatic interpretation of selected passages from the Bible, some go so far as to say that free-market economic theory is an inherent part of Christian faith.

Reconstructionists are particularly avid enthusiasts of free-enterprise capitalism. When it comes to economics, they argue, we have only two choices: Satanic centrally planned economies or godly free-market economies. One representative Reconstructionist, David Chilton, has suggested that the best way for contemporary Christians to help those in need is to pursue their own personal self-interest. "The man who makes the highest profit," he says, "is the man who is best serving the public."[25] I am not certain what he makes of Jesus' observation that we cannot serve both God and mammon or his calls to put the welfare of others before our own self-interest.

While decrying utopian socialist schemes, those on the right are relentlessly promoting their own brand of utopianism. They insist that if we simply trust our individual and collective futures to the "magic of the marketplace," all of society will prosper, and we will all realize that ideal order we long for.

Let me be clear. Almost everyone recognizes now that centrally planned economic systems don't work very well. They have been exhaustively tested during this century and have uniformly proved calamitous over the long haul. Free-market economies, on the other hand, have proved enormously successful in efficiently providing goods and services. The nations of the world have tried the alternatives and, with a few exceptions, have turned to free markets. Granting all that, and granting that the Bible does indeed encourage personal responsibility and acknowledge the concept of private ownership, I still cannot find any

25. Chilton, *Productive Christians in an Age of Guilt-Manipulators: A Biblical Response to Ronald J. Sider,* 2d ed. (Tyler, Tex.: Institute for Christian Economics, 1982), p. 146.

biblical support for the contention that the free-enterprise system is God's gift to humankind.

Frankly, the reason I believe free enterprise works so well is that its chief motive force is the naked self-interest of fallen human beings. Free-enterprise capitalism as we know it would be a disaster in a truly Christian world, because we are called not to pursue our own self-interest but every person's good. When the rich young ruler asked him for advice, Jesus didn't give him a tip on a hot stock and send him off to keep up the good work in hopes that a rising tide would raise all ships. Jesus told him to sell all that he had, give it to the poor, and come and follow him. Is his message to us different today?

You see, for the free-enterprise system to work effectively, it must operate, we are told, in a neutral ethical environment. Adam Smith recognized that it also needed a new ethically neutral "providence" to guide its work. He proposed an "invisible hand" to select winners and losers without regard to any ethical values whatever.

Obviously this is a job description that the Creator God need not apply for. The Bible makes it abundantly clear that God has some very definite ethical "hangups" about how we should operate in all life's arenas, including the economic. God calls us to high moral standards in our economic activities. God also has some very definite views as to how we should treat the poor and the marginalized. It seems to me that biblical Christians must insist that biblical ethics and social justice, not the "invisible hand," influence the operation of the free market. We need to steward the free-market system in a way that advances the purposes of God, not the power and greed of humanity.

I find it particularly ironic that leaders on the religious right who are stridently opposed to Charles Darwin and all of his theories have uncritically embraced a profoundly Darwinian approach to economics. How can Christians who claim to be collaborators with a God who is intent on caring for the poor, the widow, and the orphan support a Darwinian survival-of-the-fittest economic system and convince themselves it is God's own creation?

What has happened is that many deeply committed Christians have become adherents to two very different religions and bow their knee to very different gods. They unwittingly blend together their faith in Jesus Christ with their sincere devotion to the religion of America, nature's god, and free-enterprise capitalism. They have absolutely no idea of where the one leaves off and the other begins. Worship of God and adoration of the nation and its economic system become one and the same. This incredible fusion of two different religions dramatically alters the view of Christian mission by the religious right.

The Religious Right's Revisionist View of Christian Mission

As we have already noted, the mission of American civil religion is fundamentally different from that of the church of Jesus Christ. Its goal is not primarily to proclaim and demonstrate the love of God to the world. The mission of the religious right is to take America back around a right-wing political and economic ideology. And by "saving God's bacon," hopefully nature's god can use America to save the world.

Please understand that I am not trying to suggest that those Christians who join the religious right are abandoning their desire to see the gospel of Jesus Christ proclaimed throughout the earth. I am suggesting, however, that to the extent that they shift their allegiance to America's civil religion, they diminish their allegiance to the gospel of Jesus Christ.

To the extent that they invest their resources in the political mission of trying to take back America, those resources will not be available to invest in sharing the Good News and helping the poor. It would be tragic if evangelicals were to undermine their traditional emphasis on biblical mission both at home and abroad by pouring increasing amounts of their energy and resources into a narrow nationalistic crusade and the politicization of the church.

But there are other concerns in this regard as well. The threat to the church from civil religion is not merely a matter of diverted resources. It is also a matter of subverted principles. American civil religion politicizes the gospel in its efforts to Christianize America.

"It gives America a religious veneer and the church a political character," says Robert Webber. "America is thought to be the center of God's activity in the world and the church is supposed to become a political power base, a special agent of capitalist economics, a champion of Western liberty, and a defender of messianic Americanism. Thus the church and the gospel are made the servants of a particular ideology."[26] No one can serve two masters. And God will not be equal partners with any person or ideology. Those who try to fuse faith in Christ with faith in the American way will always end by subordinating the gospel of Jesus Christ and his church to the civil religion — which is quite simply idolatrous.

Perhaps the sharpest indictment of America's civil religion comes from Robert Linder and Richard Pierard:

1. By endorsing civil religion, Christians may unintentionally be suggesting to others that salvation comes through the nation, not Christ.
2. Civil religion is susceptible to misuse by politicians seeking to support questionable policies.
3. The church that accommodates itself to civil religion thereby diminishes its capacity to challenge the values of the dominant culture.
4. Civil religion inevitably reduces the Creator God to a tribal god.
5. Civil religion tends to promote national self-righteousness and idolatry.[27]

In pointing out some of the serious problems with civil religion, my complaint is not with America, with the principles of democratic government, or with the relative benefits of a free-market economy. I believe that American Christians should be very grateful to God for the many benefits we receive as a result of living in America. I simply believe that our identity as

26. Webber, *The Church in the World,* p. 226.
27. See Linder and Pierard, *Twilight of the Saints: Biblical Christianity and Civil Religion in America* (Downers Grove, Ill.: InterVarsity Press, 1978), pp. 168-73.

Christians is distinct from our identity as citizens of America and that we do harm to both if we confuse the two. We should not be raising barriers between ourselves and other members of the body of Christ who live in other national and cultural contexts. To the contrary, we should be searching out our links with them and celebrating the ways in which God has blessed them within their respective cultures as he has blessed us in ours.

The Christian right comes calling us back not only to a mythic golden past but to a recent past, a simpler, more stable time when most families were intact, only dad worked, gays were in the closet, and America was "kicking butt" all over the world. Part of the Christian right's vision for the better future comes not just from a selective remembering of America's founding but from a nostalgic remembering of the nifty fifties.

Retreating to the Fifties

"I kept thinking of how dramatically the world has changed since 1954," James Dobson reflected on returning from his fortieth high school reunion at San Benito High School in Texas. Leaders on the right are much inclined to blame the sixties for all that's wrong with America and to look longingly back to the fifties. James Dobson is no exception. He recently devoted an entire issue of his newsletter to a survey of how the world had changed since his graduation from high school forty years ago.

"That was before Sputnik rocketed into orbit — before John Kennedy and Martin Luther King were murdered — before Vietnam, Watergate, Roe vs. Wade, the sexual revolution, Elvis, The Beatles and the psychedelic 'Summer of Love,'" he mused. It was also before the arrival of "socialistic and humanistic colleges and universities, governmental bureaucracies with destructive purposes, oppressive tax laws, radical feminism, abortion on demand."[28] All in all, he concludes, the sixties put a stake through the heart of America.

28. Dobson, "The Year Was 1954 and We Were All Very Young," *Focus on the Family Newsletter,* June 1994, pp. 4, 7.

 135

As coincidence would have it, I also graduated from high school in 1954. I, too, remember some of the surprising changes that took place after my graduation. I remember I was sitting in a cafe in Portland, Oregon, where I was attending a Christian college, when I first heard "Blue Suede Shoes" playing on a jukebox. It was 1957, and it was my first introduction to Elvis Presley. Of course, a white lad singing black music and wiggling his hips caused quite a stir in those days.

Conservative Christians were as alarmist then as they are today. I still remember some fundamentalists banded together to start an alternative Christian radio station to counter this threat to the Christian young and the American future. They were convinced that Elvis was a Soviet plant, sent to destroy Christian youth and the American way of life. It was hard for me to believe that "Love Me Tender, Love Me True" was really hatched in the Kremlin, but my conservative friends tell me I am incredibly naive about such things, and they are probably right.

Like many on the right, Dobson remembers the fifties as America's second golden age. "The cultural stability evident when we were in high school is reflected in the personal lives of my former classmates today. Those sweet kids have become loving husbands, wives, parents and grandparents. They have worked hard to get where they are currently. Most appear happily married, some to high school sweethearts. They are 'Good people' . . . and I am honored to be counted among them."[29]

I could describe my high school class of '54 in very similar terms. Life was more stable and predictable in the fifties. I am sure most of the grads in my class are "good people" who are mostly happily married. But as I reflect back, hardly any of my classmates had any time in their lives for religious faith. Whatever morality was manifested in their lives came primarily from the norms of middle-class American culture, not their religious beliefs.

The highlight of my fortieth reunion was encountering Pat Shea as my wife and I were leaving the reunion. Pat shared his story. He had gone through some major reversals ten years ago in Fresno, California. The bottom fell away, and in desperation

29. Dobson, "The Year Was 1954," p. 7.

he had turned his life over to God. Every part of his life had been changed by his newfound faith in Jesus Christ. And now he was a leader in the Evangelical Free Church and very grateful for the mercy of God. He remembered from high school days that I was a struggling Christian. He wanted to share his story with me, and I am very glad he did.

Frankly, some of us have absolutely no desire to return to the world of the "happy days" of the fifties. While students were "better behaved," they were usually totally out of touch with the world around them. They rarely questioned or challenged the values of their society. And young people of the fifties seemed to lack commitment to anything larger than simply replicating the consumer-driven lifestyles of their parents. We were raised to put our own needs first, and most of us did.

In the fifties, for many of us the suburban lifestyle and the American dream became virtually synonymous. And the impact of the suburbs on the American family wasn't altogether positive. The suburbs and the long commutes created the absent father. Women's economic status and independence declined after World War II. And sociologists report that many suburban housewives felt isolated and led lives of "booze, bowling, bridge and boredom."[30]

With the massive migration of America to the suburbs, the extended family met an abrupt and decisive end. No longer were there aunts, uncles, and grandparents to nurture the next generation. With many dads getting home just in time to kiss the kids good night, the major responsibility for parenting was left to mom. And given her own struggles and sense of isolation, she didn't always manage that well.

I think it's important in comparing the virtues of these two decades to remember that the "fifties were pregnant with the sixties." The sixties weren't the work of a conspiratorial elite. They were a direct product of the homes, families, and society of the nifty fifties.

And it is also important for all the middle-class white folks living in the suburbs to remember that the fifties were not good

30. Stephanie Coontz, *The Way We Never Were: American Families and the Nostalgia Trap* (New York: Basic Books, 1992), p. 37.

times for all Americans. John Perkins, a black evangelical leader, told me he had no wish to return to either America's first or second golden age. He reminds us that during America's founding days, those from African heritage were enslaved and oppressed.

And while the fifties may have been a good time for all the white grads from Dobson's high school and mine, they weren't a good time for many African Americans and many other people of color. Over half of the black two-parent families in those days lived in poverty. Many were systematically excluded from opportunities in education, employment, and housing. Others were brutalized and killed by whites, who often escaped any legal sanction for their crimes against blacks.

I still remember Norris Roberts, who resigned as a major from the U.S. Air Force in the fifties. He had a masters degree in business (when that degree was virtually unheard of). No one in Portland, Oregon, would give him a job — simply because he was black. He finally had to resort to driving a cab to support his family.

John Perkins relates how his brother, Clyde, who had distinguished himself fighting for America in Europe, came home from the Army to New Hebron, Mississippi. One Saturday night, Clyde and his girlfriend, Elma, were in line in the alley with others, waiting for the black entrance to Carolyn's Theater to open.

Clyde and Elma got in an argument. And the white marshal, who always patrolled the streets on Saturday night, appeared. He shouted, "You niggers quiet down." As Clyde turned to ask a question, the deputy clubbed him. Clyde got mad and in self-defense grabbed the marshal's club to keep the man from hitting him again.

That did it! The marshal was red in the face. He stepped back two steps, pulled out a gun, and shot Clyde twice in the stomach.

Clyde died. There was no inquiry regarding the marshal's action, and those on the white side of Hebron quickly forgot about "the incident."[31]

31. For the whole story, see Perkins, *Let Justice Roll Down: John Perkins Tells His Own Story* (Glendale, Calif.: Regal Books, 1976), pp. 19-22.

But John Perkins and his family didn't forget.

If things were not as rosy in the fifties as the religious right remembers them, neither were the sixties as dark as they remember them. After all, the sixties brought the civil rights movement, which did much to make constitutionally guaranteed rights more of a reality for a whole class of Americans. The sixties also gave birth to the environmental movement, the first serious efforts to start cleaning up the fouled skies and waters of a once-pristine land and ensure a better, healthier future for a new generation of Americans.

And the sixties also saw the beginnings of important organized efforts to address the enormous challenge of poverty and hunger in our country. We finally woke up to the fact that as much as 20 percent of our population was living in abject poverty, and through a coalition of government and private agencies, we started to do something about it.

These three important areas of societal change were largely the work of a generation of young people who were no longer content to focus on their own lives, as most of the young in my generation had. In other words, contrary to the selective memory of the religious right, not all the young people in the sixties were blowing their brains on drugs or losing their innocence in free love. These young people were determined to make a difference, and they did.

Regrettably the evangelical church rarely sought either to reach out to or support the idealistic young of the sixties. Instead, they distanced themselves. As a consequence, many of the young people's causes ran out of energy because they were rooted in a superficial idealism instead of in a deep biblical faith.

Amazingly, most evangelical churches wouldn't even have anything to do with the flood of hippies who became converts to the Christian faith in the late sixties and early seventies through the Jesus People movement. And the few that did, like Calvary Chapel in Costa Mesa, California, got the Jesus People to cut their hair, move back into the 'burbs, and get back into debt. And, as a result, I believe a tremendous missionary force was lost to the church.

It's not surprising that conservative Christians are down on the sixties, because so many of us were AWOL. And much of what went wrong was not the by-product of some humanistic liberal conspiracy, "socialistic universities," or government programs. Much of the failure must be laid directly at the door of the church. We were so busy in our consumer-driven suburban lifestyles and our own upwardly mobile nuclear families that we were unwilling to spend the time or the money to try to help serve the people and steer the changes of that important decade.

Looking backward, the religious right not only deplores the sixties but adores the fifties. Pat Robertson asks, "How can somebody be considered a far right radical who is only asking for the way America was in the '50's?"[32] And he looks back longingly to the mythical lives of the Cleavers as a model for families today. What Robertson doesn't seem to recognize is that this call to return to the nifty fifties exposes the *real* foundation of the Christian right's moral agenda. It is a call to return to the moral high water mark of the fifties, to traditional American values.

Robert Webber observes,

> The idea that all people of high principle should unite to recover America's moral heritage is a moralism that feeds civil religion. It is not a distinctly Christian message that demands regeneration into Jesus Christ and absolute obedience to the moral precepts given by him to the church. . . . True moral reform comes as the result of faith in Jesus Christ, not from a desire to create "national solidarity and stability."[33]

While William Bennett's efforts to achieve a set of common moral values for a pluralistic society are commendable, our first task as Christians is to promote a biblical morality by calling people to transforming faith in the living God.

What about the Christian right's persistent call to restore "traditional family values"? Is this a call for Christians to reclaim a biblical vision for the family? Absolutely not. It is a call to

32. Robertson, "Pat Robertson Responds," *700 Club Fact Sheet,* 15 July 1994.
33. Webber, *The Moral Majority: Right or Wrong?* (Westchester, Ill.: Crossway Books, 1981), pp. 105-6.

return to the normative cultural definition of the family forged in the fifties.

Don't take my word for it. Listen to Pat Robertson. This move back toward traditional family values is not an attempt to recapture "some moment of paradise on earth, but it does represent a swing back to the norm of American life in the 1950s."[34]

Let's be candid. This so-called "traditional family" did not come with the Ark of the Covenant. It is a very modern invention. The traditional nuclear family has been around less than two hundred years. And the American middle-class suburban version that the religious right is so keen on protecting has been around for less than sixty years.

Frankly, this preoccupation with preserving and protecting the nuclear family as it is has become almost as idolatrous as American nationalism among many conservative Protestants. Some are even claiming that the "traditional" nuclear family, not the church, is God's primary institution for advancing his kingdom.

It's important to give credit where credit is due. Even the Democrats are belatedly admitting that Dan Quayle and the Christian right have been right about emphasizing the importance of family integrity. It is essential that we all work for the fidelity of the family unit. Christians of all traditions need to join in calling one another and the larger society to greater fidelity in marital vows — not because that was more common in the fifties but because Scripture mandates it.

But Scripture also calls us to reach out and care for those without families and to genuinely be family to them. That certainly was not a characteristic of traditional nuclear families in the fifties, nor is it often today. And it is not a part of the call to "traditional family values" of the Christian right.

For a moment let's set aside the traditional nuclear family as a norm for Christian advocacy and ask, "What does the Bible have to say about the family? What is a biblical view of family life? What are the biblical principles that Christians are called to live out regarding family?"

34. Robertson, *The Turning Tide*, p. 163.

First, when the Bible speaks about family, it isn't speaking about the modern nuclear family. In the Old Testament, families were patriarchal clans and tribes. And in the New Testament, the term always refers to extended families.

You won't find anything in the Bible that supports the idolatrous preoccupation with protecting the individual biological family that characterizes many conservative Christian groups today. Read the New Testament again. There is very little mention of family. There is certainly nothing in the Bible about protecting the family as it is. The call of the gospel is never to self-preservation of individuals or families. Rather, we are constantly called to take risks to extend God's love into the world.

Will the Real Biblical Family Please Stand Up

When Jesus Christ talked about family, he brought a radical new perspective to the discussion that seriously challenged normative cultural assumptions about family life then and now. And, as you will see, the family values that Jesus endorses bear little resemblance to the traditional family values of America in the fifties. Jesus Christ calls us to create much more than "Leave It To Beaver" families who go to church on Sundays.

Rodney Clapp, in his important book *Families at the Crossroads,* has done a very helpful job plowing some new ground on this important issue. Essentially, Clapp argues from Scripture that Jesus Christ fundamentally redefines what it means to be family.

Remember when someone came up to Jesus and said, "Hey, your mother and brother are over there." Do you remember Christ's response? "Who is my mother or brother but he who does the will of God?" (Mark 3:31-35, my paraphrase).

Jesus wasn't minimizing the importance of the biological family unit. He was drawing an important new circle. According to Jesus Christ, anyone who does the will of God is automatically part of a new, larger family. In other words, all those who choose to follow Christ are sisters and brothers, members of a new family that transcends our various biological families. We are all adopted into God's new transnational family, which transcends America and traditional American culture.

Remember Jesus Christ's radical call to discipleship? "If anyone comes to me and does not hate his father and mother, his wife and children, his brothers and sisters — yes, even his own life — he cannot be my disciple" (Luke 14:26). And, as you know, many of those first disciples did leave homes and biological families to become part of a new Christian family sharing God's love with a world.

Clapp insists that one of the most important things Jesus did was to institute a new family, "a first family," that transcends all of our biological families.

> It is the new first family, a family of his followers that now demands primary allegiance. In fact, it demands allegiance even over the old first family, the biological family. Those who do the will of God (who, in other words live under the reign of God) are now brothers and sisters of Jesus and one another. . . . So far as the biological family is concerned, "I have not come to bring peace, but a sword" (Mt 10:34). Those who love father or mother more than Jesus, this Jesus says, are not worthy of him (Mt 10:37).[35]

God's intention from the beginning was to create a new community that was clearly at counterpoint to the pagan culture around it. God called a people "who were no people" to become a new people, a new family through which all the nations of the world will be blessed.

Jesus was a part of this God's covenant people and their story. The first thing Jesus did at the beginning of his ministry was to invite people to follow him and become members of a new community, God's "first family." When we choose to follow this Jesus, we are called to transfer our allegiance not only to God but to the new family of God.

What does a biblical view of the family look like then? Well, it doesn't look like doing time travel back to the fifties where the

---

35. Clapp, *Families at the Crossroads: Beyond Traditional Roles and Modern Options* (Downers Grove, Ill.: InterVarsity Press, 1993), p. 77.

nuclear family was centered on its own self-involved world, conforming to the morality of middle-class American culture and promoting American nationalism.

A biblical view of family looks like that first new community of people who left their homes, families, and jobs to journey with Jesus. Even as Jesus was a man for others, we are called to be a people for others and families for others — to set aside our self-involved lives and commit ourselves to the advance of God's new kingdom.

What does a biblical view of the family look like in concrete terms? One of the most compelling expressions of God's first family for me are my friends at Ichthus Fellowship Congregation in London. Singles, couples, single parents, divorced people, widows, and others from many different cultural backgrounds come together every week in small home groups to be family to each other. These small groups not only worship and study Scripture together but also help one another with marital problems and unemployment. They share child care, resources, and vehicles — just like family.

And the focus of these believers in these extended family groups isn't the self-involved aspirations of single-family detached lifestyles. Their focus is not only on giving reality to a new meaning of family together but also on making a difference in their world. Parents and kids learn to be families for others, experiencing family bonding in service to others instead of consumerism. They are involved in doing evangelism with children caught in prostitution in London, providing job training for the poor, and caring for neglected seniors in their neighborhoods.

Warring Visions for Our Common Future

As we have seen, America's p.c. left and religious right want to transport us to very different futures. Those on the left are eager to catch the powerful waves of change and ride them into a more progressive, inclusive future in which victims wrest power from those they view as oppressors. Those on the right are more interested in trying to reverse the tide of change and return to an imagined golden age.

The vision of the left is often devoid of any sense of transcendence or spirituality. And I am troubled by the fact that many progressive Christians seem inclined to derive both their values and their images of a better future more from the secular ideologues of the left than from Scripture. Some, in fact, have bought into the left's doctrine of religious pluralism to the point that they have given up the biblical vision of the future in which the Creator God takes initiative in Jesus Christ to redeem the world.

Many on the Christian right have also capitulated to secular ideologies in their pursuit of a restored golden age. Leaders on the religious right would have us believe that their vision of a Christian America is a Christian vision. But, as we have seen, it is not. However Christian their rhetoric may seem, they are in fact promoting a civil religion that is as distant from orthodox Christianity as is the vision of the left that they so fiercely oppose.

I believe the American church is facing a grave threat from the syncretism of Christian faith and political ideology that is encroaching from both ends of the political spectrum. The syncretistic vision of the Christian left incorporates elements of Eastern religion, feminist fertility deities, and the politics of exclusion with Christian religious symbols.

The syncretistic vision of the Christian right incorporates elements of nationalism, militarism, free-enterprise capitalism, and a cultural morality with a narrowly defined personal faith in Jesus.

Both sides threaten the church by luring increasing numbers of Christians away from biblical faith to ideological substitutes. Both sides have politicized the church and undermined its unique witness in society. Many in the American church have felt that they had to choose between the Christian left and the religious right. This is a false choice.

The one thing these two warring visions for the future have in common is that they are both preoccupied with power. As we will see in the next section, their notions of how to use that power could have a decisive impact on all our lives and futures as we enter a new millennium.

 145

PART III

▼ ▼ ▼

The Politics of Extremism on the Threshold of the Third Millennium

A S WE ENTER the third millennium, we are experiencing a world changing at blinding speed. On the one hand, we are seeing a rising tide of hope in rule of law, reconciliation, democratization, and the rule of law touching countries like Germany, South Africa, Israel, Northern Ireland, and Haiti. On the other hand, we seem to be in the grip of local wars, ethnic cleansing, and political destabilization. Rapid population growth in many areas of the Third World is raising the specter of growing famine, wholesale migration, and the environmental collapse of entire regions.

Blinding change is an essential part of the American experience these days, too. Violence is epidemic in our cities. Children are gunning down children. As a people, we seem to have lost our moral and spiritual bearings, and the very fabric of our family life and our civic life is shredding. The only things we seem to hold in common anymore are our commitment to our consumer culture and our addiction to the media wasteland.

Poverty in the United States is on the rise, and children and families are its greatest victims. We are seeing the rapid emergence of a two-tier America. The burgeoning underclass is increasingly disenfranchised, cut off not only from the larger consumer culture but also from any real opportunity to be employed in the type of legitimate work that can sustain life.

On the other hand, a small but very wealthy class is garrisoning itself in high-security enclaves. And many of its wealthy members are using their considerable clout to protect their own interests and reduce the amount of money they must pay through taxes to advance the common good.

And the middle class is shrinking as increasing numbers of young people slowly lose their grip on a middle-class way of life that their parents took for granted. It will hardly be surprising if this growing stratification leads to confrontation and violence again in a new century.

Indeed, as we have seen, confrontation and violence are already evident on some fronts in America's culture war. Progressives are trying to maintain and direct the course of social change for their own purposes, while conservatives are trying to shift the engines of change into reverse.

In this part of the book we will look at the implications of the culture war for America's future. In Chapter 7, we will explore and critique the philosophy of change that has been adopted by both the left and the right. In Chapter 8 we will ask which side is likely to gain the upper hand in America's culture war and how that is likely to shape our domestic and foreign policy as we enter a new millennium.

CHAPTER 7

▼ ▼ ▼

Taking Power, Total Warfare, and Cosmic Conflict

"Born Again Bigots Go Home," screamed a huge banner strung over San Francisco's Civic Center Plaza on Halloween evening in 1990. Dozens of police escorted thousands of charismatic and evangelical Christians beneath the banner and through a huge crowd of gay, lesbian, and pagan protesters. One of the largest groups represented in this protest called itself GHOST — "Grand Homosexual Outrage at Sickening Televangelists."

Standing on a large decorated platform at the front of the auditorium, televangelist Larry Lea warmly welcomed his followers. As the last of the 6,500 participants settled in, the service began. "This is one of a series of 'Prayer Breakthrough Crusades' we are conducting all over the country," Lea announced. "Our purpose is prayer and spiritual warfare."

Lea explained that Satanic territorial spirits had taken dominion over San Francisco, and he had the ability to discern who they were. Among them was the demon of homosexuality. He explained to his audience that it was their Christian responsibility to do battle with these territorial spirits. He called them to join him in doing spiritual warfare against this Satanic enslavement of San Francisco and the people who live here. Thousands of hands extended toward the vaulted ceiling, and a mighty roar of prayer filled the auditorium, the temperature rising along with the sound level.

While the radical left and the religious right are totally polarized in their analysis of what's wrong and the future to which they would take us, they are remarkably united in how they would bring their respective visions into being. They both seem convinced that the way to change society is through political action — taking power and taking over.

However, as our look at Larry Lea's crusade suggests, those on the religious right tend to view America's culture wars as more than just a political contest: they view it as a cosmic conflict in which they can call on the supernatural powers of God Almighty to defeat their political foes and win the day.

The goals of this chapter are (1) to explore how the ideological left and the Christian right intend to change society to achieve their respective visions, (2) to look at why their approaches to change are so remarkably similar, (3) to assess the implications of viewing America's culture war as total warfare, and (4) to consider a Jesus alternative to the advocacy of taking power and total warfare.

Everything the Religious Right Has Learned about How to Change Society They Have Learned from the Radical Left

The constant claim by the Christian right is that their advocacy comes directly from the Bible. I find it truly remarkable how many people accept this claim at face value. It is particularly troubling how many who present themselves as "experts" on the religious right accept the right's claim that their agenda comes out of a "stringent use of Scripture."

As we saw in Chapter 6, that claim is largely without merit. The Christian right's advocacy comes primarily from right-wing political ideology, American nationalism, and the glorification of traditional cultural values. When it comes to how to change society, I believe the leaders of the religious right have failed to take Scripture seriously here as well. For example, there is no evidence that leaders on the right have made any effort to discern from Scripture how Jesus and his small band turned their world upside down. If they had, they would have discovered that the genius of the Jesus movement wasn't propelled by political action or the advocacy of any form of political ideology.

All evidence suggests that everything the Christian right has learned about how to change society they learned from the radical political left, not from the Bible. It seems the height of irony that the leaders of the Christian right would look to their sworn enemies to learn the best way to work for social change. But that's exactly what they have done. The religious right has not only borrowed wholesale from the tactics of the left, but some have even borrowed many of the most extreme measures from the radicals of the sinister sixties.

It is important to clarify here that the Christian right is not the first group of American Christians to borrow from the political left. Many mainline Protestants and progressive Catholics have been doing it for years. But they have borrowed not only their political strategies but often their political ideology as well.

Conservative Christians have long criticized their progressive counterparts for relying so heavily on politics and leftist activism to try to change society instead of relying on the gospel. Now right-wing Christians have adopted exactly the same tactics.

Conservative Protestants have, in two decades, made a remarkable journey. They have traveled from a rejection of virtually all political action to the enthusiastic adoption of all leftist tactics of the sixties, including political action, lobbying, political protests, and civil disobedience at pro-life protests. And, like the most extreme edge of the sixties radicals, the S.D.S. and the Weathermen, the radical fringe of the religious right is resorting to bombings and assassinations to attempt to advance its cause. And, also following the example of the sixties, both the Christian right and the p.c. left understand the importance of creating a common enemy and convincing their followers of their own victimization.

Victims R Us — Demons R Them

It's clear that both sides in this inflamed culture war are trying to recruit more troops for their ranks. Once they have recruited new candidates, the next step is to radicalize them so they support not only their political agendas but their adversarial worldview as well. The first step in the radicalizing process is to convince them of their own victimization.

Women, lesbians, gays, and various ethnic groups are indoctrinated to climb aboard the "victim bandwagon." "By converting victimhood into a certificate of virtue, minorities at large acquire a powerful moral claim that renders their opponents defensive and apologetic, and immunizes themselves from criticism and sanction. Ultimately, victimhood becomes a truncheon with which minority activists may intimidate non-minorities — thus the victim becomes a victimizer while continuing to enjoy superior moral credentials."[1]

Leaders on the Christian right have also very deliberately appropriated the rhetoric of victimization of the radical left. "The new Christian right has been most successful in the public arena," observed Steve Bruce back in the mid-eighties, "when it has presented its own cause as being that of an oppressed and hard-done-by minority."[2]

And in its most recent incarnation, religious right leaders have become even more successful in convincing their adherents that they are society's "real" victims. We are told that the attack of the religious right's common enemy, the liberal left, is meant to destroy not only the family but the church and its influence as well. "We see a deliberate effort to eradicate religious belief from every vestige of public life," claims the American Center for Law and Justice.[3] "Assault on Faith: Liberals Launch Campaign of Bigotry," shouts the front page of the Christian Coalition's September 1994 issue of *Christian America*. The article insists that a liberal elite has launched a campaign of Christian bashing.

1. Dinesh D'Souza, "Final Thoughts on Political Correctness: Some Proposals," in *Are You Politically Correct? Debating America's Culture Standards,* ed. Francis J. Beckwith and Michael E. Bauman (New York: Prometheus Books, 1993), p. 244.
2. Bruce, *The Rise and Fall of the New Christian Right: Conservative Protestant Politics in America, 1978-1988* (New York: Oxford University Press, 1988), p. 172.
3. From a fund-raising appeal letter for the American Center for Law and Justice Appeal.

One can't read the newspaper without noticing that there are indeed those who are hammering the Christian right. They include members of Congress, news commentators, and of course those from the p.c. left.

However, Michael Kinsley, writing in the *New York Times*, challenges the claim of the Christian right that they are simply innocent victims and have done nothing to precipitate the criticism directed at them:

> Religious people have every right to be involved in politics. More than that: they have every right to argue that their political positions derive from their religious beliefs. . . .
>
> But they cannot have it both ways. Having entered the political arena determined to play hardball, they cannot complain if their opponents play hardball back. Labeling themselves Christians does not give them the right to complain of religious prejudice whenever anyone takes issue with them. . . . [The religious right's] leaders are stoking the resentments of their followers, and attempting to intimidate political opponents by striking a pose of martyrdom.[4]

Those on the right who buy into their victimhood often become just as self-righteous as those on the left. Their victimhood gives them a new sense of virtue and moral purpose in their political activism, too. And finally their victimhood gives them a sense of solidarity as a persecuted minority just as it does for those on the left.

But both the politically correct left and the religious right know it is not enough to convince their followers of their own victimization. They must fabricate a common enemy that will unite them in common cause, as mentioned earlier. This was an essential ingredient that the radical left used to radicalize the young in the sixties. And of course you remember who their common enemies were: "the establishment," "the military-industrial complex," and "the pigs."

For those on the political left, as we have seen, the new common enemy is those on the religious right. A number of more

4. Kinsley, "Casting Stones," *New York Times*, 5 July 1994, p. A17.

left-leaning organizations are successfully using this enemy to galvanize support for their political causes.

For example, in Planned Parenthood's "Rights and Freedom Alert 1994," they railed against "anti-choice extremists" and "far right terrorists." The flyer to their members reads, "The dirty secret of anti-choice extremists has finally been exposed. . . . Far right terrorists have turned our nation's family planning clinics into battlefields. Now we are fighting for our lives. Please stand with us and send a generous gift today."

Ira Glasser of the ACLU characterized the Christian Coalition as an "extremely dangerous movement based upon bigotry and intolerance" in a recent ACLU appeal letter. Regrettably, even the new Interfaith Alliance has picked up on the p.c. assignment of the Christian right to serve as common enemy. "Radical right wing extremists have declared a holy war in America promoting an agenda based on hate and intolerance."[5]

The leaders of the religious right have long understood the importance of a common enemy to strike terror in the hearts of their recruits and promote a partisan, adversarial agenda, too. Nothing works like fear. And what could be more terrifying than to convince your followers that there is a liberal/humanist elite that is intent on undermining Christian faith, destroying their families, and collectivizing the planet for the Antichrist?

Some in the pro-life movement characterize the common enemy as "anti-life terrorists," "baby killers," and "fetal assassins." And some who are opposed to gay and lesbian political agendas focus their attention on gays who they insist endanger our health and economic well-being. "Gay Rights laws and executive orders elevate to a specially legally protected status a behavior that spreads AIDS and other disease and imposes huge social and health care costs on all of us."[6]

5. *Interfaith Alliance Statement of Principles* (Washington: Interfaith Alliance, 1994), p. 1.

6. "Homosexuals Have Special Rights in Washington State . . . Now They Are Demanding More!" *Washington Public Affairs Council Newsletter*, May 1994, p. 1.

As we have seen, leaders on the right have convinced their recruits that the American Christian family and "traditional American culture" are literally under siege at the hands of their common enemy — gays, lesbians, feminists, pro-choice activists, environmentalists, multiculturalists, humanists, and liberals. And it's working.

Those on the religious right demonize not only their liberal foes but any evangelicals who don't dance to their ideological tunes as well. During the early days of the first movement of the religious right, I still remember one evangelical author who deviated and paid the price. Ron Sider had the temerity in his book *Rich Christians in an Age of Hunger* both to criticize capitalism and to suggest that Christians should reduce their patterns of consumption to help bring justice to the poor. Even though the book challenged tens of thousands of Christians to reorder their lives, the political correctness police of the right were not impressed. They launched a campaign of vilification and distortion of Sider's writings that resulted in his ostracism from much of the American evangelical movement for nearly a decade. Thankfully, his exile is now ended.

But more recently Tony Campolo has fallen into disfavor with the politically correct on the right. The attack was begun by a self-appointed inquisitor who owns several Christian radio stations. Then Jerry Falwell joined the assault. Neither of Campolo's critics followed the biblical injunction to share their concerns with him before going public.

In his book *Twenty Hot Potatoes,* Campolo deals with a number of very sensitive issues including human sexuality. He makes it clear that he holds a very conservative position on issues like homosexuality. But he urges Christians to be compassionate toward gays and lesbians, showing them something of God's love for them. Tony's wife, Peggy Campolo, a Christian leader in her own right, happens to favor covenant relationships for gays. While this is not Tony Campolo's position, those on the right are trying to use this issue to discredit his entire ministry. Anyone who has taken time to hear Tony Campolo or read his writings knows not only that he is a deeply committed follower of Jesus Christ but that God has used his ministry to touch and challenge tens of thousands of people all over the world.

This demonizing of those within the evangelical community by fellow Christians has become distressingly widespread in recent years. Philip Yancey labels it "Christian McCarthyism":

> Everywhere I turn, it seems, I hear of Christians under attack — not from secular humanists or fundamentalist Muslims, but from fellow members of the Christian community. Charles Colson told me the ugliest mail he has ever received came from Christians in response to his accepting the Templeton Prize for Progress in Religion. . . . Another Christian spokesperson, Tony Campolo, has suffered from Christians who apparently printed scurrilous pamphlets purporting to be from Queer Nation in order to cast Campolo in the worst possible light. Meanwhile Karen Mains's career as a writer, speaker, and broadcaster is threatened by a boycott over what she has written about her dream life. And Eugene Peterson's New Testament paraphrase, *The Message,* has made him a target of those upset with anyone "tampering with God's Word."
>
> The list goes on. Richard Foster dares to use words like *meditation* in his writings on spiritual disciplines, which puts him under suspicion as a New Ager. Yet another author told me a Christian book distributor has refused to carry her book in France because she quotes from C. S. Lewis, who has evidently joined the enemies list posthumously.

Yancey goes on to explain that even though he hasn't read every word penned by these Christian authors, he finds the treatment of these Christians by other Christians appalling.

> Campolo, Colson, Foster, Lewis, Mains, Peterson — are these really the "enemies" of the kingdom? . . . It is time for us to remember Jesus named *love,* not theological or political correctness, as the identifying mark of Christians. Just before he died, Jesus gave his disciples a new command to love one another. "By this everyone will know that you are my disciples, if you have love for one another" (NRSV).[7]

7. Yancey, "Christian McCarthyism," *Christianity Today,* 18 July 1994, p. 72.

Can't those of us who are Christians differ very directly with one another even on political issues without resorting to demonizing and making an enemy of the other? Can't we disagree on issues without name-calling and seeking to discredit those with whom we disagree?

Both the p.c. left and the religious right have sought to appropriate the political tactics of the radical left in the sixties. And both sides in America's culture wars seem to have been successful in convincing their respective adherents that "Victims R Us and Demons R Them."

P.C. Left — Political Activists R Us

How have so many progressive and conservative Christians been drawn into such a highly politicized form of faith, life, and action? How were they seduced into believing that political action is the primary way Christians are intended to make a difference in our world?

Most progressive Christians, I am convinced, have a very different view of history than their conservative cousins. They don't see the world locked into an inevitable slide into a one-world, Antichrist takeover. Therefore, their activism is not motivated by either fear of the future or a sense that they have to save God's bacon.

For many in this group their progressive politics is born, in part, out of a progressive view of history. Influenced by social Darwinism, many tend to believe that society is progressing, and they want to do their bit. Most have no grand designs. They simply want to see their world improve, and they want to help. However, as mentioned earlier, part of their motivation also comes from their sense of identity. Progressive Christians often have almost a congenital need to be on the cutting edge of whatever is seen as socially progressive at any given moment, often regardless of biblical mandate.

By far the major influence of the political correctness movement on progressive Christians has been to define their ultimate sense of values for them. And as a consequence many progressive

Christians have totally bought into the p.c. claim that inclusivity, diversity, and autonomy are the supreme values for defining all faith, life, and action. This "buy in" has dramatically shaped how many progressive Christians worship, do theology, and seek to change society.

For example, I have discovered in speaking in a number of mainline Protestant churches that the number one issue for many is not the population crisis, world hunger, the gun deaths on the streets of America, or even the feminization of poverty. Issue number one is invariably the use of inclusive language in worship — because of a prior commitment to the supreme virtue of inclusivity. Progressive Christians will go up in flames as quickly over the use of male pronouns for God as conservative Christians will over criticism of the American free enterprise system. It's *the* cardinal sin.

Speaking recently in a United Church of Christ congregation, I went in knowing that they dealt very severely with those who were not verbally correct. As I concluded my remarks that Sunday morning, I was particularly careful to avoid using any male pronouns in referring to God. In my impassioned conclusion, I affirmed that "the God who has created all things will author the final chapter and make all things new. The God of Abraham, Isaac, and Jacob will bring God's New Order into being!"

As I was standing at the door quietly congratulating myself for not messing up, a dour older woman pressed a scrap of paper into my hand and exited without a word. The note read, "The God of Sarah, Rebecca and Rachel will also bring God's New Order into being." I left the church duly chastised and sensitized, having failed the inclusivity test yet again.

I do understand the concern regarding inclusive speech. And I work very hard in my writing and speaking to use inclusive language. But frankly, in light of the many urgent issues filling our world, I don't understand the preeminence this kind of inclusivity is accorded by many mainliners.

More serious, though, is the way in which the progressive commitment to inclusivity, diversity, and autonomy is beginning to reshape the basic theological foundation of a number of mainline churches. Not long ago I was asked to speak at First United

Methodist Church in Seattle on the theme "Global Consciousness." I prepared a message entitled "The Future of World Hunger and Our Christian Responsibility." But when the pastor introduced me, I found that I had fundamentally misunderstood both the context and my assignment. "Two weeks ago we had a Hindu in our pulpit sharing his view of global consciousness," the pastor said. "Last week we had a Buddhist. This week we have Tom Sine."

I stood there stunned for a moment. Then I set my notes aside and spoke off the cuff. "In speaking of global consciousness, I approach this topic from a very different perspective from the prior two speakers. I have a very high regard for other religious traditions. But the reason I am a Christian is that for me Christ alone offers a full disclosure of the Creator God."

Belatedly I discovered that this Methodist minister, out of a sincere desire to be inclusive and accept all religious diversity, had essentially become a "Christian Baha'i." In his quest for "global consciousness," he was trying to hammer together bits and pieces of many different world religions into a single system, apparently undisturbed by the fact that they are all based on many very different assumptions about life, faith, and reality that really can't be easily blended.

I believe that in their determination to be inclusive and welcome diversity, this pastor and many other progressive Christians are recklessly giving away the candy store. They have abandoned the uniqueness of the faith disclosed in Jesus Christ to drink from many other streams. They are letting go of the historic Christian faith in order to embrace everything from forms of latter-day animism and Canaanite fertility deities to New Age crystals and Hindu meditation.

Kwok Pui-Lan, one of the leading feminist speakers at the Re-imagining Conference, was a keynote speaker at a more recent (March 24-25, 1994) Presbyterian conference entitled "Pluralism and the Mission of the Church." A strong advocate for religious pluralism, she urged her audience not to get hung up on the myth of Christian "uniqueness." There couldn't be any movement toward a proper acceptance of diversity, she said, so long as Christians insist on holding "a vehemently exclusivist position in talking about truth, revelation, the Bible and Christ."[8]

Someone has written that for this kind of religious pluralist it is fully acceptable to believe absolutely anything you want as long as you don't believe that it's really true. Go ahead and celebrate your religious heritage, regardless of whether you are Muslim, Christian, Jew, or Druid. Just don't cross the line and start asserting that you hold a faith that you genuinely believe to be true. "The problem is, orthodoxy always appears intolerant in a relativistic culture. . . . There is tremendous pressure on the orthodox to mend their ways, to bend their beliefs to modernity in order to make them more acceptable."[9]

I am deeply distressed at the way in which many conservative Christians continue to confuse their Christian faith with the American civil religion. But I am even more alarmed that some progressive Christians, out of a rigid commitment to inclusivity, diversity, and autonomy, are moving at warp speed away from their commitment to a biblical Christology and the historic Christian faith toward any type of religious manifestation that minds can imagine.

I agree with the progressives that it is important for all Christians to be open and tolerant of other faith traditions. But I do not believe that this openness and tolerance have to entail the compromise of foundational beliefs. The rapid movement by some progressive Christians toward an all-embracing religious pluralism could have a devastating effect on the future of the mainline Protestant Christian witness. Another Methodist minister, George Geyer, speaking of similar challenges facing the church at the turn of the last century, offers some helpful counsel: "Our responsibility as Christians is not to keep up with the age, but the ages."

Historians can easily identify when the church seriously

8. Kwok, quoted by Parker T. Williamson in "Stony Point Conference Continues ReImagining Themes," *Presbyterian Layman*, May/June 1994, p. 17.

9. S. D. Gaede, *When Tolerance Is No Virtue: Political Correctness, Multiculturalism, and the Future of Truth and Justice* (Downers Grove, Ill.: InterVarsity Press, 1993), p. 47.

compromised its witness by attempting to accommodate the intellectually correct dogmas of many different ages. There is nothing within our Christian faith that requires us to bow the knee to the politically correct dogmas of inclusivity, diversity, and autonomy. And to do so could well cost us the Christian faith handed on to us by generations of believers who subscribed to its uniqueness.

While those on the radical left have been successful in persuading some progressive Christians to buy into their politically correct values, leftist movements in America are floundering primarily because of growing political conservatism in the country and their inability to attract mainstream Americans.

What has happened is that some feminist leaders have belatedly recognized that there simply are not enough left-leaning radicals to support their agendas into the next century. Therefore, several groups like Planned Parenthood are attempting, like the Christian Coalition at the other polarity, to "mainstream" their advocacy.

Over the angry protests of radical feminists and lesbians, Pamela Maraldo, the president of Planned Parenthood, is seeking to broaden the issues and moderate the tone of the organization to attract more of the American middle. First, Planned Parenthood is expanding its pro-choice agenda to include sex education, contraceptive research, and prenatal care. It is even sponsoring programs to encourage teenage abstinence.

Planned Parenthood, under Maraldo's leadership, is positioning itself as "the *real* pro-life force in America." She emphasizes "healthy women and healthy families." She also supports people pursuing their most deeply held religious beliefs.

Writing in *Ms.* magazine, Judith Warner commented, "It's a tricky approach, sharing rhetorical ground with the likes of Pat Buchanan. And in fact the kind of moral territory that Maraldo would like to reclaim has long been the domain of the anti-choice, anti-woman religious right."[10]

It's too early to tell if those on the p.c. left who are attempting to "mainstream" their message are going to be successful in

10. Warner, "Mixed Messages," *Ms.*, November/December 1993, p. 25.

reaching the more moderate members in society and church. But the attempt does indicate that some on the p.c. left recognize that they will need significantly increased support from the middle if they are to have any hope of defeating the burgeoning forces on the Christian right.

P.C. Right — Political Activists R Us

While the left is having difficulty recruiting support for its diverse agendas, the religious right is successfully recruiting record numbers for its cause. The Christian Coalition alone has just broken the 1.5 million member mark and is continuing to grow rapidly.

They have achieved this rapid growth by appealing not to people's desire for a more open society but to their fear of a more pluralistic one. Leaders on the right are masterful in playing on the fears of evangelicals of real and imagined threats to the family. They manipulate the threat-to-family motif to recruit concerned evangelicals not only to support selected "moral" legislation but to support all kinds of right-wing ideological agendas, all in the name of Jesus. It is really quite remarkable how effectively a number of right-wing religious organizations have been in recruiting sincere believers and persuading them to transfer their genuine devotion to God to various right-wing political causes.

I still remember one chilly November evening in Seattle when I went to see a new Sherlock Holmes film at the Crest Theater. As I was waiting for the main feature, the lights dimmed and a BBC documentary entitled "Thy Kingdome Come" appeared on the screen.

The film opened by taking us into the homes of Americans who had recently committed their lives to God and become active members of evangelical and fundamentalist churches in their communities. These folks very openly shared their stories of dramatically transformed lives. They described how they had been delivered from a range of addictive behaviors, from drug and alcohol abuse to gambling and spouse abuse. The authenticity of their testimonies was so powerful, I could sense that the people sitting around me were clearly moved.

The scene suddenly shifted to a very robust worship service and the evident joy on the faces of these new believers as they were singing and clapping their hands. The camera followed the converts to classes in their churches several weeks later in which they were being systematically indoctrinated in right-wing political ideology of a national religious right organization that held classes in their church.

The final scene showed these enthusiastic new believers giving active expression to their newfound faith. They weren't shown sharing their experience of God's love with neighbors or tutoring at-risk kids. Nope. The camera panned to a huge shopping mall and showed these new saints aggressively lobbying shoppers to support pending legislation for Reagan's Star Wars project and a dramatic increase in U.S. military spending.

I watched folks sitting around me. A number were nodding their heads knowingly. And it was clear that they had now found a basis to dismiss the authentic witness of genuinely changed lives they had viewed only moments before.

One of the reasons the Christian right is so successful is that it appeals to conservative Protestants in terms of their devotion to God and their concerns for family life and moral values. And then, once it has them on board, it seems to have little trouble, as was illustrated in the documentary, in politicizing and radicalizing them to become advocates of a host of right-wing political causes.

The Christian Coalition has certainly been successful in recruiting evangelical and charismatic Christians to support their right-wing political agenda. Initially, "at the local level, the Christian Coalition had pursued a combative strategy. . . . In some intraparty contests, as well as races for public offices, the Coalition's candidates kept quiet about their affiliation. Close to Election Day, bursts of church-centered politicking showed what was going on. Reed made the mistake of bragging in a few interviews about what became known as 'stealth tactics,' talking about the benefits of guerrilla methods. 'You don't know it's over,' he once said of unsuspecting opponents, 'until you're in a body bag.' "[11]

11. Reed, quoted by Laurence I. Barret in "Fighting for God and the Right Wing," *Time*, 13 September 1993, p. 58.

Since that interview Ralph Reed has sought to tone down his language and mainstream the Coalition to reach a broader segment of the American public, beyond the white conservative Protestant audience. For example, recently the Coalition has begun agressively seeking to recruit new members from the African American and Jewish communities. However, at the 1994 national conference of the Christian Coalition, there were reportedly more people of color on the platform than in the entire crowd of three thousand attendees.

Coalition founder Pat Robertson, for one, has refused to give up the inflamed rhetoric and conspiracy theories that have long filled his books. Still, he does understand the strategy of the mainstream appeal, and he knows how to appeal to middle America: "In the Christian Coalition," he writes,

> there is concern about school choice for all parents and their children, concern for lower taxes, limited government, a balanced budget amendment, and a line-item veto over the federal budget by the president. Besides that, the Coalition is against special rights for those self-proclaimed "minorities," such as lesbians and gays, and for common-sense restrictions for abortion.
>
> As Reed puts it, "We support quality education and tougher laws against crime and drugs. This is such a mainstream agenda that it is held by the majority of the American people, yet the media have done their best to characterize us as dangerous zealots and book-burners. . . . We want to assure people that we do not want to legislate our theology. We want to legislate our public policy views, and that is the basis on which our coalition was formed."[12]

I appreciate Mr. Reed's honesty in admitting that the Christian Coalition doesn't legislate their theology. One has only to read the Christian Coalition on a broad range of issues to realize that Reed is being completely truthful. There is little if any indication that the Coalition ever refers to Scripture to define its stance on issues.

12. Robertson, *The Turning Tide* (Dallas: Word Publishing, 1993), p. 68.

Well, if the Christian Coalition's advocacy doesn't come from biblical principles, where does it come from? All you have to do to answer the question is to read the books authored by the Coalition's founder, Pat Robertson. As I have shown, these books suggest that the Coalition's advocacy is based on (1) a conspiratorial view of history, (2) an allegiance to American nationalism and a civil religion to support that nationalism, (3) a confusion of American cultural values and family styles of the fifties with biblical values and biblical views of the family, and (4) a promotion of right-wing political ideology.

If I am mistaken and the Christian Coalition's agenda is not based upon the analysis and advocacy of the organization's founder, then what is it based on? And since, as Ralph Reed makes clear, it isn't based on the Bible or theology, a growing number of authors are asking on what basis can the Coalition justify calling itself "Christian"?

In any case, it appears that the Coalition is having much more success than Planned Parenthood and other groups on the p.c. left in mainstreaming itself and attracting middle America. But many who are recruited have little understanding of where these organizations secure their funding or which other right-wing organizations they are connected to.

I believe it is instructive to look back to the first incarnation of the religious right. Belatedly we have learned a bit about who funded that movement and who its members collaborated with to advance their cause.

Over the past ten to fifteen years the religious right has received funds from some very interesting sources. The Adolph Coors family, long an enthusiastic supporter of various right-wing causes, has in recent years begun to support groups on the religious right including the Institute on Religion and Democracy, the Moral Majority, the Religious Round Table, and Pat Robertson's Regent University.[13]

In 1971, Joseph Coors, a member of the John Birch Society, formed an alliance with another member, Paul Weyrich. In 1973

13. See Russ Bellant, *The Coors Connection: How Coors Family Philanthropy Undermines Democratic Pluralism* (Boston: South End Press, 1988), p. 50.

and 1974 they established the Heritage Foundation, which has since become the most influential conservative think tank in America. Weyrich has candidly admitted that although he is a conservative, he has no interest in conserving anything. He counts himself and his colleagues as a new generation of radicals: "We are no longer working to preserve the status quo. We are radicals, working to overturn the present power structure of the country."[14]

Even more remarkable and less well known is the fact that during the eighties many leaders on the Christian right accepted funds from Sun Myung Moon, the Unification Church, and associated organizations. Sara Diamond reports that in 1984 the Moonies started the Coalition for Religious Freedom (CRF). Even though its funding came from the Moonies, CRF was staffed by fundamentalist ministers who shared Moon's conservative political views. The initial executive board included Jerry Falwell, D. James Kennedy, Jimmy Swaggart, Rex Humbard, and Tim La Haye, among others.

When Moon was in trouble with the American courts in 1985, Falwell cut short a trip so that he could preside at a Washington press conference organized by CRF on behalf of the "tax martyr." A 1985 exposé in *Mother Jones* magazine revealed that Tim La Haye received "timely" and "generous" help from Moon's aide Bo Hi Pak to facilitate the "extremely expensive" relocation of La Haye's ACTV headquarters.[15] In this connection, La Haye and Moon's other friends on the right seem to be operating on the principle that any enemy of my enemy is a friend of mine. In light of these revelations, it would be very helpful to learn what the financial linkages are between various right-wing groups and the religious right today.

Declaring Total War

"I am not here to talk about the terms of surrender, but about how to fight and win the Culture War," declared Pat Buchanan

---

14. Weyrich, quoted by Sara Diamond in *Spiritual Warfare: The Politics of the Christian Right* (Boston: South End Press, 1989), p. 54.
15. See Diamond, *Spiritual Warfare*, pp. 69-70.

at the 1993 national conference of the Christian Coalition in Washington, D.C. His call to total warfare brought a rousing and enthusiastic response from the conservative Christians attending this national meeting of the Christian Coalition.

This in-your-face, attack-dog, confrontational style of politics threatens to inflame our American future and irreparably divide the American church. It has already decisively changed the nature of political discourse in America.

What has happened is that ideologues on both sides have been very successful in persuading sincere Christians to try to change their society through engaging in a very partisan, adversarial approach to political action. I am particularly concerned that many evangelical Christians have not only been swept up in this very adversarial approach to political advocacy but that they have been indoctrinated to view this contest as a "jihad" or holy war.

Since the religious right views what is wrong in apocalyptic terms, they see themselves involved in the ultimate contest — "the war to end all wars." Bernard McGinn, theology professor at the University of Chicago Divinity School, has stated that an apocalyptic worldview "has no room for moral ambiguity, for any shades of gray." By viewing foes as adherents to absolute evil, apocalypticism provides a rationale for "total opposition and dire vengeance on the wicked."[16]

As a consequence, conservative Protestants who are recruited to serve in this holy war can give no quarter to the enemy. Leaders of the religious right do not train their followers to look for common ground or give their liberal foes credit for any positive contributions they might make. Rather they are programmed to work for the total defeat of their "cosmic" adversaries.

Mark Heard, an evangelical musician who passed away recently, wrote a particularly insightful piece entitled "Everybody Loves a Holy War." The lyrics go something like this:

Some say that God has approved of their mob,
esteeming their purposes alone,

16. McGinn, quoted by Jeffrey L. Sheler in "The Christmas Covenant," *U.S. News and World Report*, 19 December 1994.

choosing sides with a definite pride
and taking their cause for his own.

Someone has suggested that politics is good theater, but our current adversarial ideological politics has turned into a dark, demented melodrama that I believe is inherently destructive. In this melodrama, each company of players has its own dramatic motif, which both characterizes its cause and is used to denigrate its foes.

For those on the Christian right, "family" serves as the orchestrating symbol of their cosmic drama. They insist that their antagonists have but one objective — the total destruction of the American family. James Dobson makes a representative charge when he says that "the family is not simply disintegrating from natural forces and pressures. Its demise is being orchestrated at the highest levels of government, and by radical special-interest groups."[17] In the fall of 1994, the Christian Coalition distributed a voting guide that promised, "On November 8 — just six short weeks from now — we can stop the anti-family train of destruction coming out of Washington."[18]

"Family" has developed into a code word that the leaders of the religious right have been able to use effectively even with regard to issues that have no clear connection to it, such as cutting the federal deficit. Gary Bauer has linked family values to such diverse initiatives as demands for tax cuts, term limits for national officeholders, and support for the National Rifle Association.[19] And it works! Many conservative Christians, legitimately concerned about the challenges facing the family, buy into this family-focused melodrama lock, stock, and barrel without really questioning the validity of the reasoning behind it all.

The other company of players on the political stage has adopted the dramatic motif of inclusiveness. Not surprisingly, the ideal of inclusiveness hasn't proved nearly as appealing to middle

17. Dobson, *Focus on the Family Newsletter,* June 1994, p. 6.
18. Christian Coalition, "Final 1994 Election Appeal," September 1994, p. 1.
19. See Bauer, *Family Research Council Newsletter,* 2 November 1994, p. 4.

America as the family theme. Those on the left have vilified those on the Christian right as "bigoted hate-mongers" and "anti-choice fundamentalists" who are dedicated to denying Americans the opportunity to make important choices for their own lives. I have found that many progressive Christians who champion the ideal of inclusivity can tolerate absolutely any kind of aberrant belief system that the human mind can imagine — except for right-wing fundamentalism. Apparently even inclusivity has its limits.

Central to both companies in this divisive political melodrama is the unbridled quest for power. In total warfare, the only way to defeat your foes and win the day is through acquiring and being willing to utilize overwhelming force. And for those on the right, who view this as a cosmic contest, this is a particularly important tenet.

Total Warfare: Taking Power and Taking Over

The old radical left, working from a Marxist critique, has long contended that the primary way human society is changed is through taking power politically. Some leftists, like Peru's Shining Path guerrillas, argue for taking power at gunpoint. Other leftists, in Eastern Europe, are trying to take back the political power they lost during the dissolution of the Soviet Empire by using the democratic processes of their newly independent states. But leftists of all stripes are convinced that change comes primarily through the acquisition and decisive use of political power.

Those on the p.c. left are equally convinced. From the radical gay and lesbian coalition to animal rights activists, they are all determined to take power for those they view as victimized. Some actually believe that their very survival depends on defeating their enemies in this total warfare with the religious right.

For decades, many progressive Christians have subscribed to much of the leftist critique and the leftist remedy — taking power to reorder society. Since the sixties, many mainline Protestant leaders have shown a continuing interest in political action as the best way to facilitate social change and assist those who are marginalized and excluded.

 169

Amazingly, leaders on the Christian right seem to have totally bought into the mythical claim of the radical left that the real way to change society is through taking power politically. As a result, conservative Protestants have done a total about-face, going from noninvolvement in politics two decades ago to becoming among the most visible political activists on the American scene today.

Of course many Christians on the right still tip their hat to evangelism as a means of changing things, one heart at a time. But the message of the Christian right couldn't be clearer. Just like their leftist opponents, they insist that the best hope they have for changing society and reclaiming America lies in political action.

Among those on the religious right, by far the most preoccupied with taking power and taking over are the Christian Reconstructionists. These theocrats have totally convinced themselves that they are called to erect the kingdom of God on earth. And their vision of what the kingdom of God looks like is the men of God taking power and taking over. Reconstructionist literature is filled with the language of "total warfare," with words like *domination, dominion, authority, power, control, hierarchy, military conquest,* and *violence.*

Gary North, one of the leaders of the Reconstructionists, candidly describes his game plan for a Reconstructionist global takeover to establish a theocratic utopia. He states that in the initial phase he will work through democratic processes. But once the men of God, including North, begin to get power, it is going to be a very different story. Once they have managed to remove the ungodly leader's power, says North, "the battered Christian should either bust him in the chops or haul him before the magistrate, and possibly both." And once the Reconstructionists have attained some degree of global power, North declares that societies that refuse to come under the authority of the men of God "are to be destroyed."[20]

I am certain that most right-leaning Christians have no

20. North, "In Defense of Biblical Bribery," Appendix 5 in R. J. Rushdoony's *Institutes of Biblical Law* (Nutley, N.J.: Craig, 1973), pp. 845-46.

interest in establishing a global theocracy or physically destroying those who resist the rule of the "men of God." But they still seem to share the conviction of both the radical left and the Reconstructionist right that the best way to change society is to take power politically.

In the eighties, the first wave of the religious right was very successful in exporting its advocacy of changing society through political action to conservative Christians in Latin America. Jimmy Swaggart and Pat Robertson were particularly successful in promoting this American right-wing political ideology to those south of the border.

There are a few less visible spokespersons who are exporting this advocacy to English-speaking countries and Europe today. For example, Dennis Peacock, a former sixties radical, is taking a "soft-core" Reconstructionist message to charismatic and evangelical Christians in Holland, Great Britain, and New Zealand. Most of his audience has no idea of the ideological origins of his message or the theocratic agenda of Christian Reconstructionists.

Joel Crawshaw of Signpost Communications in New Zealand, while appreciative of many positive contributions of American Christians, is also very concerned by the content and the power of America's ideological impact on the rest of the planet. Crawshaw states,

> I think the concern mainly arises because of the overwhelming economic and technological power of American culture generally, which is shared by the evangelical church. . . . This economic and technological muscle is then used to purvey the ideology which underlies it. And frankly, it seems to me that for the most part what we are being peddled is American idolatry overlain by a thin veneer of Christian rhetoric. The idolatry at root is consumer narcissism ladeled out with lashings of marketing expertise and pop psychology, and buttressed by militarism. In other words, the pietistic revivalism which seems to underlie much American evangelicalism has mated with the American Zeitgeist to produce a self-absorbed civic religion.[21]

21. Crawshaw, *Sign Posts Communications*, 24 January 1995, p. 2.

I have found that a number of evangelical leaders in Western countries share this concern about the exporting of both American culture and the political ideology of the religious right.

All's Fair in Love and Total Warfare

Yet another area in which ideologues on the left and right are remarkably similar is the ways in which they use information to solicit support. For example, Gloria Steinem cited another feminist author's assertion that 150,000 females die of the eating disorder anorexia nervosa each year. The American Anorexia and Bulimia Association pointed out her error. In 1985 the Association had estimated that a total of 150,000 to 200,000 women *suffered* from anorexia, but only 101 women actually died from complications associated with anorexia in 1983, 67 in 1988, and 54 in 1991.[22]

Radical feminists have long contended that anorexia and bulimia are a direct result of a male-dominated culture which dictates that all women must conform to a prescribed notion of beauty. Given their confident analysis of what causes these eating disorders, some feminists were apparently willing to believe that as many as 150,000 women a year die from anorexia.

In 1993 it was reported in the national media that wife abuse rose by 40 percent on Super Bowl Sunday. Some feminists "used the occasion to drive home the message that maleness and violence against women are synonymous." A reporter at the *Washington Post* decided to check out the story and discovered that it had no basis in fact. Police departments actually recorded no more domestic violence on Super Bowl Sunday than on any other day.[23] Again, apparently some on the p.c. left were less concerned about whether the information was accurate than whether it supported their ideological cause.

But the inaccurate use of information is not just the province

22. See Christina Hoff Sommers, *Who Stole Feminism? How Women Have Betrayed Women* (New York: Simon & Schuster, 1994), p. 145.
23. Sommers, *Who Stole Feminism?* pp. 11-15.

of the ideological left. There are those on the far right like Rush Limbaugh who seem to have a chronic problem getting their facts straight. And his supporters don't seem to mind, because he is telling them exactly what they want to hear.

> LIMBAUGH: Comparing the 1950s with the present: "And I might point out that poverty and economic disparities between the lower and upper classes were greater during the former period." (Told You So, p. 84). REALITY: Income inequality, as measured by the U.S. Census Bureau, fell from the 1940s to the late 1960s, and then began rising. Inequality surpassed the 1950 level in 1982 and rose steadily to an all-time high in 1992. (Census Bureau's "Money Income of Households, Families and Persons in the United States.")
>
> LIMBAUGH: "The poorest people in America are better off than the mainstream families of Europe." (Radio Show, quoted in FRQ, Spring/1993). REALITY: Huh? The average cash income of the poorest 20 percent of Americans is $5,226, the average cash income of four major European nations — Germany, France, United Kingdom and Italy — is $19,708.
>
> LIMBAUGH: "Oh, how they relished blaming Reagan Administration policies, including mythical reduction in HUD's budget for public housing, for creating all the homeless! Budget cuts? There were no budget cuts! The budget figures show that actual construction of public housing *increased* during the Reagan years." (Ought to Be, pp. 242-43.) REALITY: In 1980, 20,900 low-income public housing units were under construction; in 1988, there were 9,700, a decline of 54 percent (Statistical Abstracts of the U.S.). In terms of 1993 dollars, the HUD budget for the construction of new public housing was slashed from $6.3 billion in 1980 to $683 million in 1988. "We're getting out of the housing business period," a Reagan HUD official declared in 1985.[24]

Rush Limbaugh is not the only conservative who uses information and the media in questionable ways. With the demise of the Fairness Doctrine seven years ago, Christian radio has

---

24. "The Way Things Aren't: Rush Limbaugh Debates Reality," *Extra!* July/August 1994.

become increasingly more ideological and confrontational. Very few Christian stations are willing to provide opportunities for others to express dissenting opinions or to impose any ethical standards to ensure both accuracy and civility in Christian broadcasting.[25]

With few exceptions, the Christian media have become a right-wing ideological wasteland that increasingly values in-your-face programming and sometimes plays fast and loose with the facts. The views of evangelicals who don't fall in line with the politically correct dogma of the religious right are generally not welcome there.

Distortion is not limited to the electronic media. In a 1994 newsletter from the Christian Coalition, Pat Robertson asked readers if their congressional representatives reflected their values in Washington. The first question was, "Did they vote FOR or AGAINST Bill Clinton's crushing $241 BILLION *anti-family tax increase?*"

Come on. It's one thing to criticize Clinton's efforts to reduce the deficit on political grounds. But to characterize those efforts as "anti-family" is simply not accurate or fair. Almost none of the tax increase was directed at middle-income families. The Democrats are smarter than that.

Even more disturbing than the falsification, distortion, and manipulation of information that both sides have engaged in are their recent moves toward tactics of increasing confrontation and violence. Radical gays have broken into and vandalized churches that they view as anti-gay. The activist pro-life group Operation Rescue justifies confronting and stalking women who are considering abortion. And the pro-choice groups have taken to stalking pro-life protesters. Things are getting very nasty and dangerous in the trenches of those battling over the abortion issue.

Over the past ten years Pensacola, Florida, has become a center for extremist violence in America. There have been bombings of abortion clinics, destruction of equipment, and assaults on clinic employees. In 1993 Dr. David Gunn was the first person

25. See John W. Kennedy, "Mixing Politics and Piety," *Christianity Today*, 15 August 1994, pp. 42-47.

to be shot to death outside an abortion clinic as part of a protest. In 1994 abortion doctor James Barret and his escort were gunned down. And more recently two women working in abortion clinics in Boston were brutally murdered.

Michael Bray, who spent four years in prison for clinic bombings, predicts that violence will increase as more individuals become convinced that the use of violence is an appropriate way to try to change society.[26]

Most leaders on the Christian right have strongly denounced this recourse to violence, realizing that it could compromise their cause. But what they don't seem to recognize is that their polarized view of society and inflamed rhetoric are directly contributing to the growing violence. Because they are indoctrinating their followers to believe that they are involved in a cosmic contest between the forces of darkness and light, growing numbers seem to be concluding that any means they can find to defeat the enemy — including violence — will be justifiable.

Apocalypse Now — Oklahoma City

The horrendous terrorist bombing of the Federal Building in Oklahoma City has dramatically brought to our attention the reemergence of paramilitary groups all over the United States. These groups are training for violent civil conflict with assault weapons and grenade launchers, fully anticipating that they will be involved in armed conflict in our communities.

The last few years have seen in America a disturbing rise in right-wing paramilitary, white supremacist, and neo-nazi groups that see themselves at war with their own government. And the evidence is growing that this dramatic rise in paramilitary groups is directly connected to the federal raid on the Branch Davidians in Waco, Texas. This siege, reports Robert McFadden in the *New York Times* (April 22, 1995), has become "a rallying cry for scores of armed, right-wing para-military groups that have sprung up across

26. Mimi Hall, "Abortion Foes Deny There's a Conspiracy," *USA Today*, 5 August 1994, p. 3A.

the country in recent years. Styling themselves militias, the loosely organized groups — some operating in the open and others in secret — have in common the belief that the federal government plans to wage war on citizens who refuse to give up guns."

Apparently a number of these right-wing extremists genuinely believe our government is involved in a global conspiracy with the United Nations to disarm all Americans to set us up for a totalitarian, socialist, one-world government takeover. McFadden explains that members of these militia believe "that the federal government wants to utterly control the lives of citizens and will crush those who resist, using United Nations' troops with Soviet military equipment. Most believe they must bear arms and train to resist the takeover . . . members talk gravely about a coming 'new world order' in which one totalitarian government will rule. . . ."

Some of these paramilitary groups are virulently anti-Semitic. Listen to how Pastor Richard Butler, leader of the well-armed Church of Jesus Christ Christian of Aryan Nations in Hayden Lake, Idaho, characterizes the "crisis." "Here in America today, we are now prisoners of the anti-Christ — in the media, in the pulpits, in the school system," he said in his Easter sermon. And he leaves no doubt as to who he thinks is responsible: "the Jews — they are our adversaries."[27]

Daniel Levitas, an expert on right-wing extremists, reports that the Branch Davidian siege has also been "a ceaseless mantra" of these groups. He states that they have been incessantly preaching the violent overthrow of the U.S. government and advocating "leaderless resistance" in which groups of two or three people work together to commit revolutionary political crimes. If he is right, the Oklahoma City terrorist bombing might not be an isolated event. It may only be the opening salvo in an ongoing expression of this insane civil warfare against America.

Of course there are no direct links between these groups and the religious right. Conservative Republicans were among the first to call for swift and decisive justice against the terrorists guilty of this atrocity. Leaders on the religious right, like those on the

27. Brad Knickerbocker, "White Separatists Plot 'Pure Society,'" *Christian Science Monitor,* 20 April 1995.

Christian left, have spoken forcefully against this appalling act. Still, a number of these right-wing militia groups share with many on the religious right some important and deeply disturbing similarities: (1) a conspiratorial view of history, where someone is out to get them and take away all their weapons; (2) a growing rage, fueled by talk radio, toward those they believe are conspiring to undermine their freedom and collectivize them for a one-world gulag; (3) an apocalyptic, black-and-white worldview; (4) a strong commitment to right-wing political ideology and American nationalism; and (5) in many cases a view of Christian faith that glorifies American culture. The tragedy in Waco reminds us of the danger of combining a volatile mixture of apocalyptic religion with weapons. The strong warning of this book is that outrageous assumptions often lead to outrageous action.

Cosmic Warfare

As we saw in the case of Larry Lea's Prayer Breakthrough Crusade in San Francisco, many conservative Christians who believe they are engaged in a cosmic contest are now seeking to employ cosmic weapons against their foes. Increasing numbers are drawing on the arsenal of spiritual warfare to battle the liberal left.

Frank Peretti has written several novels in which the story is played out against a backdrop of this kind of cosmic warfare. He has sold over three million copies of *This Present Darkness* and *Piercing the Darkness,* making them some of the most popular books read by conservative Protestants. Rodney Clapp has written that

> Peretti's human protagonists are fundamentalists who embody "traditional" family values and empower the spiritual protagonists — angels — by praying. Strengthened by prayer, the angels engage demons in the sort of combat that might be depicted with adequate violence only in a Stephen Seagal movie. . . .
>
> This is life and destiny as ultimately agonistic. Good is pitted against evil and each struggles, with the same means (force and violence), to destroy the other. Yet, as anthropologist Paul Hiebert has argued, this *mythos* is more a species of Indo-

▶▶▶   177

European paganism than a Christian conception of reality. In the Christian story, God is a good and loving creator without counterpart.[28]

Clapp and Hiebert have it right. The Bible does tell us of the Christian's struggle against principalities and powers, but it never presents Satan as an equally matched opponent of the Creator God. God has already won the contest — and not through a violent "Star Wars" conflagration with "the force." In the Christian story of the upside-down kingdom, God wins the day not through the assertion of power but in a display of vulnerability. The powers of evil are defeated through Jesus Christ's laying down his life and being resurrected by the power of God.

I believe a number on the religious right have borrowed from the essentially pagan mythos of Peretti's fiction and other works on spiritual warfare a way of looking at their own contest. Many Christians recognize that we are all indeed involved in a spiritual struggle, but some on the Christian right have politicized it and convinced themselves that the Creator God is battling for their right-wing causes.

Others have joined Larry Lea in claiming to be able to discern the territorial demons that control our cities, our nation, and our world. Remarkably, those territorial demons tend to bear a surprisingly strong resemblance to the political foes of those who discern them. And the contest between cosmic good and cosmic evil tends to bear a striking resemblance to their political view of the total warfare between conservatives and liberals.

British evangelical author Mike Taylor undertook a study of the charismatic evangelical literature on spiritual warfare and concluded that much of it claims a deeper understanding of spiritual warfare than Scripture does. He is particularly critical of writings on territorial spirits, which he says are based more on the kind of speculation that Peretti uses in his novels than on anything found in the Bible.[29]

28. Clapp, "Calling the Religious Right to Its Better Self," *Perspectives*, April 1994, p. 11.
29. See Taylor, *Do Demons Rule Your Town?* (London: Grace Publishing, 1994).

Even the Lausanne Committee for World Evangelization has studied the topic of spiritual warfare. While acknowledging that we do indeed wrestle with principalities and powers, the committee raised a number of concerns about the current spiritual-warfare craze among evangelicals. "We heard with concern of situations where warfare language was pushing Christians into adversarial attitudes and where people of other faiths were interpreting it as the language of violence and political involvement."[30]

If conservative Christians are serious about trying to understand how the principalities and powers influence our lives and God's world, I think they would find Walter Wink's book *Engaging the Powers* far more compelling and authoritative, because it is genuinely grounded in the biblical material. And Wink's analysis is not wedded to the political ideology of either the right or the left.

Perhaps the most troubling aspect of the rising popularity of the notion of spiritual warfare among those on the religious right is the sense it seems to be giving them that the Creator God fully sanctions everything they are up to in this holy war. It gives them a sense that it is just them and God engaged in total warfare with their political enemies.

Randall Terry, of Operation Rescue, told a National Public Radio audience that he knew why thousands of midwesterners lost their homes and farms and livestock in the floods of 1993: it was the judgment of God on America for having failed to support his anti-abortion crusade. Terry added that we hadn't seen anything yet. He promised that God would continue to hammer America with additional natural disasters if people don't fall in line with him on this issue.

The Jesus Alternative

Jesus always seems to come bursting into every area of our lives, turning all our understandings of life and faith upside down. This

30. "Statement on Spiritual Warfare: A Working Group Report," *World Evangelization* 18 (December 1993): 19.

is certainly true with regard to our contemporary notions of how to change our world. What do the Gospels have to say to Christians who have bought into the claims of the political left and religious right that the primary way we work for social transformation is through taking power and taking over? What does the gospel have to say about adversarial politics, defeating one's enemies, and total warfare?

Let's visit that desert scene again at the beginning of Christ's ministry when he was being tempted by Satan. Do you remember the last temptation Satan presented Jesus? He offered him power — power over all the nations of the world. Jesus' response? "Away from me, Satan! For it is written: 'Worship the Lord your God, and serve him only'" (Matt. 4:8-10).

Satan is still in the business of tempting believers with the heady seduction of power. And our response should be exactly the same as Jesus'. "Away from me, Satan! I am not called to seek power but to worship the Lord my God, and serve him only."

There were those in Jesus' day who, with good reason, were very discontent with the conditions of life under Roman occupation and who argued that the only way to change those conditions was to take power politically, to take action against the Roman government. But Jesus did not find the Zealots' case convincing or their cause inviting. He refused to join their politically driven movement. Jesus came introducing a very different way to work for social change, a way that was clearly antithetical to the pursuit of power, political conquest, and total warfare.

In fact, I can't find a shred of evidence in the Gospels to support the Reconstructionist contention that Jesus' "real" mission was to prepare the men of God to take power and create a theocratic state. There is simply no support for this sort of thinking anywhere in the New Testament.

Reconstructionists would have us believe that when Jesus charged his followers to "disciple the nations," he was telling them in code language to take over the nations politically. Anyone trained in New Testament studies will tell you that such a claim is patent nonsense.

How can anyone possibly miss it? Jesus didn't come to take political power over the lives of others or to destroy those who opposed him. He came to love and serve them. Jesus demonstrated in the clearest terms how to change society. He lifted the fallen, set free the captives, forgave the sinners, and preached good news to the poor.

Jesus and his small band actually became an incarnational foretaste of God's loving New Order breaking into our world. The small, apparently insignificant seed that God planted in the soil of the Middle East is still quietly transforming our world. Jesus' embryonic community has given new life to people in every culture and nation. And this movement of God has not come either through arrogance of power or the insanity of total warfare. God's New Order comes through the powerless, the insignificant, the mustard seed. The Bible reminds us that the Creator "chose the foolish things of the world to shame the wise . . . the weak things of the world to shame the strong" (1 Cor. 1:27).

Don Kraybill, in his important book *The Upside-down Kingdom,* states that in Christ's paradoxical New Order everything seems upside down to the wisdom of our world. Jesus invites us to follow him into a new society in which losers are winners, the last are first, and the meek, not the powerful, inherit the earth.

Not only the Reconstructionists but many conservative Christians, including family seminar leader Bill Gothard, promote a hierarchical chain of command based on the imperial Roman military model as though it were God's model. Kraybill insists that the Bible presents God's kingdom not as a hierarchical command structure preoccupied with power and control but rather as a "flat family" in which all believers are priests before God, given to compassion and service.[31]

Jesus didn't come teaching his disciples to take power and take over. Quite the contrary. When he found two of them jockeying for a position of greater power, he gave them a very direct word. He told them in effect that the last thing he wanted to see in their lives was a lust for power and position. "You know that the rulers of the Gentiles lord it over them, and their high officials exercise authority over them. Not so with you. Instead, whoever wants to become great

31. See Kraybill, *The Upside-down Kingdom,* 2d ed. (Scottdale, Pa.: Herald Press, 1990), p. 246.

must be your servant, and whoever wants to be first must be your slave — just as the Son of Man did not come to be served, but to serve, and to give his life as a ransom for many" (Matt. 20:25-28).

Jesus' model of leadership is unique in our world. He didn't adopt the autocratic, hierarchical command structure of the powerful Roman government. He stood it on its head. Jesus led by telling stories, hugging kids, and washing feet. Jesus led by giving away power, teaching his disciples to do everything he did, and hanging out with society's outcasts.

And the ultimate paradox is that it was in fully surrendering himself to the brutal power of imperial Rome that Jesus defeated all powers and principalities. And his followers live in anticipation of that day when every knee will bow and every tongue confess that this suffering servant is both Lord and Christ.

In Mary's Magnificat we are given a brief glance at how God plans to totally reorder our society at the return of the resurrected Christ. The Creator God intends to turn the hierarchical world power structure on its head. Listen to Mary's vision again:

> He has performed mighty deeds with his arm;
> he has scattered those who are proud in their inmost
> thoughts.
> He has brought down rulers from their thrones
> but has lifted up the humble.
> He has filled the hungry with good things
> but has sent the rich away empty. (Luke 1:51-53)

I believe the Gospel narrative compellingly shows that both progressive Christians and the religious right have it wrong. The followers of Jesus should certainly seek to be leaven in all arenas of life, including the political. But the genius of God's New Order doesn't come primarily through political action and certainly not through adversarial politics, name-calling, and total warfare. God's New Order comes through the creation of an incarnational community of servants who, like Jesus, seek to change our world through telling stories, washing feet, caring for others, loving our enemies, and, if called on to do so, through laying down our lives.

You see, contrary to the message of the Reconstructionists, the inbreaking of God's New Order really doesn't depend on us.

The sovereign God will bring the kingdom into being regardless of whether we do anything or not. But what a shame to miss the opportunity to collaborate in God's remarkable mustard seed conspiracy, which is quietly changing the world through the small and the insignificant.

Isn't it past time for both progressive and conservative Christians to repudiate the contention of the radical left that the real way to change society is through political action, taking power and taking over? Isn't it past time for us to recognize that the genius of the Jesus movement is not to be found in taking power but in laying down our own lives — the conspiracy of the insignificant? Isn't it past time to admit that in order to be a part of this Jesus movement, we don't begin by characterizing ourselves as victims or denigrating our foes as demons but rather by confessing our own sins and blessing those who oppose us?

As we seek to call both sides to lay down their weapons in this unholy war, it is important to pay attention to where this adversarial contest is taking us. In Chapter 8 we will explore who is likely to gain the upper hand in America's culture war. And we will seek to discern how it is likely to shape our common future as we enter a new millennium.

CHAPTER 8

▼ ▼ ▼

Millennium III —
The Future of
America's Culture Wars

"I BELIEVE THAT EVANGELICAL Christianity is face to face with the most awesome opportunity it has ever had to penetrate the American scene," declared evangelical scholar Carl F. H. Henry at the conclusion of the Consultation on the Future and the Church sponsored by the Billy Graham Association in Atlanta in 1977.

With evangelical leaders from across the country listening intently, Henry added, "I am more afraid we will muff this opportunity than I am sure we will seize it."[1] In retrospect it seems clear that his concerns were warranted. In the late seventies American evangelicals did indeed have an awesome opportunity to penetrate the American scene. And we definitely did muff it.

This was, I believe, the first time key American evangelicals had ever come together to try to anticipate and strategically respond to the challenges filling America's future. The list of participants read like a who's who in the evangelical world in the

---

1. Henry, "Response to the Conference Findings," in *Evangelicals Face the Future,* ed. Donald E. Hoke (Pasadena: William Carey Library, 1978), p. 166.

seventies, including Leighton Ford, Francis Schaeffer, Carl Henry, Harold J. Ockenga, Kenneth Kantzer, Harold Lindsell, Warren Webster, Tom Skinner, Donald Hoke, Ted Ward, Ronald Sider, Paul Cedar, Gordon McDonald, Hudson Amerding, David McKenna, Richard Lovelace, and many others. Martin Marty was invited as an observer from the ecumenical side of the church.

These leaders did an excellent job of anticipating many of the challenges that did indeed become a part of our common future, including growing poverty and racism in America and the rising specter of famine abroad. But they muffed it by failing to anticipate significant changes that would take place in the American evangelical movement itself. No one anticipated that before we even reached the eighties Jerry Falwell, the Moral Majority, the Religious Round Table, Pat Robertson, Tim La Haye, and a host of others would take over the evangelical parade, politicize it, and give it a decisive wrench to the political right.

The whole strategic response to societal change discussed at that consultation never got the attention it deserved, in part because over the next two decades the leaders of the religious right intellectually hijacked American evangelicalism. They have subsequently defined for the movement, as we have seen, what's wrong, who the enemy is, and what the politically correct issues are.

Some at *Christianity Today*, I think, tend to minimize the impact of the religious right because they only look at the numbers of evangelicals directly involved in political action and Christian right-wing groups. They don't seem to recognize how profoundly the religious right's influence has shaped both the mind and heart of evangelicalism over the past twenty years.

During this four-day consultation on the future in 1977, I had the responsibility for facilitating a process that would enable these evangelical leaders to draft scenarios on how the church could more effectively engage the challenges of tomorrow's world. While most of these leaders were likely moderate to conservative in their political views and concerned about such issues as abortion and family values, none of their scenarios proposed trying to change America through political action.

Rather than looking to political advocacy to change society

in those days, these leaders looked to the church. All of their scenarios outlined a host of innovative ways in which evangelicals could share the gospel, plant churches, and address the growing needs of the urban and global poor. They were intent on finding creative ways to activate and motivate the church to grasp this "awesome opportunity" to make a difference for the kingdom in America and the larger world.

For example, one scenario vividly described how the church might work for the transformation of one American city. They drafted an imaginative comprehensive strategy that included (1) assessing needs and surveying available resources, (2) instituting ministries of urban empowerment among the poor, (3) sharing the gospel with the different population groups, and (4) creating new churches that would call believers to more radical biblical discipleship, Christian community, lifestyle changes, and outreach into their city.[2]

Virtually all the scenarios emphasized enabling the church to reach out more strategically and aggressively to share God's love in specific communities. They realized that if they were going to act on these visions, they had to call their members to a more serious discipleship in which they reprioritized how they used their time and money, putting first things first. Obviously, motivating Christians to reach out compassionately through their local churches to touch their world is a far cry from trying to enlist evangelicals in the adversarial politics of the Christian right.

As we stand at the threshold of the third millennium, it is time to look to the future again as those evangelical leaders did some two decades ago. In this chapter we are going to ask (1) which side is likely to gain the upper hand in America's culture wars, and (2) how they might use their influence to shape our common future. We will particularly look at how their activity might affect America's domestic and foreign policy as we enter a very demanding future.

2. See Hoke, *Evangelicals Face the Future*, pp. 17-19.

Gaining the Upper Hand

"The future belongs to the committed," I wrote in *The Mustard Seed Conspiracy* in 1981. I am more convinced of that today than when I first penned it. And I believe that the people who are most deeply committed to their cause will be the ones to gain the upper hand in America's culture war.

I also wrote in *The Mustard Seed Conspiracy* that we were entering a period in which we would see the eclipse of political liberalism and a dramatic rise of political conservatism. One has only to look back to the changes in the American political scene since 1981 to realize this forecast is proving accurate.

On Election Day 1994, I happened to buy David Frum's book *Dead Right*. The cover copy reads, "The great conservative revival of the 1980's is over. Government is bigger, taxes are higher, family values are weaker, and the Democrats are in power. What will the Right do next?"[3]

The results of the midterm congressional election of 1994 proved Frum's book *Dead Right* was dead wrong. And it also very decisively answered his question as to what the right would do next. The Republicans scored a historic landslide victory, taking control of both the House and the Senate.

The religious right played a major role in securing the Republican victories by helping to get out the vote. As the *Philadelphia Enquirer* reported, "While conservative voters turned out in record numbers, members of liberal minority groups stayed home."[4]

Steve Goldstein reported on Ralph Reed's take on the election results. Reed, CEO of the Christian Coalition, declared that exit polling "showed that religious conservatives accounted for one-third of all votes cast in the election, compared with only 18 percent in 1988 and 24 percent in 1992. He said that evangelical Christian voters provided the margin of victory

3. Frum, *Dead Right* (New York: Basic Books, 1994).
4. Jeremy Wallace, "Actively Angry Electorate Set Off GOP Landslide," *Philadelphia Enquirer*, 11 November 1994, p. A4.

for all Republicans who won with 53 percent of the vote or less."[5]

Writing in the *New Republic* before the historic election, David Frum asked, "If the Christian right is so powerful and well-organized, why does it nearly always lose?"[6] At the time Frum had a point. A number of candidates who had run as protégés of the religious right, such as Michael Farris, lost apparently because they seemed a bit too extreme to the electorate. But Frum failed to look at the broader picture.

First, Frum joined a number of journalists in refusing to take the religious right seriously. The journalists focused their attention on individual candidates and issues and totally failed to recognize the movement's impact on the broader electoral process. For example, the Christian Coalition distributed 33 million voter guides and made 2 million phone calls to get out the vote for the 1994 senate and gubernatorial elections.[7] How could a lobbying effort this enormous have failed to play a decisive role in the Republican avalanche that buried many liberal Democrats alive?

Second, the Christian Coalition has quietly become the most powerful lobby within the Republican Party. At latest count, it had 1.5 million active members and a mailing list of 30 million, and it is growing at a feverish clip. I am convinced that one of the Coalition's long-term goals is to take over the Republican Party. Skip Porteous, executive director of the Institute for the First Amendment Studies, has suggested that the Christian Coalition meetings are designed to train the group's local supporters in how to infiltrate the Republican Party and how to run for office as Republicans.[8]

The current Republican power structure is not eager to emphasize the Coalition's evident and growing influence on the party.

5. Goldstein, "Christian Right Emerges as a Major Player for '96," *Philadelphia Enquirer,* 10 November 1994.

6. Frum, "Dead Wrong," *New Republic,* 12 September 1994, p. 17.

7. Laurie Goodstein, "Christian Coalition and Vote Drive Arouses Democrat Anger," *Philadelphia Enquirer,* 4 November 1994.

8. See Rob Boston, "Stealth Candidates," *Liberty,* September-October 1994.

In an in-house memo to Republican leaders before the election, conservative strategist William Kristol sought to play it down:

> The best evidence for the new "fundamentalist dominance" of the Republican Party is pretty thin evidence, indeed. No objective review of the nationwide slate of Republican candidates for federal and state office in the coming November elections could possibly conclude the Christian Right "controls" the GOP. And in national politics generally, needless to say, the movement's agenda, though it obviously remains alive, is (unfortunately) largely defensive. Last time I looked, Bill Clinton was still President, liberal politicians and policies still owned congress and Democrats still controlled most state houses and legislative chambers.[9]

How quickly things change — with the influential help of the Christian right.

Over the past four years, members of the Christian Coalition have been working with great skill at the grassroots level to gain control in the Republican Party. At the 1992 Republican convention, as many as 33 percent of the delegates were reported to have been members of the Christian Coalition or sympathizers, and their numbers are growing. They now control eight to ten state caucuses, and those numbers are increasing as well.

That's why during the 1994 election campaign season Republican leaders including Bob Dole, Dick Cheney, and James Baker were standing in line to kiss Oliver North's ring. He was the candidate of the powerful religious right. *The Economist* states that Christian conservatives probably already have veto power in the process of selecting the 1996 Republican presidential candidate.[10]

Third, the Christian Coalition is much more adaptable than its predecessor the Moral Majority. Under Ralph Reed's skilled guidance, the Coalition is constantly reinventing itself to become more appealing to a broader range of conservative and moderate

9. Kristol, Memo to Republican Leaders, Project for the Republican Future, 16 June 1994.

10. "American Survey: Your Vulture Checklist," *The Economist*, 12 November 1994, p. 36.

Americans. I think there is every reason to believe that this strategy is working.

As part of its revised vision, the Christian Coalition is not only dropping or disguising a number of the right-wing causes it previously advocated but it is also downplaying controversial "moral" issues. For instance, it has already displayed a willingness to support Republican candidates that aren't politically correct on the abortion issue. This has provoked attacks from Randall Terry of Operation Rescue, who charges that the Coalition is becoming nothing less than the mistress of the Republican Party.

More recently, according to a report in the *New York Times* (Feb. 11, 1995), Ralph Reed, in an effort to keep pro-life supporters on board, warned the Republican Party "that religious conservatives would not support the Republican ticket in 1996 unless both candidates opposed abortion rights. . . ." Of course, such a stance could divide the Republican Party — or give rise to a serious third-party candidate.

But even though I am skeptical as to how fundamentally the Coalition is changing its social critique and its agenda for change, I think it very likely that Reed's gambit will prove successful. In fact I wouldn't be surprised to see membership in the Coalition surpass two million by the time this book is out. And I am sure that their more moderate statement of their agenda will significantly increase their already impressive influence within the Republican Party if Reed doesn't preach his pro-life rhetoric too aggressively.

Finally, in spite of their more moderate rhetoric, the Christian Coalition and other groups on the Christian right are making common cause with a number of secular right-wing lobbying groups. As Mike Casey, a spokesperson for the Democratic Campaign Committee, has put it, "The Religious Right is joining forces with other conservative issue groups to form a single fist with incredible punching power."[11]

Well, in light of the 1994 Republican avalanche and the major role that the Christian right played in it, I think it should be clear to just about everyone who is gaining the upper hand in America's

11. Casey, quoted by Leslie Kaufman in "Life beyond God," *New York Times Magazine,* 16 October 1994, p. 73.

culture wars. I don't mean to suggest for a minute that the radical left will simply fade away and disappear. I regret to predict that the more contentious and violent days of America's culture war may well still be ahead rather than behind us. Even so, I believe the Christian right is winning this contest for the following reasons:

1. The Republicans have not only gained control of the House and Senate but have a very good shot at regaining the White House in 1996. Political liberalism is not only in eclipse; it's in the trash can. Those on the right, including talk radio, have succeeded in making "liberal" a four-letter word, and as a consequence there is very little support in Washington for any left-leaning legislative agendas.

2. Even though some groups on the p.c. left have shown some modest growth in numbers, none of them comes close to matching the accelerating growth of the religious right.

3. Groups on the radical left have had a much more difficult time than those on the Christian right in packaging their radical agendas in a way that attracts the support of mainstream America — and that's likely not to change.

4. The Christian right is solidly united to begin with, and it's now entering into partnership with an expanding number of groups on the secular right. The diverse groups on the left have always been more fragmented, and they show no signs of being able to collaborate effectively on a common agenda. The Democratic Party remains as splintered as ever, even in the face of a much stronger political foe.

5. The conservative side of the American church continues to show some modest growth in numbers and significant growth in political influence. But just the opposite is happening on the more progressive side of the church. Virtually all mainline denominations are graying and declining in numbers, and their influence in society and politics is diminishing as well. Moreover, the more radical liberal element within these denominations is itself a small and shrinking minority. While these voices of radicalism continue to exercise influence out of proportion to their numbers, they tend to be older and seem to be doing little to replace themselves with a new generation

of radicals. The only exception might be a growing number of radical feminists who are becoming very influential in various mainline seminaries.

6. Finally, it is my candid opinion that more progressive Christians don't begin to match the high level of commitment evidenced by those on the religious right. Leaders on the right have successfully motivated their troops not only to act out of fear of an apocalyptic future and a sinister elite but also to transfer their profound commitment to God and concern for the family to right-wing political causes.

Looking Back from Millennium III: Anticipating the American Impact

Let's assume for a moment in light of this analysis that the Republican Party does indeed regain the White House in 1996 and retain control of the House and the Senate. Further, let's assume that the religious right generally and the Christian Coalition specifically will continue to grow in influence and play an even greater role in directing Republican policy into the next millennium. (Of course, a third-party candidate in 1996 could radically alter this scenario.)

Now let's look back from the Third Millennium and reflect on how the Christian right's influence on the Republican Party and the conservative American political scene could shape our lives and future, given their notions of what's gone wrong and what must be set right. How might their growing influence shape America's domestic and foreign policy into the next century? Let's look at some of the possible positive contributions first.

Anticipating Positive Impacts

I think it would be difficult to exaggerate the extent to which the church generally and American evangelical Protestantism in particular positively influence domestic life in America today. Our religious institutions represent, I believe, the soul of our nation. More than that, they are involved at the grassroots level all over our country in countless ways. They are building homes through Habitat for Humanity and working with kids who are in trouble with the court through Youth for Christ.

It is important to emphasize that many groups on the Christian right are also actively involved outside the political arena seeking to make a difference in their communities. Pat Robertson's Operation Blessing ministry, for example, is working to help those in need in thirty-five cities. In Seattle, Operation Blessing provides funding for the New Horizon ministry, which each year helps over a thousand kids escape the street world of drugs and prostitution and get their lives back together.

Through its political advocacy, the religious right has made all Americans more aware of the importance of moral values, family integrity, and religious faith in our society. While I clearly disagree with a number of assumptions underlying the advocacy of the Christian right, I commend its success in bringing issues of faith and values into public debate.

I particularly applaud those who are challenging America's young people to just say no to sex outside of marriage. Consistently applied, the Christian right's affirmation of the importance of moral values, family life, and religious faith could have a very positive impact on the American future.

And I sincerely hope that Christians of all traditions can both reduce the violence and gratuitous sex of American media and insist on T.V. and films making room for the transcendent dimension of life, as *The Mission, The Milagro Beanfield War,* and *Places in the Heart* have done.

With the Republican takeover of the House and Senate, it will be interesting to see how the influence of the religious right might be expressed in domestic public policy initiatives. One of the earliest indications may be the introduction of something called "The Family Reinforcement Act." It is a practical expression of the Christian right's strong emphasis on family life. Among other things, the proposed legislation would provide a $500 tax credit for families caring for elderly parents and a $5,000 tax credit for couples adopting a child. It also establishes procedures for collecting more of the millions of dollars in child support that divorced parents are now evading (a move that would have the additional benefit of reducing taxes). And it sets a minimum three-year federal prison sentence for sex offenders and people found guilty of running child prostitution rings.[12]

If the religious right could continue to inspire this kind of initiative, it could have a very positive impact on the future of both the family and American society. However, if it also gives its support to right-wing efforts to dramatically cut government agencies and social programs, it could have a devastating impact on millions of other families.

Anticipating Negative Impacts

Without doubt the domestic issue that concerns me most as we race toward a new millennium is our commitment to the common good — specifically, the way we provide for our weakest and most vulnerable citizens. All Western countries, including the United States, are finding it necessary to take a hard look at cutting back on social benefit programs. Both Republicans and Democrats have a myriad of ways to reform public welfare. But neither party seems willing to confront the major challenge to our fiscal future — struggling with entitlements.

God knows our public welfare system needs a major overhaul. We need to create a new system to ensure that those who can work do work. We need a system that provides adequate job training to move the poor out of chronic poverty. And any who are genuinely pro-family know that we need to create better health care and support structures for working poor families.

However, right now all of the programs of welfare reform that meet these goals seem to have higher initial costs for education and job-training than either Republicans or Democrats are willing to fund. In the absence of practical alternatives, conservative Republicans are promoting a balanced budget amendment to the Constitution that could result in wholesale cutbacks in social programs without putting anything in their place.

12. See Abraham McLaughlin, "House GOP Plan Aims to Bolster Family Ties," *Christian Science Monitor,* 13 December 1994, p. 2.

Some Republicans are advocating transferring all responsibility for welfare back to the states. However, based on their experience with the Reagan administration, state and local leaders are legitimately concerned that they could wind up with all of the responsibility for these programs without adequate funding to administer them.

It isn't the purpose of this book to anticipate how this debate is going to conclude. But I do want to spend a few moments looking at the role that evangelicals generally and the religious right in particular might play in this important discussion in order to get a sense of the possible consequences for our long-term future.

First, it is important to emphasize that evangelicals are among the most compassionate and socially involved of any group in America. Researchers report that the people who are most active in their churches tend to be the ones who are most generous in volunteering their time and investing their money in helping those in need. Evangelicals are among the most active of all American Christians in their churches. And, indeed, surveys show that they are consistently more generous than their mainline counterparts in seeking to help the poor.

Surveys also reveal that evangelicals tend to express concern for a much broader range of social issues than the leadership of the religious right typically does. And they tend to assign their priorities differently as well. Research conducted by a group of evangelicals headed by Lyman Kellstedt, a political scientist from Wheaton College, reveals that evangelicals generally have as high a level of concern for hunger and poverty issues as they do for abortion. Only those evangelicals that this research classifies as "highly committed" — about one-third of the total population — are aligned closely with both the ideology and issues of the Christian right. This group generally lists abortion, homosexuality, and feminism as its chief concerns — but it still expresses a significant concern for the poor.[13] Clearly the Christian right has been most successful in influencing "highly committed" evangelicals.

13. Lyman A. Kellstedt, John C. Green, James L. Guth, and Corwin E. Smidt, "American Evangelicals: Left and Right," *ESA Advocate*, April 1993, pp. 1-4.

While evangelicals have a heart for the poor and many invest their time and resources in helping those in need, regrettably that isn't the whole story. One study of evangelical missionaries working in the Third World reveals that their attitudes toward the poor seem to be shaped much more decisively by their conservative political and economic views than by biblical principles. Specifically, these religious conservatives, like secular conservatives, tend to blame the poor for their poverty. They tend to ignore the structural causes of poverty and to deny that citizens of the more affluent countries have any responsibility for the impoverished in the Third World.

At a 1991 meeting of sixty evangelical missionaries and executives, I was asked to introduce a film that told the story of Archbishop Romero's tragic story in El Salvador. Remember, the group who viewed the film was composed of evangelical Christians who had devoted their lives to working with the poor.

At its conclusion, about a third of the viewers went absolutely ballistic because their conservative political views made it impossible for them to condone Archbishop Romero's speaking out against human rights abuses and the murdering of the poor in his nation. One missionary actually declared, "If Romero had just kept his mouth shut regarding the death squads killing the people and his priests and just preached the gospel, he would be alive today!"

The Talk Radio Takeover

It's beginning to look as though the Republican landslide in 1994 was even more of a victory for talk radio than it was for the religious right. One survey revealed that hard-core talk radio listeners voted Republican three to one.[14] Frank Luntz, a conservative Republican insider, also found a very high correlation between those who listened to eleven or more hours of talk radio every week and those who voted Republican.[15]

14. Richard Corliss, "Look Who's Talking," *Time*, 23 January 1995, p. 22.
15. Luntz Research Companies, Post National Results, 8-9 November 1994, Table 35-9, Question 30.

One of the most troubling aspects of talk radio's huge victory is that these propagandists are very skilled in instilling animosity toward government, the poor, and anyone else they get in their crosshairs. Part of the problem is that, as we have seen, they sometimes tend to play pretty fast and loose with the facts. Distortion, insinuation, and rage are not a satisfactory substitute for informed civil discussion about important issues. And yet it's beginning to look as though this is the level on which America's political discourse might be pitched as we enter a new century.

These demagogues have actually convinced many Americans that they are the most heavily taxed people on the face of the earth. When compared to citizens of other Western countries, Americans are actually among the least taxed. But this kind of distortion has enraged many Americans and led them to insist on getting more of their taxes back, regardless of the cost to the common good.

Henry Aaron, of the Brookings Institution, believes that one of the most serious consequences for America's future is the creation of a survival-of-the-fittest political process that very deliberately weeds out politicians of strong principles who don't conform to public opinion as shaped by talk radio. People who don't make the grade with the talk radio crowd won't be able to get reelected. "Few of those with core principles will survive," says Aaron.[16] If he is correct, as we enter an increasingly more complex future our public policy could be shaped by the simplistic black-and-white remedies of talk radio. That is a very frightening prospect indeed.

Ten years ago the most influential person in the American evangelical church would have certainly been Billy Graham. Three years ago it would, I believe, have been James Dobson. Today I am convinced the most influential leader would be a person who doesn't even go to church — the king of rage radio, Rush Limbaugh. His syndicated sermons are received by twenty million listeners a week on 660 stations.[17] (He only needs six more stations to reach the magic number.)

16. Aaron, quoted by Wright in "Hyperdemocracy," *Time*, 23 January 1994, p. 20.
17. Corliss, "Look Who's Talking," p. 22.

I digress into this discussion of the terrifying future of talk radio because Limbaugh and talk radio hosts like him are doing more than any other force I know of to shape the public attitudes and values of many American evangelicals. Our movement has never been known for its intellectual prowess. And we seem to be particularly vulnerable to the right-wing propaganda, anger, and nonsense of both talk radio and the religious right. The combination could be deadly for our common future.

I am very troubled that American evangelicals don't have better discernment. You see many "RUSH IS RIGHT" stickers on the cars of evangelicals right next to their fish symbol. It seems to elude them that so many of the pronouncements of Limbaugh and his colleagues are often diametrically opposed to the values and teachings of Jesus Christ.

Let's look, for example, at Limbaugh's attitudes toward the rich and poor and compare them to Jesus' teachings. After railing against what he calls "Uglo-Americans" in his book *The Way Things Ought to Be*, Limbaugh launches into a diatribe against the poor:

> The poor in this country are the biggest piglets at the mother pig and her nipples. The poor feed off the largesse of this government and they give nothing back. Nothing. They're the ones who get all the benefits in this country. They're the ones that are always pandered to. . . . I don't have any compassion for the poor. Because I think they can do something about it.[18]

Limbaugh's compassion toward the rich, on the other hand, seems boundless. He sees them as society's real victims. And it is clear that he views those who are really very wealthy, like himself, as the most esteemed members of the American scene.

Doesn't Jesus Christ have a slightly different view on this subject? Wasn't he known for his compassion for the poor and his reservations toward the wealthy? Do you remember the Beatitudes?

> Blessed are you who are poor,
>   for yours is the kingdom of God.

18. Limbaugh, *The Way Things Ought to Be* (New York: Pocket Books, 1992), pp. 40, 41.

> Blessed are you who hunger now,
>   for you will be satisfied.
> Blessed are you who weep now,
>   for you will laugh. . . .
> But woe to you who are rich,
>   for you have already received your comfort.
> Woe to you who are well fed now,
>   for you will go hungry.
> Woe to you who laugh now,
>   for you will mourn and weep. (Luke 6:20-21, 24-25)

The Jesus we follow was always reaching out in compassion to those in need. And he was always challenging the wealthy to unencumber themselves to help those less fortunate. Remember, he said it would be easier for a camel to go through the eye of a needle than for a rich man to enter the kingdom of God. Isn't this categorically antithetical to the message of talk radio that despises the welfare moms as "parasites" who don't report tips but never has a harsh word for wealthy corporations that rip off our government for millions?

What will happen if talk radio becomes the ruling voice not only in the public square but also in the sanctuary? How is it likely to alter American evangelical attitudes, particularly their attitudes toward those less fortunate than themselves?

The Co-opting of American Evangelicals

Since many evangelicals' attitudes toward the poor are already apparently shaped more by conservative political and economic views than by Scripture, I am concerned that they are particularly vulnerable to the angry propaganda of talk radio and the growing influence of the religious right.

For example, talk radio has been enormously successful in recruiting conservatives of all stripes, including evangelicals, to hate government. And the spokespersons of the religious right are very skilled in using code words like "socialize," "socialistic," and "collectivize" to call up the apocalyptic images of a global takeover by the Antichrist. As a consequence, religious right evangelicals in America, in contrast to evangelicals in other Western countries, have become vehemently opposed to initiating any government-funded programs to help the poor. And they are just as strongly committed to major cutbacks in spending on social programs with little apparent awareness of the consequences for the marginalized members of our society.

Therefore, one very possible scenario for the American future is one in which evangelical Christians continue to support some private grassroots initiatives for a few of those in need but at the same time give their wholehearted endorsement to draconian cuts in government-funded programs to the huge numbers of impoverished families and children that fill American society. As I conclude this book, the first proposals for cutbacks being debated in the House are directed at poor families, children, and the elderly. There has not been a single suggestion by conservative Republicans that we should cut back on the billions of dollars in government welfare to wealthy corporations.

Recent research reveals that more than a quarter of children under the age of six in the United States are living in poverty, and tragically these figures are climbing. Three in five poor children have working parents. The number of American children under the age of six increased by a staggering one million between 1987 and 1992 according to a report by Columbia University's National Center for Children in Poverty.[19]

If conservative Republicans with the unqualified support of the Christian right get the cutbacks they want, we will see an even more dramatic increase in the number of impoverished children and families in American society as we enter a new century. And this swelling human tragedy will be supported by millions of evangelicals who claim to be followers of Jesus.

Let me be clear. As a political independent, I have been frustrated by many of the failed social programs that the liberal Democrats have initiated. I favor local initiatives and fiscal responsibility. I sincerely would love to see the Republicans create

19. "More Kids in Poverty, Study Finds," *USA Today,* 31 January 1995, p. 5A.

some new local economic programs that more effectively address the escalating needs of our cities. I particularly like some of those promoted by Jack Kemp.

But instead of selectively supporting these initiatives like Kemp's to help the urban poor to help themselves, Ralph Reed gave the Republican Contract with America the Christian Coalition's unqualified support.

Writing in *Christian American,* Marshall Whittmann states that "the Christian Coalition has made passage of the Contract its top priority for the new Congress."[20] He goes on to stress that the Contract is pro-family because it promises a $500-per-child tax credit. But nowhere in the article is there any discussion of the possible devastating impact the Contract and other proposed legislation could have on poor families in the United States or abroad.

Ralph Reed announced on January 18, 1995, that the Christian Coalition was launching "the largest single lobbying effort in our history beginning tomorrow, when all 50 of our state chairmen fly to Washington to personally work for the passage of the balanced budget amendment." Reed said that the Coalition was planning on spending more than a million dollars on a lobbying campaign that would involve "phone banks, fax networks, satellite television, computerized bulletin boards, talk radio and direct mail." Altogether, the Coalition was planning on sending out more than sixty million pieces of literature over the next two years "informing people of faith" about how their lawmakers had voted on elements of the Contract with America.[21]

Remarkably, as we know, the Republicans in the House achieved all of the goals of the Contract with America that were set for the first hundred days. No one, I am sure, celebrated the victory more enthusiastically than did Ralph Reed. The Coalition's wholesale support endeared them to Newt Gingrich and

20. Whittmann, "GOP Contract Is Now Top Priority," *Christian American,* January 1995.
21. Richard L. Berke, "The 'Contract' Gets New Ally on the Right," *New York Times,* 18 January 1995, p. A15.

leaders of the Republican House and further strengthened Reed's insider status in the Republican Party. But since the balanced budget initiative did not pass this time, the possible negative impact on poor families at home and abroad has been temporarily deterred.

But we can be sure that the Republican House will seek to finish what they started, likely with the full support of the Christian Coalition. And near the top of their list will be cutbacks in social programs to those in need in order to pay for middle-class tax-cuts and balancing the federal budget. Of course, there are already signs, even in the Republican Party, that some of the more severe cutbacks may be moderated. It is too early to tell if the momentum of the Republican House will slow.

Conservative Republicans are arguing as they did during the Reagan era that when the cutbacks come, the church and the private sector will automatically step in and pick up the slack. I worked with churches during the eighties, and they didn't step in and pick up the slack. Thousands of poor families and others were seriously hurt by those cutbacks.

Assessing these policies, Robert Plotnick, a public policy analyst, reports the telling human consequences:

> The cutbacks in welfare programs, especially AFDC and Food Stamps, were championed by the Reagan Administration as a means to reduce dependency and encourage work. Success in these objectives was minimal, and at the high cost of increasing poverty. This increase was particularly felt among persons in single parent families with children. The cutbacks pushed more than 1.1 million of them below the line and raised their rate of poverty by 3.9 percentage points.[22]

I have talked with evangelical leaders who are directly involved in providing ministries to the urban poor today. I have asked them what they would do if there were serious cutbacks in

22. Plotnick, "Changes in Poverty, Income, Inequality and the Standard of Living during the Reagan Years," Institute for Research on Poverty, University of Wisconsin, Madison Report #669 (1992), p. 40.

social programs and dramatically increasing numbers of families seeking their help. They tell me that they are having an extremely difficult time finding financing for their existing ministries. They have absolutely no idea of where they could find funds to meet this increasing need for poor families and kids. What plans does the Christian Coalition have to address this potentially devastating impact on the most vulnerable members of our society?

The Roman Catholic Bishops Conference spoke out very forcefully on the new proposed wholesale cutbacks. "We in the church stand with the unborn and the undocumented, the poor and the vulnerable, the hungry and the homeless in defense of human rights and human life," Bishop Keeler declared. "Our advocacy does not fit ideological or partisan categories, for our witness is not politically correct, but unfailingly consistent."[23] I pray that evangelicals will join Catholics, not the Christian Coalition, in calling for compassion and a witness that is "not politically correct, but unfailingly consistent."

The Prospects for America

What will the long-term domestic consequences be if the Republican Party, with the enthusiastic support of the Christian Coalition, succeeds in making wholesale cutbacks in social programs?

1. If young women who become pregnant are no longer eligible for welfare, we could see a dramatic rise in abortion rates. If they have no income and no job skills, they might well be tempted to turn to prostitution or selling drugs to support themselves. Hardly an outcome that pro-life, pro-moral, pro-family conservatives would welcome.
2. The working poor and families simply struggling to make ends meet might be hit hard by cutbacks in supplementary assistance programs such food stamps, significantly swelling the ranks of the underclass. Therefore, tax cuts for middle-

23. Keeler, quoted by David Gonzalez in "Bishops' Leader Warns against 'Punitive' Welfare Cuts," *New York Times,* 15 November 1994, p. A24.

class families might well make it harder for the working poor to hang on to such basics as food, shelter, and health care.

3. If Republicans finally succeed in passing the balanced budget initiative, even middle-class programs such as school loans could take a heavy hit, and growing numbers of middle-class young people might no longer find it possible to go to college.

4. I am very concerned that the major casualty of this right-wing crusade to promote survival-of-the-fittest economics could well be any national commitment to a sense of the common good. If we lose this central commitment, born of our Judeo-Christian past, how can we hope to survive as a nation or provide moral leadership in the larger community of nations as we enter a new millennium?

5. All of this could increasingly lead, in the next century, to an increasingly polarized and dangerous two-tier America. If the cuts go deep enough, I am afraid we could even see our cities erupt in violence and despair that could imperil our entire society. And you don't have to be a forecaster to anticipate the conservative response — major police repression.

Please understand, I am not predicting that this is our certain future. But severe cuts in social programs over the next five years could well affect our future well into the third millennium. And if this scenario, or something very like it, takes place, I think many conservative Christians could find themselves in the unenviable position of supporting political and economic policies that are shown to be diametrically opposed to the biblical purposes of the God they serve. They will discover that economic and political ideology is not an adequate substitute for biblical principle.

The biblical witness from Genesis to Revelation is clear: people are judged by how they treat the most vulnerable members of their society. That includes not only the unborn but children, widows, and families that are impoverished. The Bible teaches that they are God's special concern.

Listen to the indictment by the prophet Isaiah on those in the nation of Israel who made laws that compromised the poor:

> Woe to those who make unjust laws,
>   to those who issue oppressive decrees,
> to deprive the poor of their rights
>   and rob my oppressed people of justice,
> making widows their prey
>   and robbing the fatherless.
> What will you do on the day of reckoning,
>   when disaster comes from afar?
> To whom will you run for help?
>   Where will you leave your riches? (10:1-3)

Looking Back from Millennium III: Anticipating the Global Impact

If the Republicans gain the White House and retain control of the House and Senate in 1996 and the Christian right becomes the most influential lobby in the party, how could it shape American foreign policy as we enter the third millennium? We will look at a few possibilities, beginning with the possible global impacts of the Republican Contract with America.

First, it is essential that I emphasize that conservative Protestants have a tremendous heart for the larger world. Over the years, many evangelicals have given sacrificially of their lives and resources to see the gospel of Jesus Christ shared around the globe. And evangelicals have been much more generous than their secular counterparts in helping communities in need all over the planet. You will find thousands of schools, hospitals, and churches in Africa, Asia, and Latin America that are an expression of the caring of American evangelicals.

The Future of the Global Poor

American evangelicals have been enormously generous throughout the world. Unlike their European counterparts, they have allowed those with a very narrow political ideology to define for them the politically correct issues. And every American evangelical knows that those issues are abortion, pornography, homosexuality, traditional family values, and school prayer.

Though, as we have seen, some evangelicals are indeed concerned about a broader range of issues, everyone knows what the sanctioned list is. And few ever seem to challenge its legitimacy. So I think it is time to speak up and propose we scrap the list and start over, working for a consistently biblical agenda and a consistent life ethic.

Let's look at abortion. Leaders on the religious right would have us believe that abortion is the only pro-life issue that matters. God help us, but thirteen million children are dying every year from hunger and malnutrition, and that is a pro-life issue too! But it is never mentioned by the leaders of the Christian right.

I suspect the reason this issue doesn't make the list is that we can't blame liberals or abortionists for this criminal neglect of the lives of millions of innocent children. All of us, including stridently pro-life Christians, are complicit in these deaths through our indifference, our self-indulgent lifestyles. And too often we support policies that are likely to dramatically increase the number of deaths among these helpless children.

Let me describe in the clearest of terms how battle lines are being drawn on this issue in order to encourage genuinely pro-life Christians to consider developing a consistent life ethic. As we have seen, the Christian Coalition is giving unqualified support to the Contract with America without discussing its potential impact not only on the children of this country but on the millions of at-risk children and families in the Third World.

Listen to the concern expressed regarding the Contract by Bread for the World in a recent newsletter: "November's elections created a Congress that is likely to slash funding for hungry people in our country and worldwide. . . . Senator Jesse Helms (R-NC), incoming chair of the Senate Foreign Relations Committee, wants to cut the foreign aid budget in half."[24]

24. "Huge Struggle Ahead," *Bread for the World Newsletter* 6 (December 1994): 1.

Bob Seipel, the president of World Vision, points out that less than three-tenths of one percent of the entire federal budget goes to foreign aid to developing countries. Seipel makes a passionate plea to conservative Christians to reexamine their unquestioned support for cutbacks in foreign aid to the poor:

> The stakes are tremendous not just in terms of how to budget our foreign policy, but rather how this last remaining super power responsibly defines itself to the rest of a hurting world. Our national net worth, like an individual's, will ultimately be determined not by what we selfishly keep but rather by what we compassionately and responsibly give away. No global power can be truly great whose national interest excludes human dignity and the sanctity of every human life. Not to be an impact player in a world of desperation is nothing short of betrayal of our Christian ethics. This world and its people matter to God, and we turn away from them at our peril.[25]

Seipel and World Vision have been joined by thirty-one other evangelical agencies in opposing Jesse Helmes' and the religious right's initiative to cut U.S. humanitarian aid. Many of these evangelical agencies work directly with the poor and know what the terrible human toll will be of these proposed cutbacks. They also point out that these cuts could seriously jeopardize fledgling democracies.[26]

If the passage of the balanced budget amendment and adoption of the rest of the Contract with America results in a significant cut in U.S. foreign aid to help the world's poorest peoples to help themselves, the consequences could indeed be dire.

As we enter the third millennium we could see the number of children dying every year dramatically escalate from thirteen million to a much higher figure. Then Bob Seipel will be right. By giving our highest allegiance to right-wing economic policies rather than the biblical call to seek justice for the poor, we will

25. Seipel, in a letter to the World Vision constituency dated 13 January 1995, p. 2.
26. "Evangelicals Protest Foreign Aid Cuts," *Christianity Today,* 24 April 1995, p. 50.

have again placed ourselves in peril of the judgment of God. And one day we will be forced to ask that very painful question, "Lord, when did we see you were hungry and in need and fail to respond?"

Another pro-life issue that the Christian right tends to avoid like the plague is the millions of deaths caused by tobacco, alcohol, and guns. One of the groups that was most jubilant at the Republican landslide was a group of lobbyists that have dubbed themselves the "MOD Squad" — MOD standing for Merchants of Death. "We're going to overturn everything we don't like that we can," proclaimed Neal Knox, a vice president of the National Rifle Association. "It's payback time."[27]

The religious right is not about to speak out on those pro-life issues that anger its Republican allies. One of its strongest advocates in Congress is Jesse Helms, who gets enormous support from the tobacco lobby. I have never heard anyone on the religious right speak out on one of evangelicals' oldest social concerns, the tremendous human costs of alcohol abuse in America. And since the Christian right has made the support of the NRA a pro-family position, it is not about to be counted among those groups who are seeking to regulate children's access to guns in order to reduce the epidemic of kids killing kids in our cities. Again, their prior commitment to a right-wing political ideology and the Republican agenda seems to limit what they consider "acceptable" pro-life issues.

The National Rifle Association militantly opposed passage of the Brady Bill for a seven-day waiting period for the purchase of handguns — a bill endorsed by former president Ronald Reagan. Their argument was that "a right deferred is a right denied." For years they have convinced their constituents, including the Christian right, that any restrictions on the sale of guns is the first step down the slippery slope toward some elite totally disarming America and leaving our nation and our families unprotected, setting us up for a takeover. The same view is inflaming right-wing paramilitary groups.

When I share this line of reasoning with evangelicals in

27. "Of Tobacco, Torts and Tusks," *Newsweek*, 28 November 1994, p. 30.

Europe, Australia, and New Zealand, the response is always the same: "You can't be serious! American evangelicals couldn't be that gullible!" But I assure them that many are. That's the reason they don't dare to speak out on one of the major pro-life issues in America — growing numbers of children gunning one another down on our streets. If they did, they would have to oppose the NRA in trying to find ways to restrict gun access to those who shouldn't have guns.

Let me point out the high price in human life of their silence on just one more of these pro-life issues — tobacco. Currently three million people all over the world die annually from tobacco-induced illnesses. Since the American market for many tobacco products is shrinking, American tobacco companies are now aggressively marketing their wares in poor Third World countries.

We seem to be making up for our reduced foreign aid by the increased marketing of addictive products of death like cigarettes to the poor. Economic conservatives point to the clear benefit to the American economy without ever mentioning the high human costs to the consumers in these marginalized countries.

A missionary reported seeing one of our major American tobacco companies handing out free samples of cigarettes at a young people's rally in Costa Rica. They know if they can get them hooked early, they have them hooked for life. And several companies are marketing cigarettes with a much higher level of nicotine content than in those sold in the U.S. to further increase the addictive success of their product.

If this pro-life issue goes unchallenged in America, where most of these companies are based, what is likely to be the cost in human life as we enter a new century? The World Health Organization predicts that the successful marketing of tobacco products will cause tobacco-related deaths to soar from three million annually today to ten million annually by the 2020s. And most of this dramatic increase in the loss of human life will be among the world's poor — seven million human lives.[28]

Isn't it past time for pro-life Christians to join Roman Cath-

28. American Association for World Health, "Global Facts on Tobacco," p. 1.

olics and many of the rest of us in demanding that the Christian right develop a consistent life ethic and speak out against all of those forces that threaten the sanctity of human life, including abortion?

With the growing size and influence of the Christian right, I suspect it is unlikely that they will ever question the narrowness of their politically correct issues or the consequences of their conservative economic advocacy on the world's poor. Central to the conservative economic philosophy is the assumption that we must place America's economic interests first.

Looking back from the third millennium, I believe we will belatedly recognize the high cost of these policies to the lives and families of the poor with whom we share this planet. Again, we will have to account to a God who claims to be sole owner of this world. And we will have to answer for hundreds of passages in the Bible that remind us that God wants justice for the poor. *Justice* is a word that doesn't seem to have any place in the vocabulary of the religious right. Nor does there seem to be any recognition that we have a biblical mandate to care for creation.

Erecting a Superstate for Jesus

Let's shift our attention from America's economic policies to its political policies as we stand at the threshold of a new century. Secular conservatives are not as united on political policy as they are on economic policy. Some on the far right want to expand American military hegemony and power in the world by perhaps a couple of quick military strikes into countries such as Cuba. Others, such as Pat Buchanan, are just as militantly isolationist and advocate ceasing all aid to Mexico and putting troops along our southern border to protect us from our hungry neighbors.

Frankly, I believe both options would, in different ways, compromise our common future and would certainly undermine America's moral leadership in the world. On this side of the third millennium, it isn't clear which camp is going to gain the upper hand or whether more moderate voices can help America find a political vision in which we lead by moral principles instead of military might. What is clear is that the Christian right is four-square behind any conservatives who want to increase America's power and influence in the world.

James Skillen does an exceptional job in his book *The Scattered Voice* of describing all the different Christian groups who are active in the public square. Skillen characterizes the Christian right as "pro-American conservatives" who identify the Christian mission with the promotion of American nationalism.

> Robertson, Falwell, Tim and Beverly La Haye, Phyllis Schlafly, James Dobson, D. James Kennedy, and others decry America's moral decline and direct their indignation toward illegitimate secular humanism that is distorting the country and undermining the birthright of the majority. In the minds of many pro-American Christians, the majority of God-fearing, moral Americans are the proper owner of this estate that God gave their ancestors more than 200 years ago.[29]

Pro-American conservatives who consider America to be God's modern chosen people truly believe that their "Christian" mandate is to conduct foreign policy in a way that advances the military power and national interests of the United States. "According to those within the New Christian Right, America is a redeemer nation," says Michael Lienesch. "In embracing [this view], religious conservatives are by no means unique. What makes them distinctive is . . . seeing America's world role as both providential and politically preordained, and excluding all other views as unrighteous and un-American. For these thinkers, it is America's calling, in the words of James Robison, 'to save the world.' "[30]

Somehow the pro-American conservatives keep forgetting that at Pentecost God created a new transnational community through which God intends to reach people and redeem a world. They rarely mention that God is at work bringing into being a new transnational kingdom.

29. Skillen, *The Scattered Voice: Christians at Odds in the Public Square* (Grand Rapids: Zondervan, 1990), p. 36.
30. Lienesch, *Redeeming America: Piety and Politics in the New Christian Right* (Chapel Hill, N.C.: University of North Carolina Press, 1993), pp. 196, 197.

Mike Riddell, a lecturer at Carey Baptist College in New Zealand, relayed the following thoughts to me about his first trip to Washington, D.C.:

> I was struck by how much the monuments of the nation's founding resemble religion temples. It seemed to me that in some strange way there had been a mingling of nationalistic and patriotic symbols with the human capacity to worship. In biblical terms there was a hint of idolatry. It concerns me that many American evangelicals (and I am an evangelical) seem to have incorporated cultural values as articles of faith. As an outsider it disturbs me that national symbols such as the flag, the constitution, democracy and capitalism were spoken of in the same devotional way as Jesus, Scripture and the Kingdom of God.
>
> The other feature of life in Washington which shocked me was the poverty and violence of the central city. The paradox of beggars on the streets of such a wealthy nation haunts me still. Where is the prophetic call for justice and mercy being sounded within the American Church? I did not hear it in evangelical circles. Is it possible to follow Christ and not respond to the poor in our midst?[31]

Riddell's keen insights and probing questions should stir American evangelicals to do a little critical self-examination in light of scriptural injunctions instead of nationalistic conditioning. Perhaps the reason we don't allow Scripture to remind us of our biblical responsibility for the outrageous number of poor in American society is that we have given ourselves over to the nationalistic task of making America powerful (often at the expense of the poor) instead of to the prophetic call to make America just. This raises the question of what we as Christians owe our first loyalty to.

Doing Foreign Policy with the Religious Right

In 1988 I was invited by the World Without War Council to participate in a panel discussion at Seattle Pacific University on

31. Riddell, in a letter to the author dated 20 September 1994.

the topic "Faith and Foreign Policy." In my brief presentation I suggested that our first loyalty as Christians was not to a nation-state but to our God and to the international community of God's people.

Robert Pickus, the founder of the World Without War Council and an ardent nationalist, stepped out of his role as a neutral moderator to challenge my comments. "I understand for you Christians your first loyalty is to God," he said, "but your second loyalty isn't to the international church. It's to the United States of America." He then gave me an opportunity to retract my assertions.

I responded, "Not only won't I retract, I will add that for Christians, giving loyalty to a nation-state before loyalty to God and the people of God is idolatrous."

In fact, I recommended that American evangelicals come together with Christians from all over the world and leave our nationalism and political ideologies outside the door. Perhaps in an international forum we could study God's Word together and try to discern what the principles of God's new transnational order are. Then we could bring these biblical principles back to our respective nations to define our views on both domestic and foreign policy. But such an approach is alien to the nationalistic agenda of the Christian right.

Let me give you one example of how the religious right does foreign policy that will demonstrate their very unusual way of defining their position. We have witnessed an absolute miracle in South Africa as a nation has been born for all the people who live there. How would the future of South Africa have been altered if the religious right had brought its views to bear on this extremely difficult situation?

I believe if the religious right had been in the driver's seat, the South African miracle would never have happened. For years conservative evangelicals have propagandized themselves and others to genuinely believe that any empowerment of blacks in South Africa would inevitably result in a communist takeover of the region. Of course this is a part of their scenario of the Antichrist's collectivization of the planet. They insist on force-fitting all political issues into this very limited conspiratorial end-times mold, without regard to the real dynamics in the region or the genuine aspirations of the people.

Jerry Falwell traveled to South Africa in 1985. And, true to form, he totally bought the analysis of the white apartheid regime. "He returned to the United States," wrote Matthew C. Moen, "claiming that many black leaders opposed the imposition of sanctions, and implying that apartheid was less nefarious than it was usually portrayed."[32] Incredibly, when Falwell came back from that trip, he called Archbishop Desmond Tutu a "phony," and he lobbied the U.S. government on behalf of the white apartheid regime, as did many others on the religious right during this time.

More recently, Pat Robertson wondered aloud why in the world Western governments were imposing sanctions on virtually the only stable government in Africa: "Why, with all of sub-Saharan Africa in economic shambles, has the political left mounted such an unremitting campaign to bring about the same chaos in the only vibrantly healthy economy on the African continent — South Africa?"[33]

Of course in retrospect it is clear that those on the right were dead wrong again. It is obvious, in looking back, that those very sanctions that Falwell, Robertson, and virtually everyone else on the right opposed were directly responsible for bringing the white apartheid regime to face the hard reality that it had to change. If those on the right had been in the driver's seat, I think we would be witnessing a new level of violent repression in South Africa today instead of a relatively peaceful transition to a democratic government for all of the people.

It's been extremely difficult for those on the right to admit when they are wrong. In fact, instead of celebrating the South African miracle, the Christian Coalition's *Christian American* trotted out the old discredited communist takeover propaganda one more time: "Mandella's communist ANC has carried out a systematic campaign of terror for the last 30 years, directed pri-

32. Moen, *The Transformation of the Christian Right* (Tuscaloosa: University of Alabama Press, 1992), p. 79.
33. Robertson, *The New World Order* (Dallas: Word Publishing, 1991), p. 31.

marily against other blacks who rejected their revolutionary agenda."[34] The article goes on to hint that the old collectivist script may yet prove to be right.

But thankfully people of reason and goodwill, with the strong support of the broader church, helped midwife the South African miracle. In April 1993, Christian leaders from all over the world came together in South Africa to celebrate this transformation that seems to have had the signature of the Creator God on it. Anglican Archbishop Desmond Tutu declared with evident joy, "We used to say, We will be free — black and white together. Today we say, We are the rainbow people of God! We are free!"[35]

I think it is important to point out again that many of those on the religious right are inherently suspicious of any forms of international cooperation and fearful of the loss of American sovereignty. Because of their end-times worldview, they aren't inclined to support American cooperation with any international organization, from the United Nations to those concerned with environmental or population issues. Many on the Christian right flatly deny that there are any serious global environmental or population problems. If the religious right were to significantly increase its political influence in the Republican Party and through the party the U.S. government, it would almost certainly undermine America's ability to provide leadership in international cooperation that will become critical for our common future.

We as a nation must provide global leadership to promote the role of law, democratization, and stewardship of planet earth into the twenty-first century. Otherwise the planetary consequences could be dire. And it is clear that conservative Republicans, including Jesse Helms, are already committed to cutting back funding to the United Nations and other international organizations as well as funding for environmental efforts.

Among other things, the Republicans are determined to cut

34. Barbara V. Woerner, "Historic Vote in South Africa," *Christian American,* July/August 1994, p. 8.
35. Tutu, quoted by Jim Wallis in "The Miracle of South Africa," *Sojourners,* July 1994, p. 4.

U.S. funding for United Nations peacekeeping operations. If they are successful, with the strong support of the religious right, they could paralyze U.N. peacekeeping efforts. Again, evangelicals could find themselves working against the purposes of God because of their apocalyptic theories and their right-wing political ideology.

At the 1994 Population Conference we got a good idea of what we can expect from the new right regarding some of the urgent global issues facing our planet. Republican Congressman Christopher Smith, an evangelical, worked along with religious conservatives from the Roman Catholic Church and a number of Islamic states to change the wording of the population statement published at the conclusion of the conference so that it would read, "Abortion is not a means of population control." They effectively blocked any endorsement of abortion in the recommended plan of action.

But even leaders from these groups, including Congressman Smith, recognized the legitimate concerns raised by the out-of-control population growth for the earth's poorest inhabitants and for the global environment as a whole.

Andrew Steer, deputy director of World Bank's Environmental Program and an active evangelical, stated that "the World Bank is accepting the relationship between poverty, education, women's health and population," and he urged other evangelicals to join him in making the equation on the grounds that "our most deeply held beliefs" are at stake. The reactionary right from the United States attending the conference showed no inclination to join in this constructive conversation and cooperation.

Reporting for *Christianity Today,* Gordon Aeschliman noted "the marked contrast of respectful, sophisticated dialogue between disagreeing parties . . . and the bombastic, confrontative rabble-rousing of United States pro-life groups." The latter repeatedly interrupted the meeting and ultimately a number were arrested.

CBN journalists insulted Latin American nations on the last day by accusing them of "bowing to financial pressures from the United States." The United Nations actually had to suspend two U.S. press briefings and the final press conference was terminated early because of the out of control behavior of religious right representatives from the U.S. Both those who were arrested and those who weren't were an embarrassment to both the international Christian community and to the United States.[36]

Apparently because they were schooled in a singularly adversarial approach to political change, these religious right representatives didn't seem capable of civil dialogue. They often evidenced little understanding of the urgent global problems precipitated by out-of-control population growth, little compassion for the world's poor, and little willingness to join others in reasoned discussion of these complex issues. Convinced that there is a conspiracy afoot to impose abortion rights on poorer countries and redefine the family unit to include homosexual couples, ideologues on the right apparently believed that the only way to communicate their concerns was through unholy mayhem.

Do we really want these "flat earth" ideologues on the right, who apparently aren't capable of thoughtful and constructive dialogue, to shape the foreign policy of the Republican Party and the United States of America? We do have a choice.

As we are rapidly transported into a new millennium filled with an overwhelming range of complex new global challenges, it is pretty obvious that we can't risk placing the sensitive and difficult work of international relations in the hands of ideologues of any stripe, right or left.

In this chapter we have attempted to briefly assess what some of the consequences might be if Republicans control the House, Senate, and White House in 1996 and the Christian Coalition and religious right grow in influence and control of the party. We have identified some possible positive consequences. But we have principally raised concerns at two levels: (1) the Christian right has consistently relied on right-wing economic and political

36. Aeschliman, *Christianity Today* press report on the United Nations International Conference on Population and Development, pp. 1-5.

views and their conspiratorial view of history instead of Scripture to define their public policy positions, and (2) I believe the consequence of their conservative economic and political policies and their conspiratorial view of history could have a very dire impact not only on American domestic and foreign policy but also on America's moral leadership in the world.

John B. Judis states in the *New Republic* that the root of the problem is the fusing together of politics and Christianity in a new amalgam that is really not good for either the church or the political order. "When the two are fused . . . , when organizations acting in the name of Christianity seek political power, then religion becomes subordinate to politics. It becomes infected with the darker egoism of group and nation; it no longer softens and counters our ungenerous impulses but clothes them in holy righteousness."[37]

We must insist that both the progressive and evangelical Christians who are committed to reconciliation and reason be at the forefront of our efforts to provide leadership for America in the third millennium to fashion a new global community of peace and justice and the care of God's creation. Jimmy Carter is a model of the ways in which all Christians can bring both reason and principle to bear on the difficult issues filling our global future and in the process be agents of God's reconciling grace. He is a model of Christian statesmanship for us all.

But the only way we can do this is to develop a new critique of what is wrong and recover a biblical vision for the renewal of our lives and God's world — a third way.

37. Judis, "Crosses to Bear," *New Republic,* 12 September 1994, p. 25.

SECTION III

▼ ▼ ▼

Searching for a Third Way
beyond America's Culture War

BEAMING CHILDREN from many different cultures with mul-
ticolored streamers glistening behind them in the sun led the
jubilant parade. It was a glorious blue-sky June day as 25,000 of
us marched through the heart of London celebrating our unity
in Jesus Christ. Old-line Anglicans, enthusiastic Pentecostals, and
believers from Pakistani house churches all marched together for
two and a half hours singing, waving at passersby, and carrying
banners of praise and jubilation.

I was very grateful to be in London on this particular
weekend, marching with evangelicals, mainline Protestants, and
Roman Catholics, bearing witness to our common faith. Quite
frankly, Christine and I couldn't have marched in Jesus marches
in most American cities, because, like so many other good things,
many of the marches here have become highly politicized. And
you wouldn't find the broader spectrum of the American church
marching together. Instead of bearing witness to our common
faith in Jesus Christ, too many use these marches in the United
States to promote the political agendas of the religious right. Of
course, the implication is that their right-wing political agendas
and our Christian faith are one and the same. But they are not.

And there are demonstrations of faith by progressive Christians in America that I, in all good conscience, couldn't participate in either, because they have become so politicized. In this

▶▶▶   219

march in London, I think I began to discover some of the possible seeds of a third way. Here I found progressive and conservative Christians, not always agreeing with one another, but still able to talk to one another with mutual respect. And often they do find ways to work together on issues of both Christian faith and political advocacy. Sometimes they even march together to bear public witness to their unity in Jesus Christ.

Right now we find, in stark contrast, that America's culture war is tearing apart the fabric of both church and society. In recent years, I have heard from a growing number of Christians how absolutely fed up they are with the viciousness, polarization, and violence of America's culture war. And they want to see an immediate CEASE FIRE.

But they want more than a CEASE FIRE. They want an alternative to the highly politicized Christianity of the left and right. I find that many American Christians have absolutely no interest in the political ideologies of either polarity. They want a faith that is more vital and a basis for engaging the troubling issues of our time that comes more authentically from our faith than from any brand of political ideology.

These Christians are looking for a new reason for being and a place to stand. They are searching for a third way. In this section of the book, we are going to seek a third way. In Chapter 9 we are going to explore both an alternative analysis of what has gone wrong and a biblical alternative to the visions offered us by the Christian left and the religious right. Then in Chapter 10 I will offer a concrete, creative description of what a third way could look like if we decided to take a biblical vision for our common future seriously.

It's important to emphasize again that this third way is not a middle-of-the-road position between the polarized extremes. Rather, the third way I am proposing is a radical biblical way that transcends the highly politicized agendas of both left and right.

I am offering this third way because I find so many Christians, of all traditions, looking for alternatives. But please understand: I am not proposing for a moment that anyone adopt in toto either my analysis or my vision for what the church could become. I simply offer this approach to a third way as a starting point in the important quest to find a biblical alternative.

I understand the important task William Bennett and other conservatives have undertaken in trying to identify a common set of values in an increasingly pluralistic secular society. That is beyond the scope of this book. It is my conviction that before Christians can participate in that sort of conversation with Jews, Muslims, Buddhists, secularists, and others, we need to be very clear about our own Christian values and our biblical vision for a future made new. That is the focus of this final section.

CHAPTER 9

▼ ▼ ▼

A Third Way —
Searching for a New Critique
and Dreaming New Dreams

ONE COLD DECEMBER NIGHT, some thirty-five people crowded into our living room for a party. They weren't quite sure what to expect. Neither were we.

We called our celebration Advent II: Homecoming. Of course Advent I was when Jesus Christ came to us in Bethlehem. Advent II is when, at the return of Christ, we are going to be welcomed home to a world made new.

One of the most compelling biblical images of the future of God for me is that of a great international homecoming with people coming from every nation to the mountain of God and the city of God. It is a vision in which the blind see, the deaf hear, the lame leap for joy, and the Creator God hosts a huge banquet on Mount Zion for the family of God. And our loving God wipes all tears away.

The first thing we asked our guests to do was to share some of their most poignant memories of homecoming. I still remember Butch Holstrom sharing what it was like to come back alive from Vietnam when most of his buddies didn't. A woman shared the welcoming she saw in her mom's eyes every time she came home. People were very vulnerable for not really knowing each other.

Then we read out of Jeremiah about the captives coming home from Babylon to the City of David. And we invited our friends to join in singing Jewish folk songs and choruses as though we were the ones coming home from Babylon to the City of David. After a time of singing, we began to get up-tempo and entered into the joy of coming home.

I abruptly stopped the singing and announced, "Now we are going to dance through the streets of Jerusalem!" Terror was clearly visible in the eyes of these very staid Christians. They started edging toward the door. But we had the door locked and bolted. Unbeknownst to them, there was a Jewish folk dance instructor in the crowd. She played some Israeli folk dance music.

For the first fifteen minutes, it was painful to watch these stilted saints try to move their bodies. Finally they began to loosen up, though, and we really began dancing as though we were coming to Jerusalem and a world made new.

Then we had a buffet with dishes from all over the world. Because the great homecoming of God will be a richly multicultural celebration in which we share our gifts with one another, we enjoyed festive food from Asia, Africa, Latin America, and Europe. We ate until we were absolutely full. Then we ended our celebration as we will begin our homecoming celebration, with the bread and the wine of the eucharist.

I am convinced that we Christians can do better than celebrating the Home Shopping Channel, playing Trivial Pursuit, or watching MTV. We can, if we choose, celebrate our Christian faith in every aspect of our lives. And I firmly believe that one of the most important parts of our faith to celebrate is our sense of God's vision for both our lives and our common future.

That's the point of this chapter. It is my contention that both the p.c. left and the religious right have misdefined what's wrong. As a consequence we have all embraced dreams and aspirations for our future that have little to do with the purposes of God. And we have missed the biblical imagery of a God who intends to make all things new.

Therefore, in this chapter we are going to present a third way in attempting to answer the two questions we have asked of the respective polarities in America's culture war: (1) What is wrong with American society and who is the enemy? and (2) What is a biblical vision for the human future and the created order?

I am convinced that if we can find a new vision for our common future in Scripture, it will inevitably lead us to discover a new reason for being and a new place to stand. Then we will all be able to come home to the future of God.

A Crisis of Vision

Crisis number one facing the American church, I believe, is a crisis of vision. When I use the term "vision," I don't mean anything hyper-spiritual in the clouds. I simply mean that image of the better future we want for ourselves and those we care about.

Aboriginals have a saying that comes out of their experience with Europeans in Australia: "White man got no dreaming. Him go another way." Essentially this aboriginal saying suggests that they feel that Europeans don't have any soul or spirituality. It also implies that Europeans have no vision for the future that comes from their spirituality. I believe this indictment could be applied to much of our American culture as well.

Kenneth Boulding, a scholar and Christian author, has stated, "No people, society or organization can long exist without some compelling vision of the future that calls us forward into tomorrow." The Bible insists, of course, that "where there is no vision, the people perish" (Prov. 29:18, KJV). We are not the only ones perishing for lack of this biblical vision; those to whom we are supposed to be extending God's love are perishing as well. The only vision that many of us are offering them has little to do with our Christian faith and everything to do with our secular culture.

I am convinced that in all our Christian traditions, we have allowed our modern culture instead of our ancient faith to define our views of the good life and our images of the better future. And in the process, all of us, progressive and conservative Christians alike, have been seriously co-opted by a secularism we haven't named — Enlightenment secularism.

224 ◄◄◄

Will the Real Secularists Please Stand Up!

As you will remember, those on the left have attempted to persuade us that we can fully understand what has gone wrong in our culture by analyzing how power is used and abused. Their power critique variously designates the enemies as males, whites, heterosexuals, Eurocentrists, and biocentrists. But for a number on the left, the religious right has really become public enemy number one.

As we have seen, many on the Christian right have attempted to explain what has gone wrong by asserting that planet earth is destined for a one-world takeover, based on their questionable reading of a handful of passages from Daniel and Revelation. A number of them link this foundational end-times claim to a conspiratorial view of history. With the collapse of the Evil Empire, they are no longer certain who the global conspirators are. But they have absolutely no doubt as to who the American conspirators are — a liberal/humanist elite.

Their critique of what's gone wrong points the finger at secular humanists. And they basically put in that category anybody who is for abortion, gay rights, and a liberal political agenda. Since conservative Christians don't find themselves anywhere on that list, they mistakenly assume that they are untainted.

Even those on the Christian right who might not buy into a conspiratorial view of history are dead certain that "secular humanism" is an accurate portrayal of what's gone wrong. And they sincerely believe the real enemy is a humanist liberal elite that is intent on destroying our families, undermining our faith, and subverting the American way of life.

I have already explained why I believe the critiques of both the liberal left and the religious right are dead wrong. They both define what's wrong in largely political terms. I am going to argue that the real secularism that is seducing us needs to be understood primarily in cultural, moral, and religious, not political, terms.

I call this alternative critique "Enlightenment secularism." I think Francis Schaeffer was mistaken when he coined the term "secular humanism." I believe history shows that the real secularism that bedevils us doesn't come from the humanistic period as he contended. It is certainly true that certain themes began to emerge during the humanistic or Renaissance period in the fifteenth and sixteenth centuries that contributed to the secularization of the West. And one of those was indeed, as Schaeffer points out, "that man was seen the measure of all things."

However, most historians seem to agree that the greater influence on modern culture is not the humanistic period but rather the Enlightenment. The Enlightenment, or the Age of Reason, spans the sixteenth to eighteenth centuries. It introduced a new way to understand our world, through scientific empiricism. Spokespersons of the Enlightenment began to recognize the possibilities of using empirically derived knowledge to subdue and control the larger natural world. Francis Bacon, writing in the seventeenth century, asserted that "knowledge is power." He saw the potential to use scientifically derived knowledge to master nature for the benefit of humankind. This marked the beginning of the Modern Age.

The roots of the real secularism that has co-opted Western society can be found right here. In this worldview, much more of the initiative to master the natural environment and order human society was given over to rational human control. As a consequence, the Creator God became increasingly marginalized and for many became largely irrelevant to the "Enlightenment project." We suddenly awakened to a modern world freed from any sense of divine presence or purpose in which we were told all values were relative.

And through modernity, the images, ideas, and values spawned by the Enlightenment are engulfing and secularizing a world. Everywhere traditional values are collapsing before the relentless onslaught of modernization. Speaking at a conference on modernity, evangelical scholar Os Guinness declared that "modernization is not something simple, local, transient or inconsequential. At its most developed level it confronts us with such relentless power and pervasiveness that it has been aptly described as an 'iron cage' around human life (Max Weber) and a 'gigantic steel hammer' that smashes traditional institutions and communities of faith (Peter Berger)."[1]

As we have seen throughout this book, the politically correct left and many progressive Christians welcome modernization and the eclipsing of traditional structures and values. Fundamentalists, on the other hand, from Islamic fundamentalists to Christian fundamentalists, are engaged in furious battle with the forces of modernization.

Conservative Protestants in the United States are particularly battling against those who would deny the authority of a Creator God and the existence of absolute moral values. But while evangelicals are engaged in opposing the encroaching modernization of a few selected battlefields, they seem largely oblivious to its larger impact on their lives, faith, and even their political advocacy.

John Seel, an evangelical scholar speaking at the same conference, observed that "modernity defines what is real for modern people . . . the way things are." Seel adds, "So the uncritical acceptance of modernity within evangelicalism is a serious matter. For modernity does not first lead to heresy but to idolatry. Modernity's potent rewards will come to replace our need for God."[2] As we will see, Seel's forecast that modernity leads to idolatry is chillingly accurate.

Perhaps no area of modern culture and Christian life has been more seriously affected by Enlightenment views and values than our image of the better future. Let's look at the vision for the better future that is at the core of modernization and the idolatry it has unobtrusively fostered among people of faith.

1. Guinness, "Reflections on Modernity," *World Evangelization* 18 (December 1993): 8.
2. Seel, "Evangelical Myopia," *World Evangelization* 18 (December 1993): 14-15.

An Enlightenment Vision:
Progress, Economic Growth, and
Technological Expansion in the Here and Now

The storytellers of the Enlightenment told us a new story. It goes something like this: If we cooperate with natural law, all of society is going to progress economically and technologically. The future will bring ever-increasing levels of economic growth, technological mastery, and social progress. Someone has written that "Marxism says all there is is matter, and capitalism says all that matters is matter," but these are both inherently materialistic visions for the future, lacking any larger sense of transcendence.

Essentially what happened was that the vertical quest for God and God's kingdom, which had been at the center of European culture through the Middle Ages and the Renaissance, got tipped over on its side in the Enlightenment. It was transformed into the horizontal secular pursuit of progress, power, and ever-increasing material bounty. And in essence there was little place for the Creator God in this dream. It was a dream created by the initiative of humankind for the benefit of humankind. And it is focused singularly on the here and now.

Francis Bacon sketched the first vision of a technological paradise in Western literature in his book *The New Atlantis*. As one of the early leaders of the Age of Reason, he saw clearly the possibilities of scientifically subduing and utilizing the resources of the natural realm to create an opulent new future of wealth and technological wizardry. Bacon envisioned new energy, transportation, and war-making technologies. He even foresaw the scientific fabrication of artificial fragrances and foods and a very comfortable way of life that anticipated the rise of a technologically based consumer culture.

Today, in our post-Enlightenment culture, our images of the better future are drawn directly from this Enlightenment vision for the human future. I am convinced that most of us, including both progressive and conservative Christians in the United States, have uncritically bought into this materialistic secular view of the better future that is solely preoccupied with the here and now. In the American dream, the Enlightenment values of progress, economic growth, and technological innovation have been translated into an ever-expanding consumer culture. Lesslie Newbigin charges that "the effect of the post-Enlightenment project for human society is that all human activity is absorbed into labor. It becomes an unending cycle of production for the sake of consumption."[3]

In the American dream, we have come to define the good life and the better future in largely economic and materialistic terms. We aspire to ever-increasing levels of personal consumption, affluence, and status. For many, consumerism and happiness have become virtually synonymous. Increasingly, moderns not only want all the material benefits of the American dream but self-actualization too.

The Enlightenment has also placed tremendous emphasis on the importance of control, power, and mastery. At the very center of the Enlightenment vision is an obsession with scientific and technological power. The leaders of the Age of Reason lusted to know as God knows and to be powerful as God is powerful. They were strong advocates for increasing the rational human initiative to order and control our world. I suspect that some of the contemporary pursuit of power that preoccupies the political right and left finds part of its origin in the Enlightenment's growing hunger for human power and control.

While the Enlightenment has clearly brought us many benefits, some of the ideas and values generated by this period have had unintended negative consequences for our modern age. Chief among these is a vision that sees the better future in largely economic, materialistic terms with no larger sense of transcendent purpose. This vision of the better future is both the driving force of modernization and a major corrupting force of traditional faith.

The reason for the growing rage coming through talk radio and paramilitary organizations is that entire segments of our society are beginning to lose their grip on this essentially economic middle-class dream. Somehow they seem oblivious that

---

3. Newbigin, *Foolishness to the Greeks: The Gospel and Western Culture* (Grand Rapids: William B. Eerdmans, 1986), p. 30.

the downswing of their economic privilege had more to do with the downsizing and downscaling of corporations than with anything the federal government or some imagined conspiratorial elite are up to. But those on the far right are not about to direct their anger on a free market system that is systematically reducing their economic power while increasing the wealth and power of corporations and a wealthy few.

Buying into the American Dream:
The Hidden Costs of High Living

We are all in serious trouble, progressive and conservative Christians alike, in that we have allowed the secular impulses of the American dream to define the aspirations that drive our lives and the values on which our lives are premised. And in all candor, I believe the aspirations and values of Enlightenment secularism are often categorically in opposition to the aspirations and values of God's New Order. How did we get into this mess?

First, since we have been conditioned to see the better future in largely economic terms, it shouldn't be surprising that we have come to see the created order and indeed ourselves in largely economic terms, too. For many in our modern world, the universe has been stripped of any sense of divine presence or purpose. It is seen by many in starkly utilitarian terms as the place where we drill for our oil and set up our campers. It is nothing but a storehouse of passive natural resources we use to erect our consumer-centered technocracy.

In a world robbed of a sense of God's presence and purpose, many see humanity in starkly reductionistic terms as well. We are simply the sum of our organic core and behavioral surface. In such a world, many of us, including many within the church, seem to derive much of our sense of identity and self-worth from our success in the economic arena.

Don't we almost always introduce ourselves in terms of where we work? Our very identity as persons seems to be largely derived from the kinds of homes we live in, the cars that we drive, and our success in our consumer culture. Many people actually seem to believe that they are what they own. And therefore the more they own, the more they are. For too many, the ability to upscale in our career and consumerism has become synonymous with happiness. In fact, the only thing that seems to hold many Western societies together is a commitment to keeping the consumer culture growing.

But deep down I think we realize that we can't find the sense of ultimate meaning we all long for in the pursuit of the American dream. Furthermore, as Christians believing we have a destiny beyond this life, we also know that our self-worth isn't derived from our success as producers and consumers. It is innate, because we are image bearers of the Creator God.

Second, we get caught up in this consumer culture to find not only meaning and identity but also community. Psychologist Paul Wachtel suggests that another reason we have succumbed to the seductions of consumerism is that we have tried to replace intimacy, a sense of belonging, and the security of community with the consumption of a never-ending stream of consumer goods and services.[4] Again, deep down we recognize that consumerism can never replace our need for human community. But many, apparently not knowing how to find meaningful community, settle for a very unsatisfactory substitute.

Third, we have been seduced by this essentially materialistic vision for the better future to believe that we have a fifth human need. In addition to the basic survival needs of air, water, food, and protection from climatic changes, "the fifth need is the need for novelty — the need throughout our waking life for a continuous variety in external stimulation of our eyes, ears, senses or organs and all of our nervous network."[5] In this constant quest for novelty, yesterday's luxuries become today's necessities.

However, the only way to keep this free-market engine producing more and more economic growth is for all of us to develop a huge and ever-increasing appetite for novelty and a cornucopia

4. See Wachtel, *The Poverty of Affluence: A Psychological Portrait of the American Way of Life* (New York: Free Press, 1983).

5. Stuart Ewen, "Waste a Lot, Want a Lot: Our All-Consuming Quest for Style," *Utne Reader,* September-October 1989.

of consumer delights. We will constantly have to develop new "needs" when many of us seem to be struggling with declining discretionary resources. Is this kind of ever-increasing appetite for materialism and consumer novelty congruent with the biblical vision for the future? Isn't this what the Old Testament prophets labeled as idolatry?

I think any fair assessment will demonstrate that this American obsession with upscaling and consumerism is putting enormous stress on our lives and families. Fully 89 percent of American adults report that they are chronically stressed out. Sixty percent state that they are regularly struggling with stress and doing nothing about it.[6] This stress is directly responsible for many of our ills and is sending many Americans to early graves and fragmenting many families.

I find that the number one problem of people I work with all over the country is that they are absolutely out of control in their timestyles. The economic demands of the American dream have pressured most women to go back to work. And more and more couples are taking additional part-time work. Some are doing it to stay even, others to increase their capability to participate in the consumer rat race. Recent research reports that, on average, Americans lost ten hours of discretionary time per week over the past fifteen years. This out-of-control busyness has been labeled "The Applauded Addiction" in American culture. But the rat race is a fraud. It never was the good life. And it is taking a tremendous toll on our lives and families.

The pro-family folks need a wake-up call. The real threat to our Christian families isn't some sinister elite living in Washington, D.C. The real threat is Christian families unquestioningly buying into the secular aspirations and addictions of the American dream. Christian parents trying to get ahead in their careers and in their upscale living are often among those working the longest hours. As a consequence, their lives are more stressed, and they have less time for their kids, their faith, and one another. This is one of the major contributors to the breakup of the family

6. Louis Harris, *Inside America* (New York: Vintage Books, 1987), pp. 8-9.

and the alienation of the Christian young. And frankly, this "rich in things, poor in time" modern lifestyle is not preparing the next generation to be successful in creating healthy families either.

Buying into the American Dream: The High Costs to a New Generation

Ivan Illich wrote an educational classic called *Deschooling Society* in which he coined the term "hidden curriculum." What is the "hidden curriculum" in a Christian family in which the kids all have their own CD players, TVs, VCRs, and phones, and, when they get to be a certain age, their own cars? With each succeeding generation, Madison Avenue, the media, and pop culture are gaining greater control over our youth.

Do you know what I'm talking about? Every Christmas looks like the department store blew up in the living room! In this "hidden curriculum," the clear message to the Christian young is that "things" are what matter most. Generation X has gotten the message, and many, including the Christian young, have become disciples of a celebrity culture and devotees of the religion of instant gratification. We are losing huge numbers of our young people from churches, but we are not losing the Christian young to the cults. We are losing them to the new shrines of worship in America, where too many Christian families go to do their devotion — the shopping malls.

For all the talk on Christian radio about "raising up a child in the way he should go," the real message to the Christian young is to "get the best you can for yourself." We are promoting a driven, acquisitive individualism. Robert Coles, a Christian psychologist who specializes in working with children, states, "Very little is asked of a lot of American children with regard to compassion and thinking of others. The emphasis is on using psychology to cultivate the individuality and self-importance of a child. One sees that in home after home. Children are encouraged to look out for themselves and get what they can. Very little emphasis is put on pointing the child's eyes and ears, and even heart and mind, away from himself or herself and toward others."[7]

I am convinced that we can't just blame that larger modern society for the growing sexual promiscuity of the young. Part of the responsibility must also lie with Christian parents who have conditioned their young from the time they were infants to focus on meeting their own needs and desires and get the best they can for themselves. We are raising the Christian young with a driven, acquisitive individualism that affects every facet of their lives, including the development of their sexual behavior and their moral values. It is very difficult for the young to discipline their sexual appetites when they are often encouraged to freely satisfy their consumer appetites with little discipline at all. They need to learn to just say no to all the seductions of secular culture, not just premarital sex.

For all the talk about the lordship of Jesus by evangelicals, the real message to the Christian young is to get their careers underway, their houses in the suburbs (if they can afford them), and their upscale lifestyles started. Then, if they have anything left over, they can follow Jesus like the older generation.

But since the American dream is so much more expensive for this generation than it was for their parents, if they follow the script, they are going to have much less left over. They are likely to lead even more stressed lives than their parents do, with even less time for their kids. And, if they go for it, many of them will have virtually no time for prayer, church, or caring for anyone else. This vision is hardly congruent with pro-family and pro-faith values. Nor is it congruent with those progressive values that focus on the marginalized.

I suggest that Christian parents raising their children in upper-middle-class homes aren't doing their children any favors. Many of these kids will never again be able to afford the lifestyles they were raised with. And if they try, they will face chronic financial problems.

I am running into growing numbers of young couples who

7. Coles, "Our Self-Centered Children — Heirs of the 'Me' Decade," *U.S. News and World Report,* 25 February 1980, p. 80.

are going through plastic melt-down because they have been programmed to emulate the secular affluent lifestyles of the families in which they were raised. What has happened is that we sold the Christian young the wrong dream. Christian families, churches, and schools have all sold them the American dream with a little Jesus overlay.

The real secular threat to our families is not some pack of secular humanists out there trying to do in our families. The real threat is Christian parents who unwittingly allow the aspirations and values of Enlightenment secularism to order their private world and dictate the values they pass on to the next generation.

Frankly, our unqualified commitment to ever-increasing levels of consumerism isn't doing the environment or the poor any good either. And to the extent that we Christians give our unqualified allegiance to constantly upscaling our lifestyles, I believe we are misappropriating large quantities of the resources of time and money God has entrusted to us — resources that could be used in Christian mission to make a difference in the lives of those in need both in the United States and throughout the world. Our unbridled love affair with this idolatrous notion of the better future is coming at a very high cost to our lives, families, the next generation, God's creation, and the poor and marginalized with whom we share this small planet.

Finally, with the coming of postmodernism, the Western dream and all the assumptions on which it is based are under increasing assault anyway. Doesn't it make sense for Christians to provide leadership in seeking a new biblical vision to which we can devote our lives, raise our young, and order our society?

Enlightenment Secularism and the Visions of the Religious Right

American Christians of all stripes seem to be content to allow the American dream to define the aspirations that drive our lives and the values on which our lives are premised. But some on the Christian right have elevated the economic theories that are at the core of the American dream to the level of highest religious dogma. As we have seen, many seem to have more confidence in the magic of the marketplace than in the power and promise of the Creator God to transport us to a better future.

For example, conservatives have joined their conservative economic theories with individualism born of the Enlightenment to formulate the doctrine of economic self-interest. They contend that the best way to benefit the larger society and help the poor is to pursue our own individual self-interest. One spokesperson on the right actually argued that the best thing he could do for those in need was to purchase a fleet of luxury autos. The idea is that the more lavishly we spend money on ourselves, the more money will be pumped into the economy and spread around for the benefit of the larger society, including the poor.

In other words, Jesus had it wrong. We are not supposed to "lose life" for the good of others as he did. We are supposed to follow the gospel of the Enlightenment and modern culture, which encourages us to pursue our own personal happiness and seek our own personal economic gain. I believe that this is just one more expression of the idolatry of the self that is burning incense at the altar of materialism and egoism.

Ironically, at the same time that conservative Christians are fully caught up in this modern society and the materialism of the American dream, they also show signs of being drawn to a future that is singularly nonmaterialistic. Influenced by Western dualism, evangelicals are often profoundly schizophrenic when it comes to their visions of the future. As we have seen, they tend to be as committed as anyone else to getting a piece of the great American pie, but many are also looking forward to a transcendent future that is, I believe, more a product of Greek philosophy than of biblical hope.

Plato and other Greek philosophers despised this material realm and looked forward to a nonmaterialistic existence in the beyond. Influenced by Hellenistic thought, many evangelical Christians also look forward to a Christian version of this nonmaterialistic existence in the clouds.

Many evangelical Christians find themselves therefore looking forward to two very different visions for the future: getting a piece of "fat city" now and getting their souls rescued for a

disembodied existence in the clouds by and by. Most who subscribe to this very materialistic vision for the here and now and
a nonmaterialistic vision for the future of God don't seem to
recognize how incongruent these two images are. Nor do they
seem to recognize that neither one is compatible with the biblical
vision of God's New Order. Of course, there are many evangelicals
who reject this disembodied notion in favor of a biblical view of
the redemptive future of God.

Evangelicals who are members of the religious right also
entertain a third vision for the future that really has no support
in Scripture either. It, too, is a by-product of Enlightenment
secularism. In fact, the primary vision of the religious right, as
we have shown, involves making the American political and
economic system great and powerful. One can certainly understand citizens in many countries wanting their national governments to be more powerful and influential. However, where in
the world can one find any hint in the Bible that our Christian
mission is to make a modern state great and powerful? As Gabriel
Fackre said, this "adds to the Christian story a chapter which is
not in the Book." For biblical Christians, working for the advancement of a nation-state is as idolatrous as pursuing the self-
interested aspirations of the American dream.

Leaders of the religious right, recognizing that they can find
little biblical support for the advancement of this nationalistic
agenda, have looked elsewhere. Many have turned to civil religion.
I was honestly surprised to see Ralph Reed, in his book *Politically
Incorrect,* trying to persuade Christians to embrace civil religion in
order to advance the religious right's nationalistic cause.

Reed states, "What religious conservatives want is to accommodate the historic role of faith in American civic life. In short,
they seek to restore the time-honored civil religion — not to
establish Christianity by law or create an official church."[8] I
applaud Reed's not wanting to "establish Christianity by law,"
but surely he must recognize that Christianity and "time-honored
civil religion" are two very different faiths.

8. Reed, *Politically Incorrect: The Emerging Factor in American Politics*
(Dallas: Word Books, 1994), p. 135.

I wrote and asked him what biblical basis he had for urging Christians to embrace both civil religion and Christian faith. He responded as follows:

I am not urging that Christians embrace civil religion in their function as Christians. I am merely suggesting that civil religion has been an important glue that has held American society together that we should adopt as citizens. As a Christian, I embrace an evangelical personal faith. As a citizen I embrace a different kind of faith that encompasses virtually all of our citizens. Similarly, I place emphasis on advancing the United States because it is my function as a citizen of this country.[9]

Reed's response brings us directly to the heart of the matter. Civil religion and Christian faith are two totally different faiths that bow the knee to two very different deities and work for two very different agendas. Civil religion supports the nationalistic agenda of "advancing the United States," while Christian faith is committed to advancing God's transnational kingdom. It is absolutely incomprehensible to me how a follower of Jesus Christ can worship at two very different altars and serve two very different Gods. It violates the first commandment — "You shall have no other gods before me."

Evangelical scholars Richard Pierard and Robert Linder make the point forcefully: "Christianity and civil religion are not the same thing. American Christians do the cause of Jesus Christ an enormous disservice when they communicate a contrary understanding. . . . In fact, civil religion simply becomes more intense and often dangerous to the survival of genuine Christianity when it is hitched to an evangelical bandwagon."[10]

The god of civil religion is nothing but what Southern Baptist leader Foy Valentine calls "a homemade god" that can "neither judge us nor save us." He adds that "in fact civil religion comes dangerously close to blasphemy when it identifies God

9. Reed, in a letter to the author dated 30 January 1995.
10. Pierard and Linder, *Civil Religion and the Presidency* (Grand Rapids: Zondervan, 1988), p. 294.

with national destiny and in essence reduces the universal God of the Bible to the tribal God of America."[11]

As we have seen, many Christians on the religious right are working for three different visions of the future — buying into the American dream, looking forward to a disembodied existence in the clouds, and making America great and powerful. These three visions not only lack biblical support but contain elements that I believe seriously undermine the values and vision of biblical faith.

Enlightenment Secularism and the Visions of the Radical Left

Progressive Christians tend to much more wholeheartedly embrace modernization and everything that goes with it, including the upwardly mobile aspirations of the American dream, just like everyone else. While they do at times denounce materialism and rail against "the evils of capitalism," they still seem to buy into the Western myth of progress and often seem to be influenced by social Darwinism.

Typically they are not just interested in getting a piece of the pie for themselves. Many want to try and build an escalator into the system to help the poor get a taste of the dream, too — as long as the personal costs aren't too high.

When it comes to transcendence, progressive Christians are all over the map. Unlike many of their conservative counterparts, few are looking forward to a disembodied existence in the clouds. Some have been totally secularized by the political correctness movement to view the better future simply as a reordering of political power with no sense of transcendence or spiritual transformation. Some look forward to a modern future that focuses exclusively on the here and now.

As we have seen, others, influenced by Eastern spirituality, look for a future in which there is a growing oneness between the natural and the sacred realms. A few even embrace reincar-

11. Valentine, "Civil Religion: A Biblical-Theological Assessment," *Search* 6 (Winter 1976): 50.

nation and view themselves as being reincarnated through time and space.

But I find few on the radical edge of mainline and Roman Catholic faith that seem to be willing to consider a biblical vision of God redeeming a people and restoring a world. In other words, many progressive Christians not only share in an idolatrous involvement in our modern consumer culture with the Christian right and the rest of us but also subscribe to visions for the human future that contradict the biblical vision. One area in which this is most evident is the Christian left's unqualified support for another form of individualism — human autonomy.

The political correctness movement is the most vocal champion of the value of human autonomy. It is a very modern "virtue." You simply don't find it promoted by either traditional cultures or religions. It is a child of modernization and those who support the advance of modernization. Traditional cultures and religions believed that selflessness was a virtue and stressed the individual's responsibility to others. Only modernity has suggested that selfishness is a virtue and argued that the individual's primary responsibility is to him- or herself.

In describing the emergence of what he calls the "strange new moral principle" of radical autonomy, Daniel Yankelovich notes that in turning inward, our culture has seriously discounted the importance of tradition, rules, and self-denial.[12] The therapeutic principle drawn from this value is "I have to do what's best for myself first."

Through the past two decades, countless individuals, guided by this "strange new moral principle," have put themselves first, divorced their spouses, fragmented their families, and sometimes abandoned their children — all because they bought this modern notion that they should place *their* needs first.

One of the cardinal doctrines of the politically correct both in secular society and in many progressive churches is a brand of modern autonomy that encourages individuals to place their own needs first in all areas of life. The doctrine specifies that in

12. See Yankelovich, *New Rules: Searching for Self-Fulfillment in a World Turned Upside Down* (New York: Random House, 1981).

matters of sexual behavior, reproduction, and the ways in which we end our lives, the decisions belong to the individual alone.

I can certainly understand why secularists would support this perspective born of modernity. But for the life of me I can't understand why progressive Christians do — unless it's that they feel that in order to stay on the cutting edge of progressive change they have to embrace all the values that go with the progressive package, including this modern notion of autonomy.

All traditional faiths, including Judaism, Islam, and Christianity, have always understood that in issues dealing with human sexuality, reproduction, and the termination of life there is no such thing as autonomous choice. These are always decisions that must be made in the context of community, in which we are all ultimately accountable to the God who created us.

Placing modernity's value of autonomous choice above community and God isn't just a problem for the Christian right. It is a problem for believers of all traditional faiths. And I believe that this kind of idolatry of the autonomous self, if left unchallenged, could rend the fabric of our common life and undermine our religious belief more profoundly than any of the other idolatries we have discussed.

Will the real secularists please stand up! The real secularists cannot be identified by simply doing a leftist analysis of who has power and who doesn't. Nor can we identify the real secularists by asking all political liberals to raise their hands. It just isn't that simple.

If this brief assessment of Enlightenment secularism and modernity has any validity, we have all been profoundly secularized by the aspirations and values of Western culture and the American dream. Additionally, I believe a number of us, including those on both the left and right, are caught up in idolatries that are drawn, in part, from the values of Enlightenment secularism as well. Some Christians have, as we have seen, embraced the modern secular values of human autonomy, apparently unaware of the destructive consequences for the larger society.

And a number of the leaders on the Christian right have not only embraced the economic and nationalistic idolatries of American conservative culture but have gone so far as to encourage other Christians to bow the knee to the civil religion of America. For biblical Christians, all these modern secular visions should be anathema. We all need to search for a new reason for being and a new place to stand.

Will the Real Enemy Please Stand Up!

The religious right is on target in expressing concern about declining moral values and the increasing secularization of American culture. The Christian left is spot on in its concern about growing poverty, violence, and intolerance in America. Both sides are struggling to identify who the real culprit is in America's culture wars. The problem is that they are both looking for someone else to blame. And they are both working from inadequate critiques of what is wrong. They are looking outside, not within, to identify the real enemy.

Will the real enemy please stand up! Since the influence of Enlightenment secularism pervades all our lives and families, it should be clear who the real enemy is. It isn't someone else. It isn't right-wing fascists or a secular humanist elite. Pogo had it right. We have seen the enemy, and he is us! We have all been co-opted and seduced by modernity's values and the worldview of Enlightenment secularism.

So let us all put aside our accusations and our unkind characterizations of those with whom we disagree. Let's all come down from our arrogance and do what Christians are always supposed to do when we get it wrong — repent. Let's ask God to forgive us for our secular obsessions and idolatries and seek to return again to true faith and a biblical vision for tomorrow's world.

A Third Way — A Biblical Vision
of the Now and Not Yet

Looking back, I think many of us recognize that we have been taken in by views and values that are alien to a biblical faith. I think most of us are looking for a vision of the future to which we can give our lives that would make a difference in the world and at the same time give a sense of meaning to our existence. In this section, we will try to discover a new vision, a third way.

If we are going to find "a reason for being" that transcends the idolatries and ideologies born of the Enlightenment, may I suggest that we reconsider returning to an ancient faith? I am proposing that we define a vision for our future that isn't drawn from our modern world but rather from our ancient past, that we look to Judeo-Christian Scripture to help us define our reason for being. I am persuaded that people of all Christian traditions have been content to allow modernity and secular culture instead of Scripture to define both the direction of our lives and the terms for our engaging urgent social and political issues. We simply haven't taken Scripture seriously.

Catholic and Orthodox traditions place a high emphasis on using Scripture liturgically. Many mainline denominations use Scripture prominently to undergird their social agendas. Evangelicals place a high priority on using the Bible devotionally. What I am recommending is that we also use Scripture *culturally*, to define an alternative vision for our lives, something different from the American dream.

I am proposing that we intentionally use the Word of God to redefine our notion of the good life and the better future. I am convinced that if we use Scripture for this broader purpose, we will all be able to find a new reason for being and a new place to stand that not only transcends the ideologies of the religious right and the progressive left but gives more compelling meaning to our lives.

As I present this alternative biblical vision, please understand that this enterprise represents only one person's attempt to make sense of the Story of God and God's purposes for the human future. It is not offered as definitive but only as a starting point to bring Christians from many different traditions together to search in Scripture for a new sense of meaning and a new basis for engagement.

Looking to an Ancient Story
for a New Reason for Being
and a New Place to Stand

I begin this journey toward the renewal of vision by asking a very specific question of Scripture: What are God's purposes for the future of humanity and the created order?

I want to suggest that if we can discern from the Story of God something of God's purposes for God's people and God's world, then we will be able to find a much clearer sense of direction for our lives, our families, our churches, and even the ways in which we engage the urgent issues that fill our world. I am convinced that we can find in Scripture not only a vision that provides a sense of meaning for our lives but also a premise for hope and for action.

As I seek to relate my sense of this vision, essentially I am going to be doing very informal narrative theology. I am going to seek to share very quickly some of the images and values that I find in the Story of God.

Obviously there isn't space to do an exhaustive study of Old and New Testament Scripture to answer our question about God's purposes for humanity and the created order. So we will focus our attention on selected material out of Isaiah and Luke that I believe captures something of the flavor of the larger biblical story and God's intentions.

I am assuming here that the writings of Isaiah can be understood as a unity. While these ancient writings spoke into a very particular cultural context, I believe that many of the images and values have implications not only for our lives today but also for our common future tomorrow.

An Ancient Vision for the Now and Not Yet

Pierre Teilhard de Chardin once wrote, "The future belongs to those who offer it hope." In a world drowning in cynicism, nihilism, and polarization, people are looking for a reason for hope. And I am convinced that the people of God have no higher calling than to offer hope to the world. The only problem is that we cannot offer what we do not possess.

I find that many deeply committed American Christians have a private hope for their own salvation but have virtually no larger corporate hope for the redemption of a people and the restoration of a world. Therefore, I want to stress again that I sincerely believe that the number one crisis in the church today is a crisis of vision. It is my contention that Christians of all traditions have largely failed to take Scripture seriously in defining a compelling corporate vision that could lend focus to our lives, families, and communities — an alternative to the American dream.

To set the stage for this journey, I want to invite you to join me in a brief trip to the British Museum in London. Shortly after we enter, we see a huge relief sculpture that fills a long corridor. As we look more closely, we see scenes of a savage battle carved into the stone. The sculpture portrays scenes of a battlefield with armored figures in chariots running over the bodies of their foes. The field is littered with headless torsos, body parts, and dying victims. Those who are responsible for this bloody slaughter are the armies of the Assyrians.

In the seventh century B.C.E., the Assyrians were at the gates of Jerusalem, and the future of the children of God was imperiled, as described in Isaiah 1–39. In the final chapters of the book, it is the powerful Babylonians that threaten the very existence of Israel.

In those desperate times, the prophet Isaiah brought a ringing word of hope that must have bolstered the courage of his listeners. Contained in the prophetic word is a glimpse of the future of God that I believe can also offer hope to those who have chosen to follow God in our times.

So let's examine Isaiah and try to raise to the surface something of the compelling vision of God implicit in that book. I take a bit of literary license in trying to connect different biblical images of the future of God and allow the compelling vision of Isaiah to affect both our hearts and our minds.

In seeking to answer the question of what God's purposes are for God's people and God's world, Isaiah shares a glimpse of the panoramic vista of God:

▶▶▶   245

Behold, I will create
> new heavens and a new earth.
The former things will not be remembered,
> nor will they come to mind.
But be glad and rejoice forever
> in what I will create,
for I will create Jerusalem to be a delight
> and its people a joy.
I will rejoice over Jerusalem
> and take delight in my people;
the sound of weeping and crying
> will be heard in it no more. (65:17-19)

That realm in which God dwells that we call "heaven" and the earth on which we dwell will somehow be fused into a single realm.

Obviously this passage must have held a tremendous sense of promise to the children of Israel, whose very survival was imperiled at this time. But even today, as the people of God we still live in eager anticipation of God's new creation, in which we will dwell in greater intimacy with our God.

Isaiah's vision for the future of God shifts from a new heaven and a new earth to a new mountain and a new city. Throughout the writings of the prophets, Zion and Jerusalem consistently seem to be identified as the focal point of God's renewed creation.

Picture yourself in barren wasteland, with not a single blade of living grass in sight. Rising up unexpectedly out of that wilderness we are shown in Isaiah 2:2-4 a mountain that transcends all other peaks. That isn't true of Mount Zion today. But according to Isaiah it will be then:

In the last days
the mountain of the LORD's temple will be established
> as chief among the mountains;
it will be raised above the hills,
> and all the nations will stream to it.
Many peoples will come and say,
"Come, let us go up to the mountain of the LORD,
> to the house of the God of Jacob.
He will teach us his ways,
> so that we may walk in his paths."

The law will go out from Zion,
  the word of the LORD from Jerusalem.
He will judge between the nations
  and will settle disputes for many peoples.
They will beat their swords into plowshares
  and their spears into pruning hooks.
Nation will not take up sword against nation,
  nor will they train for war anymore.

Look to the horizon, as far as the eye can see — small dots. As they get closer, we see that they are people — people from every tongue and tribe and nation. As this vast throng converges on the mountain of God, we see that they are singing and dancing. Arm in arm from all directions, they begin to climb the mountain together, as both valley and mountain suddenly burst into bloom. Color, blossom, and fragrance explode across the barren landscape. Listen to Isaiah's description:

The desert and the parched land will be glad;
  the wilderness will rejoice and blossom.
Like the crocus, it will burst into bloom;
  it will rejoice greatly and shout for joy.
The glory of Lebanon will be given to it,
  the splendor of Carmel and Sharon;
they will see the glory of the LORD,
  the splendor of our God. (35:1-2)

As this vast multicultural throng surges toward the summit, not only is the valley below transformed but so are the surprised climbers. Suddenly the blind see, the deaf hear, the lame run. Praise and jubilation sweep through this huge human ocean. Isaiah counsels his readers:

Strengthen the feeble hands,
  steady the knees that give way;
say to those with fearful hearts,
  "Be strong, do not fear;
your God will come, . . .
  he will come to save you."
Then will the eyes of the blind be opened
  and the ears of the deaf unstopped.

> Then will the lame leap like a deer,
> and the tongue of the dumb shout for joy. (35:3-6a)

On top of this mountain we are shown a spectacular scene of the great homecoming in which the Creator God welcomes the people of God to a festive international family reunion. God's "first family" will be the guests of honor at this lavish multicultural homecoming.

> On this mountain the LORD Almighty will prepare
> a feast of rich food for all peoples,
> a banquet of aged wine —
> the best of meats and the finest of wines.
> On this mountain he will destroy
> the shroud that enfolds all peoples,
> the sheet that covers all nations;
> he will swallow up death forever.
> The Sovereign LORD will wipe away the tears
> from all faces;
> he will remove the disgrace of his people
> from all the earth.
>   The LORD has spoken.
> In that day they will say,
> "Surely this is our God;
> we trusted in him, and he saved us.
> This is the LORD, we trusted in him;
> let us rejoice and be glad in his salvation." (25:6-9)

The Old Testament is filled with a tapestry of breathtaking imagery of the loving purposes of God for a people and a world. These loving purposes will be expressed most fully in the coming of the promised Messiah, one from the lineage of David. He is the one who comes from the Creator God to offer hope and meaning to our world and our lives.

In Isaiah's narrative on the coming of God's Chosen One, we are given a further glimpse of the Creator's loving intentions:

> The people walking in darkness
> have seen a great light;
> on those living in the land of the shadow of death

a light has dawned.
You have enlarged the nation
    and increased their joy;
they rejoice before you
    as people rejoice at harvest,
as men rejoice
    when dividing the plunder.
For as in the day of Midian's defeat,
    you have shattered
the yoke that burdens them,
    the bar across their shoulders,
    the rod of their oppressor.
Every warrior's boot used in battle
    and every garment rolled in blood
will be destined for burning,
    will be fuel for the fire.
For unto us a child is born,
    to us a son is given,
    and the government will be upon his shoulders.
And he will be called
    Wonderful Counselor, Mighty God,
    Everlasting Father, Prince of Peace.
Of the increase of his government and peace
    there will be no end.
He will reign on David's throne
    and over his kingdom,
establishing and upholding it
    with justice and righteousness
    from that time on and forever.
The zeal of the LORD Almighty
    will accomplish this. (9:2-7)

The zeal of the Lord of Hosts will indeed accomplish all of this!
The initiative for this vision comes from God and God alone.

In James Michener's book *The Source,* we are shown a small,
jovial, rotund rabbi residing in Israel during the intertestamental
period, who lives for little else than the coming of the Messiah.
Michener portrays him as always arriving to synagogue first on
the Sabbath so he can get the best seat in the house. He always
positions himself so he will be the very first one to see the Messiah

coming down the road. For thousands of years a great company of believers has lived in anticipation of the coming of the Messiah and God's New Order.

In the New Testament we are told that in "the fullness of time" the Messiah did indeed come. The Gospel of Luke tells us that Mary somehow understood that the coming of the Chosen One would not only dramatically change her life but turn the whole world upside down.

> His mercy extends to those who fear him,
>> from generation to generation.
> He has performed mighty deeds with his arm;
>> he has scattered those who are proud in their inmost
>>> thoughts.
> He has brought rulers down from their thrones
>> but has lifted up the humble.
> He has filled the hungry with good things
>> but has sent the rich away empty.
> He has helped his servant Israel,
>> remembering to be merciful
> to Abraham and his descendants forever,
>> even as he said to our fathers. (1:50-55)

Later, as the Story of God continues, we see Mary's son Jesus, who is now an adult, stand up in the synagogue in his hometown of Nazareth. He stands to read the Scripture at the inauguration of his ministry.

> The scroll of the prophet Isaiah was handed to him. Unrolling it, he found the place where it was written:
>> "The spirit of the Lord is on me,
>>> because he has anointed me
>>> to preach good news to the poor.
>> He has sent me to proclaim freedom for the prisoners
>>> and recovery of sight to the blind,
>> to release the oppressed,
>>> to proclaim the year of the Lord's favor."
> Then he rolled up the scroll, gave it back to the attendant and sat down. The eyes of everyone in the synagogue were

fastened on him, and he began by saying to them, "Today this scripture is fulfilled in your hearing." (4:17-21)

I believe that for Jesus, being the Messiah of God meant, quite simply, devoting his life to working for the purposes of God. John the Baptist didn't get it. He sent two of his disciples to find out if Jesus was the one or not.

Listen to the evidence Jesus offers to John's disciples to demonstrate that he is indeed the Messiah of God: "Go back and report to John what you have seen and heard: The blind receive sight, the lame walk, those who have leprosy are cured, the deaf hear, the dead are raised, and the good news is preached to the poor" (7:22). The proof of his Messiahship was that Jesus committed his life to working for the purposes of God as they are described in the vision of the prophet Isaiah.

One of the first things Jesus did was to create a new community that was something of a foretaste of God's New Order. To be a member of Christ's countercultural community, you couldn't do what American Christians do today: you couldn't commit your life to God and then go about life as usual.

Christ's first disciples had to make the same radical commitment that Jesus did. They committed their lives not only to God but to working for the purposes of God — preaching good news to the poor, bringing freedom for prisoners, recovery of sight for the blind, release for the oppressed, and proclaiming the year of the Lord's favor. The vocation of this small band was not to take power politically. Like the one they followed, their new vocation was one of suffering servanthood.

In other words, following Jesus has always meant committing our lives not only to God but to a radical biblical vision that is ultimately destined to change a world. The Hebrew word for this vision of a world made new is *shalom.*

In the shalom vision, God the Creator intends to reconcile us to God, to one another, and to God's good creation. God purposes a world in which all things will be made new, beginning with a new heaven and a new earth.

Jesus Christ, therefore, isn't just the full disclosure of the Creator God, though he is most certainly that. Jesus is a preview of coming attractions. He is the shalom future of God made present. Every time he heals the blind, sets free the captive, and forgives the sinner, we are given a glimpse of the future of God and a foretaste of the in-breaking of God's New Order.

Walter Brueggemann characterizes the life and ministry of Jesus and that first community in terms of the shalom vision of God: "Jesus' ministry to the excluded . . . was . . . the establishment of community between those who were excluded and those who excluded them. His acts of healing the sick, forgiving the guilty, raising the dead and feeding the hungry are all actions of reestablishing God's will for *shalom* in a world gone chaotic in callous self-seeking."[13]

Jesus Christ came proclaiming a single message: "Good news! Good news! The future of God has broken into our midst!" Jesus' compassionate acts and the incarnational quality of his messianic community lent authenticity to his claim that God's New Order was indeed bursting into the world.

While all the visions flowing from the Enlightenment deal exclusively with the here and now, the vision of God deals with the now and not yet. In Christ, God's shalom future has broken into the world. The death and resurrection of Jesus Christ make the outcome clear. God's New Order will be established, the people of God will be redeemed by Christ's death on the cross, and God's creation will be restored. The best that's ever been will be alive again.

However, in this inaugurated eschatology, God's New Order is both present and coming, both now and not yet. I don't believe God's future will be fully realized until the return of Jesus Christ. But thankfully we still see it breaking into the world today through the festive lives and the compassionate service of the messianic community of Christ all over the world.

Reflecting on the biblical material that we have briefly reviewed, let's go back to the future and answer the central question of this chapter: What are God's purposes for the future of humanity and the created order?

13. Brueggemann, *Living Toward a Vision: Biblical Reflections on Shalom* (Philadelphia: United Church Press, 1976), p. 19.

▶ At the very center of the shalom vision of God is the redemption of the people of God through the atoning death and triumphant resurrection of Jesus Christ.

▶ It is also apparent that God is intent on creating a new, truly inclusive, transnational family — the messianic community of Jesus. This new first family of servants is called to be clearly at counterpoint to the self-involved secular societies from which it emerges.

▶ God intends to create a *more just* social order in which the poor, meek, and marginalized inherit the earth. The pyramids of power will be turned upside down.

▶ God purposes to bring wholeness, healing, and shalom to those who are disabled and partial, bringing an end to all evil, suffering, and death through the death and resurrection of the Messiah Jesus.

▶ God intends to bring peace and shalom to the nations, transforming the instruments of warfare and violence into the implements of peace and reconciliation. And Jesus calls those who follow him to be peacemakers working for the reconciliation of God in a divided and violent world.

▶ God is committed to the completion, not the destruction, of God's good creation. And we are called by Scripture to be God's faithful stewards of God's sacred created order.

▶ God is planning to welcome God's new transnational family to a future of banqueting and joy in which we reign with our God and celebrate with our new multicultural family forever.

How is the biblical vision of the shalom of God different from the American dream? One of the most striking features of the biblical vision is that it's a corporate vision for all peoples. The American dream is intensely individualistic — all of us pursuing our own piece of the pie. While Isaiah's vision embraces the material world, it isn't materialistic. While it is certainly concerned with the individual, it isn't individualistic.

The American dream emphasizes the values of acquisition, accumulation, materialism, consumerism, self-interest, and a driven individualism. As we have seen, the biblical vision of shalom emphasizes the values of worship, community, celebration, healing, righteousness, reconciliation, servanthood, justice, and peace.

Frankly, the acquisitive appetites of the American dream are, for a biblical people, nothing less than idolatrous. The individualistic pursuit of our own self-interest, status, and power is totally antithetical to the vision of Christ, who devoted his life to the service of God and the benefit of others.

In other words, the goal for the followers of Jesus is not to give allegiance to the upwardly mobile aspirations of the rat race but to commit our lives to advancing the shalom purposes of God.

If we choose to commit our lives to the vision of God instead of the secular aspirations of American culture, we will find what we are all seeking — a new reason for being that makes a difference in the world. Our commitment to this new reason for being will also help us to fundamentally redefine, in the light of biblical principles, what is important and what is of value. We will raise our children to put God's purposes ahead of the expectations of the secular culture.

What are the implications of embracing this biblical vision for progressive Christians and those on the religious right? First of all, I believe it is obvious that if progressive Christians embrace a biblical vision, it will transcend those modern visions that deal exclusively with the here and now.

There is no way progressive Christians could any longer support the modern notion that autonomous individuals should put their own interests first and make decisions regarding their private lives outside of the context of community. In the biblical vision, the community of God, not the individual, is the primary reference point. Scripture makes clear a view that is not accepted by the secular left — that ultimately we are all accountable to the God who created us.

Leaders on the religious right are unequivocal in their assertion that the primary mission of American Christians is to make America great. This assertion is not only unsupported by the biblical vision but is in fact pointedly condemned by it as idolatrous. We need to see God's love extended to all nations. The biblical vision is of a God creating a new community that transcends nation, race, and culture. And the Bible makes clear that God intends to use the church, not a nation, to advance God's loving purposes in the world.

Finally, contrary to the message of modernity and Enlightenment secularism, the initiative for change resides primarily not with us but with God. Listen to the affirmation of Isaiah:

> The LORD Almighty has sworn,
> "Surely, as I have planned, so it will be,
>   and as I have purposed, so it will stand. . . ."
> This is the plan determined for the whole world;
>   this is the hand stretched out over all nations.
> For the LORD Almighty has purposed, and who can
>   thwart him?
> His hand is stretched out, and who can turn it back?
> (14:24, 26-27)

Welcome to the great homecoming festival of God! I think we can find in this compelling biblical imagery not only a new basis for hope but also a new reason for being and a new place to stand. In Chapter 10 I will try to give practical, creative expression to what a third way, a radical biblical alternative to the polarities of right and left, might look like.

CHAPTER 10

▼ ▼ ▼

A Third Way — Searching for a New Reason for Being and a New Place to Stand

I FIRST HEARD ABOUT the community of the Gentle Bunyip in 1980. It is a Christian community in Melbourne, Australia, that is named for an imaginary animal that is searching for its lost mate.

A group of adventuresome Christians under the leadership of Athol and Judith Gill formed this unique Christian community out of a strong desire to be something of the family of God together. They came together not only to be a sample of God's new family but also to try to flesh out some of the values of God's New Order by reaching out in compassionate ministries to the poor. These ministries include "The Truffle Hunters" (an outreach to street kids) and "Billabong Arts and Crafts" (for young people struggling to find themselves).

One of their most intriguing innovations was something called the "Monk for a Month Club." Simply put, the club was created for those who are seriously looking for a new reason for being and a new way of living. People can come and stay for a couple of days or a couple of weeks and see if Christian community is as scary as they thought it was.

Like many others, I have been affected by the witness of the community of the Gentle Bunyip and the writings of Athol Gill. In 1992, I finally had the opportunity to travel to Melbourne and visit the community. As I arrived in Melbourne, I received the tragic news that Athol had died of a massive heart attack two weeks earlier. I was deeply saddened for his family, the community, and the many others of us who had been challenged by his writings.

I made my way to the community of the Gentle Bunyip with some hesitancy on that bright Sunday morning. I arrived just as the church service was letting out. I introduced myself, and the members immediately invited me to join them for their weekly community potluck.

I still remember the large meeting room, filled with people from different cultures and lots of kids and young people. We sang, we prayed, and we ate together. And one stray Yank felt very welcomed.

After the meal, I had the opportunity to spend some time with Judith Gill and offer my condolences. Like the other members of the community, she was still grieving the tragic loss of Athol.

"You know, I never had appreciated our Christian community as much before as I have in the past two weeks," Judith shared. "My biological family came to the memorial service and were very supportive. But as soon as the service was over, they had to get back to their homes and their work. These people you see here in our community have supported me and my kids through the whole ordeal in a way that has simply been a godsend. And I know they will stand by us and pray with us all the tough days ahead."

I think deep down all of us are longing for the kind of love, support, and sense of purpose that characterize those who are a part of the family of the Gentle Bunyip. But too often in the American religious scene we settle for much less, and we are the poorer for it.

In this chapter we are going to ask what our lives and communities of faith would look like if we, like those in the community of the Gentle Bunyip, decided to put the vision of God at the center of life. We are going to consider concrete, creative ways in which our lives might change if we replaced the aspirations and idolatries of modernity in American culture with the aspirations and values of the shalom future of God. We are going to journey together in search of a third way that not only transforms our lives and communities of faith but ultimately, by the power of God, has the potential to renew our nations and the larger world.

A Crisis of the Spirit

Zbigniew Brzezinski, the national security advisor during the Carter administration, declares that our nations are experiencing a crisis of the spirit. In his important new book *Out of Control,* Brzezinski states that this "global crisis of the spirit has to be overcome if humanity is to assert command over its destiny."[1]

He indicts Western society generally and American society particularly for buying into a secular consumer culture devoid of any transcendent values. The only thing that seems to bond our Western nations together is our common commitment to keeping our consumer economies growing. He calls this culture, which he says "focuses largely on the immediate satisfaction of individual desires," a "permissive cornucopia."[2]

His critique is very similar to the one I present in Chapter 9. He decries the eclipse of vital faith in Western culture and American society. He joins conservatives in being alarmed by the breakdown of the family and the decline of strong moral values. But he also joins liberals in pointing out that no society can remain moral if it allows huge inequalities to develop between its richest and poorest members.

Essentially Brzezinski is arguing that the only hope for our global and our national future, as we enter the third millennium, is a profound spiritual renewal. As I have already argued, Christians will not be able to meet this unprecedented challenge by turning to political action. True spiritual renewal will come only

1. Brzezinski, *Out of Control: Global Turmoil on the Eve of the Twenty-First Century* (New York: Macmillan, 1994), p. 230.
2. Brzezinski, *Out of Control,* p. 65.

through a revival of strong biblical faith that calls us beyond ourselves, that transforms every aspect of our lives and our churches. Only such faith has the potential to help create an inspired new vision for America — and other lands as well.

If we are to pray and work aggressively for the renewal of the church in a way that can change our nation, we must seek fresh answers to the following questions:

▶ What does it mean to be a follower of Jesus Christ?
▶ What does it mean to be the church, the people of God?
▶ How are we called by Scripture to share the good news of God's love in a way that renews our communities, nations, and the world?

And after we have answered these questions — and only then — we can ask

▶ How are we to share our prophetic witness in the political arena as well?

Welcome to God's Mustard Seed Conspiracy!

First, I want to emphasize again that God's strategy for transforming the world doesn't begin as those on both the left and right contend, by taking power and taking over. In fact, the shalom vision of God doesn't begin with either the pursuit of power or the pretensions of position. In *The Mustard Seed Conspiracy* I wrote,

> Jesus let us in on an astonishing secret. God has chosen to change the world through the lowly, the unassuming, and the imperceptible. . . .
> That has always been God's strategy — changing the world through the conspiracy of the insignificant. He chose a ragged bunch of Semite slaves to become the insurgents of his new order. . . . And who would have ever dreamed that God would choose to work through a baby in a cow stall to turn the world right side up! "God chose the foolish things . . . the things that are not. . . ."

It is still God's policy to work through the embarrassingly insignificant to change his world and create his future.[3]

Realizing that God works through the foolish things gives me some hope. How about you? I think most of us are relieved when we realize that God is not looking for the prominent or the powerful to collaborate in this cause. God is simply looking for ordinary folks with willing hearts and ready lives.

Remember that the Story of God did indeed begin with that ragtag, stiff-necked band of Semite slaves. God was determined to create from this unlikely lot a new community that would be a foreshadowing of God's promised future. In every area of life from worship and moral behavior to diet and economic practices, they were called by God to be a clear counterpoint to the peoples who surrounded them.

Regrettably there were repeated failures. But God didn't give up. In fact, this Creator, Liberator God seems to have the remarkable ability to transform every defeat into a building block for the new order.

Isaiah, like the other prophets, had a great deal to say regarding Israel's sin, failures, and defeats. One of the images he used to characterize Israel's devastated condition was that of a dead stump — no fruit, no leaves, no boughs, no trunk, nothing but an apparently desolate stump. But this prophet of the living God saw in every defeat the promise of a new beginning:

A shoot will come up from the stump of Jesse;
    from his roots a Branch will bear fruit.
The spirit of the LORD will rest on him —
    the spirit of wisdom and understanding,
    the spirit of counsel and of power,
    the spirit of knowledge and the fear of the LORD. (11:1-2)

With the coming of Jesus, God's purposes burst the dry, aging wineskins of Jewish faith and culture and reached out to embrace a world. It all began when this itinerant teacher formed

3. Sine, *The Mustard Seed Conspiracy: Making a Difference in Tomorrow's Troubled World* (Waco: Word Books, 1981), pp. 11-12.

a new community. It, too, was composed of anything but the powerful and prominent. He called unemployed fishermen, IRS agents, prostitutes, and the social outcasts of that day.

When these people chose to follow Jesus, something quite remarkable happened. They discovered in this itinerant band not only a new faith in God but a new reason for being. Obviously they wouldn't have so readily quit jobs and left homes unless they had discovered in following Jesus something that gave their lives a new sense of meaning, that called them beyond themselves.

Jesus did not simply proclaim the good news that the future of God had broken into human society. His new community was a living expression of it. This "first family" became an incarnational model to those around it, an expression of the shalom future of God.

I love the way Michael Green, a British evangelical leader, describes this first family as it spread across the Mediterranean world:

> They made the grace of God credible by a society of love and mutual care which astonished pagans and was recognized as something entirely new. It lent persuasiveness to the claim that the new age had dawned in Christ. The word was not only announced but seen in the community of those who were giving it flesh.
>
> The message of the kingdom became more than an idea. A new human community had sprung up and looked very much like the new order to which the evangelist had pointed. Here love was given daily expression; reconciliation was actually occurring; people were no longer divided into Jews and Gentiles, slave and free, male and female. In this community the weak were protected, the stranger welcomed. People were healed, the poor and dispossessed were cared for and found justice. Everything was shared. Joy abounded and ordinary lives were filled with praise.[4]

In the revised edition of his classic study of ecclesiology *Models of the Church,* Avery Dulles adds a tenth model for the

4. Green, *The Call to Conversion: Recovering the Gospel for These Times* (San Francisco: Harper & Row, 1981), p. 15.

church to the nine he had discussed earlier: *community*. I believe the biblical narrative indicates that the primary characteristic of the people of God is the fact that it is a new community that bears witness to a new way of being in the world.

A Call to *Being* Rather Than *Doing*

You see, the first call of the gospel of Jesus Christ is not to *doing*, but to *being*. It is a call not to progressive or conservative political action but to a new way to be in the world. The foundation of God's radical third way lies in the family of God, in the eucharist, in worship, and in Scripture.

I believe that the biblical narrative makes clear that the church was not called into existence to promote political ideologies of any brand. Nor is the church, all appearances to the contrary, primarily intended to be a religious institution. According to the biblical story, those who choose to follow Jesus are meant to be more an organism than a bureaucracy. God created a new community in which all are invited to come home and become a part of God's first family.

A Call to Christian Commitment

When I was sixteen years old, I was offered a free plane trip from San Francisco to Los Angeles to attend a missionary conference. Frankly, I had little interest in the conference, but I had never flown and was very intrigued with the opportunity.

I wasn't going to church at the time, nor was I at all religiously inclined. I was hanging out with a group of aspiring young delinquents. Quite honestly, during my high school days, nothing went very well. My grades were an abomination. I was small and too uncoordinated to do well in sports. The group I hung out with wasn't even any good at delinquency.

However, I got more than I bargained for when I accompanied my missionary uncle to Southern California. I wandered in and out of the conference and spent a lot of time exploring the neighborhood where it was held. But I did, out of courtesy, sit through the entire concluding service.

It was during that service that I unexpectedly found myself confronted by the Creator God in a way I never had been before. I had always intellectually believed in God, but I suddenly found myself transported into God's presence with a reality that's hard to put into words.

In that blinding moment of awareness, I knew with certainty that God lives and that God loves. Somehow I found myself included in the circle of that love. And I was deeply moved.

But I was also confronted with a scalding awareness of my own selfishness and sinfulness. After the service, I collapsed in a corner and sought God's grace and forgiveness with tears and earnest prayer.

I found not only the forgiveness I sought but also a new relationship to God that revolutionized my life and gave me a new reason for being. And I was very grateful for the mercy of God.

When I returned home, I started attending a Methodist church, because my grandparents were Methodists. I immediately made an appointment with the pastor and shared with him the dramatic change that had taken place in my life and my desire to serve God. He told me that skid row alcoholics sometimes undergo conversions, but not young men in high school. He assured me that nothing had really happened to me. But I knew better.

I was very active in the northern California conference of the United Methodist Church for the final two years of high school. But never once, during that time, did I ever hear young people or adults called to commit their lives to God. Even though I was a very young Christian, I knew something was missing.

In later years, I found that some mainline Christians seem to be involved in what I call "commitment by assumption." A number — though by no means all — of the mainline Christians I have worked with seem to assume that if they hang around church buildings and are active in the institutional church, that signifies that they have made a commitment. But it isn't any more possible to become a Christian than it is to get married in that way. We don't become Christians without a deliberate decision and a vital living encounter with the God who calls us.

Roman Catholics, Lutherans, and Orthodox, through their confirmation process, call those raised in those traditions to commit their lives to God. Many who do so enter into a spirituality that also has become a vital resource to many of us from other backgrounds.

Many evangelicals, charismatics, and Pentecostals regularly invite people to commit their lives to God. Usually such commitments result, as in my case, in the development of a sense of intimacy and relationship with God and a decisive change in moral behavior.

Conservative Protestants have always emphasized that the only effective way to change the moral standards in our society is not through legislation but through calling people to vital faith. "If anyone is in Christ," says the apostle Paul, "he is a new creation; the old is gone, the new has come! All this is from God, who reconciled us to himself through Christ and gave us the ministry of reconciliation: that God was reconciling the world to himself in Christ, not counting men's sins against them. And he has committed to us the message of reconciliation" (2 Cor. 5:17-19).

After being an evangelical believer for many years, I belatedly discovered that the Bible teaches that there is more to following Christ than being reconciled to God and changing one's moral behavior, as important as those things are. Scripture teaches that God wants to transform every part of our lives, including our life directions and our cultural values.

Many evangelicals are taught, as I was, to accept a very compartmentalized view of discipleship that focuses exclusively on personal piety and private morality. This kind of compartmentalized faith is easily overwhelmed by the aspirations and values of secular modern American culture. As a consequence, the American dream is more influential than the Christian faith in ordering the private world of many evangelicals and determining how they use their time and resources.

I am convinced that this prior commitment to the secular values and worldview of American culture also makes many evangelicals easy pickings for the ideologues of the political right. As we have seen, many sincere believers have been conned into transferring their commitment to God to a host of right-wing political causes.

It is my contention in this chapter that if we are serious about finding a new reason for being and a new place to stand that is authentically biblical, we must do what those first disciples did: we must commit our lives not only to God but also to God's purposes. In other words it isn't enough to do what most conservatives do — invite God to change our hearts and clear up our moral behavior. If we are to be whole-life disciples like those first followers, then we must also invite the Creator God to transform the aspirations that drive our lives and the values on which our lives are premised. And that isn't easy. Modernity has its claws deeply embedded in us.

Listen to the apostle Paul again as he calls us to commit not just the spiritual compartment of our lives but everything in our lives to God: "I urge you, brothers, in view of God's mercy, to offer your bodies as living sacrifices, holy and pleasing to God — which is your spiritual worship. Do not conform any longer to the pattern of this world, but be transformed by the renewing of your mind. Then you will be able to test and approve what God's will is — his good, pleasing and perfect will" (Rom. 12:1-2).

Be warned: if we do indeed invite God to change not only our hearts but our entire lives, everything will begin to change. If God transforms our life direction from upwardly mobile lives to outwardly ministerial lives, it could mean changes in our occupations as it did for some of those first disciples. It will almost certainly mean changes in our timestyles. If God transforms our values from the materialistic, individualistic values of secular American culture to the other-serving, celebrative values of God's new order, it will definitely alter our priorities and change our lifestyles. And we will likely become part of a new family where we are known, loved, and held accountable.

I am convinced that the gospel of Jesus Christ calls us not only to whole-life discipleship but to whole-life stewardship. Biblical Christians aren't content with doing the American dream with a little Jesus overlay. We must, like those first followers, reorder our personal lives to put the purposes of God's New Order first.

In a little book entitled *Live It Up! How to Create a Life You*

Can Love, I offer a host of imaginative, practical ways in which whole-life disciples can create timestyles and lifestyles that are much less driven and acquisitive but also more festive and celebrative. Those who succeed in making these sorts of changes find that they have more time and resources to invest in a life of prayer, care for others in the body of Christ, and advancing God's loving purposes in the world. Let me emphasize that this whole-life discipleship is rooted in a life of prayer, the study of Scripture, and worship of the living God.

In Search of the First Family of God — Getting Serious about Community

If we become whole-life disciples, it will also change the way we parent our kids and nurture the Christian young. We will shift the emphasis from making a living to making a life. We will help our young to create lifestyles they can afford, centered in the values of God's new order instead of the addictions of our modern culture. We will develop family mission statements for the raising of our young drawn from the purposes of God instead of the aspirations of our secular culture.

But there is absolutely no way we can be whole-life disciples or whole-life stewards alone. We can find this new way of being only in community. And spilling coffee on one another on Sunday morning isn't community. We need to be a part of groups where we are truly known, deeply loved, and genuinely held accountable. I believe we will need to be a part of God's first family, which transcends race, culture, national identity — even political affiliation.

There is a broad spectrum of ways in which Christians today are discovering how to be whole-life disciples and stewards and flesh out something of the values of God's right-side-up kingdom in an upside-down world. There are those who, like the community of the Gentle Bunyip, choose to live together residentially. For many, that sort of life affords the greatest opportunity to create the sort of Christian community that actually has something more of the aroma of God's kingdom than of American culture about it. But it can also pose the greatest risks. Regrettably, even deeply committed Christians don't always get on well with one another in their own biological families, let alone with others in the body of Christ.

The Bruderhof in Woodcrest, New York, is a Christian community that I believe makes the pro-family values of Scripture come alive. This Hutterite community is composed of 280 people, including widows, singles, two-parent families, and even a few single-parent families. But, like the early Christian churches, it operates more like one large extended family.

Biological families and single people have their own separate living units. But in the evening, the whole community comes together for the evening meal and a period of song, prayer, and the reading of Scripture.

While parents have primary responsibility for their own kids, the entire community also takes responsibility for the nurture and raising of all the young. Likewise, care for the senior members of the community is the responsibility of the entire Bruderhof family.

This remarkable community has no life insurance or health insurance. When a person becomes ill, the community's doctor is summoned. If a person needs hospitalization, the community pays the bill. And when a member of the community dies, they all celebrate his or her passage into God's kingdom and take over responsibility for the surviving family members.

By the way, one of the major free-time activities of families in the Bruderhof isn't hanging out at the mall or paying other people to entertain them. On the weekends you will find parents and their kids ministering to prisoners at a penitentiary down the road. Or you will find Bruderhof families in New York City working with homeless families.

I believe these folks have it right. The pro-family values of the Bible do not call us to try to protect self-absorbed suburban lifestyles. The Bible calls us to reach out to the family of God in our churches in real mutual care. And like these Hutterites, the Bible also challenges Christian families and singles to take the risk of reaching out, with our kids, to those who are in critical need in our cities, our prisons, and our own neighborhoods.

Creating Alternative Housing for a New Generation

Because of the changing economy in the United States, I think Americans — particularly young Americans — are going to have to reevaluate our love affair with single-family detached homes. Scripture repeatedly calls us as the body of Christ to community, cooperation, and mutual care. Single-family detached living reflects the cultural values of autonomy, individualism, and alienation. If we are going to find a new way of being, we must bring Scripture to bear on all areas of life, including the ways in which we shelter ourselves.

For the past twenty years, some folks in Denmark who aren't particularly religious have come to the conclusion that single-family detached living isn't really the good life after all. They have created a cooperative lifestyle that, unlike the Bruderhof, is not communal.

Essentially they have erected clusters of condominiums in which every couple or family owns its own private unit. Instead of the backyards and front yards of the suburbs, they have one area where residents garden together and another cooperative area where kids play together.

Instead of having a huge recreation room in each home that only gets used two to three times a year, they have one large recreation room that doubles as a dining room for a complex of seventy-five people. Residents can eat the evening meal there, if they want, for about 90 cents per person. Each couple cooks once every two months.

If we are serious about giving the Christian young an alternative to the thirty-year mortgage trap and the stress that goes with it, I believe this model deserves consideration. I have created one modest alternative concept of what a cooperative housing model for the next generation of the Christian young might look like.

Today in Seattle, a two-bedroom starter house costs $150,000. In reality, the real cost is closer to $500,000 over thirty years. Typically young couples buying one of these homes have to work at least two full-time jobs to make the mortgage and do the whole nine yards that goes with home ownership. As a consequence, they have very little time or money left over to invest in the work of the church, the advancement of the gospel, or anything else.

My proposal is to construct a six-plex cooperative housing model on a one-third-acre lot. In other words, this cooperative would comprise six three-bedroom, one-bath homes with a shared recreation room, a shared laundry, shared workshop, and an enclosed central courtyard where the kids could play and families could visit together.

These units, including the cooperative area, could be constructed for about $60,000 a unit, financed with a five-year no-interest loan. So, instead of paying $500,000 over thirty years for a $150,000 single-family detached house, these six couples would only pay $60,000 over five years. I suggest that each couple pay an additional two years beyond payout for the kingdom. This kind of whole-life stewardship would free up $144,000. That would be enough to construct a hundred homes for poor families in the Third World or four or five Habitat for Humanity houses in the States.

At the end of the seventh year, these six couples would no longer have any mortgages. Nothing in the Bible indicates that we have to work thirty years for a mortgage company. The couples would then be set free from the mortgage trap.

This would provide another opportunity for a creative approach to whole-life stewardship. Since these six couples would no longer have any mortgages, they could, if their employers cooperated, cut back to twenty-hour work weeks. What could be better for family life than having more time for the kids? And then perhaps these parents and kids could, like the Bruderhof families, take some time to reach out to others and place God's mission purposes at the very center of family life.

Of course these six couples could become a small Christian community together. Not only could they come together every week to pray and study Scripture and support each other in their daily lives, but they could also explore imaginative ways to show hospitality, celebrate together, and create lifestyles that more genuinely reflect the values of the shalom future of God than of the American stress race.

Where would the no-interest loans come from for this venture? From the family of God. Instead of relying on biological parents to help the next generation, why not rely more broadly on the older generation in the church? The membership of many churches includes people over fifty who could easily loan the $360,000 necessary to create this six-plex alternative. They would of course get their $360,000 back in five years. All they would be out is the interest.

While I am not suggesting for a minute that all Christians should live in residential communities or cooperative housing projects, we do need to create an expanded array of options for the next generations. And I firmly believe Christians could be pacesetters in designing an array of new Christian settlements that would more authentically reflect the biblical values of community. And, like the Bruderhof, they could include intergenerational care and outreach to those in need in the community.

If living together residentially in some form of cooperative lifestyle isn't an option, simple proximity may be. Eight faculty couples at one Christian college purchased homes together on the same cul-de-sac, and they report that this physical closeness helps them to experience a more genuine sense of shared life and Christian community.

In Search of Community in a Small Group

Minimally, all who choose to take Christian discipleship seriously need to be in small groups that meet weekly and in which each individual is known, loved, and held accountable. For example, all the active members of Assembly Mennonite Church in Elkhart, Indiana, are members of small groups in their church.

During their weekly meetings, these small groups study Scripture together, pray together, and support one another just like an extended family, dealing with marital problems, unemployment, and health crises. But twice a year they do something that reminds me of the first-century church.

Twice a year all the couples and singles open their time schedules and budgets before everyone else in their small group. They ask for discernment as to how they might better order their priorities during the next six months to put God's purposes first. If we are going to find a new way of being in whole-life discipleship and stewardship, I believe it will take the support and the accountability of the family of God.

Contrary to the message of modernity, there is no way we can find a reason for being if we remain isolated from others. I believe we can find it only in a community centered in the worship of the living God, devoted to the study of Scripture, sharing in the eucharist, and fully entering into the fellowship of the family of God. God's agenda is forcefully at counterpoint to the world around us. To the extent that we truly bear witness to God's radical new order in our common life, I believe God will use our witness to affect both our neighborhoods and the larger society.

It is my contention, therefore, that God's primary vehicle for changing society is not political advocacy or any strategy for taking power and taking over. The primary vehicle is the mustard seed. The Creator God still seems to be in the business of calling people that many folks wouldn't put much stock in and creating new incarnational communities. These churches, home groups, and residential communities not only bear witness to a new way of being but provide the primary way in which God's counter-cultural New Order is breaking into our secular godless society and offering hope and a glimpse of God's new future. Ultimately, I believe the primary way God renews a nation is through the vitalization and expansion of incarnational communities of faith that march to a different drumbeat than the larger secular society.

Doing the Gospel of Jesus

Once we have found creative new ways, in community with others, to flesh out something of the values of God's New Order, then and only then do we have any basis to speak out or act on the basis of the gospel of Christ authentically. And when we shift our attention from the gospel as *being* to the gospel as *doing,* we find that there is little biblical support for the preoccupation with political action that typifies both progressive Christians and the religious right in America.

George Gallup speaks of a growing hunger in America for spirituality. Gallup's recent surveys "document the increasing number who are searching for the meaning in life with a new intensity and want their religious faith to grow."[5] People all over the country seem to be searching for God, vital faith, and a new reason for being. But frankly the American church in its many traditions seems to be doing little to respond to this growing hunger by finding creative ways to share the love of God.

Human needs are increasing across America. And there is a very high probability, as we have seen, that there is going to be a dramatic cut in federal funding for the country's social programs. This will mean an urgent challenge for all of our churches to respond. But again, many churches seem to have very little sense of their biblical responsibility to reach out to those in need.

If the church in America is going to respond to the crisis of spirit so forcefully described by Zbigniew Brzezinski, we are going to have to pray for a renewed passion for evangelism. We are going to have to place much more emphasis on sharing our faith in both word and deed ministries. And we are going to have to work much harder in creatively communicating the gospel in a way that engages those who are fully immersed in modern secular culture.

We particularly need to reach out strategically to those under thirty. They are the population disappearing most rapidly from all our Western churches. They are the ones being most fully seduced by the secular consumer culture. And they, of course, are the ones that will lead both church and society into the third millennium.

The kind of activism to which the New Testament repeatedly calls Christians involves proclaiming and demonstrating God's love to the world. Evangelical college students working with InterVarsity are actively sharing their faith in Christ with fellow students on the UCLA, Occidental, and Claremont campuses in California and effectively reaching many people in Generation X. In Pasadena, John Perkins and his wife are working with other

5. George Gallup Jr. and Robert Bezula, "Seeking Spiritual Renewal," *Philadelphia Inquirer,* 25 December 1994.

black and white evangelicals to take back a drug-infested neighborhood from dealers and gangs. In Seattle, the mainline Seattle Church Council is actively involved in providing housing for the homeless.

On March 16-18, 1995, Billy Graham and a team of evangelical leaders from several different countries shared the gospel of Jesus Christ, through a global T.V. hookup, with undoubtedly the largest single international audience in history. It is estimated that over a billion listeners, all over the world, listened to these speakers calling people to commit their lives to God. And Christians were instructed in how to advance God's kingdom in their own nations through both serving those in need and sharing a word of hope.

The church at its best all over the world has always been involved in both word and deed ministries. But frankly, I often find that churches in other countries are much more involved than American churches in acting out the love of God in their communities. If we are serious about working for the renewal of a vital spirituality in American society, we must have all of our congregations make the commitment to become churches for others.

Creating Churches for Others

Many of the churches I work with in the United States don't sponsor a single ministry to those in need outside their building. The story is very different in New Zealand. Most churches I have worked with there give a priority to making a difference in their communities. They not only consistently work at sharing faith with neighbors but they take a keen interest in reaching out to those in physical need.

For example, Ponsoby Baptist Church in Auckland, New Zealand, is a small congregation of 150 members. And yet they have five thriving ministries for at-risk kids, the homeless, and urban outcasts. Spreydon Baptist invests almost 60 percent of its income to address the needs of those in their immediate community in Christchurch, New Zealand, as well as supporting missions throughout the world.

I have found that Christians in Great Britain are not only more activist in ministry than many of their American counterparts but they are also more innovative and open. A group of young Anglicans in Manchester has created an alternative worship service to reach their under-thirty peers who would never set foot inside a church. They rent a multi-tier parking garage on weekends, bring in a cutting-edge rock band, have skateboarding down the ramps, offer a ten-minute message, and call it "rave in the nave."

A group of older mainline and evangelical Christians in Britain does evangelism through an organization called Springboard, sharing the Good News in shopping malls, village centers, and churches all over Great Britain. People are responding and committing their lives to God. Broken families are being reunited, people are being delivered from addictions, and Christians are learning how to share their faith with their neighbors.

Joe Stowell, president of Moody Bible College in Chicago, confided to me that he has never found it more difficult to share his faith in the United States than he does today. "The difficulty is not the offense of the cross. I find people drawn to Jesus Christ," he said. The difficulty is that "they are turned off by the offense of a right-wing political ideology. They are under the false illusion they have to accept the whole political package of the religious right if they are going to become evangelical Christians!"

One of the major tasks of the church of Jesus Christ is to get a hearing for the Good News. We need to become much more effective in finding ways to share the gospel with those who are looking for a vital spirituality and are hungry for God. And we must remove all impediments to evangelism, including political ideology.

But we are called by Scripture not only to proclaim but to demonstrate God's love to a world. I am troubled by the fact that when American churches do become involved in addressing the needs of those at the margins, they often get involved at a handout level. They start soup kitchens and food and clothing banks. While there is a place for that kind of ministry, these programs tend, like public welfare, to foster dependency. What we need are programs that promote self-reliance.

For example, Tom Skinner Associates has rented an office building across the street from an inner-city high school in Newark, New Jersey. The group refurbished the building and persuaded local businesses to donate computers. They use the computers to give basic literacy skills and job skills to high school students. The students beat a path over to this office building, because they know that once they have gotten the skills being offered there, they need never be unemployed the rest of their lives.

Guess what Skinner Associates uses as software to teach these young people literacy skills. They use Scripture. Many of these students are coming to faith in Christ while developing the skills necessary to break out of the cycle of poverty.

Jim Wallis, from Sojourners community in Washington, D.C., has been successful in persuading the Evangelical Lutheran Church in the United States to provide financing for Barrios Unidos in Los Angeles to start "micro-enterprises." Former gang members, drug dealers, and felons have gotten their lives turned around through this ministry and have created thirteen chapters in eight states. These chapters are seeking to improve the quality of life in their communities and offer opportunities to those in the inner city.

Jim Wallis calls the widespread efforts in America to demonstrate our faith in ways that actually change our communities a "prophetic spirituality."

> It draws evangelicals with a compassionate heart and a social conscience. It brings together mainline Protestants who desire spiritual revival and justice. It invites Catholics who seek a spirituality for social change. It includes African-American, Latino, Asian, and Native American faith communities . . . and it attracts those who, long alienated from established religion, are hungry for a personal and communal spirituality to undergird their struggle to live more justly.[6]

In other words, the Creator God is at work quietly changing our world and manifesting God's subversive new order not only

6. Wallis, *The Soul of Politics: A Practical and Prophetic Vision for Change* (Maryknoll, N.Y.: Orbis Books, 1994), p. 44.

in our communities of faith but also through the words and deeds of love we express in response to the urgent needs in our world.

Lesslie Newbigin, an esteemed leader not only in the World Council of Churches but also in the international evangelical community, reminds us of the mission of the people of God in the following way: "The word is essential, because the name of Jesus cannot be replaced by anything else. But the deed is equally essential because the gospel is the good news of the active presence of the reign of God, and because this presence is to be made manifest in a world that has fallen under usurped dominion of the evil one."[7]

If the American church could be ignited by the spirit of the living God to reach out to those around us, we could see the renewal of a vital spirituality in our nation. That could inspire a new vision for the third millennium born of biblical faith instead of civil religion.

A Third Way — Searching for a Place to Stand and a New Basis for Political Responsibility

If the first call of the gospel of Jesus Christ is to "being" — fleshing out something of God's New Order in community with other members of the family of God — and if the second call of the gospel is to "doing" — demonstrating God's love in word and deed to the urgent needs in the world around us — then is there any place at all for Christians to speak explicitly in the political arena?

Most Christians in America (with the exception of a few fundamentalists, Pentecostals, and old-line Anabaptists) would answer yes. But we have to recognize that our involvement must be totally different from that of our secular counterparts, because we are committed to the in-breaking of a New Order that we believe is destined to transform all areas of human society.

7. Newbigin, "Cross-currents in Ecumenical and Evangelical Understandings of Mission," *International Bulletin of Missionary Research*, October 1982, p. 148.

As Jim Wallis observes in his important book *The Soul of Politics,*

> This is a new time. It is a time when the spiritual nature of many crises we face is increasingly clear to many people. The failure of ideology on all sides and the now-dysfunctional character of old political categories are also increasingly apparent. If discerned truthfully, religious faith will not be squeezed into predetermined positions of Left, Right, or Center. . . . At its best, religious perspective and conviction will transform categories by bringing independent moral values and social conscience to the public square.[8]

God knows the American public square desperately needs some independent moral values and social conscience that have the potential to inspire new vision for an uncertain future.

There are charismatics in Scotland who are convinced that God could never countenance any political system other than Scottish socialism. And there are charismatics in Virginia Beach who are just as convinced that God is a right-wing Republican and decidedly partial to America.

If we are going to be a biblical people, we must recognize that God's agenda transcends liberal and conservative agendas and indeed all dysfunctional political systems and national identities. There is not a shred of evidence anywhere in Scripture to suggest that God's agenda includes making any particular modern nation-state great and powerful — the United States of America included.

Scripture testifies that God's agenda is to create a new transnational community of the people of God in which our national identity will be eclipsed by our new identity as the international family of God. James Skillen insists that we must begin our involvement with "a full and unhesitating acceptance of the fact that the kingdom of God . . . cannot be identified with any state in this world."[9]

8. Wallis, *The Soul of Politics,* p. 34.
9. Skillen, *The Scattered Voice: Christians at Odds in the Public Square* (Grand Rapids: Zondervan, 1990), p. 215.

It is also essential that we remember that Scripture is very explicit about where the initiative for the transformation is coming from. The initiative for the transformation of the old and the ushering in of the new rests solely with the God who originally spoke all things into being. It is not up to us to save God's bacon.

God most certainly calls us to be leaven in all arenas of society, including the political, but we dare not come crashing in to take power and take over. Instead, we must seek to discern from Scripture something of God's purposes and then seek to advance those purposes as best we can. And since we still see only as through a glass darkly, we have absolutely no basis for either arrogance or triumphalism. We must approach the task with genuine humility and a willingness to learn from others . . . even our foes.

I believe our role is principally to be a prophetic witness for God's New Order. We are called to speak out against the injustice and immorality that fill our world. We are called to unmask the powers, expose corruption, and challenge arrogance within both society and the church. But at the same time, we are called to offer positive policies and programs that are clearly drawn from biblical principles, not threadbare political ideologies.

We need to be involved in the public square — not in the contentious, adversarial spirit of partisan politics but in the reconciling spirit of Jesus Christ. Mother Teresa passionately presented her concern for the unborn before a large audience in Canada. She didn't stoop to vilifying and demonizing those who held a different viewpoint on the abortion issue. Instead, in the spirit of the living Christ, she reached out to her entire audience. "You don't want your children?" she said. "You bring them to me. I will love them and I will care for them."

Like Mother Teresa, we need to reach out in the spirit of the reconciling Christ to those who disagree with us. All Christian political involvement must take place before the cross and must fully participate in the agonies of the cross. We need to remember that it is only through the mercy of the cross that any of us has any hope for the future.

Our political involvement as followers of Jesus Christ

doesn't begin in party caucus rooms or in lobbying for a piece of legislation. It certainly doesn't begin with the American civil religion advocated by some on the religious right, in which there is no crucified or resurrected Christ.

Our involvement must begin in the shadow of the cross. Like Jesus Christ, we are called to enter fully into the suffering of the poor, the marginalized, and the outcast. And our involvement also looks forward to the hope of the resurrection, when the shalom future of God will fully burst into our world and make all things new.

A Third Way — Coming Together

The cause of Jesus Christ offers absolutely no grounds for going to war with those with whom we differ. There is certainly no room for the scandalous name-calling and demonizing that goes on in America's culture wars. Rather, we are reminded by Scripture that the primary evidence we have to offer the world that the gospel of Christ is valid is the way that we love one another.

We need to take the initiative to reach out to those with whom we disagree. For example, when conservative Catholic ethicist George Weigel lived in Seattle, I routinely invited him to speak in my class at the University of Washington entitled "Ethical Dilemmas in a Technological Society." I wanted the students to hear an informed conservative viewpoint. And I too wanted to learn from one who saw the world in different terms than I do.

In 1984, believing very strongly in the importance of Christian reconciliation, I invited Michael Farris, then the head of the Washington state chapter of Moral Majority, to come to Seattle for a meeting with the local chapter of Evangelicals for Social Action. I asked Farris to bring a few of his folks, and we brought a few of ours. We took time that Saturday morning to get to know each other a bit, to break bread together, and to worship together. We began to see the defenses come down on both sides, and we began developing relationships.

Then after lunch we broke up into small groups to discuss issues. When we reconvened, we started with the education group. Regrettably, things broke wide open. One of our folks got into a rather heated exchange with Farris, and the day ended differently than we all had hoped. Even so, it was certainly worth doing.

More recently, religious leaders from both sides of America's culture war and others came together in Colorado Springs to sign a "Covenant of Mutual Respect." James Dobson is to be commended as one of those on the Christian right who signed this covenant and is working for mutual respect and common understanding of difficult issues that divide too many of our communities, such as public policy issues related to the gay community.

I would urge evangelicals, mainline Protestants, Catholics, and Orthodox to follow the example of these religious leaders in Colorado Springs and come together in a covenant of mutual respect to listen to one another's sincere concerns and work toward reconciliation.

I also encourage all of us to begin the cease fire in America's culture war by taking the initiative of inviting someone from the other camp to lunch. Don't make the mistake we did in Seattle. Check your burning issues at the door and simply work at building a relationship. I believe it is particularly important that we reach out not only across the religious and political spectrum but especially to our Christian sisters and brothers from ethnic backgrounds that are different from our own. What a powerful witness it would be for the Christian faith if the body of Christ could enter the third millennium united, marching together in common faith and action.

A Third Way — A Sampler of Alternatives

In addition to beginning the important work of reconciliation in the American church, it is also important that we be aware of a few of those Christian organizations that are dealing with public policy issues from nonideological points of view. Perhaps one of the most important groups I have discovered in my wanderings is the Center for Public Justice. This group seeks to address important issues from a Reformed biblical perspective. James Skillen, who heads the Center, has led in the examination of a broad spectrum of issues including trade, racism, the environment, social justice, democratization in Africa, and reform of the American welfare system.

For example, the Center recently produced a proposal on welfare reform that takes an approach to this issue very different from that of either the conservatives or liberals. It suggests that change in the underclass must begin with "spiritual transformation." It points out that faith-based programs have proven to be the most effective in enabling those at the margins not only to develop job skills but also to become more responsible parents, more active community leaders, and more responsible workers.[10]

Charles Colson's Prison Fellowship organization works with a broad spectrum of mainline and conservative Protestant groups not only in ministering to offenders and their families but in working for the reform of the criminal justice system. Colson's positions on public policy issues avoid the ideological overtones of either the religious right or the liberal left. He and his staff are intent on working for policies that both reflect biblical values and make sense.

For example, Colson has spoken out strongly against mandatory sentencing minimums, which are often favored by political conservatives. "With mandatory sentencing we're hoping to keep criminals off the streets. Ironically it does just the opposite," says Colson. "By slapping long mandatory sentencing on minor offenders, we're using a prison space we desperately need for serious offenders."[11] We need Christians of all persuasions to reflect this kind of independent thinking.

Evangelicals for Social Action recently formed an environmental organization called Green Cross. The group is com-

10. For a copy of the proposal, entitled "A New Vision for Welfare Reform," write to the Center for Public Justice, P.O. Box 48368, Washington, D.C., 20002-0368.
11. Colson, "Mandatory Madness," *Justice Report*, Spring 1994, p. 3.

mitted to looking at issues regarding the care of creation from a distinctly biblical perspective.[12]

As I have mentioned repeatedly throughout this book, the captivity of American evangelicalism by the ideological right makes it an aberration in the larger global evangelical world. Nowhere else that I have traveled are evangelical Christians expected to wed their faith to a narrow political ideology, right or left. Let me provide a few examples.

In April 1991, evangelical mission theologians from all over the world convened a conference in Yugoslavia in which they drafted a document entitled "Freedom and Justice in Church State Relationships."

In this document they insist that "evangelical political praxis must be based on and critiqued by deep reflection on the social dimensions of biblical revelation. . . . Since God measures every society by how it treats the poorest and weakest, the voiceless and the marginalized (Prov. 31:1-9), it is an important responsibility of government to create just conditions within which the welfare of such groups can be actively promoted."[13] This is a welcome contrast to the growing hostility toward government assistance to help the poor that characterizes much conservative advocacy in America these days.

Brian Stiller, the president of the Evangelical Alliance in Canada, recently interviewed me for a television show called *Cross Currents*. Nothing comparable to this program is offered by religious broadcasters in the States. First, Stiller doesn't narrow his focus to the politically correct issues of the American Christian right — opposition to abortion, pornography, and gay rights. He discusses everything from human rights and peacemaking to teenage suicide and the world population crisis. And he doesn't insist, as do most hosts of religious television shows in the States, that all his guests endorse the same politically correct viewpoint.

12. For a copy of Green Cross's quarterly publication or ESA's *Prism* magazine, write to Evangelicals for Social Action, 10 E. Lancaster Ave., Wynnewood, Pennsylvania, 19096, or call 1 (800) 650-6600.

13. "The Declaration of Osijek: 'Freedom and Justice in Church State Relationships,' " *Transformation: An International Dialogue on Evangelical Social Ethics*, July/September 1991, p. 4.

In fact, he routinely invites representatives of points of view from the complete political spectrum in Canada, including some who are not believers. I am thankful that the Southern Baptist channel and Vision Network are bringing this important Christian program into a few U.S. markets. I pray to God it will become available all over America.

In Australia I found people from evangelical and charismatic churches joining with those from uniting churches (their mainline Protestant denominations) to speak out for Aboriginal rights and to show concern for the urban poor. While there is also a strong pro-life lobby among conservative Christians in Australia, there is no comparable culture war tearing apart society and church. Christians from all sectors of the Australian church are finding ways to work together.

The people of New Zealand are experiencing the same kinds of societal change we experience in America — declining moral values, growing pressure on families, and the like — but evangelicals there don't blame these changes on some sinister elite. Nor have they narrowed their concern to the short list of issues that concerns the religious right in America. They are concerned about family values and abortion, but they are also concerned about the poor and homeless, the unemployed, single-parent families, drug addicts, and the disabled. And evangelicals in New Zealand are in the forefront of those lobbying *for* government-funded programs to help these people.

The European Evangelical Alliance also focuses on a much broader array of issues than those championed by the American religious right, including care for AIDS victims, relief for refugees from Croatia, and care for the special needs of the young and the elderly in the cities. Evangelicals are working with traditional churches in Europe to develop a multilevel strategy called "Hope for Europe." The goal is to attempt to help each European nation develop a new national vision that reflects something of both its Christian past and God's promised future.

Perhaps the most exciting model I have found — and one that I believe has the greatest potential for offering a biblical alternative to adversarial extremes in the United States — is the Evangelical Alliance in Great Britain.

A Third Way — The British Evangelical Alliance

Under the leadership of Clive Calver, the Evangelical Alliance in Britain is finding ways to make a positive Christian witness in British society.

First, I need to emphasize again that the primary focus of evangelicals in all the other Western countries I have mentioned is not political advocacy but rather the call to follow Christ faithfully in their communities and to share God's love with the world. Political advocacy is at the bottom of their list of priorities, not the top.

While the Brits have a few right-wing ideological groups (e.g., the Christian Institute), these are in the decided minority, as they are in all other Western countries save the United States. The Evangelical Alliance is by far the largest evangelical organization in Great Britain and includes Christians from such non-evangelical communions as the Anglicans and Methodists as well. It represents 1.2 million Christians from over thirty denominations and seven hundred Christian organizations.

The aims of the Evangelical Alliance are:

▶ to promote unity,
▶ to stimulate prayer,
▶ to encourage evangelism,
▶ to promote, explain, and defend biblical truth, and
▶ to enable Christians to act as salt and light in society.

The final aim of acting as "salt and light in society" is the one that relates to their political advocacy.

Martyn Eden, one of the leaders of the Evangelical Alliance, has outlined five major ways in which Christians in Britain can be salt and light:

The first of these is to exercise a prophetic ministry in society. As former President of Zambia Kenneth Kaunda has written, "what a nation needs more than anything else is not a Christian ruler in the palace but a Christian prophet within earshot."

A second role for the Church is to serve as an agent of

reconciliation in a divided society. One of the characteristics of Jesus' life is that he brought people together like Matthew the tax collector and Simon the zealot, who were virtual enemies. He also befriended Samaritans who were certainly enemies of the Jews. He not only reconciled people to God but people to each other. . . . In a political system like Britain's which is adversarial in nature, the Church acting as an agent of reconciliation can be very political, yet non-partisan.

Thirdly, the Church can spearhead a ministry of prayer for the nation.

Fourthly, the local Church will also respond to social needs in its local community insofar as it has the resources and God's prompting to do so. . . . Churches offer emergency housing for homeless people and counseling services for families' debt, bereavement or marital problems.

The fifth function which the Church can perform is one of teaching and training individual Christians for consistent socio-political involvement.[14]

As you can see, this list — particularly the call to promote reconciliation instead of indulging in adversarial politics — suggests an approach entirely different from that of Christians involved on either side in America's culture war. And members of the Evangelical Alliance, like Christians in other Western countries, are interested in a longer list of issues than those that interest the American religious right. Among other things, they are addressing issues of housing and homelessness, unemployment, disability, racism, obscenity, pornography and violence in media, euthanasia, homosexuality, human rights and religious liberties, drug abuse and prevention, Sunday trading laws, the environment, Third World development, and education.

During his period of secondment from his position with the senior staff of the Alliance on which he served as executive secretary of the World Evangelical Fellowship's Religious Liberties Commission, Mike Morris worked to turn the spotlight on people persecuted for their faith worldwide. Since its inception in 1846, the Alliance in Britain has also consistently campaigned for reli-

14. Martyn Eden, "Salting Caesar" (unpublished paper), pp. 7-10.

gious freedom for members of Catholic, Orthodox, and Jewish as well as evangelical communities. The creation of a united international approach offers genuine potential for a still more effective voice in the future.

I particularly appreciate the way in which the Evangelical Alliance develops its public policy positions. It is more member-directed than leader-directed — just the opposite of the Christian Coalition. A friend who is an active member of the Christian Coalition told me that he has never been at a local or national meeting of the organization where he was asked for his input on what the issues should be or what stand the Coalition should take. The leadership always makes those decisions for the members and expects them to fall in line.

He also said he has never been at a meeting of the Coalition in which the biblical basis for the organization's positions was spelled out for the members. I believe I know why he has never heard the Coalition's biblical rationale for its various public policy issues: it doesn't have one. While those on the religious right in the U.S. pride themselves on taking the Bible *literally,* I believe they staunchly refuse to take the Bible *seriously.* I have yet to find any group on the Christian right that does the hard work of drafting a statement of biblical principles as a basis for its advocacy. Evangelicals in Britain and other countries do this sort of thing as a matter of course.

Martyn Eden told me that the Evangelical Alliance "is emphatic about not being a right wing moral majority or fundamentalist. We look upon those Americans who are the focus of your book as seriously adrift and in error in the way they have hijacked the Gospel for political ends."[15]

The Evangelical Alliance has chosen a very different approach than that of America's Christian right to developing its public policy positions. While the perspective of the British evangelicals has been shaped in part by John Nelson Darby's end-times views, they don't work from a conspiratorial view of history. And while few would give any credence to the assertion of America's Christian right that an elite group of secular humanists is at work

15. Eden, in a letter to the author dated 28 September 1994, p. 3.

trying to undermine their families and destroy their faith, they do work against government policies that they believe would undermine the integrity of the family. And they show no interest in promoting nationalism — British, American, or any other variety — or in returning to the traditional family values of the fifties. They take Scripture much too seriously for that.

Clive Calver points out that the Alliance welcomes the participation of Christians from across the political spectrum, from conservative to progressive. They have wedded a positive pro-life stance with an active concern for political advocacy for the poor, for example. Freed from captivity to either the political right or the political left, they have formulated public policy positions in a way that has significantly enhanced the evangelical witness in Great Britain.

The Evangelical Alliance would never dream of leaving the development of its positions solely in the hands of the leadership and then expecting the membership to fall obediently in line. British evangelicals insist on a participatory process.

Martyn Eden has designed a systematic way in which groups of Christians in local churches and parachurch organizations develop their own positions and then the Alliance seeks to draw from these a common position. In a book he wrote with Ernest Lucas entitled *Being Transformed: Applying the Bible to Modern Life,* Eden outlines the following steps:

1. Assemble all the facts available on the issue being considered.
2. Analyze the elements of the issue. "Complex issues become clearer and more manageable when they are broken down into various factors," says Eden.
3. Decide what moral and spiritual principles are involved in the issue.
4. Identify the relevant biblical material. Eden notes that there will seldom be passages that apply clearly and directly to the issues. Where there is no immediately applicable text, he urges the group to secure the input of those who are biblically trained to help discern the broader biblical *principles* that most directly apply to the issue.

5. Corporately draft a statement of how the biblical principles apply to the issue.
6. In light of the relevant biblical principles, formulate a plan for personal action and advocacy of public policy.

Obviously this involves a lot more work than simply accepting the directives of an elite leadership. And, as a consequence of this rather involved process, views endorsed in the Evangelical Alliance are rarely unanimous.

As you might imagine, when you deliberately use Scripture instead of political ideology to define your position, it dramatically changes the outcome. The Evangelical Alliance's public policy positions are not uniformly conservative or liberal. They are all over the road map politically. And the fact that the Alliance clearly isn't captive to any one partisan viewpoint allows it to serve more effectively as a prophetic witness from outside the government.

The Evangelical Alliance has lobbied the British government on issues ranging from drug addiction to civil rights for disabled people. Recently over two thousand Christians lobbied members of Parliament to increase funding for the care of the homeless. I can't imagine any group on the Christian right in America lobbying Congressional representatives for increased government funding for any social program, given their right-wing political fears about big government.

The Evangelical Alliance has been successful in securing a new system of classification for videos that will help to make violent material less accessible to children. And, working with Catholic M.P. David Alton, they are also seeking to introduce new criteria with regard to violence on British television programming.

Overall, the Evangelical Alliance offers a superb alternative model of political participation for American Christians. The organization's informed, nonadversarial, reconciling approach and the fact that it is not captive to any partisan political ideology make it highly regarded not only by those in government but even by secular groups who may at times differ with its strong biblical advocacy. They don't view themselves as either society's victims or the power brokers of Britain's future. Rather, they view themselves as a prophetic witness in the political arena for the gospel of Jesus Christ.

A Third Way — A Call for the Renewal of Vision for the Third Millennium

As we approach the third millennium, one of the welcome signs of hope is the number of nations all over the world moving toward democratization and the rule of law. This presents a historic opportunity for democracies throughout the world, including the United States, to provide leadership for the advancement of freedom, the rule of law, and the promotion of human rights.

However, there are troubling signals that suggest the world's most powerful democracy might miss this opportunity to provide global leadership because of troubling internal changes in the United States that are directly connected to America's future. E. J. Dionne Jr., in his important book *Why Americans Hate Politics,* argues, "With democracy on the march outside our borders, our first responsibility is to ensure that the United States again becomes a model for what self-government should be and not an example of what happens to free nations when they lose interest in public life. A nation that hates politics will not long thrive as a democracy."[16]

As we have seen, talk radio is conditioning millions of Americans to hate their government and despise their leaders; and cynicism in our country is widespread and growing. Observers are also expressing concern that talk radio is seriously endangering our representative form of government. How in the world can we lead other nations into a more democratic future when we seem to be actively involved in undermining our own representative democracy?

The only way that the United States can, in partnership with other nations, provide moral leadership into the next millennium

16. Dionne, *Why Americans Hate Politics* (New York: Simon & Schuster, 1992), p. 355.

 289

is, I believe, to respond to the challenge of Zbigniew Brzezinski and call for a revival of spiritual life and a renewal of moral vision.

We have already discussed how, through the church, prayer, community, witness, and service, those of us from Christian faith traditions can work toward the renewal of vital faith and responsible moral action in American society. This renewal, however, will not come through hysteria, rage, invective, and demonizing those with whom we disagree. It will come only when we reach out of our own brokenness to embrace our opponents in reconciliation and mutual regard and seek a new vision of hope and responsibility for our common future.

How can we work toward the creation of a new moral vision of hope to help direct our nation's destiny and give it the moral authority required to provide leadership in calling other nations to democratization and the rule of law? Glenn Tinder makes a convincing case in his book *The Political Meaning of Christianity* that we cannot be good without God. In other words, any moral vision must ultimately be grounded in some sense of transcendence. And this sense of transcendence must be drawn from something larger than the impotent tribal deity offered by American civil religion.

If those of us from evangelical Christian backgrounds are going to participate in this process with others in calling America to a new moral vision, we must begin by demanding a cease fire in America's culture wars and repudiating the adversarial rhetoric and agendas of both the far right and the far left. And we must begin this journey by first finding a new biblical vision for our lives and communities of faith.

Millennium III: A Call to a Third Way

In *Cease Fire* I have sought to explain how the assumptions on which those on the politically correct left and the religious right are working have directly contributed to the increasingly adversarial nature of America's culture war. And I have intentionally spent much more time examining those on the Christian right because they are a part of the evangelical movement in America I claim as home. And I have not only offered my forecast as to how this culture war might play out, but I have also offered a third way — a biblical alternative to both extremes. Though I have disagreed very directly with those at both polarities, I don't for a moment question their integrity or their motivation — only their assumptions.

Recently, I learned of other evangelicals who were fed up with America's culture wars and were seeking to offer an alternative. On February 2, 1995, Tony Campolo, Ron Sider, and Jim Wallis convened a conversation at the National Prayer Breakfast in Washington, D.C., with evangelical leaders from all over the country. Their purpose was not only to call for a cease fire in America's culture war but to invite these leaders to join with those from other Christian traditions to find a new place to stand that is based on Scripture, not partisan political ideologies.

They drafted a preliminary statement entitled "The Cry for Renewal: Let Other Voices Be Heard." It reads in part:

> Our times cry out for renewed political vision. And vision depends upon spiritual values. We believe that the language of morality and faith can make a critical contribution to political discourse. The crisis we face is a spiritual crisis and must be responded to by solutions that address the "spirit" of the times that often lies beneath our political and economic problems. We believe further that the old political language and solutions of Right and Left, liberal and conservative, are almost completely dysfunctional now and helpless to lead us into a different future. But if politics will be renewed more by moral values than by partisan warfare, the religious community must play a more positive role.
>
> Christian faith must not become another casualty of the culture wars. Indeed, religious communities should be the one calling a cease-fire. The ideological polarization of the church will not contribute to the spiritual discernment of politics the country most needs. Inflamed rhetoric and name calling is no substitute for real and prayerful dialogue between different constituencies with legitimate concerns and a gospel of love which can bring people together.
>
> We are Evangelical voices who seek a biblical approach to politics, not an ideological agenda. We are Catholic voices who assert our own church's social teachings are a vital alter-

291

native to both the Left and the Right. We are African American, Latino, Asian, and Native American church voices whose commitment to personal faith and social justice leads us to visions of transformation beyond both political parties. We are voices from all the Protestant churches who feel represented neither by old religious liberalism nor new right fundamentalism.

Together we proclaim an evangelical, biblical, and catholic faith that must address a nation in crisis. We believe that our impoverished political process needs the moral direction and energy that spiritual and religious values can contribute to the public debate. Separation of church and state rightly prevents the official establishment of any religion, but does not and must not prohibit the positive influence of religious communities on the nation's moral and political climate. . . .

Conformity to the options offered by either the Religious Right or the Religious Left will not take us forward. Both conservative and liberal religion have too often become culturally captive forces that merely cheer on the ideological camps with which they are now identified. But religion as a political cheerleader is inevitably false as religion.

The almost total identification of the Religious Right with the new Republican majority in Washington is a dangerous liaison of religion with political power. With the ascendancy and influence of the Christian Right in party circles, the religious critique of power has been replaced with the religious competition for power.

Likewise, the continuing close identification of religious liberalism with political liberalism and the Democratic Party has demonstrated a public witness often lacking in moral imagination or prophetic integrity. Liberal religious leaders have sought access and influence with those in power no less than their Religious Right counterparts. Neither right-wing religious nationalism nor left-wing religious lobbying will serve us at this critical historic juncture. Such faith is often more ideological than truly evangelical.

Today, the body politic is buffeted by polarized extremes. Instead of helping a politically war weary public find common concerns and values, the religious community on both sides has often given sanction to the perpetuation of tragic divisions. . . .

Politics cannot solve all our problems. Spiritual renewal

will be required — of our personal values and communal values, of our religious congregations and neighborhood organizations, of our educational institutions and economic enterprises. But genuine spiritual renewal must not be self-righteous or mean-spirited. And spiritual sensitivity must replace ideological predictability as the touchstone of religion in politics.

Our definition of politics must be widened to include new solutions and leadership. In particular, new community-based and value-centered solutions must be found to our seemingly intractable problems. The wall between "public" and "private" solutions must come down in favor of new partnerships and configurations that involve everyone. And our religious communities must become meeting places and experimentation grounds where these new solutions are shaped and carried out in partnership with other cultural, economic, and political institutions.

The issues of political morality we now confront are too important to be left to only one voice. We testify that there are other visions of faith and politics in the land. New voices are critically needed. We especially appeal to the media to let new voices be heard. We appeal to the politicians to listen to the voices of religion rather than seeking to manipulate them.

Our commitment is to diligently apply spiritual values to the vexing questions of our public life and where necessary to offer a Christian alternative to ideological religion. Let a new dialogue begin at national, regional, and local levels around the country. Let politicized religion be replaced with prophetic faith to forge new coalitions of Christian conscience across the land.

On May 23, 1995, Tony Campolo and Jim Wallis held a press conference in which evangelicals and leaders of Catholic, mainline Protestant, and ethnic churches joined together in endorsing "The Cry for Renewal." They called for an end to America's culture wars and invited Christians of all traditions to unite in finding a new biblical place to stand and a new compassionate, non-adversarial approach to political engagement.

A few of those who have signed this "Cry for Renewal" are the following: David Bechman, President of Bread for the World;

Marie Dennis, Maryknoll Justice and Peace; Margaret Cafferty, Executive Director, Leadership Conference of Women Religious; Ted Keating, Conference of Major Superiors of Men; Dan Weiss, American Baptist Churches USA; the Rt. Rev. Edmond L. Browning, Presiding Bishop, Episcopal Church; Dr. Richard Hamm, General Minister and President, Christian Church/Disciples of Christ; Johan Maurer, Friends United Meeting; Rev. Dr. Gordon Sommers, President, National Council of Churches Executive Committee; Bob Seipel, President, World Vision; Steve Hayner, President, Inter-Varsity Christian Fellowship; Roberta Hesteness, President, Eastern College; James Dunn, Baptist Joint Committee.

Other signers who didn't list their affiliations include Myron Augsburger, Manfred Brauchy, Karen Mains, Daniel R. Chamberlain, Harvie Conn, Ted Engstrom, David Fischer, Lois McKinney, Richard Foster, Luis Madrigal, Eldin Villafañe, and Howard Snyder.

Anyone who would like more information about this call to a third way can contact

> Tony Campolo
> Eastern College
> St. Davids, Pennsylvania 19087
> (215) 341-5800

or

> Jim Wallis
> *Sojourners*
> 2401 15th St. NW
> Washington, D.C. 20009
> (202) 328-8842

A growing number of other evangelical leaders are beginning to speak up and decry the religious right's hold on American evangelicalism and are calling believers back to a biblical faith. For example, recently Os Guinness, an evangelical scholar and political commentator, spoke out against the fear generated by the religious right. He told an audience that "evangelicals must now decide whether to continue to live in fear . . . or to regain their historical and biblical roots in kingdom values."

What would happen if American evangelicals responded to

this call and repudiated the hysteria and fear-mongering of the religious right and reclaimed the positive biblical values of God's kingdom? What would happen if we evangelicals decided to take our movement back, depoliticize our churches, and give our primary attention again to advancing God's shalom vision for the human future? What would happen if, when we choose to speak in the public square, like our British counterparts, we used Scripture instead of political ideology to define our sense of Christian responsibility?

Donald Argue, the new president of the National Association of Evangelicals, has publicly repented of the racism of the NAE and has asked that the NAE and the National Black Evangelical Association join forces. He has also stated that he wants to help lead American evangelicalism out of its unquestioned identification with the political right and the Republican Party. "We need a strong voice to government on moral issues, especially today, but we must speak biblically," Argue says. "I want to undrape the Republican flag that has draped evangelicals in recent times. There are some wonderful evangelical Democrats."[17]

What would happen if the National Association of Evangelicals in the United States, like the Evangelical Alliances in other countries, demonstrated the courage to call evangelicals to a higher plane of engagement that transcends fear-mongering and adversarial politics? Perhaps the NAE could play a critical leadership role in helping conservative Protestants to find their way out of this embattled war zone to reclaim a prophetic biblical witness in American society again.

The majority of evangelical organizations in the United States, such as World Vision, InterVarsity, and the Billy Graham Association, have staunchly refused to choose sides in America's culture wars. What would happen if these organizations joined with the growing number of evangelical leaders in calling for a cease fire in this contentious conflict and challenged us to return to our biblical mission?

The reason the religious right has been so successful in

17. Argue, quoted in "First Stride in a Long Walk" and "Argue to Assume NAE Helm," *Christianity Today,* 6 February 1995, pp. 48-49.

subverting much of the consciousness of the evangelical movement is that they have gained near total control of evangelical
media. One rarely hears evangelicals who do not adhere to the
religious right party line on Christian T.V. or radio. The political
correctness police on the Christian right are very effective. As a
consequence, people in both the church and the larger society
are left with the clear impression that all American evangelicals
are right-wing ideologues who view complex policy issues in very
simplistic, conspiratorial black-and-white terms. And what we
lack in understanding we seem to more than make up for in
bombast, belligerence, and arrogance.

What would happen if the evangelical radio and T.V. stations
instituted their own fairness doctrine and invited evangelicals
from a full spectrum of our movement to share their views? If
they did, we might hear for a change from an African American
pastor I know in Detroit who is not celebrating the deep cuts in
social programs proposed by the Republican Congress. Rather we
would hear his genuine concerns for likely impacts on families
in his community. We might even hear from Mennonite Christians in Elkhart, Indiana, voicing strong concern that U.S. weapons firms are manufacturing land mines explicitly designed to
destroy civilians, including women and children.

It would be a particularly welcome change to hear from the
brightest and best in the evangelical community instead of right-
wing ideologues who too often have not done their homework.
These men and women, while reflecting a range of views on
current issues, are typically well informed and committed to civil
discourse rather than angry harangues. What would happen if
we regularly heard over evangelical radio and television from a
broad spectrum of these evangelical leaders who head our organizations and teach in our colleges and seminaries?

What would happen is that both church and society would
rapidly discover that, at its core, American evangelicalism is less
ideological and belligerent and more reasoned and compassionate than most people ever recognize. And Christian radio
and T.V. stations that are genuinely interested in broadening their
programming could begin by contacting the Coalition for Christian Colleges to secure the services of evangelical faculty on any

subject from the future of the family to the epidemic of violence sweeping our nation.

I am firmly convinced that evangelical Christians could play a significant role in the revitalization of the church and the spiritual renewal of the United States if we would return to our biblical roots and recommit ourselves to our biblical mission — extending God's love into the world by both word and deed.

Millennium III — Dreaming New Dreams

If evangelical leaders in the United States called the movement both back to its roots and forward to its biblical mission in the world, then we would have an opportunity to join much more fully in partnership with Christians all over the world in the advance of God's kingdom. Working through organizations like World Evangelical Fellowship and the Lausanne Committee, we American evangelicals would not only have expanding opportunities for partnership, but we would also discover how much we have to learn from those in other cultures.

We evangelicals would also have the opportunity to join with Christians from ethnic congregations, mainline Protestant denominations, and Orthodox and Roman Catholic traditions in discovering together within Scripture and our ancient past a compelling new vision for our common future. The recovery of biblical vision could both renew our churches and provide a much more significant sense of direction for our lives and the raising of the next generation. And when it comes to speaking in the public square, we could draw on resources like the Evangelical Alliance in Britain and also promote a nonadversarial biblical approach to public witness.

Perhaps we could also follow the model of the Evangelical Alliance in Europe and seek to join with other Christians as well as those from other faith traditions in helping to fashion a new dream for the American future in the third millennium. People of religious faith could provide an invaluable service by joining with others in helping our nation at this critical threshold time to define a new moral vision that calls our country beyond itself.

 297

I am not exactly certain what this renewed American dream would look like. But I am certain that if we drew on our Judeo-Christian heritage it would look less like Pat Buchanan's belligerent, self-interested isolationism and more like Dr. Martin Luther King's dream of a people united in compassionate cause for the common good — a dream that embraces the world.

In a very real sense American society and the church in the United States are at a historic watershed time. The decisions we make in the next few years could define the quality of moral life in America and moral leadership in the world well into the third millennium.

Our options seem to be rapidly narrowing to two starkly different alternatives. Either out of our faith and tradition we recover a vision for the common good and aggressively invest enormous private and public resources in working for the renewal of our communities, or we invest enormous resources in razor-wire fencing, guns, and prisons and settle for a permanently polarized society.

I believe that those of us from the Christian faith have it in our power to tip the scales in either direction. It is my sincere prayer that Christians from both sides in America's culture wars will lay down their arms and join with Christians from all traditions in working to see something of God's shalom vision of righteousness, justice, and peace become a reality in our nation and our world as together we enter a new millennium.

INDEX

▼ ▼ ▼